SPEAKING OF LIFE, DEATH AND HOCKEY . . .

Bulk orders of this book may be available for educational,
promotional, fund raising or business use. Please email the
publisher at walkonwaterbooks@gmail.com for more information.

Cover and interior illustrations -
James DeMarco – www.smallsaves.com

Editor – Mike Valentino

ISBN 978-0615557182
ISBN 061555718X

10 9 8 7 6 5 4 3 2 1

For Gitanah

With thanks to Karalyn and Lorinda,
for listening, reading and providing your insight,
but most of all for motivating me to finish this novel

SPEAKING OF LIFE, DEATH AND HOCKEY . . .

a novel

by

SCOTT NOBLE

WALK ON WATER
BOOKS

Denver, Colorado

CHAPTER ONE

SECOND-TIME LUCKY?

Things started to take a turn for the worse that morning when Rory didn't shoot his neighbor's dog.

The sun was a hung-over, half eyeball peeking lazily above the horizon when Rory Clark rose. With a caustic groan, he rolled out of bed at the insistence of his clock radio. As the gray dawn brightened the shades he fumbled for the appropriate button to silence the song before it inexorably forced its way into his brain for the remainder of the day.

The rumpled covers and wildly splayed hair on the other side the bed indicated that his wife had slept through his alarm.

Scratching himself with one hand while stretching the other arm, Rory shuffled into the bathroom. He regarded the man in the mirror thinking *that man* looked older than the one on his side felt. Yes, his brown hair bore a trace of gray if one were to inspect closely. A few wrinkles could mostly be blamed on his pillow. The redness in his blue eyes would clear up shortly after his morning cup of coffee. But neither man was exactly old by any stretch of the imagination.

He inspected his teeth and found them all in place and in the same condition as when he last inspected them. He rubbed his chin. While he wished he could skip the razor, it was apparent that his stubble was in dire need of maintenance.

Though still many hours away, his mind was preoccupied with thoughts of the adult league championship hockey game tonight. He had drifted to sleep visualizing numerous heroic saves he would make en route to victory.

Despite having slept well, he felt somewhat spent from stopping several thousand shots and breakaway chances during his nocturnal sojourn.

Six miles away three sheets of ice sat ghostly quiet. A light fog hung above the ice, embraced by the dasher boards and glass as if they longed for the whirling skaters that would fill their void. For now the vaporous mist would have to suffice. In an hour a dozen brilliantly festooned young ladies would become whirling acmes of grace upon one rink.

High school boys swearing, spitting and crushing one another for the sake of sport would fill the other rink with a reckless abandon and near ceaseless energy, their crudeness every bit the counterpoint to the girls on the opposite rink. Yet each group would spin and fly and chase away the morning fog.

It would be fourteen and a half hours before Rory's feet would touch that hallowed ice. The musty odor of the locker room and contrasting sweet, clean fragrance of the ice wouldn't be his to savor until the workday had passed. It was no less on Rory's mind for the interminable wait.

The day would crawl by with nearly unbearable slowness. Even as he opened the valve on the shower, his mind was on the coming game.

Rory closed the shower door and while he waited for the water to warm up, he peered through the bathroom blinds to determine what type of day awaited him. There was a downside already. A huge, black Newfoundland was slowly circling about his side yard looking for a place to offload a batch of cookies. The pooch, which belonged to Davis Jennings, Rory's troublesome neighbor, obviously had no real understanding of the many regulations pertaining to illegal waste disposal.

Rory's first thoughts were what a dire omen it was to witness such a thing on the morning of his big game. Being both a goalie and quite tired he was momentarily very superstitious and muttered to no one in general, "You have to be kidding me."

He shifted from irrational worry to anger in a heartbeat, even while remembering that he made a point never to be superstitious about anything. Never mind that he ate the same meal before each game and wore the same un-laundered game-socks for the last five years. These things were not superstition, but pre-game rituals. The meals wouldn't cause him indigestion and the socks were quite comfortable.

He made a point of wearing number thirteen on his jersey just to indicate his complete and total lack of superstition. In fact, he was so adamant about not being superstitious, that when he once forgot his jersey he refused to play until he found another with the number thirteen on it.

Although Rory didn't know it, the large Newfoundland squatting in his yard was named Thunder. Thunder was taking care of his morning business in an area of the yard that had been turned into a minefield of doggy bombs (of this Rory was *acutely* aware). Though vaguely cognizant that finally knowing which dog was polluting his manicured lawn was a good thing, Rory was mostly interested in venting his displeasure. His first impulse was to put a quick end to this day's incursion.

He opened the window and yelled, "Get out of here!"

Thunder stopped in mid-squat and looked at him. The giant black dog cocked its head as if trying to comprehend what on earth any man or beast could be so upset about on such a fine morning. Thunder contemplated Rory for a moment, perhaps considering the validity of his request. Perhaps again, Thunder was simply wondering, in the sort of wisdom that only a dog seems to possess, just what might be in it for him. He apparently decided that his slight case of constipation was more important than whatever the man wanted. Thunder gave a slight snort, which might be interpreted as a as a contemptuous laugh by a man (but never another dog). He then returned to the important business of fertilizing the lawn.

Rory leaned from the window yelling again, "Get! Knock it off. Get, you mutt!"

This time Thunder didn't even acknowledge him. His anger rising, Rory weighed his options. He could run down with a broom to physically drive off the dog. But visions of becoming the crazy neighbor chasing dogs out of the yard wearing nothing but a pair of boxer shorts didn't play out well in his head. Visions of the dog eating the broom as an appetizer played out even more poorly. Then one of those ideas smacking of wisdom before the sun fully rises, although obviously quite absurd thereafter, took hold.

He found himself a moment later leaning out the window with a pistol. The percussion of the shot brought a frightening clarity to the situation. Rory stood, ears ringing, contemplating the pistol in his hand, like a man glaring at a golf club which offended him by sending a ball in the wrong direction. Thunder was not a dog prone to skittishness, but he jumped five feet at the blast, spun toward the open window and launched into an intense round of accusatory barking worthy of his name. A moment later Davis Jennings came dashing around the corner in his bathrobe.

Jennings' wiry gray hair twisted around the bald dome of his shiny head like a gaudy version of Caesar's wreath. Even the expansive, powder gray robe he wore couldn't disguise the vastness of his girth as he came puffing into view, a steam locomotive about to explode. His round face closely resembled an atomic fireball in both shape and color. Rory suspected the man drank too much as this was a normal color for him even when he wasn't out of breath. His eyes twitched back and forth between the second story window and his now barking dog as he sputtered, "What the . . . ! You're shooting at my dog?"

Meanwhile, Rory found himself surrounded as his wife, Stephanie, appeared behind him in the bathroom. Rory spun as she burst into the bathroom; her blonde hair was as wild as her eyes were wide. Her slender body heaved through the tight, pink nightshirt she wore. Apparently unable to decipher the story her eyes were telling her, she stopped short of Rory. He looked in her direction momentarily, suspecting that she was torn between striking him in the head with something heavy or dialing 911. Instead she stood with her hand over her mouth, shaking, and asked in a frightened whisper, "What's going on, Rory?"

Rory held a finger up to indicate he'd answer her in a moment and leaned back out the window to yell at Jennings, "You've got to be kidding me, Davis. I've been getting letters from the HOA about crap in my yard and I don't even own a dog. Have you been standing there every morning watching your dog take a dump all over my lawn?"

"What if I have?" he responded.

"Are you actually so lazy that you'd do that?"

"Maybe."

"That's absurd and intolerable."

"You'd shoot my dog because of it?"

"Wouldn't you want to shoot *me* if I crapped in *your* yard every day?"

"I don't know. You've never crapped in my yard."

"I didn't shoot your dog either."

"Lucky you're a bad shot."

"I don't think so."

"How could you miss a dog that big?"

"What? I wasn't trying to shoot your dog! Do you *want* me to shoot him?"

"You'll be hearing from the police. It's against the law to fire a gun in city limits, jackass! It's just a lucky thing you're a bad shot," Davis screamed as he took his dog by the collar. Thunder wasn't finished barking at Rory though and refused to move until Davis gave him a good pull.

"I wouldn't shoot your dog. He's fine—you're the idiot. It's also against the law to not pick up after your mutt, you . . ." Rory left off as Davis disappeared around the corner toward his house. He shut the window disgusted that this was the best counter he could muster this early. He suspected Davis had the upper hand if he called the cops. Firing a gun in city limits probably trumped dog crap. The one thing Davis didn't know was that the only gun Rory owned was the starter's pistol he'd fired to scare Thunder; the starter's pistol fired nothing but blanks.

As Davis Jensen slipped inside his house most of the neighborhood was upset. Davis was angry at Rory, not realizing that he had fired a blank. He was also angry with himself for getting caught. He pondered if it might be better if Thunder crapped in a different lawn each morning. Rory was disturbed at making a fool of himself. The neighbors were upset by gunshots and yelling so early. Rory suspected that each and every one of them had peered out the window and chose a side before Rory shut his blinds. He knew that most (if not all) of them would side with the guy who *wasn't* firing a pistol first thing in the morning. Thunder was angry that he still needed to relieve himself.

Inside, Rory found an angry Stephanie glaring at him, her arms crossed over her chest. She opened her mouth to say something, let out a deep sigh, shook her head and stomped away from the bathroom. Rory was glad that he wasn't superstitious. A superstitious man might have seen an angry neighbor, disturbed neighborhood, pooping dog and speechless wife as a very bad omen indeed.

The house where Rory and Stephanie slept and Thunder defecated in the side yard, though somewhat desecrated in the aforementioned area, was otherwise immaculate. The two-story home sat on a corner lot across the street from a municipal golf course. The yard was pleasingly arrayed in colorful flowers, fruit trees and a neatly trimmed lawn. In keeping with this state of spotlessness, Rory was opposed to pets of both the canine and feline variety. In the case of cats he could claim a severe allergy. More than an hour in the presence of a feline was enough to make him nearly give up on attempting to breathe. While the same was not true of dogs, he wasn't fond of the smell associated with a house frequented by wet canines. He was equally disturbed by the gifts they left for unwary barefoot pedestrians and holes dug at random. To his belief, such things went quite poorly with immaculate.

One odd aberration existed in his logic. He enjoyed having a clean, fresh smelling house as much as the next man. Mostly he hoped if the carpets were tidy, furniture pristine and the air odor free (save for the pleasant scents of chocolate chip cookies) that it would be an impressive experience for his friends and guests—a testament to his prosperity and happiness even. The problem with his hope—there were almost never chocolate chip cookies in the oven or guests on the couch.

Stephanie, on the other hand, begged her husband to bring home a dog every few months. She would tell him, "You don't understand how lonely I get while you're out in the morning working or out in the evening playing hockey. If I had a pet I'd be so much happier."

The irony here was that while Stephanie was not allergic to cats, she did react violently to dogs. So deep was her love for animals that she swore she'd suffer through it. Rory was sure that her suffering would become his own.

Invariably, Rory would dismiss this telling her, "It's not even open for discussion. I'm not suffering through a cat in the house and I'm not suffering through you suffering through a dog in the house. How about a goldfish?"

It wasn't as if Rory didn't want his wife to be happy. In fact, there was nothing he'd admit to being more important to him than her happiness. To the contrary, he'd seen her ask, in fact beg, for more than one thing that he suspected would be of little interest once obtained. The bread maker was nice for the first month and used perhaps twice in the years that followed before eventually finding a permanent place in the basement. Her bicycle hung unused in the garage with 12 miles on the odometer. The Ultimate Chocolate Chip Cookie Cookbook . . . well, its disuse goes without saying.

After showering and shaving, Rory emerged from the bathroom to discover, much to his dismay, Stephanie wide-awake sitting in bed. He found her with a raptor's gaze fixed upon him from her perch on the edge of the bed. It was more than a little unnerving since she was certainly not a morning person. In fact, on the rare days that her blaring alarm preceded his, Rory often had to wake her up to turn it off. Thus he was slightly confused, but mostly terrified, to see that she hadn't returned to bed with the odd events of the morning a bleary uncertainty in her head and was instead staring furiously in his direction.

He gently tested the waters, fearing them to be dangerously frigid, "Good Morning, honey . . ." It came out more a query than a greeting.

She continued to glower taking a moment before speaking. "So now we know the truth, don't we?"

"I . . . I'm not sure." Rory stammered, certain that there was no correct answer to his wife's question. It was too early in the morning to step into bear traps. "Do you think you could yell at me later? I've had a rough morning already."

"You hate dogs! How could I be married to a man who hates dogs?"

Lord Stanley's Cup of Java is an appropriate enough name for a coffee house residing in the shadow of an ice rink. Interlaced aromas of fresh ground Arabica, warm assorted pastry and toasted pannini punctuated the air. The fifteen hundred square foot space contained an overstuffed distressed leather couch and two matching armchairs arranged around a small gas fireplace, six small tables with chairs, a fifteen thousand dollar La Marzocco espresso bar, and momentarily, two hard-working, young employees behind the counter. A little further back one would find Rory Clark, entrepreneur.

It was ten in the morning and the frenetic pace subsided into a stable trickle of customers. By lunchtime things would pick up with bleary-eyed office workers and well-exercised skaters stopping by for a second dose of caffeine and a grilled sandwich or burrito. Rory sat in the office chipping away at the computer's dosage of daily paperwork. He looked through the one-way mirror behind the counter at the whine of the bean grinder.

A cop ordering something gave him pause to consider the morning's events. He wondered if Davis would actually call the police. He also pondered Steph's remark. He thought, *I don't hate dogs. I just don't like them enough to clean up after someone else's!*

His assistant manager, Mark, handed a cup of drip coffee to the cop while Lisa sent him on his way with a smile and nod. As the uniformed officer disappeared around the corner, Rory relaxed a little. He was about to start the weekly order when Mark stuck his head in the office, the rest of him following shortly thereafter.

"Hey Rory, I don't know if I told you, they're shipping the decaf in five pound bags now instead of cases. So, order double if you want the full ten pounds."

"You told me yesterday, but thanks."

"That's right. Hey, Lisa and I are going to order a pizza from Abo's in a little bit. You want in on it?"

"What kind of pizza?"

"Dunno, we were waiting on you to decide that."

"In that case, no thanks."

Mark, momentarily puzzled, started to head back out the door but paused. "Oh yeah, there's a cop out here looking for you."

Rory rolled his eyes. He'd told Mark about the morning's events and figured the kid was playing a practical joke on him. Rory guessed that he was using the convenient ploy of the cop at the counter for his amusement. He wondered for a moment why they were called practical jokes when they were indeed so impractical. Trying to gauge whether Mark was serious or not, Rory looked at him for a moment before replying.

His assistant manager was just out of college with a degree in business management. Rory found that Mark reminded him of Mark Hamill before the car accident and new nose. They shared the same piercing blue eyes, slightly too long sandy-brown hair and even the sometimes whiny attitude of young Skywalker. It might have made it easy for Rory to remember his employee's name, but he slipped once calling the kid Luke. Mark had looked at him inquisitively upon the gaff.

Rory explained that the kid looked like Mark Hamill, to which Mark replied, "Who?"

"He's the brother of a famous ice skater, Dorothy Hamill," Rory had fallaciously explained, feeling a bit decrepit in light of what seemed a silly question.

To this, Mark became even more perplexed. "Then why Luke?"

Rory continued the misdirection. "It was a famous hairstyle named after her."

"After who?"

"His sister, Dorothy."

"Oh."

Rory was never sure who was putting on who was putting on whom in that conversation. Mark didn't have an obvious tell as far as Rory had determined. He knew the kid liked to yank his chain sometimes. Yet, he hadn't figured out how to tell when he was up to something. He made a mental note to invite him to poker sometime. For now he probed him a little just to see. "Is it about the dog thing?"

Mark shrugged. "He just asked for you after he ordered a coffee."

"What did he get?" Rory asked. He wasn't convinced that the cop was even still in the store. Asking about the coffee would display an attitude of nonchalance, just in case. If this was a prank, he was determined to have the upper hand.

"Ethiopian Harrar."

"Good, my favorite!" Rory replied standing up from the desk.

In the lobby, Rory found the officer and immediately had a feeling that something was wrong about him. His uniform was a little baggy. He had the confidence and swagger of a cop, but was missing something of the imposing nature Rory expected. Instead this officer seemed quite approachable even though Rory's feeling was that this would be an uneasy meeting at best. Rory looked at the man's shoes. They were so shiny he could almost make out his reflection. The gun and taser seemed convincing enough.

"How's the coffee, officer?" Rory asked as he approached. The man wasn't quite six feet tall, a lot younger and bit skinnier than most of the officers who frequented the shop. He was scanning the newspaper when Rory approached him and stood up. The fact that he had been perusing the Want Ads didn't escape Rory.

"Not bad," the officer replied, "Ethiopian, I think they told me?"

"Ah, that's the Ethiopian Harrar. It's one of my favorites. Frankly, I think it's a lot better than not bad. Did you notice the subtle blueberry cheesecake notes in the flavor?"

"This is a flavored coffee?" the cop asked, suddenly holding his cup as if it contained a urine sample. It was an odd reaction for a cop. Rory knew most of them were generally used to drinking lots of caffeine in whatever quality might be available.

"No, no, it's a single origin coffee. Most of the Ethiopian beans have a natural fruitiness. Harrar has one of the most obvious layers of flavor, a pronounced blueberry undertone." Rory noticed the cop's badge with immense reward. His gut feeling had been right. The badge read, Officer Feelgood, Fun City Police Dept.

The officer replied, "Huh, I didn't notice it at all."

"Here, let me show you," Rory told him, rounding the corner to the counter. "Get me a sample cup of Harrar please, Mark."

Officer Feelgood was right behind him when Rory retrieved the tiny cup of coffee. In fact upon turning, he nearly ran into the man. Feelgood told him, "I really don't know if I have time for this. Unfortunately, I do have a warrant for your arrest here."

Rory stole a look at Mark and Lisa behind the counter. Mark had an impressive poker face, but Lisa had to stifle a laugh with a cough. Turning his full attention back to the officer, Rory nodded. "Nonsense officer, you haven't even asked who I am. If you do have a warrant, I'll come along peacefully. But, you really should fully enjoy your cup of coffee first. Here's what you need to do. Take a small sip and lean forward. Then suck air bubbles through your teeth and allow them to flow over your tongue—like this."

Rory demonstrated, finding it difficult not to laugh while doing so. Officer Feelgood mimicked the demonstration, swallowed his java and nodded. "Yeah, I taste it." He was practically beaming. "I really do taste it. Wow! That is good coffee —really good coffee."

"Excellent!" Rory replied. "Let me get my coat and I'll be right back so you can take me downtown." He didn't wait for the so-called-officer to respond before dashing to the office.

As Rory's mind spun, looking for a plan to turn around the prank he watched the officer through the one way mirror in the office. The man was stripping down to his skivvies, a banana hammock to be exact. After a cringe and shudder, Rory took a moment to thank no one in specific for his timely departure from the lobby. There was only one escape from the office. If it really were the police after him, it would be worthless, as it led to a very high roof with no other way down. Rory climbed up the iron ladder, through the hatch and onto the roof. He shut the trap door and sat on it. For a while his emotional state gyrated, one moment snickering to himself for getting away, the next fuming about the mostly naked man possibly frightening customers in his shop.

Eventually, he heard someone climbing the ladder below him. He expected upward pressure on the door. Instead, he felt the click of the latch being locked below him. He stood up and pulled on the door, confirming that he was trapped on the roof. Rory yelled, "Mark?!"

Mark's muffled reply from the other side of the hatch was, "You don't get off the hook that easily, Rory. I'll let you in if it gets busy . . . besides, you don't want to even think about what the *officer* is doing in the lobby right now."

Then the rain began. Rory didn't so much mind it. The late summer weather was still warm. It felt nice, even though he knew being soggy later would be less pleasant.

He sat on the roof stewing in silence about the poor quality of his day and reflecting upon how lucky he was to not be superstitious. Certainly a lesser man would have found issue with the day he'd been having. Instead, he concentrated on the game ahead once again. He visualized making numerous amazing saves, until he began feeling the sting of the puck and realized that the rain was turning to hail. *Seriously? Now hail,* he thought.

Rory banged on the hatch. Knowing that his hopes of sanctuary from the hail were slim, in that direction, he quickly abandoned that escape route. Covering his head from the growing intensity of the climatic attack, he ran to a nearby hatch and pulled on the lever. To his surprise, it was unlocked. He lowered himself down the ladder, cutting off the hailstorm above with a thump of the sturdy steel door and realized that he was in the back stairwell of the ice rink. With a slight grin he sat on the floor and thought to himself, *Yep, it's a good thing I'm not superstitious.*

CHAPTER TWO

LORD FANCY PANTS

It was a great day to be a hockey player. Dashing anonymous strangers into the glass that partitioned the game from the rest of the world could be strangely therapeutic. It's been said that the glass isn't there to keep the puck in, but to keep everyone else out. Rory always found some truth in this. The fury that was about to take place on the ice offered a moment of, if not peace, at least escape from the perils of the outside world.

     The violent pace of the game would momentarily absorb everything, bringing a sense of solace to those it temporarily embraced. Ironic perhaps, given the ferocity of the sport. Yet, by its very nature, the game is engrained with the ability to encompass everything else, forcing a singular focus. Hockey is completely impervious to any disquietude of the outside world. Yes, it was a great day to be a hockey player. Unfortunately, Rory was a small business owner who played hockey, which isn't quite the same thing.

     Even had he not been a goalie, true therapeutic violence was never a viable part of recreational hockey. This league was filled with twenty-something show-boaters, thirty-something wanna-be's and forty-something has-beens. Most of them had jobs requiring a presentable set of teeth and un-broken limbs. So, body-checking was never a true option. In fact hitting another player, no matter how obviously they might deserve it, almost always resulted in a penalty. Most nights this was a good thing, but to Rory, on this particular night, it was slightly disappointing.

It wasn't as if Rory wanted to hurt anyone. Were he about to play tennis or baseball, he might have been looking forward to venting his amassed aggravations on the ball. There was something satisfying about indulging primal violence on inanimate objects. When much younger, Rory had occasionally flown into a rage smashing things. While these things were usually his own, he knew it to be an unhealthy act even in his youth. Certainly the physical aspect of ice hockey had helped to channel this aggression into a more creative outlet. It had been more years than he could remember since he had smashed anything in a rage. Perhaps during his first, very difficult year of marriage he had, although he was fairly certain that he vented such frustrations on objects far too sturdy for him to damage or too temporary to matter. Stephanie's homemade biscuits came to mind as an example of both types of objects (although there was a time when he had severely damaged a wall by throwing one in anger).

Rory claimed the corner of the locker room assigned to his team. They'd been unimaginatively named *The Lucky Pucks*. He was wedged in behind the stick-rack where he felt there was more room for the acres of equipment his gear bag contained. Despite the name, he'd never seen a hockey locker room which actually contained lockers. He supposed that extremely-cramped-hockey-player-changing-room-with-no-lockers was a bit long winded, even if it was a more accurate description. Perhaps that's why the locker-less rooms were generally referred to as locker rooms.

Now locker rooms exude certain aromas, none of which could accurately be described as pleasant. The air on this day was laced with the rancid odor of funky hockey equipment (which wasn't likely to be washed even if it were possible), sour beer, sweat, chewing tobacco, urine and a pinch of bleach. The bleach had no doubt been the work of some misguided or overly-optimistic cleaning person; it was a futile attempt to subdue the olfactory attack. Nonetheless, the pungent air in the cramped room carried a welcoming, if unsavory, smell. Much like manure might beckon fond thoughts of a favorite beast to the zookeeper, to Rory this was the scent associated with his dysfunctional family, also known as a hockey team.

Overhead, one of the bare fluorescent bulbs flickered and buzzed angrily, creating slightly more noise than light. The walls were painted in colors that reminded Rory of his run-down high school. They were colors that an institution had agreed were cheerful, imaginative and bright. However, once on the wall these were watered-down hues that evoked intense sentiments of indifference and boredom. The rubber floor was peeled back in several places. It apparently hadn't been dry for twenty years (never mind that the rink was only half that old).

On the poorly-shellacked, maple bench that flanked the walls, his teammates told humorous stories, cursed and laughed loudly. They complained about referees and boasted of carnal conquests, which generally smacked of fabrication. Their voices were always loud, straining to part the conversation for a moment to interject what seemed an important addition to the banter. Insults were generously ladled out and even those that bore the sting of truth were both delivered and received in good nature, filling the room with gregarious laughter.

Next to Rory sat Gary Gilden, the team's most intimidating defenseman in three areas. These included a cannon-like shot, his seeming inability to turn or stop his 280-pound frame while skating, and his approximately two-hundred pounds of facial hair. Gary generally spoke in a slow, awkward drawl. The effect of this somehow portrayed a man contemplating whether anyone in the room was intelligent enough to understand his words rather than any slowness in his own thought. Despite the labored approach of his speech, his booming voice and smoldering glare over-rode anyone who tried to sneak in a word while he addressed the room. Those foolish enough to ignore the warning in his eyes were sometimes introduced to his cantaloupe sized fists.

In fact, the previous year's championship game had ended abruptly for the Lucky Pucks as a result of Gary's raging fists. Rory had backstopped his team to a 3 to 1 lead. With a mere seven minutes on the clock, time was on their side, or so it had seemed. A loose puck baited Gary and Brad (the only man on the ice close to Gary in size) into its deadly trap. Neither of them had their head up. The collision which followed should have required an inventory of brain cells before either of them were allowed to take further action.

Unfortunately, there is no mandatory moment to reflect on such things in hockey. Both players threw down their sticks at once and began to hammer on each other. In recreational hockey, taking one's gloves off to fight is the acme of foolishness since the imprudent player who does so ends up punching the wire cage on the his opponent's helmet with bare hands . . . such an act tends to hurt the puncher's hands a lot more than it does the punchee's head. The fact that Gary and Brad kept their gloves on was perhaps the only intelligent part of the melee.

Conversely, the most ignorant portion of the fight was the fact that Gary and Brad both played for the same team. It was widely agreed that the fight could be cataloged among the lowest points to which the game of hockey has ever descended. Two members of the same team pummeling each other with fists and profanity no doubt had Lord Stanley clawing at his coffin lid in the hopes of rapping them each over the head with his favorite walking stick.

So it was, fists flew in the absence of sanity. Gary ripped off Brad's helmet after losing a glove. Both lost some blood. Brad lost a tooth. Finally, the officials came in to help the team captain, Dan, break up the fight.

The referee that night was a guy named Johnson. No one was certain of his first name aside from perhaps his mother, but even this was widely debated. Johnson was apparently so proud of this fact that he was the only ref at the rink with his last name emblazoned across the back of his striped jersey. While Rory never had any issues with him personally, Johnson was the annual recipient of the most hated league official award.

In fact, the players annually awarded Johnson two titles: "World's Worst Ref" and "World's Best Mustache." (Although technically it was his mustache winning the second award). The mustache indeed was a work of art, resembling the bristles of a push broom in volume. Johnson waxed the tips and rolled them into a couple of silver-dollar size curls. Apparently he had not been not informed that mustache wax went out of style when men stopped wearing six-shooters on their belts. In spite of the voluminous cookie duster, the title World's Worst Ref was by consensus far more deserved than that of World's Best Mustache.

After interceding, Johnson and the linesman sent Gary to the penalty box and made Brad sit in the far corner of the rink in order to sort things out. The officials conferred for a moment, debating quietly to themselves before borrowing a rulebook from the scorekeeper's desk. For more than five minutes Johnson pored over the book, while the jeers on each bench grew more urgent. Dan skated across to the scorekeeper's bench three times to add to the discussion. Each time Johnson's increasing ire was displayed by the volume of his voice yelling, "Get back to your bench!" The third time he punctuated the not so subtle request with a bit of profanity then added, "and shut up!"

The opposing team grumbled loudly from their bench about the time trickling away from the clock. Rory gained confidence. The longer the officials took, the better his chances were for victory. After all, his team was ahead by two goals. Since the game was stretching the schedule for the night, the clock would continue to run until it hit the five minute mark; only then would time stop when play was interrupted. He confidently thought, in a manner that amused him, *they need to get a sense of humor over there.* Rory was feeling smug without even saying it aloud.

Johnson eventually stabbed at a section of the rulebook with a copious finger. He flashed a page triumphantly in front of the linesman. After nodding in agreement, the linesman let Gary out of the penalty box and called Brad over. In the meantime Johnson skated across the ice and told The Lucky Pucks' bench, "I need three guys to serve penalties. Those two are out for fighting." Then nodding to Dan he added, "And you're out for third man in."

"Third man in?!" Dan shouted, his angry response more than a little tainted with confusion. Third man in was a rule meant to keep one team from ganging up on the other, "I was trying to break it up!"

A fight meant a $50 fine and a suspension for the first game of next season. Gary and Brad, despite being bloodied by one another, were suddenly allies.

"You can't give us a penalty for fighting. I never landed a punch," Gary protested, slowly, but with a great deal of menace.

"Yeah, we're on the same team and I'm not pressing charges," Brad sputtered through his bloody lip and missing tooth.

"You two shut up and get off the ice or you're done for next season too!" Johnson yelled. His face was turning a frightening shade of red. Rory half expected the ends of his mustache might straighten out and blow steam. Johnson shook the rulebook at Dan, looking a great deal like a fire and brimstone evangelist, although the profanity flying from his lips quickly shattered that impression. Johnson worked himself into a frenzy, explaining, "It doesn't matter who was fighting! Anyone who fights gets a game and five minutes. And it doesn't matter if you're trying to break up a fight. You get a game infraction for intervening in a fight. Since you dropped your stick to do it, I have to give you a minor penalty too. Easiest call I'll make all night!"

"If it was so easy, why did you have to look at the book for ten minutes?" Dan shot back.

"That's two more minutes!" Johnson shouted, "You want to make it harder on your team, just keep talking!"

Dan never liked making things easy. He launched into an impressive refrain of profanity. Gary and Brad sang harmony along with him. The entire bench chimed in as the backing chorus. Rory watched in amazed disbelief for a moment before skating to the bench and yelling at his team to calm down. It didn't matter. Three minutes later, Johnson had amassed a litany of charges so long that most of the players would still be sitting in the penalty box well into their eighties if the game weren't over. Instead of time served, the Lucky Pucks forfeited on too many penalties. Several players were asked not to come back next season. Johnson swore he wasn't going to be back to ref again. Rory left the ice knowing he had played brilliantly and lost nonetheless.

A year later, Rory looked around the locker room contemplating what might be different from last season's debacle. It was essentially the same team. All the villains were intact. Even those who'd been asked to leave had pleaded their case, paid their fines and returned. He hoped that the penalties and ignorance wouldn't become the story of the night. Little did he realize, neither would be a factor this time around.

Despite the rather mundane quality of recreational adult hockey as a spectator sport, there existed something of a festive atmosphere in the rink that night. It was the championship game after all. Both teams looked crisp. The Lucky Pucks were adorned in their green and silver jerseys crested with a royal flush above a puck bearing the team name. Their opposition, Red Army, wore white and red jerseys with the rather uninspired CCCP on the front. Though unimaginative, at least all of them had matching jerseys. Gary had apparently misplaced his team jersey mid-season and wore a plain green jersey with a 98 haphazardly slapped on the back with white hockey tape.

The scorekeeper announced each player's name and number before the game in a flowing voice. His voice boomed impressively over the PA system as if he were announcing an NHL all-star. "At gooooaaaalie for the Lucky Pucks, Roorrrryy Claarrrk!" Rory joined his team on the ice, at once pleased and embarrassed at the announcement. He wasn't sure if he should wave, bow, or blow kisses. Instead, he skated carefully to his net not wanting to accent his entrance with a silly fall. After depositing his water bottle on top of it, he casually leaned on the crossbar feigning indifference as the other team filed onto the ice, their names being similarly announced.

The assembled mass of approximately twenty-seven spectators applauded. They did so with almost the force one would expect from the gallery at an amateur golf tournament celebrating a two-foot bogey putt. The one exception to the subdued cheers was Dan's girlfriend, Shelly. She had shouted, "Go Daaaaan!" when his name was announced. She yelled, "Go you Green Puck guys! Woohoo!" when Rory's name finished off the team roster.

Shelly was often a source of conversation in the locker room. Gary had decided she was bad luck because every loss was a game she had come to watch. Rory, dismissing talk of luck (along with all other things superstitious), attributed the losses to the fact that Dan's girlfriend was about two seconds of airbrushing from being a supermodel. She also wore obscenely short skirts even in the cold rink. The Lucky Pucks always seemed to have a harder time concentrating on important things like the puck when she was watching. No one seemed to consider that she was more a distraction than bad luck.

More intriguing to Rory was the matter of what a potential supermodel might see in Dan, even considering that she had the I.Q of a paintbrush. In Rory's consideration, Dan was the least eligible guy on the team. There was abundant evidence backing Rory's assumption, including Dan's career, his wardrobe choice, his hockey skills, looks and even his personality. To say that Rory considered Dan below average was to akin to inferring that water might be wet.

Perhaps the worst strike against Dan was that he sold pianos for a living. To Rory's reckoning this, without a doubt, was the lowest denominator in career choices. Piano salesman was indefensibly the sleaziest occupation on the planet. In fact the profession was so bad that were Rory to have asked Dan, he'd have found that Dan not only wholeheartedly agreed with such an assessment, but longed for the respect garnered by used car salesmen and personal injury lawyers. Before taking up hockey, Dan considered killing himself on a daily basis.

The piano salesman is caught in a profession where it is impossible to survive without lying. While used car salesmen might have similar difficulties, at least people actually require a car. A piano is certainly a luxury for most. Piano shoppers typically know very little about what they are buying beyond the fact that they don't want a Chinese made piano. However, with an American made piano costing more than a pair of full-sized luxury SUVs and any decent European make equally out of their reach, Dan justified his career with a fabricated belief that shoppers needed someone to deceive and pressure them. Anyone truthful about pianos would be crushing their dreams. Furthermore, any would-be piano salesman who let a candidate escape without pressure, risked a potential buyer spending their money on something frivolous, such as a new roof or braces for their child. Even worse, they might buy a piano somewhere else.

Thus when a piano shopper would ask for an American made piano, Dan would steer them to the Lindermann and Son's line—a piano his employer deviously purchased as a custom labeled brand from a Chinese piano maker. The shop, Antonelli's Music, could land a six-foot baby grand with this private label for about $4,000. The Chinese expedited the building process and kept costs down by using plywood sound boards and wood that had been seasoned for less than a year. Of course, there was no way that a customer could know this as any evidence of the piano's Chinese origins was quickly removed when the instruments arrived in the shop.

Dan would hand them a glossy printed brochure detailing Lindermann and Son's 100-year history building pianos in New York, complete with a toll free phone line that conveniently redirected to the back office at Antonelli's. He'd start out truthfully telling them, "There are only a couple companies left making pianos in the United States, Steinway and Mason Hamlin." That was about the end of honesty (as it would be with any successful piano salesman). "Sadly, Lindermann is not among them anymore. The company moved their piano operations to Korea last year and this is one of their last American made pianos. We were extremely fortunate to get a deal by buying all of their remaining American piano stock. I believe this may be the very last grand we have from that purchase." (Never mind that there were typically a couple dozen more in the back warehouse).

He'd play an open chord with the sustain pedal down and follow it with an arpeggio to demonstrate the full range of the instrument's voice. The chord and simple scale were as close as he'd ever come to learning to play the instrument. It sounded strained and thin, but he'd smile and nod asking, "Amazing isn't it? Hear that richness?" He'd found that most buyers agreed with whatever he said as long as his head was bobbling. Then he'd launch into the benefits of the solid Englemann Spruce soundboard which had been seasoned for 25-years, the lifetime warranty, the keyboard action which was superior to that of Steinway, the solid maple pin-block, the high-tech, precision-cast plate . . . all of which were fabrications leading up to the eventual deal where he reluctantly dropped the price from $24,999 to $20,000 and threw in free delivery and tuning.

He'd claim that he wasn't making a penny on the sale, but he liked the couple and their freckled, punk kid with the crooked teeth. He'd invariably rub the kid's head saying, "You remind me of myself at your age. I don't know how I would have made it through my teens without a piano to express myself. That's what this job's all about for me." They'd leave thinking they'd made the deal of the century and Dan would pocket a $1,500 commission check. Buyers didn't need to know that he hated kids, was more than a hundred pounds overweight a year ago, and that their piano would possibly be warped so badly that it wouldn't play properly in six months. *That* would be a disservice.

Dan's nearly complete lack of scruples was often an asset on the ice, where a cleverly-timed, malicious barb had prompted players on the other team to take a dumb penalty more than once. No one on the Lucky Pucks was sure of the verbiage or tone he used. Dan's words were for his prey alone. As easily as his silver tongue could turn a lump of plywood and tin into the world's finest piano, it could also raise the ire of his opponents on the ice. Years of reading people's reactions had revealed a personal aptitude in swaying emotions. However, the more important portion of this art was his detailed study of the opposing team's penalty minute leaders. He memorized their numbers, looked up their names on the league website and found out a couple things from each of their backgrounds. He paid $45 a week to dig into their secrets on an Internet background-check website.

Dan would congratulate an opponent on having his car repossessed, or an impending bankruptcy. Wives were always a good choice for making a guy angry. Kids were better. First names of family were easy to find and Dan had no qualms about telling someone that he'd enjoyed racy pictures of their wife on the net. He'd been hit with sticks and be-gloved fists more times than his customers had been disappointed when they tried to have their pianos repaired under warranty. And darned if the brands that Antonelli Music sold didn't keep going bankrupt only to be replaced by another venerable, although completely unknown, piano manufacturer. But he was as proud of selling that junk as he was of his role in helping his team by taking lumps while his opponents racked up penalty minutes.

Despite his shady vocation and unscrupulous moral character, Rory thought that Dan's biggest issue was that he didn't have a neck. The apparent lack of a proper pedestal for Dan's head was not the result of lifting weights for so long that it had simply disappeared beneath a bundle of muscle. In fact, he was an average sized guy with the neck of a two-foot tall man. The astute observer would realize that in addition to the apparent lack of vertebrae C1 through C7, Dan's torso was disproportionately small as well. Even assuming that this infirmity which left Dan all arms and legs was unimportant to Shelly, his head was rather flat on top and his eyes seemed too small for his face.

It was enough to make the entire team wonder if his trophy girl didn't need to have her eyes examined *and* to find a better piano. Not only did she have bad taste, she was bad luck. While Rory didn't believe in luck, as luck was akin to superstition, he did realize that Shelly had a profound effect on the team's performance. Even discounting the effect of the short skirts she wore, the team believed she was bad luck, and Rory knew they'd have it as a result—not because such a thing actually existed, but because of their belief in it. Such things could only exist within a deeply-abiding faith since they didn't actually exist at all.

Despite this concern, the game proceeded in a civilized fashion. This was both to Rory's surprise *and* satisfaction. By the third period each team had taken only one penalty. More pleasing to Rory was the fact that the red LED lights of the scoreboard indicated The Lucky Pucks were in a scoreless goalie battle with only three minutes and six seconds left. A feeling of near invincibility had washed over Rory. He was calmly intense and completely in control. When scoring opportunities came, he welcomed them, knowing he was up to the task. He relished each puck that hit him—the slap against the pads, the snap of the goalie glove in his hand, the hard crack of rubber bouncing off his stick.

He wasn't worried when the other team's center drifted between his defensemen at the far blue line. No one was a match for him that night. Never mind that the shooter was the one who scored all three goals against last time they'd played Red Army. Rory found it hard to take him seriously, as he was the only guy he'd ever seen playing recreational hockey in a pair of purple pants. After the previous game, earlier in the season, the team had dubbed him, "Lord Fancy Pants" over beers smuggled into the locker room. It was a name he would be stuck with forever, though he would likely always be clueless about it.

Rory watched as Gary failed in a diving, desperate attempt to block the inevitable pass. Fancy Pants caught the puck near center ice. He shifted the puck ahead shoveling it with one hand and accelerated to open ice. Rory calmly moved out from his net to meet the challenge. A slight smile lit upon his lips as he thought, *it's down to me and a guy in purple pants.*

Rory wasn't really contemplating who might win a blue ribbon in a head to head accounting of fashion sensibility, although he was pretty certain he'd prevail. This was hockey—there is no fashion-sensibility-award in hockey. There's just basic black or the odd-assortment of shades in the clearance bin. And in that moment, Rory was, aptly enough, focused on that moment—not upon the clearance bin.

It seemed an eternity, the sheer moment of vivid clarity in which Rory found himself engulfed. Everything slowed down from the instant the pass slipped through and slapped loudly against Fancy Pant's stick. Rory looked at the scoreboard with time to memorize each detail. Two minutes and fifty-one seconds remained. Both teams had one timeout left. The score was nil with 28 shots against and 26 for his team. Then all on the ice faded to oblivion, except for his rival and the puck.

He could clearly see the slight mist of breath from his opponent, the ripple of his jersey, a bead of sweat just above his left eye. The scritch of each stride of his skates and the clack of puck on stick drowned out every sound from the yelling of his teammates to the jeers and cheers in the stands. He smelled the clear, cold, dry air of the rink as keenly as he felt the ice beneath his skates and the stick in his hand. The tenths of seconds seemed to take several minutes each to roll off the score-clock and in the immense amount of time this apparently provided, Rory found himself musing about what type of person might wear purple pants.

He considered, there were three types of players who would wear purple pants. Someone who lost a bet, a guy who didn't realize that purple was lame when he bought his first set of gear on the Internet, and the guy who played organized hockey at some level where purple pants were acceptable garb for the team.

He pondered, *so which of these is Lord Fancy Pants? Well, he proved three times last game that he was good enough to score on me. He must have played growing up. So, the purple pants are a badge of honor from his high school days when he really was something. Maybe he won a state championship in those pants, or maybe he's just too cheap to replace them. If he only knew his nickname was Lord Fancy Pants. Now he has the game on his stick. If he only knew I'm about to stop him cold.*

It was an odd sensation, but Rory had time to contemplate the exact size and weight of the puck, attempting to determine if a missing chunk of rubber, apparently clipped out by someone's skate, might affect its flight during a shot. He could read the embossed script spelling out, "Made in Slovakia," as well as the league sponsor's logo on the top of the puck, "Edward Crickbaugh and Associates—Divorce Attorneys." It dawned as odd that a divorce attorney sponsored the league. A microbrewery seemed more logical.

Rory drove hard, coming out of his net, almost to the top of the circles, before digging in to adjust his speed to the attacker. Fancy Pants had just gained the blue-line and settled into a steady gait. He'd returned both hands to the stick. Rory noticed hints of his opponent's skill in everything about him. His strides were long and powerful. He watched Rory's eyes rather than the puck, which he knew was firmly under his control; he effortlessly flipped it from forehand to backhand. Fancy Pant's jaw was set in determination. Despite his effort, he appeared relaxed. Mostly though, it was the purple pants that Rory noticed.

As Rory started backing toward the goal, accelerating to match his rival's speed, he shouted, "Come on! Shoot it!" It was petulant, even cocky and Rory knew it. It was part tactics to intimidate his opponent and part a war cry to pump himself up. But mostly in that moment it was a truthful assessment of his confidence in his own skills. He knew the worst thing he could consider was any inability to stop this shot. This was Rory's first rule of goaltending. *The goalie has to want to the shot. The moment he decides he doesn't want the shot is the moment in which he is beaten.* Thus, Rory focused on the fact that the game was entirely his own to win.

However, he had underestimated the intimidating nature of his war cry. Fancy Pants, apparently quite adept at sizing up an opponent, suddenly stopped moving his legs. He still had enough momentum to maneuver very quickly around the front of Rory's net. But a moment of hesitation slowed his legs and a flicker of doubt crept over his face. Rory spotted the hesitation and sprung upon it like a cat.

That moment of hesitation changed things for both defender and attacker. Fancy Pants cut hard to his right, the puck on his forehand. He was suddenly thinking shot, rather than deke. It was a mistake. Rory had the depth and angle on him. Rory's move made sure the net was covered. He decelerated, adjusting his angle to protect the net as he prepared to drop to his knees. He knew there wasn't any part of the net that Fancy Pants could hit, and no longer enough room for him to make a move.

Fancy Pants pulled the puck back. Gritting his teeth, he set up for a big shot. Rory dropped for the save, a certainty in his mind. However, when Fancy Pant's stick came down, the puck was gone. Dan caught up and had picked his pocket taking the puck and the game from Fancy Pant's stick in one fell swoop. Rory, down for the inevitable save, felt suddenly deflated. Dan had stolen his moment. He tried to reconcile the disappointment with the fact that the game was still tied. *The puck isn't in the net. Am I content to win, or do I need to be the hero?* Most days the win was enough, but in this moment Rory wasn't sure.

Fancy Pants wasn't content either. He put the brakes on wheeling hard toward the puck. Dan pulled up in the circle sidestepping as his momentum pulled him right beside Fancy Pants. Dan had the puck and half a step to the outside. All he needed to do was pull up and send it back out of the zone.

Instead, Dan did something Rory never expected. He came hard toward the goal line as if to cut behind the net. Fancy Pants had the angle to cut him off in that direction. At the bottom of the circle, Dan apparently realized he was running out of room. He attempted a move that failed to elude Fancy Pants. His back to the man, Dan spun and shot the puck. Rory, still down on his knees to stop a slap shot that never came, watched in revulsion as Dan's shot spun into the net just out of his reach.

Three minutes later, that goal was the game winner, credited to Fancy Pants for a shot he'd never made. Had he shot it, Rory knew he would have stopped it. But Dan took the shot and scored the last goal of the season, a game winner for the other team. The locker room was silent until Rory finally walked in, having been the last one on the ice.

Gary cajoled, "Hey Rory, how'd Dan score on you? He hasn't had a goal all season."

Despite the gregarious laughter in response Rory did not receive this jibe in good nature. He spoke not a word and despite being the last one in, he was the first one *out* of the locker room that night.

CHAPTER THREE

THE RULES

Rory tossed his bag contemptuously. The bag and its sixty pounds of wet gear landed on the garage floor with a thud. He stood looking at it for a full minute without moving. If the bag had a neck he would have strangled it even though nothing in the bag was to blame for the bitter taste in his mouth. His team was likely still *celebrating* in the bar at the rink. There was no call for jubilation. Looking at the hockey bag, which had no neck to strangle, Rory suspected that there *had* been a reason to actively pursue a drunken stupor. Regardless, he was in no mood to waste time with idiots celebrating mediocrity. First place was the *only* reason to celebrate. Rory's thoughts resonated between the fiasco he'd just left behind and the next season, flickering from foul to hopeful, but generally residing in the foul.

Eventually he gave up his vain attempt to stare down the bag. Before leaving he did give it a sound kick for good measure. As he turned the doorknob to the house he remembered that he hadn't seen Steph since that morning. It was easy for him to surmise that she still wasn't happy with him. There was an infinitesimally small chance that she went right back to bed and forgot the entire morning circus act. However, Rory knew that counting on such a thing was akin to expecting to win the lotto . . .

maybe even expecting to win the lotto without buying a ticket. However, he did earnestly hope for it. He pushed the door open wishing for the best, yet braced for the worst.

"Hey, I'm home."

Stephanie's arm flopped in a half-hearted wave above the back of the couch. She was watching *Dancing with the Stars*. Obviously engrossed, she simply replied, "Hi."

Uncertain what her response indicated, Rory skirted an encounter by tossing his towel and hockey clothes in the washer just a few feet inside the house from the garage. Of all the appliances in the house the washer was, in Rory's opinion, the only one with a proper brand name. Like the dryer, it was a Whirlpool. The oven and microwave were Frigidaires and the dishwasher was a Jenn Air. Once the washer was filling, Rory headed through the family room to the kitchen. He grabbed a banana from the Hotpoint refrigerator, poured himself a glass of milk and joined Steph on the couch. The program was about as interesting to him as those home makeover shows that turn best friends into angry neighbors. Stephanie enjoyed them though. Once in a while she punished him for sitting beside her on the couch by forcing him to view one. At times he tolerated such drivel simply for her company.

Rory picked up the remote, just to test the waters. He found them to be chilly with a strong chance of shark attacks. Normally, *Keeper of the Remote* was his domain. However, even when she was in a good mood, it was a risky move to claim his title by interrupting one of her programs. Without looking, she pointed a finger at him in mock threat. In light of the morning he wasn't sure of her temperament even when she growled sarcastically, "Don't even think about it, buddy. I was here first."

"There has to be something better on," Rory groaned, trying to sound like he was kidding. In fact, having his toes smashed one at a time with an eight-ounce, ball-peen hammer would probably be less painful than what she was watching. Some unrecognizable minor celebrity who had apparently spent half of her lifetime earnings on facelifts, silicon augmentations and Botox was doing a tango. At least that was Rory's impression. He knew himself to be no expert, but there were two people dancing and he did recall hearing the tango required two. Stephanie was strangely engaged by the program.

When the horrific tango mercifully ended, she finally looked at him and replied, "There was some airplane fighting show, a Clint Eastwood movie and a hockey game on . . . boring." A little twist formed at the corner of her mouth. Some of the tension fell away when Rory saw it. Such was the little verbal dance that they had perfected in six years of marriage. She was teasing him, which meant that she was still upset about the morning. However, she hadn't broached the subject, which meant she didn't want to talk about it. Further, the fact that she had to force the containment of a smile told Rory that there wouldn't be a fight tonight. A discussion would take place eventually, but these clues indicated that it would not be today.

Rory hadn't always been this cognizant of her mood. The first year they were married he planned their entire Christmas holiday without bothering to fill her in on the details. He ignored the possibility that *she* might actually want to make any plans for Christmas. After the day with his parents she had blurted out in anger, "Did you ever even bother to consider that I might want to visit *my* parents today?"

While this to her seemed an impossibly stupid gaff, he did remind her that they were Jewish after all. She informed him that they weren't so Jewish as to miss a holiday as important as Christmas and stormed off to the furthest corner of the house. Rory was then unaware of her three-step process designed to make him suffer. First came the silent treatment. No matter how hard he tried, she wouldn't talk to him for an indeterminate period of time. Thus he pleaded, apologized, reasoned, wept, complained, screamed and eventually threw a biscuit severely damaging the wall but leaving the biscuit mostly intact. Over the course of several hours he attempted to wear her down and got nothing. No name, no rank, no serial number—she didn't even ask for an attorney. It was then that he became certain he wanted her on his side in a war or any sort of criminal caper, but against him in nothing.

Two hours after this attempted interrogation, stage-two began. This stage was somehow even more frustrating to Rory as it made even less sense to him than the total shutdown that preceded it. Stage-two was the *act like nothing happened stage*. Stephanie's tactic suddenly shifted to talk about the weather, work and the dinner menu. She'd even crack a joke from time to time. In his first encounter, Rory mistakenly believed he was out of the proverbial doghouse. He hugged her and told her he was sorry only to be shoved away by his tearful wife who dashed out of the house with her car keys.

When Steph returned three hours later she told him about the weather in Kansas. Rory knew that either she had been driving very quickly or slightly exaggerating since it took three hours just to *get* to Kansas. Nonetheless, he learned a valuable lesson that day—wives can be insane. Perhaps even more importantly, he learned never to apologize until she reached stage-three. This was the stage when she would tell him, "I'm ready for you to apologize to me." Why she couldn't have told him early on, "I'm not ready to hear your apology, but I will let you know when I am," he would never understand. Further complicating things, he still did not understand that she would sometimes change the rules when she realized that he figured them out.

The television announced that Stacey Keibler would be dancing next. Rory watched the pre-commercial teaser showing the long-legged beauty learning her dance routine and nodded without looking at Stephanie. "You're right, this probably *is* better than any of that other stuff."

Stephanie turned from the television to abruptly put her feet in his lap. "Hmm, if you're going to act like that you owe me a foot rub."

Rory chuckled. It was a laugh born of equal parts, nervousness, confusion and mirth. Kneading her feet he replied, "Hey, if I can watch Stacey Keibler dance in that short skirt, I will rub your feet all night."

With a sigh, she pondered it for a moment. "I guess that's fair, but you're still a pig."

"Rumor has it we're all pigs," Rory told her warming up to their playful patter. He was half starting to believe that perhaps there would not be a fight at all. Steph sat quiet for a while, chuckling lightly at a humorous soft drink commercial, but allowing his concern to rebuild. For lack of conversation he brought up the subject of his game asking her, "So how was your hockey game tonight?"

"I didn't have a hockey game, silly."

"Oh, really?"

"No, I don't play hockey."

"I thought you were playing goalie in the championship game tonight."

She smiled at him even though her show had come back on. "Oh that. Nope, it was *you* playing in the championship game and I didn't want to ask, because I knew you lost. Did you want to talk about it, or would you rather watch Stacey Keibler?"

"Wait, how did you know I lost?"

"When you win you come in the house and yell, 'Who's the goalie?' When you lose you come in and say, 'I'm home.'"

"That's not true," Rory protested. "I never yell, 'Who's the goalie?' . . .well, not if you're in bed anyway." Suddenly he wondered if this wasn't all a ploy to keep him from watching Stacey Keibler. Sadly, if it was a ploy, it was a very effective one. Rory hadn't caught a second of her dancing.

Rory knew that no matter how angry Steph was with him, she was still a fixer at heart. She was generous to a fault at times. He once came home and puzzled for a moment on why they no longer had living room furniture. She informed him that a friend's had been destroyed when their roof collapsed after a snowstorm. He thought it a ploy to get new living room furniture until a year later she gave away their brand new bed to a couple who had been sleeping on the floor and replaced theirs with the same model. Stephanie finally became serious. "So what happened in your game?"

"It was plain stupid. No one had scored. I played one of the best games of my life. Then with three minutes left, that idiot, Dan, takes the puck from the other team, turns around and shoots it right into my net. We lost one to nothing. Can you believe it? Dan scored the only goal and it was against me. The rest of the team thought it was a big joke."

She put on her best sad look and sat up to put her hand on his face. Her frown and kiss on his forehead were more sarcastic than sympathetic. She smirked and told him, "There's always fall season, honey. Maybe you'll win that one. But at least the night isn't all bad."

Rory looked at her for a moment waiting for an explanation. Her only addition was a growing smirk. Finally he bit, "How's that?"

"At least you can watch Stacey Keibler dance."

He looked at the television just in time for them to cut away from a pair of long legs protruding from a short dress to a commercial. For a moment he was almost amused at the horrible perfection of it. Perhaps if the roof leaked that evening, allowing a continuous dribble directly on his forehead while he attempted to sleep, things would be somewhat *more* perfectly horrible. Rory considered that his only good fortune that day was the fact that he hadn't considered such a possibility. *That* would have been superstitious.

It was in Peaberry Coffee at 28th and Arapahoe in Boulder, years earlier, where Rory had first noticed Stephanie. As he recalled, the day was bright and unseasonably mild. It was the type that no one who lived outside of Colorado would ever expect a November's day to be like in Boulder. College students came in the shop wearing shorts and sunglasses and left carrying frozen drinks. Convertible tops were lowered in reverence of the sun. A few quickly fading piles of snow evaporating into eerie steaming tendrils were the only evidence that this wasn't May.

Rory was behind the counter when four women entered the coffee shop. They were a mother and her three grown daughters, by Rory's correct guess. Rory would later find out that this stop was a new one in an excursion that took place several times weekly, a long morning of scouring nearby Crossroad's Mall for bargains. All four women were certainly attractive, but it was Stephanie who garnered all of his attention.

He wasn't able to say if it was her long, blonde hair, which hung in long, flowing curls, her deep-brown eyes or her perfectly plump red lips that first caught his attention. He did know it was her smile that made him keep on staring. He kept on staring until he realized that the four ladies were waiting on him to wait on them.

Departing his reverie with an embarrassed start, Rory took their order and started making the drinks. He was barely conscious of what drinks he was making, working more by instinct than cognition. Stephanie, who still had not decided what she wanted, distracted him as she stood at the register waiting for the drinks while her companions staked their claim to a table on the porch. His derision at being left to man the store alone melted away. Suddenly he'd *not* been left alone to do the work of two people, but left alone in the presence of a beautiful, young woman, which was decidedly an improvement.

Rory would never forget her order that first day in the shop. She'd asked him what was good. Her voice was liquid and smoke all at once without enough of either to conceal a faint angelic chime. Rather than the droll, uninspired answer he normally gave, *everything here is good*, he asked her if she was feeling brave. She cocked her head slightly and the corner of her mouth turned up into a smirk as she replied, "What if I am?"

"Then I'll make you the best coffee drink you've ever had. But you don't get to find out what it is until you taste it."

Her smirk bloomed into a full-blown smile. Rory hoped he wasn't blushing. She asked, "What if I'm on a budget? You might make me an eight dollar drink."

"I'll tell you what. If you're brave, your drink is on me today."

"Now why would you do that?"

"Maybe I have ulterior motives," Rory wryly confessed, certain that he was blushing now.

There was a pause in the banter as she ran one hand through her curls, the other tapping a set of perfectly manicured nails on the copper counter-top. Rory perceived this more as flirtatious than uncertain. "And if I *don't* like it?"

"I'll let you buy a mocha for regular price," he said with a grin that fell just short of a wink.

A sweet trickle of laughter fluttered from her throat as she replied, "Well, with a deal like that, how *could* I refuse?"

The problem Rory suddenly encountered was he hadn't expected her to agree. Now he had offered her the best coffee drink she'd ever had, with no idea of *what* she'd ever had. For all he knew she grew up immersed in the great coffees of Italy, or even worse, Seattle!

With less than five minutes to ponder the solution to this dilemma, an answer which might ensure he would see this girl again one day (hopefully tomorrow) he finished the drinks for her family. One thing that he had going in his favor was approximately a month's worth of the recommended daily allowance of caffeine coursing through his veins. There was little doubt in Rory's mind that his mind was spinning at twice its normal speed. Otherwise he wouldn't have been able to simultaneously ponder the speed it was running at, make three drinks, flirt with the lovely girl across the counter, contemplate the perfect drink and feel self-conscious about the glistening spot of amaretto syrup that he'd splattered on his black polo shirt earlier that day.

The perfect drink came to him in a flash of brilliance, or so he believed. He set the first three drinks by the espresso bar for her to pick up and asked her, "Before I do this, I need to know." She raised one eyebrow in anticipation of his query. "Do you have any allergies?"

She smiled at him again. "Just cats."

He feigned dismay. "Hmm, that might make this difficult."

"Well, now I'm pretty sure I made the wrong choice," she told him with a wonderful laugh.

As she whisked the first three drinks outside, he reached into the basket in front of the counter and retrieved a large raspberry caramel. He fished a single-origin, dark Ghana chocolate from another basket. After dicing them up Rory tossed the pieces into a warm mug from atop the bar. Adding two shots of espresso to the caramel and chocolate, he swirled the concoction until he was sure it had melted. The drink was finished off with heavy whipping-cream that he'd steamed and frothed for a breve latte with a perfect half inch of foam.

Rory was so engrossed in the project that he was surprised to look up from the bar and find her waiting patiently. She watched him with a slight smile on her lips. He'd hoped to mark in the foam with a heart, but the heavy cream was thick, muddling his effort. It was hard to make out even with an active imagination.

Still, his hand shook a little as he placed the cup on the counter for her.

"Is that a heart?" she asked.

"Probably." His face felt warm.

"So, Mr. Barrista, does this concoction have a name?"

"I'm not sure what to call it yet. If you like it, I will name it after you," Rory replied, thinking himself clever for a moment. She certainly wasn't offended by the heart. He'd find out her name before she left.

At that moment a group of four students walked in the door, deviously interrupting his clever plan. Behind them a pair of senior ladies arrived. Stephanie lifted her cup and smiled at Rory. "I guess I will have to let you know then." With that she headed toward the patio, turning back momentarily to say, "Thanks!"

Rory spent the next twenty minutes making drinks non-stop. He spent every moment attempting to determine if he might extricate himself from the counter to check on whether she liked her unique beverage. She'd been sitting with her back to him enjoying the mountain view, the sun and laughing with her family. Rory was once again annoyed at being left alone to do all of the work. The twenty-seven dollars that had accumulated in the tip jar in less than half an hour would have normally made up for it, but not today.

He was distracted and giving poor service to everyone who wasn't Stephanie at that moment. Even when Jerry returned to the shop and helped out at the register it was too busy to leave the counter. Rory pumped drinks from the espresso bar as quickly as he could. When the rush ended, she was gone and his hopes evaporated like a final sputter of steam from the espresso machine.

After first meeting Steph, who was but a nameless smiling-face to him still, Rory thought of her often. He held a deep belief that there were moments in life that were meant to be taken by force or regretted forever. Once while skiing with two friends on a double chairlift, he'd lost in a rock, scissors, paper match to determine who went solo. He wandered to the singles line only to find himself paired with an attractive brunette with a bunny hat and great personality.

In the ten-minute lift ride Rory felt a connection, not unlike the one he'd made with Steph. They parted company with him failing to ask if she'd like to ski with him the rest of the day. This happened despite his knowledge that she was looking for her father on the slopes and that she lived mere minutes from him. He spent the rest of the day on the lookout for bunny hats, but never saw her again. It was regrettable.

"Coffee Girl," as he had dubbed Steph, was somehow less regrettable as the situation hadn't really been in his control. He'd made the most of the moment they'd been given. After that Rory was certain she'd stop back in the shop. Days passed and she didn't return. He tried to convince himself that this was a sign of an obvious personality flaw that rendered her a dismal choice. He failed in this constantly, only managing to remember her smile.

A profound and inexplicable unhappiness settled over him. This was odd and annoying. Rory was used to rolling with the punches and smiling through whatever came his way. But the more he thought about her, the more distraught he became and the more distraught he became, the more annoyed he was at himself for being foolish about a girl he'd only met briefly, a girl with no name. Then he'd wonder what her name was, only find himself thinking about her and becoming distraught, repeating the entire dismal process.

His studies at the University of Colorado began to suffer for lack of attention as did his work. He chastised himself for the way he was acting. *Rory, you're no fool. You knew her for five minutes, move on.* But there was no chasing the thought of her from his mind. The harder he tried, the more obsessed he became.

Thus, it wasn't surprising that within a week he was paying more attention to the empty cups before him and the instructions thereupon, than he was to the clientele. While deeply contemplating an empty paper cup that would shortly become a skinny-half-caf-latte, better known as a *Why Bother,* his ruminations were interrupted by a voice repeating for the third time, "Hello, I'd like to order a Stephanie."

Without really looking up, he murmured, "Sorry, not familiar with that one."

The voice replied, "That's a shame. You invented it."

He turned his attention to the voice. The darkness that had lingered over his soul immediately lifted. There before him was the face of the girl that had permeated his waking thoughts.

"I didn't think I'd see you again," he replied with a smile so genuine and involuntary that she had to know in that moment that he was more than a little pleased to see her. He felt his face redden slightly, feeling she probably realized that he'd been thinking of little other than her for the last seven days.

She smirked, apparently pleased by this reaction. "Well, I tried some other places, but no one wanted to name a drink after me anywhere else."

"You obviously didn't go to that dump on 30th by the bowling alley. They'll name a drink after anyone; of course everything they make tastes like dirty socks. Who wants to have a drink that tastes like dirty socks named after them?"

She laughed. "Maybe I should head over there instead then. You seem a little distracted and I don't have all day."

He looked to his right where three customers were impatiently waiting for their drinks. They were not nearly as impressed by his banter as Stephanie was. He nodded to them turning back to the machine as he talked to her.

"No problem, miss. One Stephanie coming up right after I take care of these fine folks."

Two minutes and seven shots of caffeine later they were alone in the shop. This time she watched as he recreated the drink that was apparently good enough to bring her back. As he handed her the cup he asked, "So you liked it enough to put your name on it?"

She nodded as she took her first sip.

"It's too bad that we're changing all the drink names to numbers next week. Maybe I could name it after your phone number."

She made a sour face. "So the drink wants my phone number?"

Rory shook his head. "No, but I do."

CHAPTER FOUR

OFFICER FEELBAD

It was far too early for the chiming doorbell that commenced Rory's day off. Yet this was what roused him from his sleep. He pulled on a pair of ragged sweatpants noting that the clock read 7:42. Cursing whoever was outside, he stumbled down the steps. Through the peephole his bleary eyes made out a female police officer standing on the porch. The fish-eye lens in the door indicated that she was blonde, maybe 5 foot 6, 140 pounds and far more attractive than any police officer he'd ever seen before.

Rory, a regular insomniac, spent the night in bed not sleeping. In spite of any sleep-deprived lack of clarity, he was struck by a singular thought—it was disappointing what little imagination his employees displayed. He also made a mental note to double check what he was paying them since they could apparently fritter away their paychecks with such little thought. He considered the possibility that they hated him after the Officer Feelgood incident. Since they didn't send a male stripper on the second attempt he wondered if maybe they liked him, at least a little bit. As he pondered this, his hand brushed the doorknob making it rattle. He cursed aloud at the mistake.

"Police, open the door. I hear you in there," came a gruff female voice from the other side of the door.

"It's awfully early, I didn't realize you people worked at this hour," Rory replied. "Listen, let me just get you some tip money and they don't need to know you didn't do your thing here. I'm not really in the mood this early."

"Excuse me, sir, you're offering me money?"

"You don't work for tips?"

"This is the police, sir."

"Maybe we can just skip that part. I know you're a stripper."

"You're not making things any easier on yourself."

"Sorry, dancer? I didn't realize that *stripper* was offensive."

"Sir, open the door."

"Singing telegram? What *do* you call yourselves?"

"Open the door, now."

"Only if you promise to leave your clothing on."

"Sir, if you don't open the door, the way that you're acting is enough probable cause for me to force it open."

Rory turned the knob, wondering what his wife would think if she woke up to a stripper in the living room. Even in his bleary state it suddenly didn't make sense to him. *Why would someone want to embarrass me without witnessing it?* He opened the door just enough to peek through the crack. The officer outside had shrunken about 4 inches from his previous estimate and had put on about seventy pounds. Her head, which appeared perfectly shaped through the peephole, was actually almost perfectly square. She had the build and smile of an angry fullback. In fact for just a moment he thought she might have been his middle school gym teacher (were she a man). Rory noted that her right hand was on her gun.

"Mr. Clark?" she asked.

He nodded, suddenly unable to speak. He wished he'd been struck mute much sooner. The woman behind the door was far too ugly to be a stripper. For a moment he cursed his bad luck before remembering that he didn't believe in such things.

"I'm Officer Doyle, with the Broomfield Police department. I need to ask you some questions. Open the door."

Rory looked at her for a moment, trying to remember what early morning idiocy had left his mouth a moment earlier. He nodded again before regaining the power of speech. "Uh, yeah . . . let me get the chain here."

As soon as he unchained the door, she pushed through it. Before Rory knew what was happening, he was handcuffed and facing the wall. This was clearly the most dismal start to a day he could remember. (There were a few in college that came close). She patted him down for a weapon, then roughly escorted him to the couch. Rory was deposited there in the manner one might toss a bag of garbage into a dumpster. At least the couch was comfortable. He'd hate to have the police brutalize him while he was uncomfortable.

Without taking her eyes from him, she pressed the button on her shoulder-mounted microphone and said, "I have him. Front door is open."

The tiny speaker crackled a static-laced, "On my way."

"Who else is in the house?" Officer Doyle asked.

"My wife is upstairs in bed sleeping. What's going on?" Rory's voice was a tiny crackle itself.

Officer Doyle said nothing until her partner wobbled into the room. He was following a belly several hundred doughnuts larger than an average belly should have been. Doyle told him, "Wife's upstairs in bed."

Her partner stood waiting. Doyle finally acknowledged him with a glare, "Go, I've got him."

He shook his head. "Well, procedurally . . ."

She snapped at him, "I said, I've got this one."

"Uh . . . yeah . . . I'll call her down," her partner replied and began calling loudly, "Mrs. Clark, Broomfield Police. Would you come downstairs please?" The officer had as much success as Rory thought he might. Rory sat helpless on the couch considering what type of fury his wife might rain down upon him after having a police officer wake her up. He was speechless again for a moment when he realized that the officer was heading upstairs. Short of firing a gun in the bathroom, Rory was pretty sure the officer would have to give her a good shake to wake her up.

Cop or not, Rory was livid at the thought of a man heading to his bedroom to wake his wife. Some things were worth taking a nightstick to the head. He stood up to protest, sputtering, "Hey . . . Hey! That's my wife up there!" He was expeditiously reminded that Doyle was in control of the situation. She shoved him back down on the couch as her partner disappeared from the landing.

"Relax, Mr. Clark, your wife will be fine. Now, we're here to talk to you about illegally discharging a firearm in city limits. But before we get to that I need to ask you something else. Your behavior at the door seemed a little odd. Have you been taking any drugs, medications or alcohol, sir?"

Rory's mind was wandering to how he could keep the three-hundred pound cop from wandering into the bedroom. He played several scenarios through his mind on how to accomplish this and how Steph might react. None of them ended well. Two ended in his incarceration without bail, two ended in divorce, one in his own death.

"Mr. Clark, are you listening to me?"

"I'm really sorry, officer," Rory said, hoping that Officer Doyle didn't want to go through three phases before being ready to accept an apology. "My employees tried to pull a prank on me last week with a stripper dressed as a cop and failed. I thought they were being sore losers and trying again this morning. That's why I was acting oddly when you came to the door, ma'am . . . er officer. I'm not on anything. But listen, my wife has nothing to do with . . ."

She interrupted, "We can get to that later, Mr. Clark. First thing I need to know is whether you own a firearm."

"Not really."

"Not really?"

"Nope."

"Either you do or you don't."

"I own a starter's pistol. It's a cap gun, a toy really."

"So you fired a *toy* gun out your window last Wednesday?"

"Pretty much."

"Can we stick to yes or no, Mr. Clark?"

"Yes."

"We had several complaints because you fired a toy gun."

"Yes?"

"I'm asking the questions."

"Sorry, I didn't know if that was a question."

"So we had complaints because you fired a toy gun?"

"I don't know."

"What?"

"I don't know if you had complaints."

"There were and our investigation pointed to you as the culprit."

"I resent that! I've never been a culprit."

"Mr. Clark, *did* you fire your toy gun Wednesday?"

"I thought we established that part, yes."

"Why would you do that at five a.m.?"

"My neighbor's dog was er. . . pooping in my yard. I yelled at it to go away and it didn't. I thought a loud noise would scare it."

"How'd that work out for you?"

"Well, the dog still soiled my yard, my wife wasn't pleased, apparently I made several neighbors angry enough to call the police, and you woke me up early today, so not very well. Listen, could you *please* let me wake up my wife?"

His plea, despite being at the forefront of his thoughts, came too late. Steph was awake and screaming. The officer upstairs was yelling for her to calm down. Doyle glanced toward the stairs and back at Rory. She asked, "Is your *wife* on anything?"

Rory sighed. "She just doesn't wake up very well and the last couple Wednesday mornings have been extra challenging."

The officers had inspected Rory's starter pistol and made a cursory search of the house. They didn't find any drugs, weapons or ammo. Doyle had expected at the very least to issue a summons for disturbing the peace, although she'd have preferred hauling Rory off in cuffs. However, after her doughnut toting partner conferred with her at length regarding policies, angry women and potential lawsuits, they departed leaving Rory with a stern warning and an enraged wife.

In what seemed a logical choice, Rory headed upstairs to comfort Steph once they had gone. Little did he know that she'd changed her three-step process to a new one of indeterminate steps. When he rounded the corner to the bedroom a thrown pillow hit him squarely in the head. It was one of the heavy pillows so he exclaimed, "Hey!"

She yelled at him to get out. He stood dumb for a moment before she added, "I mean it! I'm not in a mood to talk to you, or even see you for a while."

He backed away, hands up in surrender. "OK, I'll go to the shop. If you need anything call me."

So it was. One angry spat with a neighbor (who was clearly wrong) and Rory was in the proverbial doghouse. He'd nearly been arrested, his wife was not only livid, but was violating the rules which she herself had created. At least there was the upcoming fall hockey season. Aside from that all things seemed for naught.

Rory sat in the shop for a couple of hours annoying his employees, drinking too much coffee and browsing the Internet to kill time. Mostly he felt an empty shell while sitting there waiting and wondering what might go wrong next. The times between anger and forgiveness were always bleak ones for Rory.

Eventually Steph called, confirming his thought that the rules somehow didn't apply. She was all business, nonetheless he was pleased to hear her voice. "Don't forget, I have my work dinner tonight at 6:30 p.m."

He *had* forgotten. "Am I supposed to be going with you to that?" he asked, both dreading her answer and cringing at the thought that he didn't already know it. There was a sinking feeling that she'd told him the details and he'd forgotten. Rory braced himself for the reply he suspected would be coming.

"Yes, I've been telling you about this for two weeks now. We're meeting everyone at the Walnut Brewery for our employee meeting tonight. The company is paying for it. Remember?"

Sitting at dinner with fifteen nurses wasn't as exciting to Rory as it might have sounded in high school. For starters Steph was the only one in her group under forty years old and under two hundred pounds. Then there was the rather unsavory conversation during dinner. Listening to talk about blood, guts, urine, stool, vomit and strange items that patients had to have removed after "accidentally sitting on them" wasn't exactly something that Rory felt like doing ever, let alone during dinner.

He wasn't sure they did it on purpose. If they did, it was well practiced and smoothly delivered. A typical mealtime conversation might proceed like this:

"That new CNA, Jules, left one of my patients lying in his own stool for over an hour last week."

"Is she the one who broke the light bulb by mistake when that guy came in with it in his butt?"

"No, that was Cindy. Who is Jules?"

"You know Jules. She was the one who got peed on, crapped on *and* puked on her first day."

"Oh yeah, she *is* worthless."

The husbands were typically just as interesting to Rory as the conversations the women were having. Most of them were in such bad shape that Rory suspected their doctors advised them not to even *watch* sports. Even if they had something in common with Rory, there wasn't ever much chance of getting a side conversation going with the raucous monopoly the women had on the table chat. The men mostly drank too much and kept quiet.

Rory normally wouldn't make any attempt to hide his sarcasm. Instead, he'd tell Steph something to like, "Of course I didn't forget, I can *hardly* wait." However, he knew she wasn't his biggest fan at the moment. He simply and wisely replied, "OK, I'll be there."

"I know you don't like these dinners, but I forgot to tell you something. There's a new nurse in our group, Helen. Her boyfriend plays hockey and he's going to be there," Steph said.

Suddenly the dinner sounded a little less dull to Rory. "What's his name? Maybe I know him."

"She said he hasn't played for over a year, but he's going to play again this season. I think his name is Rob, Rob *Weller* maybe?" Steph answered.

He promised to be on his best behavior before they finished the conversation. However, after hanging up, he realized that probably didn't mean much. His behavior hadn't been too impressive lately.

While it seemed trivial in light of how life in general was treating him, Rory was still annoyed that the championship had eluded him, twice. His dream and goal fell short by the slimmest and most unlikely of margins. Despite this last failure being in the less serious summer season, he was angry about it. In hockey he wore the badge of loser if only by association with the other players who called themselves Lucky Pucks. *Luck, bah!*

In life, all things seemed like they were brimming with bad luck . . . assuming he believed in such things. He'd heard bad things came in threes and wondered if there was some scientific evidence to support that. If it was just superstition, he wasn't buying it, although he did seem to be the victim of a group of three himself.

In fact, he considered the possibility that he was the victim of not one, but *two* groups of three. In life, he had an angry wife, a neighbor re-purposing his yard for a canine restroom and wake-up call from law enforcement officials. Still, these were secondary in his thoughts to the likelihood of a third straight championship loss. Despite the lack of any silver cup on which his name would appear for eternity, little was more important to him than the championship. It wasn't about accolades or the rather cheesy T-shirts proclaiming victory to anyone who might bother to read them. For Rory, it was about the competition. He felt the true measurement of a man lay within knowing that he'd brought his best and succeeded. Unfortunately, the measurement of his particular team was recorded in heaps of failure.

The worst part of the day was undoubtedly going to be the team meeting that Dan had scheduled for Fall season sign-ups. Memorial Day weekend marked the bye-week between seasons. After a fourteen day hiatus, they'd return to the ice for yet another championship run. In light of Rory's rage, which required some time to properly cook, ingest and subsequently digest, a longer wait would have been a good thing. As for the team meeting, the fact that the cops woke him up that morning certainly didn't bode well for his chances of remaining civil.

Nonetheless, later that day, Rory sat with the entire team on the patio of Jackson's Grill, conveniently located in the same building as the rink and his shop. A strange quiet had overcome the normally robust group as they sat filling out paperwork for the next season. Rory's pen paused while he worked on a Fat Tire Ale in a mug so big it should have read 7-11 Humongous Gulp. He pondered why anyone would actually want a beer that big at lunchtime and assured himself he wouldn't finish it.

Directly across the table from Rory, there came a groan. Dan, team captain and piano salesman, was gazing across the parking lot to where a man in a wheelchair was unloading himself from a van. The whir of the hydraulic ramp lowering was barely audible across the lot. Dan turned to Rory, an apologetic look in his eyes. Rory didn't catch the look since he was wondering how Dan turned his head despite not having a neck.

Dan muttered, "This isn't good."

"What's not good?" Rory asked.

"That's our old goalie."

"Funny," Rory replied after following Dan's gaze to the wheelchair exiting the van.

"Not really."

Rory was immediately chagrined. "Oh geez, I'm sorry. Was he in an accident?"

"What? No . . . well yeah, but that's not why he's the old goalie."

Confusion set in. "This *is* a joke, right?"

Dan stood up and motioned Rory to follow. The Lucky Pucks had the patio pretty much to themselves despite the warm day. Dan maneuvered Rory toward some empty space away from the rest of the team. He pulled off the Lucky Pucks ball cap that he'd ordered online. Few men could have been as proud as Dan to have a one of a kind Lucky Pucks hat, even if it was even uglier than the $8 price might indicate. Thus, Rory knew he was in trouble when Dan began twisting his prized piece of head wear in his hands.

"I'm sorry, Rory. I didn't think that Wheels was coming back." The man in the wheelchair was closing the access ramp on the van. He could have been Grizzly Adams if the meeting with the bear had gone differently. *Perhaps the character would have been Grizzled Adams instead,* Rory thought momentarily amused at how clever he was, then ashamed for thinking it. The man's face was covered in approximately forty cubic-feet of beard. He was wearing sweats and a pair of top-end running shoes. It struck Rory odd that a man in a wheelchair would wear a pair of expensive running shoes. Perhaps it was a fashion statement, or a subtle sign to proclaim, "Look, I've made it big! I can buy something as frivolous as expensive running shoes."

Dan continued, "Wheels is the goalie you replaced. He started the Lucky Pucks a few years ago. He was having some health issues and couldn't play. I didn't know he was going to come back this season. I'm sorry. I would have told you if I knew he was going to play."

"What are you telling me, Dan?" Rory asked, his voice rising. This smacked of some sort of joke. Rory was trying to piece it together, the problem was that while Rory was pretty good at reading a lie, he suspected that Dan was even better at telling one. Rory had to go with the evidence alone.

He pondered the facts. The first among them was simple— the guy was in a wheelchair. Rory wondered, *How could he play hockey in a wheelchair?* Second was the mysterious timing. *How did "Wheels" know about the sign up session if no one knew he was coming back to play?* The nickname was certainly suspicious. *What kind of person in a wheelchair let people call him Wheels?*

On the other hand, Dan was a known prankster, although his pranks were typically only funny to him. Several times the team was left aghast at something Dan thought would be funny. One such prank involved a gallon of mayonnaise heaped into a fellow player's skates while the rest of the team showered. No one was sure why Dan thought this would be funny or how long he carried a gallon jar of mayo in his bag waiting for the opportune moment. Nonetheless, the player left the team after Dan refused to replace or clean the skates. Rory wondered if this wasn't Dan's plan from the start.

Nonetheless, a slight sense of dread was creeping over Rory. A forced smile concealed his concern when he asked, "You're really going to replace me with Rasputin in a wheelchair? This is our year to win. Third time's the charm right? I mean come on, the guy's in a wheelchair. It looks like the health issues just might still exist."

Dan was nodding. Rory wondered, *is he messing with me?* He couldn't tell, but Rory's sense of humor was receding beneath a growing layer of ire. Dan still wouldn't look Rory in the eyes. His prized hat was almost in a knot now. Still Rory couldn't tell if he was joking and trying not to laugh or he was ashamed for not having mentioned this detail to earlier.

"Listen," Dan continued, "this has always been Wheels's team. He's always been on the team email list in case he wanted to come back. I don't know why he didn't reply to let me know he'd be playing." Dan paused almost apologetically before continuing. "Wheels has been in the chair since I've known him. He put this team together. I'm not telling him he can't play just because I didn't hear from him in time. You're welcome to skate with us. We need a left wing since Jeremy isn't coming back."

The electric chair was rolling closer now. Rory could see something resembling a smile through the tangle of facial hair. Despite the unkempt nature of the man's beard (Rory was pretty sure he saw a whole crouton hanging in it) the man appeared smug. Grizzled Adams was driving the chair by blowing into a couple of tubes. Rory reeled in anger at the sight. He wasn't just being replaced by a guy in a wheelchair—this guy was barely moving from the neck down. *How could he play hockey? He probably can't even dress himself.*

His lungs apparently worked though. He rolled up the patio ramp past Rory to greet the rest of the team with a hearty, "Hey guys!" The Lucky Puckers looked up from their registration forms returning his greeting. Oddly, it dawned on Rory that they looked like a bunch of high school students taking their SAT tests right up till Wheels arrived when suddenly they looked like a bunch of hockey players once again. The greetings were sincere at first, then slightly awkward. The team apparently knew there were suddenly too many goalies on the patio at Jackson's.

"So what do you think? You want to skate out this season?" Dan asked.

The offer was empty. Rory knew little about playing left wing. He thought, *seriously? Moving from goalie to another position is like asking a quarterback to move to defensive end, or a pitcher to pinch hit, or a point guard, aw, who cares about basketball? I don't even own the proper gear to switch positions. I am a goalie. Anything else is a demotion.*

He'd turned down offers from three other teams even after *not* winning the championship. A lingering possibility that Dan knew this might be coming and said nothing made Rory as angry as the offer. Now with seven days before the fall season started, it might be too late for him to find a team at all. Furious was not a strong enough word to define Rory's state of mind.

Regardless, of what Dan's intentions were, or were not, it was impossible for Rory to reign in his anger. He found himself screaming, "You don't want to tell him he can't play but you don't have an issue insulting me? Why would I play for you after you just cost me my championship season for the third time in a row? Let Wheels skate out."

Not playing again until spring season was unfathomable. Rory also realized that Dan had been a part of both championship game losses and was about to cost him a third attempt. Rory completely blamed Dan for all of his woes past, present and future. Despite this, his anger was inexplicably directed at Wheels. This feeling manifested itself in an inferno of profanity. It came spewing from his mouth with inexplicable precision and automation as Rory stormed off the patio. He heard himself stringing together four letter words while punctuating them with terms like cripple and invalid. Rory was embarrassed even as they erupted from his mouth.

Dan looked hurt, but even if that were a possibility, Rory couldn't stop himself. Momentum and rage spun like a flywheel in his brain, driving his speech. He was ashamed of every word. The venom that he attached to the old goalie's nickname, Rory found particularly detestable even as he spat it out. Try as he might, he could not stop himself.

He took one last glance at the team sitting around the table with enormous mugs of beer in front of them. He recognized the dismay on each of their faces. The old goalie's chair spun around and Rory saw that the smug smile on his face had been replaced with a look of intense sadness. Rory turned his back feeling a wave of shame and embarrassment finally quelling the embers of his outburst. He wasn't quite ready to give up the anger, but muttered to himself, "You're an idiot, Rory."

CHAPTER FIVE

THE TROUBLE WITH NICKNAMES

The Rock Bottom was filled to capacity that night. Fortunately, Steph's group called ahead and five tables had been shoved together in anticipation of their arrival. Animated nurses and their comatose spouses occupied the chairs corralling them. Despite the numerous patrons filling the restaurant, the cacophony of voices from the other tables was unable to overwhelm the nurse's shop talk. The dark wood, mood-lighting and specialized conversation cleverly conspired to make Rory feel somewhat sleepy.

When Helen finally arrived with her boyfriend in tow, Rory had already downed several beers. These he deemed requisite to improve his endurance for the drivel that passed as conversation. He'd just finished a brown ale, which by his best guess was about 92% alcohol. This he judged by the near opiate state of relaxation he found himself enjoying.

He vaguely noted that a young, mousy-haired woman had joined the table. She was a tiny girl with big brown eyes on an otherwise unremarkable face. But when she flashed a friendly smile at the table it was, Rory thought, a refreshing and unexpected change from the dour, old-nurses convention. He hoped that the new blood would revive the conversation, momentarily musing to himself that new blood or not, less talk of blood would be a good thing.

Out of the corner of his eye, he noticed her already-seated date. The "hockey player" rolling up to the table was none other than Wheels. Beneath the man's acres of beard Rory spotted a Lucky Puckers T-shirt. Rory hadn't even ever *seen* a Lucky Puckers shirt, let alone owned one. He quickly re-calculated the alcohol content of his drink. It was probably closer to 6%. He certainly felt sober as he flew into a rage.

"You've got to be kidding me! You're the hockey player?" he shouted, bolting out of his chair and pointing an accusatory finger in Wheels' direction. Conversation at the table (and several nearby) withered in reply to the indignation in Rory's tone.

The wheelchair bound goalie flashed his best Grizzly Adams smile and nodded. "That's right, I'm Rob. Have we met?"

Rory was shaking with rage. His head swam. "Really? You stole my team this morning and now you're not going to acknowledge that you even know me! If you weren't in that chair I'd break your jaw."

Rory was oblivious to the looks of horror among the nurses at the table. Nor did he feel Stephanie tugging on his shirt sleeve even though she was pulling with effort as hard as the look she was giving him. The husbands at the table, as novocained on alcohol as Rory had been a moment earlier, were mildly interested in the possibility they might see a guy in a wheelchair get throttled.

Wheels was moving his mouth, perhaps to apologize, but Rory didn't hear a word of it. Then with the impeccable timing of someone who asks questions while her clients have full mouths, the waitress arrived with the tray of food. Oblivious to the threat of violence at the table, she asked, "Who had the bacon burger?"

Rory took this as his cue to leave, which he did promptly, leaving his flabbergasted wife and more than a few gawking diners behind. He walked swiftly out the door without looking back. The gathered mass at the table watched him depart and exhaled a synchronized sigh of relief.

After reaching the car, Rory collected himself enough to realize that he'd left his wife stranded in the restaurant. Equally important he realized that he was in no shape to drive. He leaned on the roof of his Porsche for a moment watching the plumes of mist generated from his deep breaths. He exhaled slowly trying to calm down. His hands were still shaking as he put the keys back in his pocket.

He strolled slowly past the theaters contemplating what he should do. *What is it about this guy in a wheelchair that infuriates me to irrational acts? I don't even know this guy. It's Dan who's to blame anyway, isn't it?* These things were all true. Yet twice he'd met Wheels and twice he'd publicly made a complete and total fool of himself.

For a moment Rory paused to peruse the film list at the theater. There were a couple titles he thought might be interesting, but not interesting enough to watch alone. A hundred yards away he could wile away some time at Dave and Busters playing video games while drinking another beer . . . probably not the best plan. Crossing the bridge to see what was on the ice at the rink was an option. The bowling alley he didn't really consider, recalling bowling as a sport for irredeemably depressed alcoholics. He did worry for a moment that seemed like a place he'd fit in pretty well at the moment.

The only other real options were to catch a cab home or head back to The Rock Bottom with his hat in his hand. He'd certainly put Steph through enough for one day. So, despite not actually having a hat, he stumbled back in that direction hoping to make amends . . . or at least amends enough to muddle through the dinner without a reasonable expectation of divorce papers being delivered in the near future.

Rory walked back to the restaurant as slowly as if he were facing his own execution. He passed through the doors and approached the table. He had no doubt they were still talking about him as the conversation wilted and died at his approach. All eyes turned to him and he felt suddenly as if he were standing in a spotlight on stage and had forgotten his pants.

He cleared his throat. "Um, I apologize. I didn't mean to ruin everyone's dinner tonight. I've been having a bad week and I'm sorry to air it out here."

Rory then turned to Wheels. "I've behaved irrationally and been unacceptably rude to you twice now, and for that I'm terribly sorry."

To Rory's surprise, Rob smiled. "You're forgiven. Have a seat here. I'd like to talk with you," he said indicating an empty chair beside him.

There was no way Rory was sitting next to the guy. It was bad enough to have to apologize and then eat near him. It was a sour tasting apology, even though he wasn't sincere in delivering it. Rory declined with as much grace as he could muster.

"It's a kind offer, but if you don't mind, I'd like to sit with my wife."

The ride home that night ensued in silence. Rory wasn't sure what stage this was. There were so many reasons for Steph to be angry with him that he had to consider that she might be on several stages at once. Besides, the rules were apparently no longer the same even if he *had* only given her one excuse to be angry. It began to rain on the drive home. Rory found himself blinded by the glare of traffic lights on the rain spattered passenger window as a numbing wash of emotions passed though him. Catching his reflection in the window he saw a very unhappy man.

At home, Steph went straight to bed, telling him goodnight in a terse voice. There was no customary hug, no kiss. Rory, unsure if he should join her or not, sat in front of the television hoping to escape the dire reality of his existence for at least a moment. It didn't help. His mind wandered, always falling back on how utterly alone he felt.

Wondering what it would be like if he had to live without Steph, he pondered their first date. It was a mild November night. After dinner they strolled the Pearl Street mall hand in hand finding one busker, a magician with a small audience. His act was amusing although mostly forgettable. There was one moment that Rory would never forget; for his finale the performer conscripted Steph as his assistant.

She was to retrieve his sword after he had swallowed it. Just to work the crowd he put a large bib on her, claiming it was so no blood would spoil her shirt in the event of an accident. Under the pretense of adjusting the bib, he managed to steal her necklace, a feat he proudly displayed to the audience with a wink.

Of course, she removed the sword without any blood letting. When he retrieved the bib from her, it was attached to a bra of tremendous, granny size proportions. He handed her the necklace she'd been wearing telling her, "Here's a little something to remember me by." Then displaying the bra, he arched his eyebrows to the crowd as told her, "and a little something for me to remember you." Rory was embarrassed for her. He worried that the joke at her expense was a little much. However, she returned to him laughing and planted a little kiss on his cheek. She'd taken it in such good humor that Rory was certain he'd fallen in love with her that very moment. He was pretty sure he'd wither and die without her now.

Rory fell asleep on the couch, finally crawling into bed at two in the morning. He'd get a few more fitful hours of rest before his early morning shift. At 5:00 a.m. he was showered, shaved and anything but refreshed. He kissed Steph on the forehead without waking her and slipped out of the house to work.

The day found Rory working like a politician trying to find a vote. Sadly, he was finding it impossible to gain the single vote he needed. He'd neglected his real work leaving Mark to run the shop.

Rory hung up the phone in frustration and gazed through the one-way mirror. The lobby was empty aside from Mark who was back-flushing the espresso machine. The slight throbbing hum of the pump and hiss of water leaking through the porta-filter seal was barely audible above the piped in music.

The phone call Rory had just finished marked the end of his options. There were no other teams in the B-league to call. All of them were set at goalie. Three of the captains indicated that they wished he had called sooner. It was pretty much official, he was without a team for the next season. His name was on the free agent list, so if someone got hurt or another league needed a goalie, there was still a chance he'd get a call, but that fact did nothing to sate his disappointment with the situation.

He was about to go complain to Mark about the quality of his life, figuring that a $12 an hour employee was a lot cheaper than a therapist. Before he moved from his seat the phone rang. Rory picked it up. "Thanks for calling Lord Stanley's, this is Rory."

"Rory, this is Josh," came the reply. Rory had played pick-up hockey with Josh for a couple years. He knew Josh to be a decent guy off the ice and an outstanding player on it.

"Hey Josh, what's going on?"

"Just wondering if you'd like to play A-league this season."

"Seriously?"

"Seriously."

"I just spent the last hour and a half on the phone calling every captain in the B-league for a team."

"B-1?"

"The entire B league, B 1 through 5."

"So you found a team already then?"

"Nope, everyone had a goalie lined up. I'd love to play A-league."

"Good deal. Call my team captain, Tim. He'll get you the details. I'll text his number to your cell."

"Great."

Rory finished the call and hung up the phone. He still felt the slight wave of anxious nausea that had been chasing him since he stormed off the patio at Jackson's the previous day. But while it was still there, it shifted from an emotion born of loss to one born of anticipation. He would be playing in the A-league! True, there was still no Stanley Cup and he would still be about a million players removed from playing any level of hockey that anyone would pay to watch. But there perennially were a couple of former NHL players in the league, a dozen or so former minor-league players and quite a few more who played in college. It was the highest level of hockey a guy who started playing in his twenties could hope to attain.

He stood up and started walking to the lobby as he dialed Tim's number. The second ring was interrupted by a gruff, "Yeah."

Put off for a moment by the demeanor on the phone, Rory stammered, "Uh, yeah . . . is this Tim?"

"Who is this?"

"My name is Rory Clark . . ."

"Not interested."

"Excuse me?"

The line was dead. Tim had hung up. Figuring he'd dialed the wrong number somehow, Rory continued to pace through the lobby, then dialed again. The phone rang four times and went to Tim's voice mail. Rory hung up and dialed from the store phone instead, deciding that Tim was ducking his call back due to some inexplicable and misguided fear of telephone solicitors.

This time the "Yeah?" was more angry than gruff.

"Tim, I'm a friend of Josh's. He said you were looking for a goalie for your A-league team."

There was a long pause, so long in fact that Rory thought that Tim had hung up the phone again. He looked at his cell phone's display to make sure he was still connected and put it back to his ear.

Eventually, Tim did reply. With no attempt to hide his irritation he said, "I *am* looking for a goalie, but that was pretty presumptuous of Josh to line one up. I don't really have time for this right now. I'll call you back tomorrow at noon, this number. We can do a phone interview."

"A phone interview?"

Once again Tim had hung up not even hearing Rory's question. A normal person might have made sure that the number and time were convenient. The nervous feeling in Rory's stomach returned to a less positive origin. He called Josh.

"What's up, Rory?"

"I just talked to Tim."

"And?"

"He didn't seem to expect my call."

"Huh, I just talked to him."

"Well, he hung up on me twice."

"Ah, I didn't know he'd do that to goalies too."

"So he's pretty much a tremendous tool then?"

"I wouldn't say that. He just has a . . . well . . . a process. Did he set up a phone interview?"

"Yeah. This seems ridiculous though. Tell me why I want to be on this team. I'm not sure about jumping through these hoops, Josh."

"It's a great team, Rory. We've played for the championship the last four straight seasons, and that's because Tim is that particular about who plays for the team."

"Alright Josh, is there anything else I should know?"

"Not really. You'll be fine with the phone interview. The tryout will be Friday night during our practice ice time."

Rory simply replied, "OK, see you then." But as he hung up the phone, he wondered what he was getting into. He'd never heard of a recreational team having a tryout or practice ice time, let alone phone interviews. Most of them were lucky to have uniforms that matched and 10 or 12 players who showed up on game night.

As Rory pondered these things, he watched a woman tethering her English Bulldog to one of the outdoor tables. Despite having the appearance of wrought iron, weighing as much as a small car, the tables were aluminum. They, in fact, weighed about as much as a very heavy pocket watch.

Rory started toward the front door to warn the woman about the unsuitable nature of the table as a hitching post. His act, though well intentioned, was too late. The pooch pulled against his leash then looked back to see what was keeping him in place. In perfect reply, the table complete with umbrella toppled in the in dog's direction.

Despite his master's command, more a plea, "Nigel, stay!" the dog was off and running. Nigel's owner was a slight woman who might have been five feet tall. She had the unhealthy pallor of a vegan. This somehow matched the vague look of confusion in her eyes as well as an overall lack of understanding of how her dog (who likely weighed twenty-five pounds more than she did) was able to pull over a table that weighed about five pounds.

If ever Rory had witnessed a look of terror in the eyes of a dog, it was in this English Bulldog. After one bark of disbelief, eyes bulging, Nigel spun and took off at full speed. He dodged the umbrella. Taking a hard right, Nigel not only dislodged the canopy from the table, but the legs as well. The top of the table rolled gaining momentum then slowing with each revolution as the leash urged it along. The faster the tabletop spun, the more frantic Nigel's progress became. His head would swivel back to determine if he'd lost the pursuing table or not and then he'd surge ahead once more.

All the while Nigel's imbecile owner stood mute. If she had been standing in that location when the concrete was poured she couldn't have been any less mobile. Even the slight breeze could not cause her saggy hemp dress to flutter.

Rory made it to the patio and passed her just as the dog made it to the parking lot. He wasn't sure if he should feel bad for the dog or angry at the owner, so he did both. The table smashed into a parked car somehow increasing poor Nigel's level of terror. With a yip, he slashed left between two more parked cars, the table scraping both of them. Nigel apparently couldn't understand how no amount of maneuvering or speed could evade the dreaded saucer of death that was apparently determined to kill him.

For a moment Rory thought this might be the pooch's undoing. With no escape in sight, Nigel turned toward Westminster Boulevard, a busy four-lane byway, and dashed down the hill. Traffic screeched to a halt with cars swerving to miss the dog. Suddenly, as if realizing the table wasn't as scary as traffic, Nigel stopped in the middle of the road. The table top rolled past pulling him a couple feet before falling down. Nigel took the opportunity to pounce on it and begin barking to proclaim his ultimate victory.

The shaken pooch was picked up by a squad car among the traffic affected by his impromptu roadblock. The top of Rory's table was unceremoniously tossed on the side of the road. Nigel got a free ride in the back seat to where the police spotted his anxious owner waving them down. She'd moved almost three feet.

While Nigel, upon his return, was being praised like a hero for his efforts in traffic disruption and destruction of property,

Rory hoofed down the hill to retrieve his tabletop. He suspected that it was pointless since it was likely destroyed, but the way things had been going, he figured he'd get a littering ticket if he didn't go pick it up.

As Rory returned up the hill, two police officers stood talking to Nigel's oblivious, vegan owner, who now held his leash. The lanky officer knelt by the dog scratching behind its ears and reassuring the still slightly skittish dog, saying, "That's a good boy."

The other officer, muscled and tonsured like a marine, stood with a notepad in hand, nodding as the woman spoke. All three of them ignored Rory as he set down the remains of the table. He waited for a moment assuming his turn would come. After a while he was struck with the thought that he wasn't interested in talking to more police officers. He pushed through the doors and passed behind the counter.

"Everything alright? The dog didn't get hurt did he?" Mark asked as Rory proceeded to the office.

"E tu, Brute?" Rory asked, not noting Mark's puzzled look as he swept into the office. Rory made his way up the ladder and through the roof hatch for the second time in his life. He closed the lid, but this time more for a place to sit rather than to fully escape.

Rory breathed deeply the cool crisp air and thought to himself what a mess he'd made of things. It all felt so futile. His wife was angry at him and despite a dozen guys that he played hockey and drank beer with once a week there was no one he could count as a true friend.

His best friend, the one person who he could call at a moment's notice and count on to drive right over, had moved to Pittsburgh four years earlier. They stayed in touch, but it was hard to really dump your woes on a buddy over the phone. Though Rory would never admit it aloud, a hug would be nice too. Even the rough, awkward embrace of a two hundred pound bearded friend would suffice. He'd lost close friends several times in his life. But never had the void been left unfilled for so long.

Through this he had his wife, but with the issues he faced now, his one rock was gone. Now with the lack of even his superficial once a week friends, Rory felt the pang of emptiness suffocating him. Thus he sat alone on the roof watching the traffic far below, feeling utterly and totally alone.

CHAPTER SIX

CLEARING THE AIR

Rory winced as he cleaned Thunder's personal doggy-log disposal area after work. He'd paid a premium for the corner lot that they lived on. The landscape was lush, green and of his own design. He liked to think it was creative and attractive. At least it was until Thunder had claimed a spot beside the drive leading to the side-loading garage. Numerous brown bulls-eyes marked that area. He pondered planting a fruit tree there to give the impression that the brown spots were nothing more than fallen fruit. Rory dismissed this plan quickly with the realization that he'd have to pick up two kinds of fallen fruit in that area . . . assuming Thunder didn't just eat the tree.

    The neighborhood, though pleasant enough, had been beaten into submission by an overachieving homeowner's association. They allowed every shade of boring on the homes which resulted in each of them being painted tan or gray. Rory found this ironic since patches of either shade cropping up in one's yard always resulted in a letter demanding that the homeowner correct the situation.

    It was his determination that the HOA simply existed to make enemies of neighbors. He had once been chastised for his mother-in-law's car being parked in front of their house for more than two days. When he called to inquire if they'd considered using strong laxatives to improve their mood and judgment, they told him one of his neighbors had complained. Complaining neighbors, that was always the story with the HOA, although on three occasions he had spotted HOA representatives stopping to write notes a couple days before a letter from them arrived.

Using a hoe, shovel and some carefully muttered four-letter words, Rory transferred three large mounds of recycled dog food into an enormous seventy-five-gallon, wheeled trash can. He'd purchased the vessel specially for this very purpose. The odor from the trash can was more noxious than anything he could imagine despite the fact that it was less than a quarter full. Rory wasn't entirely certain why he was saving fifteen gallons of mutt muffins, but somewhere in the most devious part of his mind he thought mailing it to the HOA would be fun.

On a warm day the odor sometimes took on a life of its own. Several occasions left Rory thinking he'd seen a writhing, ethereal, green wisp glaring at him above the can. Though reasonable enough to chalk this up to a methane related hallucination, Rory did once have a nightmare that the malodorous visage escaped the confines of the can and was attempting to choke him. He'd awoken gasping and ran to the bathroom thinking he might throw up.

Now, as he finished his manual labor, Rory's mind was running through the possible ways to rectify the rump raisin problem. He'd earnestly believed that Davis Jennings would stop using his yard as a poo depository after their previous run in. If anything, the situation had become worse. Rory wondered, *do dogs like to take care of their business in a place where another dog previously left a calling card?* He had no idea, but regardless of whether Davis had allowed his pooch to mark a corner of his yard as suitable for general doggie dung disposal or Thunder was solely responsible for the enormous scale of the fecal invasion was irrelevant to Rory. The bottom line in his mind was, Davis

Jennings was to blame. Just what he might do about this was as of yet unresolved.

Thinking that he needed to shower, despite the fact that he hadn't come within five feet of contacting any of the offending land mines in the yard, Rory stepped back into the house. He watched the overhead door close before turning his attention to the direction he was headed. As the entry door closed, Steph stood in front of him. She wore as fearsome a countenance as any guard dog on duty. Rory stopped in his tracks. Startled, he accidentally asked aloud, "What stage is this?"

Steph's frightening glare didn't falter as she replied, "What *stage*? What's that supposed to mean?" Without waiting for an answer she continued on. "I'm tired of whatever you're doing, Rory. It has to change. I don't like having gunshots and police officers wake me up in the morning. I don't appreciate you embarrassing me by acting like a total buffoon in front of my friends. But mostly I don't like you acting like someone that I don't know."

Rory was trapped in the hall with his back to the garage door. He didn't ponder escape, although he was certain it was impossible. A drill sergeant poking a finger in his chest and screaming at him couldn't have made that point any clearer. In fact a drill sergeant wouldn't have been half as scary.

Finding himself pressed against the door to the garage and his wife suddenly silent, Rory determined that perhaps it was his turn to speak. He struggled to find the words thinking, *how can I explain behavior so irrational that I'm not sure where it came from? How can I assure her that the man she married is the one in front of her?* Most confounding was the question of whether something really was wrong with him.

He wanted to defend himself. Yet he knew that defending himself was akin to going on the attack. Surrender was the only viable plan for peace. Every fiber of his being knew it. Despite this obvious truth, Rory found himself explaining . . . explaining and thinking he was apologizing.

"Tinkerbell," he started, as this was what he often called her, "you know I'm not like that. I've been under a lot of stress with the hockey team."

Rory paused for a moment thinking how badly things might go if anyone from hockey knew he called his wife Tinkerbell. Then he continued, "I *am* the man you married. You know me. It's just a rough patch."

She looked at him for a moment before reminding him, "You screamed at a man in a wheelchair . . . no, Rory, you told a man in the wheelchair that you'd like to punch him out. That's not the man I know and it's a lot more than a rough patch. You used to be easy going and now *everything* gets under your skin. What's going on with you?"

It wasn't the first moment in the crisis that Rory thought he realized what the issue was, or even that there was an issue. But with that moment came the first realization that he could put into words what he was feeling. He wasn't alone until Steph was decidedly against him. His shoulders slumped as all of the fight went out of him.

"Steph, I'm so sorry. I know I made some bad decisions, horrible decisions. I've lost my temper too. The problem is that you're the only one that I can talk to and for more than a week, I've done nothing but upset you. You're my wife and my best friend, Steph . . . my only real friend. So who do I talk to when my wife and best friend is angry at me? I've felt so alone in this."

He took a big chance and stepped closer, pulling her into his arms. If things went poorly, he was pretty sure neither car had enough gas to get to Kansas, but at least a triple-A card was in the glove box in case she tried. Steph was limp in his arms, but he held on to her telling her, "I'm so sorry" several times.

She finally yielded and wrapped her arms around him in return. Eventually, Steph put her head on his shoulder. He held her until he felt the warmth of her tears soaking through his shirt. In a small voice, Rory asked, "Are you OK?"

She nodded and with a sniff told him, "Rory, I'll always be here even if your best friend or wife is angry at you . . ." Pulling away she forced a smile and told him, "but honey, you smell like dog crap right now. Maybe you should go shower and change."

He nodded in agreement. "Meet you on the couch in ten minutes?"

She smiled. "Fine, but the remote is mine tonight."

Rory picked up the phone on the second ring answering, "Thanks for calling Lord Stanley's, this is Rory." The voice on the other end was female and a few bricks shy of a wheelbarrow load. He looked at the clock. It was straight up noon. Tim's call was due any moment.

His caller had a voice that wavered in anger. "Rory! You're the manager right? There's a problem that you need to fix with your employees or your process or something.

"I was in this morning on my way to work. I ordered a decaf latte. I even twice asked the girl who was making it if it was decaf, yet I received a regular latte. Now Rory, this is the fourth time that this has happened to me in your shop. I have a severe caffeine sensitivity and this is simply unacceptable. Why is it so difficult for you to me make a decaf latte there?"

Rory was stunned. He was pretty sure that she was insane. He knew mistakes were going to happen from time to time, but a tale of someone getting the wrong coffee four times was pretty hard to swallow. Even if his employees *were* making that mistake, she'd never called before to complain. The fact that she gave them three more chances with her "severe caffeine sensitivity" made the story all the more absurd.

Biting back on his true feelings, he replied, "I'm so sorry that your drink wasn't to your expectations. I assure you that we have solid procedures to prevent mistakes like that from happening. Whenever there are people involved, there is a potential for mistakes though. Did your cup have a decaf sticker on it today?"

"Yes it had a sticker on it, but it wasn't decaf. I'm not stupid. I know when you people screw up. I'm so shaky that I can't even drive myself. I'm having to pay for a cab to take me to detox. You've essentially poisoned me."

Rory wanted to beat the phone repeatedly on the desk and scream. Part of the process in making a bar drink was to pull the decaf sticker off the roll attached to the decaf espresso grinder. This process was in place to make sure that the barista grabbed a sticker only when remembering to grind the proper beans.

"Again, I'm very sorry. Let me ask you, what I can do to make this right?"

"Unless you want to pay me for four lost days of work, there's nothing you can do to make it right."

"So I guess I don't understand the purpose of your call then."

"I'm calling to keep you from poisoning other people."

"Caffeine isn't poisonous."

"It is to me!"

"I see. Did you call the other times you were unhappy with your drink?"

"No."

"So you didn't think it was important the other times?"

"I was in detox."

"Do you live in Boulder, ma'am?"

"Yes I do, why is that important?"

"I'd suggest the little shop by the bowling alley on 30th."

"They poisoned me eight times there . . . and they tore down that bowling alley years ago. It's a computer store now."

"Really?"

"Really, you should get out more."

"Ma'am, did you ever think that maybe you should just give up coffee altogether?"

"You're just being rude now. I'm hanging up."

Rory looked at the handset for a moment after it clicked wondering if there really were people who could be poisoned by caffeine. He decided it was more likely drug abuse, mental health issues, a prank call or even all of the above. He hung up the phone, suddenly realizing that he'd been waiting for Tim to call. It was seven minutes after twelve.

He waited three more minutes, nervous about whether he'd be castigated for his inability to follow directions if he called instead of waiting for the call. Finally he decided that he should just go ahead and dial. On the third ring Tim picked up, "Yeah."

"Tim, it's Rory Clark."

"Our appointment was at noon. It's ten minutes after."

"Sorry Tim, I had a call right at noon. I figured you were getting a busy signal."

"Why would *I* be getting a busy signal?"

"You were going to call me at noon."

"If I called you then how would I have known you could use a clock?"

"It's pretty much irrelevant, I was on the phone at noon anyway."

"Let's say the time issue isn't important for now. There *is* still another problem. Following instructions is important to me. I asked you to call *me*. I need coach-able team players, Clark."

Rory was speechless. He was sure that Tim had said he'd call at noon. He distinctly remembered him saying he'd call on the same number. Perhaps the issue was more a case of Tim's communication skills than it was of Rory's inability to follow instructions. He was half tempted to just tell Tim no thanks.

Before he could, Tim told him, "Listen, I'm headed over to Uncommon Grounds near the rink in a couple hours. Meet me there at, let's say 2:30. We'll meet in person and talk about the team there."

Rory contemplated whether this guy was purposely rude or just a complete tool. *Now you want to meet at a rival coffee shop across the street?* he thought. While every part of him wanted to pass, he relented. "I can make it at 2:45 if that works."

"Fine, but be on time. I'll have my Hartford Whalers shirt on." And with what Rory had decided was his customary style, Tim ended the call by hanging up.

At 2:30, as Rory's pessimistic side had predicted, the coffee shop was packed with customers seeking a cup of warm pick-me-up. Lisa walked through the door right on time, rather than her customary ten minutes early. Nonetheless, they managed to move through the line of customers quickly. This left Rory seven minutes to get across the street.

After grabbing his jacket and briefcase, Rory shouted his good-byes and dashed to the door. He pulled it open as none other than Wheels was rolling in. The bristle-faced man had a big dopey grin that Rory was starting to think was pasted on permanently. He held the door as Wheels passed through it.

"Hey it's Rory, right?" came a gruffly pleasant voice from somewhere beneath the beard and mustache. Rory noted that the man was once again wearing expensive running shoes. In contrast he also sported a well-worn pair of jeans and a T-shirt depicting a long-haired, bearded goalie making a glove save. The caption on the shirt read, "Jesus Saves!"

"Yeah, and it's Rod, right?"

"Rob, actually. Glad I caught you. Do you have a sec?"

"Actually, I'm running behind for a . . . meeting."

"Well, maybe we can set up a time to talk?"

"I'm sorry, I am really late already. You know where to find me though."

Rory passed by with an apologetic nod. He was a little worried that the guy was selling insurance or something. No one had a right to act so nice to a person who had treated them so poorly unless they had an ulterior motive, did they? Still, he felt a pang of remorse as he took a glance back. Wheels seemed to be somewhat upset that Rory hadn't made time for him.

As Rory dashed into the parking lot and dropped himself into the seat of his Porsche 968, he once again realized that Wheels had never wronged him in any way. Here he was running across the street to meet someone who seemed to be the prototype for the perfect dill weed and in the process treated a man in a wheelchair rudely. If there weren't a season of hockey on the line, he might have seriously questioned his motives.

All of the things running through his head were translated to his right foot. He careened out of the parking lot onto Promenade Drive. The tires protested slightly against the asphalt as the rear end of the car whipped out under power. As he straightened the wheel, the perfectly balanced Porsche shuddered back on line with a pop. He stopped at the light just as a police car came around the corner. The smell of burning rubber was still strong in the air and a wisp of blue smoke wafted away on the breeze. From the corner of his eye, Rory could see the cop looking at him. Feeling guilty, Rory drummed on the steering wheel and whistled along to the tune on the radio, never mind that the radio wasn't on.

The police apparently had better things to do for a change. The car continued on, allowing Rory to make his destination without intervening. Rory was a little nervous about meeting with Tim. The way things had been going lately, there was more than a small chance he might end up punching the guy in the face.

He walked into the shop. Passing the counter, he ignored the greeting from the cashier at the counter as he didn't intend to order anything from his nearest competitor. It was, however, pleasing to see that there were only four patrons in the entire place; even more pleasing to Rory was the fact that they all had sat with empty cups, nothing to eat and their eyes glued to a computer. The place was full of freeloaders cruising the web. They weren't selling coffee, they were giving away Internet access.

Among the laptop surfers, Rory quickly identified one in a Whalers shirt. Though he looked vaguely familiar, Rory wasn't sure where he'd seen him before. A Whalers shirt was pretty much a dead giveaway that a guy was a hockey player. Everyone Rory had ever met wearing the defunct team's logo had in fact been one.

Approaching the table, Rory asked, "Tim?"

The man at the table typed for a moment before looking up and replying, "Yeah, you're Rory?"

"That would be me." Rory stuck out his hand. Tim looked at it as if he were proffering a rotten mackerel. Without shaking Rory's hand he nodded to the seat across the table.

"Rory? Is that short for something?" Tim asked as Rory eyed the seat. Everything Tim did seemed to expand the definition of rudeness. Rory was considering simply leaving the shop instead of talking with him, but couldn't seem to lower himself to Tim's level of civility.

"Not normally," Rory replied, being intentionally vague. He surrendered and sat down.

"How about in your case?"

"In my case, yes it is."

"And in your case, what would that be?"

"Robert. It's short for Robert."

"And your last name is Clark?"

"That's right."

"So you have the same name as Philly great, Bobby Clarke, but you play *goalie* and go by Rory?"

"Not exactly."

"You're not a goalie or you don't go by Rory?"

"There's no 'e' on the end of my last name."

Tim gave a little snort. Rory wasn't sure if it was of contempt or mirth. Either way he forged ahead with what seemed more an inquisition than an interview. He'd become certain he would have been more comfortable across the street getting an insurance pitch from a guy in a wheelchair.

"I have your stats in front of me here. It looks like you led the league in save percentage the last two seasons. That's impressive. On the other side of that it also looks like you lost the championship game two years in a row. That's not so good."

He paused as if there were a question for Rory to answer. Rory sat quiet and waited. Eventually, Tim continued, "What do you think could have gone differently for your team to win those two championship games?"

"Well the first of those two championships was lost due to a forfeit. We lost after two members of my team started a fight. The rest of the team took so many penalties we went over the limit.

"In the second one my team captain scored the only goal which turned out to be the game winner for the other team. So I guess that we would have done better on both fronts if my team had played smarter."

Tim interjected, "Let me rephrase, what could you have personally changed about *your* game to win those championships?"

"You did hear? The first one was a forfeit? I'm not sure how I could have changed that."

Tim nodded slowly and typed furiously. Once he was finished typing, he looked up and asked Rory, "We need a goalie who can be a leader on the ice at the A-league level. So what I'm trying to glean here is what your leadership skills are, Rory Clark. Looking back on the game now, what do you think as an on ice leader you might have done to change the outcome of either game?"

Rory sat for a moment perplexed by the question. His fears about punching the guy out were apparently not unfounded. Tim's horrible phone manners were just the tip of the iceberg. In person he was at least as rude as on the phone—that or he was a terrible listener. Rory looked at Tim for a while trying to decide what to do. The options in Rory's mind were: get up and leave, punch Tim in the face, or come up with a fittingly trite answer. After a moment of consideration he opted for trite answer, followed by getting up to leave with the possibility of punching Tim in the face depending on his reaction.

Rory opened his mouth to speak, but before he could Tim interrupted, producing a Lord Stanley cup from inside his Uncommon Grounds cup. "Hold on, I almost forgot. I brought you some decent coffee."

It suddenly dawned on Rory that he'd seen the guy in the shop. He'd been wearing a ball cap, jacket and sunglasses when he'd ordered, a deviously simple but effective disguise. Rory had handed Tim his drink less than 20 minutes ago—two drinks in fact.

Tim added loudly, "This Uncommon Grounds stuff is vile swill." Producing another cup from a bag at his feet, he stood on his chair and held it up announcing, "Ladies and gentlemen, your attention. This is much better coffee than you are currently drinking. Conveniently located right across the street in the Ice Centre, Lord Stanley's Cup of Java. Thank you very much."

The collected clientele and employees of Uncommon Grounds shot him looks that varied from mildly amused to downright displeased. However when he sat back down, they apparently assumed he was done and went about their business. Rory, however wasn't sure what to think. Tim continued after he sat down.

"Sorry. I've been razzing you. Josh said you had a good sense of humor. I did want to meet you before we put you on the team. Your attitude is important. I don't need a team of hot heads and you seem like a pretty patient guy, so that's good. Most hockey players would have wanted to punch me in the face for the way I was acting."

"You don't say?" Rory asked. "Am I on the team then?"

"As far as I'm concerned you are. We have practice ice Friday night at 9:30. It's more like a pick-up game really, but sometimes we discuss strategy. I do expect everyone to show up on a regular basis. As long as the rest of the team doesn't hate you, you're the goalie, Rory."

Tim stuck out his hand this time. Rory pretended to regard it as a rotten mackerel for a as long as he could. Two seconds later he smiled and shook Tim's hand with a vigor that left him slightly embarrassed by his own exuberance.

CHAPTER SEVEN

MAKING THE BIGS

Finding a new hockey team had seemingly rendered Rory immune to the less agreeable events that came with the rest of his day. The fact that he'd found a team with a sense of humor had given him a warm, fuzzy feeling that he barely recognized. Even an insanely long line at the bank (where two of the ten windows actually featured a teller) didn't dampen his mood. While this was usually an event that caused his blood pressure to rise seven to ten points, he found himself whistling a little tune as he left. At the gas station, a guy who cut him off to steal the last open gas pump did not disturb Rory. He didn't momentarily considering smashing the guy's windshield with a tire iron or even swear under his breath. Pulling into his garage at home, Rory didn't give a thought to the new deposit of pooch pies left by Thunder.

     A moment after walking into the house Rory had KBCO blaring in the family room. He was singing along to "If I had a Million Dollars" as he walked into the kitchen. Steph would be home in a couple hours. After pulling out the cookbook, he flipped to the bread page. Assured by the instructions that he had the time and ingredients to bake his specialty, *The Enormous Pepperoni Calzone*, he rolled up his sleeves and started mixing dough.

The Calzone was one of Rory's few culinary skills. Of course he could make a mean omelet (even down to the chef style flip which he was proud to have mastered at the slim price of four dozen eggs and a pound of both cheese and ham). He also considered his skills to border on heroic when it came to grilling. The gargantuan grill on the deck was capable enough to prepare burgers, dogs, chicken breasts, brats, warmed buns and baked potatoes all at the same time for about seventeen thousand people. Rory knew given the chance, he was the one man to perfectly grill all of that food. He only hoped that one day he might get to try.

While the dough was rising on top of the warm oven, Rory, found a head of lettuce. Wondering how fresh produce had actually found its way into their fridge, he tossed a couple plates in the freezer. Not long afterward, the plates were nicely chilled and garnished with nice looking salads. Within ninety minutes he had the calzone stuffed into the oven and was in front of the television watching the Avalanche game while smelling the exquisite aroma of baking bread and bubbling mozzarella.

When Steph came home, he had the table set complete with candles and a couple glasses for red wine. He'd even found cloth napkins and invested far too much time fluffing and folding them into a pleasing shape. Rory quickly turned off the television, somewhat relieved that the Avalanche were winning by three goals in the third period. It would have been a shame to turn off the game if it wasn't a done deal.

"What smells so good?" Steph asked as he put down the remote.

"I just whipped up a little something famous, legendary even," Rory replied.

"Not The Enormous Pepperoni Calzone I hope?"

"Of course The Enormous Pepperoni Calzone! Why not?"

"I'm on a low carb diet, honey. Don't you ever listen?"

"Of course I do. Are you sure a calzone has carbs?"

"I can't eat bread for the next six weeks, Rory."

Rory thought he actually heard the air of excellence slowly hissing away as her words deflated his unflappable attitude. Of course, a calzone *was* mostly bread. This feeling was not improved when Steph saw the spread and informed him she couldn't drink wine or eat the salad due the high carb dressing he'd coated it in.

She tried to make the best of it telling Rory, "It looks really nice, hun. I appreciate the effort. I have a chicken breast that I will boil. I'll toss it on the stove, go get cleaned up and join you in twenty minutes."

With a bit of a dent in his splendid day, Rory moped back to the family room returning to the hockey game. Before Steph came back downstairs the Avalanche had frittered away their lead and ended up losing in overtime. Rory turned the television off in dismay just as the oven timer signaled Steph's chicken was ready.

He was setting the anemic, gray lump of chicken on the table as she came down the stairs. They sat at the table, Rory with a masterpiece of Italian culinary bliss which was now as cold as penguin's backside and Steph with a warm piece of meat every bit as exciting as last week's leftover carnival food. At least that was what Rory thought as he looked at it vaguely remembering a rule about never eating carnival food and something to do with a 20-year-old hot dog.

They started eating in silence. Steph was downcast because she couldn't appreciate Rory's efforts. Rory was despondent that his calzone was cold, the Avalanche had lost and that his inspired plan to create a blissful wife had fallen so pathetically short. Eventually, they found time to start talking between bites of the less than savory meal.

"How was your day?" Rory asked.

"Tiring, we were short handed, as always," Steph replied. "How about yours?"

"I thought you'd never ask. I had a good day for a change."

"Oh, did Rob meet with you today?" Steph asked.

"Rob?" Rory asked, not confused who Rob was, but how Steph might have know he was going to stop by the shop.

"Yeah, Rob from dinner the other night—the one who you threatened."

"Yeah, I know who he is and he did stop by, but how did you know about that?"

"Helen said he felt really bad about taking your spot and he was going to talk to you about it," Steph told him. She sounded slightly defensive. Rory realized that her posture was reasonable since he had probably gone on the offense at the mere mention of Rob's name.

"Oh, I didn't get a chance to talk to him."

"Really? So why was your day so good?"

"I found a team!"

"Oh, good." In Steph's tone, Rory sensed as much excitement for this fact as she had demonstrated for his high carb dinner. Regardless he forged ahead, trying to regain the enthusiasm he had earlier in the day.

"I'm taking over the goalie spot for a really good A-league team. I think it's going to be a lot of fun."

"Is this the team with the captain that you referred to as . . . was it a world class idiot?"

"Yeah, that's the team!" Rory was practically beaming as if Steph had said the captain was a world class hockey genius.

"So I'm confused. Suddenly you want to play hockey with a world class idiot?"

"No, he was just messing around with me. He's pretty funny actually. It was kinda an initiation I guess. I'm meeting the rest of the team on Friday night."

"Friday night?"

"Yeah."

"When does that start?"

"Tomorrow."

"I know tomorrow is Friday, Rory. What time?"

"Oh, it's at 9:30 in the evening."

"Tomorrow?"

"Yeah, tomorrow."

"On date night?"

Rory realized that he'd completely forgotten that detail. He suggested that that they change date night to another evening. This plan fell on deaf ears, especially when he reminded Steph that he had poker in a couple hours. There was no consensus that two nights in a row with the guys was a good idea. Canceling or re-scheduling date night was like tossing sticks of dynamite into a burning house as far as Steph was concerned. As the negotiations stalled Rory's impenetrable bubble of bliss finally and completely popped.

Lord Stanley's closed at eight in the evening, as it normally did. Thirty minutes later with shades drawn tight, any passerby might have thought the shop empty or at most pictured some secret society whispering conspiratorially behind the window glass. The true atmosphere was a bit more raucous as seven hockey players huddled around a large folding poker table. The conversation was not unlike that of a boisterous locker room. Chips were counted and card decks shuffled in preparation for tournament style game—Texas Hold-em with a $20 buy in. A few more players were expected, so Rory left the door unlocked.

As the others discussed the rules of the night, Rory retrieved beers from the backroom fridge. He returned to the lobby just in time to find Boomer preparing to light up a cigar (no one was entirely sure why Boomer was called Boomer, but they did know that calling him by his real name, Arnold, was a big mistake).

Boomer was all of about five-foot-two and might have tipped the scales at a hundred and twenty-five with his hockey gear on, sopping wet. As always, he wore a huge, easygoing smile on his face. The smile seemed somewhat in contrast to his bent nose, which seemed to point to his left ear.

"Whoa Boomer! You can't smoke that in here."

"I don't think the Board of Health is going to show up tonight to bust you on a smoking violation."

"I could care less about that. But I do have several thousand dollars worth of coffee beans that I don't want to throw away because they taste like cheap cigar smoke."

"Well that shouldn't be a problem," Boomer offered sliding the cigar under his nose as if he were an aficionado. "This is definitely *not* a cheap cigar."

Rory shot him a look. "You can take your stogie outside after I have all your chips."

A spattering of laughter rounded the table barbed with remarks on both sides of the equation such as, "Yeah Boomer, you always go home early." or, "Rory, your feeling pretty confident considering you're the dead money hand tonight."

Regardless, Boomer smiled and slipped the cigar back into his shirt pocket. "I'll smoke it in celebration of my win tonight."

The game progressed slowly. Several players used their opportunity to buy back into the game early on. Two more guys showed up. Rory was pleased in his progress. He'd been patient all night. His decisions were good ones and he'd amassed the largest pot at the table by his estimation.

Eventually, they were down to the last three players. The others, those who had been relegated to spectator status, turned off the television and came back to the table to watch the finale. Standing around the table, beers in hand, they heckled the remaining players. Remarks were made such as, "Just go all-in, boys. We can get another game going that way."

Rory suddenly became aware that Wheels had rolled into the shop. He was watching the game quietly. Catching Rory's eye he nodded. Boomer, still in the game, caught the look in Rory's eyes and turned toward Wheels.

"Hey! The shop is closed, dude. It's a private game." Boomer's friendly demeanor had faded after a few beers. The money on the line didn't help it either.

Wheels apologized and was rolling out the door before Rory could do anything to stop him. He was torn between the poker game, where he was going to get a cut of the $220 pot (of which his preference was the first place cut) and the fact that Wheels was getting the short end of the deal from him once again.

Rory called to the retreating goalie, "Sorry Rod, come by tomorrow if you can."

Wheels muttered, "It's Rob," as he passed through the door and into the night.

The next evening even a couple of perfectly grilled steaks were not enough to improve Rory's status in light of the cancellation of date night. It might have helped if he'd known that potatoes were not appropriate for a low carb diet. He made a mental note to look into just what foods had lots of carbohydrates.

While the meal was civil, there was no small amount of tension at the table and the negotiations were tough despite the extra $140 Rory had won at poker. Steph obviously thought that Rory was admitting to his guilt by offering up a gourmet meal two nights in a row (or at least his version of a gourmet meal). While Rory had intended to simply show his wife that he was thinking of her, despite, or perhaps precisely because of his carb confusion, he had given her the upper hand.

She asked him, "So you're going to hockey practice tonight then?"

"Yep, I thought I'd take you out to eat tomorrow night instead. I hope it's alright if we just move date night to Saturdays."

"And where did you think you'd take me?"

"I was thinking pasta." He paused, remembering pasta to be a good meal for marathons and such. An inkling of the term *carbing up* popped into his head. He quickly retreated with a chuckle. "Just kidding of course. I thought I'd let you pick since you have your diet. I'm obviously not doing too well with the carb counting thing."

She softened slightly at this. "I'll think about it and let you know. Anywhere I want?" she clarified.

"Within reason, yes. Let's just not empty the savings account to do it," he replied, lulled into a false sense of victory. Little did he know that she was simply setting the trap for phase two.

"Sounds good. What are we doing after dinner?"

Rory hadn't contemplated this portion. He opened the store on Sundays, which meant he was in the shop at six in the morning. This was the reason they they'd originally made Friday their date night.

"There are a couple good movies playing," he suggested, pretty sure she'd pick a chick flick. This could actually work to his advantage since he could simply sleep through it. Later he could complain vaguely about it not being a movie meant for men. She'd never know he'd taken a nap.

Instead, she simply vetoed the idea. "I think you need to take me dancing, Rory."

"Dancing?"

"Yeah, when was the last time you took me dancing?"

"That would have been our wedding, Tinkerbell."

"Good it's settled then. You're long overdue."

Rory sighed. Among the things he thought that no man should ever do were drive the new Volkswagen Beetle, wear pajamas, listen to poetry readings, arrange flowers and go dancing. He was strongly opposed to this and knew that Steph was aware of the opinion.

He asked, "Can we compromise on this one?"

"I don't know. What do you have in mind?"

"Maybe we can go see a show."

"A show, like a play?"

"A band, you can dance if you feel so inclined."

"So what you're saying is you won't take me dancing?"

"Sure."

"You will then?"

"No, sure, as in that's what I was saying."

"I don't know, that's a pretty lame compromise, especially since I'm compromising on the date night."

"How about I take you to a place where there is dancing, but I don't have to dance?"

"Really, Rory?"

"Wait, *did* you want to see a play?"

So the conversation went until Rory suddenly realized that not only had Steph somehow talked him into going dancing, but that he was going to be late for his first practice. He jumped up from the table when he spotted the time on the clock. "Oh no! I have to go!"

The next four minutes consisted of a frantic number of trips through various parts of the house. He collected his keys upstairs in his office. In the garage he tossed most of his gear in the car. Back in the house he filled his water bottle. He tossed it in the bag in his car and opened the garage door. Then realizing that he'd nearly forgotten his laundry, Rory ran in the house and retrieved it. He backtracked to the kitchen to plant a quick kiss on Steph and dashed back to the garage where he put the laundry in his bag and zipped it up. A quick inventory, ensued: sticks—check, leg pads—check, gear bag—check. He closed the rear hatch, jumped in the Porsche and sped out of the driveway. From the corner of his eye he saw Thunder sitting on the lawn chewing something—a bad omen if he believed in such things.

Ten minutes later the Porsche slid into a parking spot about as far from the building as possible without being in another state. Rory felt like a berserk, medieval salesman running across the parking lot with 60 pounds of goalie gear flailing around him. People stared even though a goalie was far from an uncommon sight at an ice rink. Passing though the automatic rink doors, he had to execute a spin move to avoid running over an oblivious five-year-old who didn't see Rory's bag of gear coming and jumped right in front of it. Milliseconds later he was in the locker room filled with his new would-be-teammates.

Tim introduced Rory to the team members, who were a little less frenzied in their efforts to get dressed. Rory was hopping on one leg pulling up his jock when Tim introduced someone named Kelly. Rory was quite surprised to find a woman sitting directly across the room from him.

His face reddened with the realization that aside from the jock strap at knee level he wasn't wearing anything else. He pulled it up, fully embarrassed. "Sorry, I didn't realize the room was co-ed," Rory explained, certain his face was pretty close to the color of a tomato.

Kelly shrugged, tossing her long ponytail. Her face was pleasant, neither entirely attractive nor unattractive. Rory smiled at her in a weak attempt to reduce his discomfort. She rolled her eyes. "Don't flatter yourself. It wasn't like I was paying attention."

The rest of the team filtered out onto the ice as Rory finished getting dressed. Pleased that he wasn't too far behind them, Rory pulled on his helmet, grabbed his blocker and reached for his catch glove. Strangely, it wasn't where he expected it to be. He looked under the bench, under the bag, in the bag, even in the rafters twice. It was nowhere. It suddenly dawned on Rory, with all that had been happening to him lately, maybe he should consider that there *was* such a thing as bad luck. He dismissed the idea quickly, annoyed that he'd even allowed it to enter his head.

Grabbing what gear he did have, Rory ran to the lost and found box in the dark recesses under the bleachers. It was as bleak and eerie place as any ice rink might have. Rummaging through it he finally found one catch glove. It was a junior sized glove that appeared to have had about one-hundred-years of use. Although it was at the bottom of the very large box, indicating it had probably been there for an indeterminately long period of time, it was still damp. It smelled something like Rory imagined the basement would in the Tower of London. With no other options coming to mind Rory put it on. He was partly fearful that the smell of the thing indicated several strains of flesh eating bacteria and partly concerned that the ancient glove would simply disintegrate out of fear the first time a puck came within a foot of it. But mostly he feared that the stench of it might never wash off.

Bravely putting aside these concerns, he hit the ice. The smell of the rink invigorated him, but not enough to put the butterflies in his gut to rest. After skating to his net, he deposited his water bottle there. He took a couple laps around the rink to start warming up his muscles. Ignoring the skaters who were starting to look desperate to take some shots on him, Rory spent another couple minutes finishing up his pre-game ritual. He began roughing up the entire crease area in front of his net. Sliding back and forth on his skates he shaved snow from the ice surface and then with his stick swept the snow to the sides of the net along with any excess water left from the Zamboni.

Rituals complete, Rory took a deep breath, thought to himself, *I want the shot,* and looked up. The warm-up shots came, as hard as any he'd ever faced. The volume of shots combined with power and pinpoint placement was overwhelming. After five minutes he felt like he needed to take a nap and a goalie refresher course. He also felt like he hadn't stopped many of them. At least the catch glove hadn't disintegrated, but the few shots that hit it had stung severely.

At the other end, his teammates were warming up a second goalie. The warm-ups ended after ten minutes. When the pick-up game began in earnest, Rory found himself quickly falling into a rhythm. Pucks were bouncing off him, but not going in the net. At moments, his level of play rose to a pinnacle that he'd never experienced. Still the skill on the ice was far superior to anything he'd ever seen. Even Kelly, who he'd dismissed as simply being a girl, was capable of putting harder shots on net and making smarter passes than most of his former teammates could boast even in their most drunken tall tales.

The skill level wore him down after a time. A few pucks began squeaking into the net. He realized they had probed for his weakness. Identifying the tiny and ancient catch-glove as a good spot to shoot, almost every scoring attempt ended up there. To his chagrin, they not only shot there, but scored there. By the end of the session, they scored at will it seemed.

The Zamboni doors opened signaling the end of the scrimmage. While the skaters filed off the ice and back to the locker rooms, Tim came to the goal cage and helped Rory pull up the net pins.

"You did OK tonight."

Rory nodded. "It was a lot better hockey than I'm used to playing."

"One thing though, we need to get you a bigger glove. They tore you apart on that side."

"Yeah, this isn't my glove—lost and found special."

"Lost yours then?"

"I think it's at home, I so hope anyway."

"Well, don't hang onto that one, it looks a little small."

"It's a lot small, but the smell is the biggest issue."

Tim laughed as he started pushing the goal toward the Zamboni doors. "I got your net. See you in the locker room."

Rory headed off the ice. He barely managed to hang onto a beer flung to him as he walked through the locker room door.

After bobbling it a few times, he sat down slightly embarrassed. His catching glove already in question, barely being able to catch a beer seemed like affirmation of what was lacking in his game—the ability to catch things. Sheepishly, he sat down and started stripping off his gear, very aware this time that there was a female in the room.

Tim came in a moment later. He jumped on top of the bench at the end of the room and bellowed, "Alrightly people listen up! I don't want any comfortable players, right? We should always try harder to be better. So in the spirit of discomfort, who hates Rory?"

Kelly coughed and raised her hand.

Tim replied, "Shut up, Kelly, you hate everyone."

She nodded and said, "That's true, but I hate you more than the rest of them, Tim."

"Anyone other than Kelly hate Rory?"

One player, whose name Rory couldn't remember, spoke up, "He seems OK, but his glove hand is about as reliable as a Colorado weatherman."

Another player harrumphed, "Hey! That's not fair." Then turning to Rory said, "Ignore him, Rory. That was more about me than you. I'm a meteorologist."

Tim conceded, "Well, it looks like we need to put this to a vote. Rory, why don't you hit the shower. We'll let you know the verdict when you get back out here."

Rory stood up and nervously told everyone, "Just so you know, my glove hand isn't that bad. That was a borrowed glove."

They booed him and laughed as he headed to the showers. Rory smiled at it. Years of experience with hockey mockery told him that this particular style of jeering was actually friendly. He was pretty sure he'd made the team.

A few minutes later, his feeling was confirmed. He exited the shower. On the mirror in lipstick was a message, "You're in,

Rory. As a welcome present, we left you a towel and carried the rest of your stuff upstairs for you. P.S. It was Kelly's idea."

Rory was so pleased with himself that it took him a few moments to realize they'd left him a tiny hand towel and carried off all of his clothes. Nothing like a team prank to welcome a new goalie. He wondered though if most guys would consider it good luck or bad.

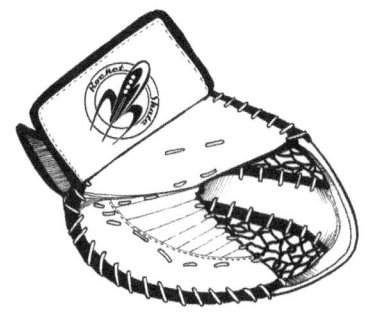

CHAPTER EIGHT

UNWANTED GUESTS

Ask any restauranteur if they'd like to see the Board of Health Inspector walking into their store and they'll tell you, "No!" Ask them how they feel about seeing one on Saturday and their answer will still be no, but more emphatic and likely accented with a bit of profanity. Rory for one, was pretty sure they didn't work on weekends unless there was some sort of hantavirus outbreak. So when a guy with a metal clipboard, two thermometers in his pocket and a county name badge around his neck walked through the door, Rory's mind wandered toward mouse feces and his stomach did a back flip. The man introduced himself, holding up the badge and telling Rory, "Larry Birch, Jeffco Board of Health, I'll be doing a full inspection today."

Larry was a slight, gray man, maybe five-foot-five. The neatly trimmed salt and pepper beard gracing his face seemed ironic to Rory as few food service employers would have allowed him to sport a beard. The others would have certainly made him put one of those ridiculous bags over it. Yet, here was one of the few men who could walk into any kitchen in the county, anytime of the day and he was sporting an abundance of the very facial hair restaurant owners constantly attempted to eradicate.

In his years of experience, Rory had found that it was best to walk the rounds with health inspectors. Obviously it was important to cooperate with them, but he also had a sense that they enjoyed elucidating their victims. He wasn't sure if it was a benevolent sense of making the world a better place or just the thrill of their own power. They could, of course, simply decide to close down any restaurant on a whim—so their power was certainly not illusionary. Rory just hoped that Larry Birch's motivations were benevolent.

They walked about behind the counter. The inspector poked various items in the two refrigerators and the display case with his thermometers. He shone his flashlight under the counters and pulled out everything that had wheels to take a look at the floor. Though he made notes on his clipboard several times, Rory was confident that his marks were excellent. His last inspection had yielded a 98% score. Still, Rory had a bad feeling that there was something special about this weekend inspection—special in a *bad* way.

"What sanitizer are you using?" the inspector asked as he stopped at the red bucket by the dishwasher.

"Liquid bleach," Rory answered.

"Not the best option out there right now," Larry said matter of factly. He dipped a test strip that he'd fished out of his kit into the bucket. "It certainly works though. How often do you change it?"

"Hourly," Rory replied. There was a timer above the bucket to remind them when the hour was up. It wasn't running. Rory hoped that they remembered to change the bucket and had merely forgotten to set the timer.

The strip came out. Larry compared it to his chart and nodded making a note. As Larry headed to the back room, Rory tapped Mark on the shoulder and pointed to the bucket behind the man's back. Mark nodded and turned back to the espresso machine finishing a customer's drink.

The process continued in the back room with a thorough inspection of the area that doubled as storage room and office. After getting all of his temperatures, Larry was on hands and knees looking under all the shelves. Eventually he exclaimed, "Aha!" then crawled nearly completely under the ice machine, which would have been impossible if he were a bigger man. When he retreated, he had a single bottle cap in his hand.

Rory's mind raced as he realized that it was a bottle cap from the previous night's beer in the man's hand. He wondered, *did Larry exclaim, "Aha!" because he is about to close down the shop for a liquor license violation? Is that even his department?* Rory chastised himself for allowing the game in the shop. *Sure, I had some fun and won a few bucks, but am I about to lose my livelihood as a result?*

Larry stood up, holding the bottle cap as if he were Indiana Jones holding Delilah's golden scissors. The pure look of evil victory was unmistakable in his eyes. Inwardly, Rory trembled in fear. He was certain that what came next would not be a giant rolling-boulder threatening to crush Larry for his impertinent intrusion into a place that contained things meant to remain lost. Thus it came much to his relief when Larry chuckled, "It's so clean in here, I didn't think I was going to find *anything* on the floor."

He tossed the bottle cap into the trash. "Rory, could I trouble you for a cup of water? I'll go finish this paperwork and be out of your hair."

The inspector then sat in the lobby for about ten minutes scribbling notes. When he was done, he headed to the counter and handed Rory a copy. "You have one major violation which is the reason for my visit today. I was actually called in by the Westminster Police department due to animals in the establishment."

"Animals?" Rory inquired, genuinely surprised.

"Dogs, well one dog to be specific."

"I've never allowed dogs in the building."

"Ah see, there's the issue. This was a dog on the patio."

Rory turned it over in his head. "Oh, Thursday?"

Larry looked over his notes. "Right, um, apparently a bull dog named Nigel who ran into the street. A police report was turned over to my department."

"So when someone attaches a dog to one of my tables outside I'm going to get a health code violation for my shop?" Rory asked, perplexed.

Larry nodded apologetically. "I know. I don't agree with this one either. It's more of an error in the way the health codes were written than any type of rule that makes sense, but that's how it is right now."

"So seven days to correct it, right?" Rory asked.

"I think you can handle this one more quickly than that. You run a clean shop. How about a sign in the front window by the door saying, 'no dogs on patio, please.' I'll swing back by in the next few days and if it's there, I'll submit your major as corrected."

"Fair enough," Rory replied. As Larry left the store, Rory was glad that someone with power possessed both common sense and compassion.

Twenty minutes later, someone in power who had neither visited him. Matt Morgan, the Director of Operations for the ice rink, and more importantly Rory's landlord, swept into the store with the intensity of a hurricane. The line was short, but he jumped right to the front of it, much to the dismay of the four customers waiting their turn. Ignoring their grumbles, he asked Mark, "Where's Rory?"

Mark pointed to the back. "He's in the office."

Rory looked up from the computer as Matt stomped through the doorway. Matt was, in most ways, the opposite of the friendly heath inspector who had just left. He was tall with a clean-shaven, chiseled face, strong chin and jet black hair. Morgan always wore a crisp suit and tie. Ignoring the rather angry appearance on the man's face, as he always seemed wound too tight anyway, Rory asked in a friendly tone, "What's going on, Matt?"

"What's going on? For starters there's video of you sneaking around my rink yesterday with no clothing on."

"Oh, that."

"Yes that, you want to tell me what that was about?"

"I was the victim there—team prank, Matt."

"There were a lot of kids at the rink."

"No there weren't, it was almost 11 p.m. Besides, it wasn't as if I *wanted* to be left in the locker room with no clothing."

Matt exhaled, reducing his storm rating to a Category Four. He seemed to concede that Rory had a point. It was pretty obvious to anyone watching the video that Rory wasn't quite as comfortable as the emperor had been in *his* new clothes. Much the opposite, no one had ever moved through the Ice Centre with such stealth. Aside from the cameras it was unlikely that Rory had been detected by anyone before donning a pair of hockey pants from the lost and found bin.

Rory cringed as he recalled putting on the pants, every bit as disgusting as the glove that he'd borrowed earlier that same day. Not only were they nauseatingly rank, they were way too small and he'd had a hard time squeezing into them. After retrieving his gear from his laughing teammates in the lobby, he returned to the locker room wanting little more than a very long, very hot shower. He'd settled for getting dressed in the fear of finding his gear gone again and having to restart what might prove to be an endless process.

"Look Rory, I don't care how you ended up naked in my building. Just make sure it doesn't happen again," Matt told him finalizing that particular subject. However, he had other ammunition that he intended to expend before leaving.

"There's another issue. It came to my attention that you've got a poker game going on here after hours."

Normally Rory liked to make people ask an actual question before he responded. This was practically an uncontrollable pet peeve. Where some people corrected grammar or trivial misinformation, Rory simply refused to answer a question until it was actually phrased as one . . . unless it made him angry.

"Come on, Matt! You make it sound like I'm running a casino in here."

"Well, are you?"

"Absolutely not! It was a social gathering with a few friends. We got together and played cards last night."

"How often is this happening?"

"Once."

"So, once a week?"

"No, once an ever."

Rory suspected that this made Matt tremendously happy. He seemed the type of man who wanted people to feel like he knew everything that was going on in the building. Perhaps it was the fact that he spoke about the rink as if he owned it, rather than managed it. Regardless of how pleased Matt was, he did not back down on this issue.

"Rory, you realize that this is a government funded facility. Because of that everything that happens here is under extreme scrutiny. You follow me?"

"Yeah Matt, no poker in the shop."

"It's more than that, Rory. No screw-ups from you. I'm not losing my job over your little chunk of rent here. This facility loses two million a year and no one bats an eye. You think they'll care if it's two million and twenty four thousand a year? I don't."

Rory was irritated. He started his own business to get away from people like Matt who enjoyed pointing fingers and lording over everyone around them. He'd begun to realize that no one really ever had the luxury of completely escaping from power-hungry, time-wasting idiots. The best plan was to simply placate them so they'd go away quickly.

"Matt, you're right. I screwed up on both fronts. I'll be more careful about being trapped in the Ice Centre without proper apparel and I assure you that last night's poker game will never happen again. You don't have to worry about me causing any ripples. What's bad for you is probably bad for my business as well."

Matt stared at him with the intensity of one dog trying to establish dominance over another. Rory didn't flinch. Finally with neither man backing down, Matt nodded. "Don't screw up, Rory. I have my eye on you."

After he left, Rory took a moment to consider how Matt found out about the poker game. The only conclusion he kept coming to was that Wheels had ratted them out. The question was, why? As to that, he could only divine that the gloves were off. Rory started the fight and if Wheels wanted to continue it he would finish it as well.

Dinner wasn't great. Steph decided that Greek food had the proper amount of carbs and chose a place named Pete's to indulge that need. Rory felt the name Pete evoked thoughts of Greek food like the name Nigel made him hungry for a taco. This he found odd since upon thinking about it, Pete was short for Peter, which is indeed an indisputably Greek name. Name issues aside, Kabobs and Gyros were not on Rory's list of things that were good to eat—in fact they resided on another list which he called, "Barely Edible Things." The only positive thing about Pete's, in Rory's opinion, was the relatively small price he paid for food he normally would not have eaten. Unfortunately, he was still quite hungry after dinner.

Adding to Rory's dismay was the fact that Steph had decided *The Church* in Denver was the place to force him into the humiliating contortions that he knew weren't really quite dancing, but were as close as he might ever come to it. Though the building *had* once been a church, it was now clearly a nightclub. Inside, the dark spindly beams and stained glass of the club's Gothic architecture stood in stark, even surreal, contrast to the lasers and strobes fluttering across the throng of people within. Rory wondered, if the strains of an enormous pipe organ were to once again fill the hall, would the partiers have stopped dancing to look at one another in dazed confusion or just continued to sway.

All of this was a drastic change from the strip-mall clubs of Rory's younger days but one thing remained the same. It was a huge space filled elbow to elbow with sweaty people looking for something or someone they probably wouldn't find in a nightclub. The gut wrenching beat of the music, like a hammer on his head, wasn't Rory's idea of a nice relaxing date night. Doing it while hungry and tired was even less appealing. He was pretty sure there was a secret room at Guantanamo Bay just like this place into which they tossed terrorists to soften them for further interrogation. If the atmosphere wasn't torturous enough his memory of the obscene cover-fee was certainly was.

They danced for fifteen minutes, Steph energetically, Rory begrudgingly. Then they reversed emotional roles and sat down as Rory was feeling lightheaded. His rest period was short lived; Steph sent him to get drinks. Rory knew a libation was not going to help with his lightheaded feeling. However, his place was not to protest. This was apparently some sort of test and he was determined not to fail it (if only so he never had to repeat it). When he returned to the table, the vultures had already begun to flock. Three guys were lingering hungrily in the vicinity of his wife.

Rory set down the two beers, on which he'd just spent eighteen dollars, and took Steph by the hand. He held her hand up so the diamond on her finger caught the light, hoping they were sober enough to see it. Pulling her from the table he announced, "Guys, you can fight over the beers, but I'll be taking the lady home tonight."

With that he escorted Steph to the exit. Rory calculated it to be the most expensive thirty-minute date he'd ever had. His companion aside, it was also the worst date he'd ever had. At least Steph didn't protest. In fact she thanked him.

"See Rory, that wasn't so hard. You rescued me without losing your temper."

Rory smirked as he replied, "If there were only one of them, I would have punched him in the eye."

Sunday morning came six hours earlier than normal. At least that was Rory's feeling when the alarm had gone off. He made it to work and put in a rather mundane nine-hour shift. The tired feeling which, exceeding all expectations, extended to his bones, fingernails and hair. Despite this Rory was in a pleasant enough mood.

He'd joked with the regulars. Seeing a septuagenarian in a bright yellow Hawaiian shirt he greeted him, "Morning Bob, you need to take the batteries out of that shirt before you come in here. It's blinding the other customers."

Later an older female customer who he hadn't seen in quite a while came dancing in and did a spin in front of the counter asking Rory, "Notice anything new?"

"You had the tattoo on your forehead removed?"

"No silly, I never had a tattoo on my forehead."

"Hmm, beats me then."

"I lost twenty-two pounds!"

"Aw, that's too bad, where did you last see them?"

The nine hours passed quickly enough. Rory realized that he felt good after the worst date night of his life. Perhaps it was because the date had been something Steph wanted and he'd been able to give it to her. Yes, she'd hated most of the night as much as he had (although they'd disagreed heartily on the quality of the Greek food). Perhaps he was happy at sharing a miserable experience with her. Perhaps he was happy that even if she liked Greek food, he knew she would not want to go dancing for a long time, perhaps ever again.

Regardless he was pleased when the shift was over and he was headed back home to spend some time with her in a less miserable capacity. He was humming along to the radio as he eased the Porsche into the driveway. Seeing a freshly baked batch of yard cookies, courtesy of Thunder, only slightly dampened his mood.

Before entering the house, he grabbed the shovel and hoe and tossed them in the side yard. Behind the gate he retrieved the trash can which was now more than half full. He never had looked in the can to take a formal inventory as the stench now made his eyes water whenever he came within ten feet of it, but he knew the deadline for any devious plot involving a copious amount of excrement was coming up fast. While he'd secretly entertained ideas of sending it to the HOA, he'd resigned himself to a near certainty that he'd simply put it on the curb next trash day.

Rory started depositing the latest installments into the can he'd now dubbed, "Thunder's savings account." He was scooping up the final chocolate-twinkie when it split in two, revealing a blue and gold center. Rory stopped in mid scoop and stomped into the garage. He rummaged through his hockey bag, checked all of his gear hanging on the wall and looked through the backseat and hatch area of his car.

He'd mostly forgotten about the debacle with his missing glove. His assumption was that the catch glove was simply left in the garage when he rushed off for practice. However, he knew when he couldn't produce it that he'd discovered its mortal remains in Thunder's most recent special delivery of fanny funk. It was suddenly clear just what Thunder had been chewing on the night Rory had rushed to practice.

Rory retrieved a garden spade from the garage. Thus armed he moved closer than he'd ever ventured before to any of Thunder's mud bunnies. He carefully tilted the shovel, using it as a tray. With the spade, he made what he felt was a surgical incision to reveal most of the undigested chunk of his catch glove. It was the portion that had been embroidered, the exact spot where his custom glove read, "Clark." To his surprise it was legible even through the mangling.

Momentarily blinded by anger, Rory shifted the evidence to his trowel and marched to Davis Jennings' door. He was certain that faced with such damning evidence, Jennings would have no choice but to pay for the destroyed $350 glove. He rang the bell and stood on the porch step for a moment until Davis opened the door.

Poking his head of receding, white steel-wool out the door, Davis feigned pleasure at seeing Rory. "Rory, how are you?" Once he spotted what was certainly *not* a Snickers bar resting on Rory's trowel, his tone changed. "What the . . . why are you standing on my door with crap on a shovel?"

Rory held up the trowel a little closer to Davis' face. He spat, "Take a look at that, Davis. What do you see?"

"A piece of crap, get it out of my face!"

"That's evidence."

"Evidence! Evidence of what?"

"Evidence that your mutt ate my goalie glove."

"How's that?"

"That's a piece of my goalie glove there."

"Your glove was made from crap?"

"No! In the crap."

Rory realized that he needed to turn the mess so Davis could see it properly. He tilted his arm and pointed.

"Right there, see it now?"

"Oh yeah, it has your name on it."

"Irrefutable proof that this was part of my goalie glove."

"OK, but what's that have to do with Thunder?"

"Your dog left this in my yard after eating my glove."

"I don't follow why you think it was my dog."

"History, Davis."

"History?"

"Your dog craps in my yard."

"Prove it."

"Seriously? You're not going to own up to this?"

"Sure, my dog has crapped in your yard, you moron. But you can't believe that turd proves he ate your glove."

Rory suddenly realized the fault in his rage-tainted logic. Even he himself wasn't sure that Thunder was the only dog polluting his front lawn. While there was no doubt in his mind that Thunder had indeed ingested and digested his glove, he only had evidence to prove that *some* dog had done so. It wasn't as if the police were going to subpoena DNA samples and run labs over a dog complaint.

Still, there was no uncertainty in Rory. He knew full well that he saw Thunder chewing something the night his glove disappeared. He also knew that Thunder had the means, the opportunity and the motive. Clearly Thunder was big enough to eat a goalie glove. As far as Rory was concerned any dog given the chance to eat a goalie glove was probably stupid enough to try. The garage door had been open for only a couple minutes. His glove would have been at the top of his open bag in his car with the hatch up. Thunder was at the scene moments later. Perhaps, most important to his case was the obvious fact that Thunder simply didn't like him. Why else would Thunder leave such evil things in the yard?

Another telling detail to Rory was how collected Davis seemed. Yes, he had been surprised to open the door to poop on a shovel, but he didn't seem at all surprised that Thunder had eaten the glove. There were no questions from him about how Thunder might have gotten the glove and no real denial. This alone seemed to overwhelmingly point to his guilt.

Rory stood for a moment glaring at Davis while contemplating all these things. At last he pulled back the turd like it was some sort of prize, looked him in the eyes and said, "This isn't over Davis. Not even close!"

Turning on his heel, Rory stepped angrily, just short of stomping, back toward his house. As he approached the garage, he heard the honk of a tiny car horn. His mother-in-law was pulling up to the house in her neon-green Honda Insight. In her typical fashion she was hunkered over the wheel as if its purpose was an upper body ottoman, or perhaps she was so near sighted that she needed to lean forward to see the road. Either way, Rory figured that if the airbag ever was deployed it would propel her through the rear window of the car.

She was without a doubt, among the top seven people that Rory didn't want to see at that moment. Rory ducked into the garage without acknowledging her. He tapped the button to close the overhead door, only then realizing that he was still holding his little gift from Thunder. He growled to himself, "Perfect."

CHAPTER NINE

RESTLESS MUSINGS

At two in the morning Rory had been lying in bed for almost four hours—not sleeping. This wasn't the garden-variety insomnia that so often plagued him. Instead it was the manifestation of the very annoying chain of events rattling about in his head. Especially disturbing was the visitation by his mother-in-law. The longer he lay awake, the more agitated he became that he wasn't sleeping. The more agitated he became, the more he dwelt on the woes keeping him awake. This quickly became a self-perpetuating situation. Rory tossed in the bed and sighed loudly, annoyed that Steph had the audacity to sleep right through his anxieties.

With a vague sense of resignation concerning sleep, he remembered how once upon a time, his mother in law, Colette, had been a reasonable person. Rory even found her company enjoyable. She was intelligent, happy and blessed with a great sense of humor. Before he married Steph, Colette would have them over to her house a couple times a month for dinner and a movie or a board game. Steph never had to twist his arm or beg him to go. This hadn't been the case with visiting the dysfunctional households of many previous flames. With Colette it was always an enjoyable time whether it was just the two of them visiting or Steph's sisters were there with their boyfriends.

Despite divorcing her husband about a year after Steph and Rory's marriage, something inside Colette cracked when her ex died from lung cancer. The last three-years had seen a steady degradation of her mental faculties. Colette hadn't started pushing a grocery cart full of cat food around the streets. She didn't she dress in purple hats or wear several different animal prints at the same time. No one ever heard her mumbling nonsense to herself. Thus, the average person on the street might not have seen Colette's fading sanity, but Rory did.

Steph's sisters saw it too. They'd pretty much cut Colette out of their lives except to let her know in vague terms that she needed the assistance of a mental-health care provider. Colette was in a downward spiral of depression and self-loathing that effectively pushed away the most important people in her life. She spent all of her waking efforts finding something to be unhappy about and complaining incessantly about the most benign things. Even her friends had deserted her. Only Steph still put up with her shenanigans.

Rory understood that Steph's mother was important to her. Her mother would always be her mother no matter what. But Rory himself often felt as if he were trapped in the middle. He was constantly forced to choose between his wife's happiness and his personal sanity.

While Colette had a beautiful and spacious home twenty minutes away, she felt it important at times to join Rory and Steph for a few weeks. These extended stays, like the one she'd stopped by to start today, were her attempt to affect a group nervous breakdown. This was much less excruciating than having one alone, apparently. Of course, Rory and Steph didn't exactly see it that way; without her intrusion wouldn't have suffered *any* sort of nervous breakdown at all.

Colette's timing was perfectly imperfect. Rory was stewing in his anger due to the catch glove debacle. He'd wanted to grouse about it to Steph but was foiled when Colette demanded a monopoly on his wife's attention. His only defense was to retreat. He'd taken to hiding when she visited, so tonight he'd turned in to bed early.

Rory sighed impatiently staring at the faint shadows the streetlight cast on the ceiling while considering his multitude of personal demons. He mentally listed his woes: Colette's visit, Matt Morgan pressuring him, Wheels starting a war, Davis Jennings refusing to take responsibility for his dog, the impromptu health inspection . . . he suddenly realized that he forgot to make a "no dogs" sign to hang in the window. He also realized that he needed to buy a new goalie catch glove. His last one was custom made, but that wasn't much of an option since it took almost three months; he needed to be back in net on Tuesday night.

These things rolled about in his head conspiring to keep him from sleeping. He didn't have a solution to most of them. However, as he lay in bed he came up with a solution to one issue, or so he thought. Further, he decided there was no time like the present, even if the present was two in the morning. Actually, for this solution, *especially* because it was two in the morning. He got out of bed and dressed in dark clothing. As expected, Steph didn't stir, even when he knocked over one of the many knickknacks on her dresser while fumbling in the dark. He then headed to the garage where he donned a pair of work gloves.

Opening the garage door would be loud enough to wake even Steph, so Rory trod back through the house and out the sliding glass door to the back yard. On the deck he was surprised how bright it seemed outside. A few long, wispy clouds framed the half full moon. It shone like a beacon on his enormous stainless steel gas-grill. The night was quiet though. The only sounds were a hum of white noise from the highway a couple miles away and the faint barking of a dog. The air was cold. Inhaling it was invigorating and Rory felt wide-awake.

With as much stealth as he could manage Rory opened the back gate and rolled Thunder's savings account through it and down the driveway. Despite the cool night, his eyes burned from the stench of it. Rory wasn't sure if he should move slowly to avoid detection or quickly to get this task over with. The plastic wheels of the trashcan chattered across the pavement, sounding to his ears like someone shouting into a megaphone, "Hey, look at Rory! He's up to something."

He turned the corner, headed down the walk and was about to venture across the street when he heard a car coming. Rory dove behind a bush suddenly feeling like he was a twelve-year-old playing hide and go seek on a summer evening. The trashcan was just barely in the street in front of his neighbor's house, looking as if someone simply forgot when trash day was. The car was a slow moving police cruiser. Rory suddenly realized that his mission wasn't as fun as hide and go seek, it was more like war. To his relief the police car simply passed by on the cross street, not venturing down his cul-de-sac.

Rory waited in the bushes for a moment. He was concerned that whoever just started playing the drums might give away his location. He looked around trying to determine the source of the staccato tempo. Eventually, he realized that the pounding he heard was the blood coursing through his head from his racing heart. After a few deep breaths, he tried to admire his neighbor Linda's fine job of landscaping. Finally calm, he felt it was safe to uproot himself from his hiding spot.

He opted for speed this time. He figured that no one had windows open as the outside temperature was below freezing. Thus no one would hear the angry wheels. He rolled the trashcan to Jennings' yard continuing right across the lawn which crinkled with new frost. Determining a proper location for his foul deed was easy. s had a two-foot-tall garden gnome right under his front window. It was an eyesore that somehow slipped the scrutiny of the otherwise overzealous HOA.

Rory hated garden gnomes.

He tipped the trashcan toward the gnome, spilling the abhorrent contents. He shook it until all of Thunder's butt cookies rolled out covering the smiling gnome. The only visible part of the garden gnome was the tip of his pointy red hat. Rory almost laughed as he pictured the gnome, no longer smiling given his current dilemma. In fact, the gnome's predicament might have caused Rory to start reciting synonyms for jubilant had he not inhaled deeply. Many of Thunder's chocolate doughnuts had apparently become quite dry and he was concerned that he'd breathed in the dust from them. The smell was suddenly more a taste in his mouth and his eyes watered uncontrollably.

Rory picked up the empty trash can and ran back toward home, coughing the entire way. He was pretty sure as he slipped through his gate he'd made it undetected. However, the sheer force of the pungent attack on his olfactory senses sent him to his knees. He retched twice. This was something of a relief—maybe he'd purged all of the repulsive particulate matter from his system. He wiped his face, stood up and walked back to the sliding door.

To his dismay and surprise, the door was locked. For a moment he panicked thinking, *I didn't pick up my keys on the way out of the house. Why would I? Who was awake to lock the sliding door behind me? Steph? Colette? What now?*

He calmed slightly remembering that he could still get in through the garage. He wasn't locked out, but he'd be in the open, dressed like a criminal just moments after completing his dastardly act. He looked up and down the street. No one seemed to be awake. No cars were coming. Rory punched in the code for the door. It crept up so slowly he was pretty sure he could have made a good start on reading *War and Peace*.

He slid under the door as soon as it was high enough for him to do so. After slapping the button to close the door, he stepped back into his house. Colette was sitting on the couch in her bathrobe watching television. In one hand she held the remote, in the other a very large glass of wine. Her gray hair was tangled about the top of her head. The effect was much like Rory would have expected to see on a Disney movie witch. She gasped when she saw Rory coming in through the garage.

Rory shushed her whispering, "Colette, it's just me. Sorry to startle you."

It apparently the reason he was whispering didn't register with her. Colette replied quite loudly, "Rory Clark, you scared me half to death. What on God's green earth are you doing sneaking about in that outfit at dark o'clock in the morning? I'm sure it's nothing good!"

Rory chuckled to himself. The adrenaline wearing off, he felt good about dumping fifty gallons of dung on Davis Jennings' garden gnome. Revenge had brought with it a sweet sense of relief and accomplishment. These were both feelings that Rory didn't yet realize were misplaced and hollow. For now he was euphoric.

"Actually Colette, I think it was the *best* thing that I've ever done."

At that moment the doorbell rang. Rory's first impulse was to run to the basement and hide in the crawlspace. *I've been discovered!* He tried to compose himself. *Who could have seen me? Do I have plausible deniability?*

Colette looked at him as if he was insane to *not* answer the door at two in the morning. "Well, you waiting on the maid to get that or what?"

His options limited, Rory headed to the door and peered through the peephole. In the dim darkness of the porch light he could see a police officer. His heart leaped to his throat. *Did they see me? Am I going to jail? Why is life so cruel to me?* There was a knock at the door. The officer obviously wasn't going away. Rory opened the door putting on his best bleary face. He looked at the cop trying to mask his fear with confusion. The officer looked him up and down for a moment before speaking.

"Are you the homeowner, sir?"

"I am."

"I couldn't help but notice you crawling under your garage door there, sir. It seems a little irregular. I'm just wondering what had you out at two in the morning?"

"Two in the morning?" Rory asked, buying himself a moment to cook up a reasonable excuse. "There was a cat in my back yard keeping me awake. I went to shoo it away and my mother-in-law accidentally locked me out." It seemed a little too much like a Flintstone's episode as it came out of his mouth. Rory regretted his effort immediately.

"Any reason you're dressed like that?"

Darn the luck! The all black ninja outfit meant to render him invisible was going to end up putting him in prison. He looked down at the condemning outfit and realized that in the dark he'd grabbed a pair of green sweatpants and a red turtleneck. He actually looked like an elf. The surprise in his reply was genuine. "Huh! It was dark when I grabbed these clothes. I didn't turn on the light since my wife has the good fortune to sleep through just about anything except me turning on the lights. I didn't want to wake her."

"Do you mind if I come in so we can get this sorted out?" the officer asked.

"Please." Rory stepped out of the way.

Colette came around the corner in her robe. "What's going on here?"

"Do you live here, ma'am?"

"He's married to my daughter. I'm just visiting."

"Your daughter a sound sleeper?"

"Like a log, ever since she was a baby."

". . . and you locked your son-in-law out of the house tonight?"

"I did find the sliding glass door open a few minutes ago and locked it."

"Sorry to bother you both. If I can just get your names for my report, I'll be out of your hair."

Rory showered and slept like a rock for three hours. Steph, of course, never awoke. Despite the short nocturne, Rory felt refreshed when his alarm roused him. Driving out of the neighborhood, he was slightly disappointed that it was still too dark to see his handiwork. He nonetheless snickered to himself at the thought of Davis walking out in his robe to see the horrendous mess his pooch was capable of making in a month. Rory pictured Thunder slightly confused by the mound, peeing on it to claim it as his own. Lastly, he imagined the gnome weeping uncontrollably.

At Lord Stanley's, it was a typical, busy Monday morning. Rory, Lisa and Mark were slinging espresso and the time flew by. When things slowed down, Lisa emptied the self-service drink fridge to clean it. Mark helped her get into the cold drink case to wipe the inside glass. Being small, she found this the easiest method even though the sliding doors lifted out. She stood inside alternately waving to amused customers or pretending she couldn't escape. Finally when one elderly man exclaimed, "Dial 91 or whatever that number is, she's trapped!" they ended the game.

Once Lisa was finished, Rory headed to the back for his routine paperwork. Eventually his feeling of euphoria evaporated into fear of reprisal. *Jennings will know I did it. How will he respond? What if he calls the police?* Though Rory felt that his act of revenge was justified, he started to actually feel badly about what he'd done. Guilt was such an odd feeling to follow his righteous rage.

He called Mark into the office since it was slow. While he didn't understand the Catholic notion of confessing to a priest, he suddenly felt like talking to someone. But Rory wasn't seeking to unburden himself from his sins. Rather, he hoped for confirmation of his virtuousness. Mark came in and sat on the only other seat in the backroom, a barstool.

"What's up, Rory?"

Rory suddenly felt quite short in the office chair and moved to sit on the desk before answering, "I have to get your opinion on something."

"Fire away."

"Remember the incident with me shooting at the dog?"

"Of course, it was epic."

"The same dog has been using my front yard as a toilet ever since that day. It's been more than a month."

"You called the cops, right?"

"The day I shot blanks at the dog any sympathy on that front ended, so no. But that's not the point. The issue has escalated since then."

Mark raised his eyebrows in anticipation and asked, "Really?"

"The dog ate part of my goalie equipment the other day, a $350 glove. I confronted his owner in the hopes he would remedy the situation, but he flat out denied it happened."

"Are you sure it was his dog?"

"Absolutely sure, but not really able to definitively prove it. So let me ask you this, do you think a little payback is out of order?"

"I don't know. What type of payback are you talking about, Rory?"

"Returning a month's worth of dog waste to him."

Mark was quiet for a moment. Rory thought he looked surprised, perhaps even shocked. Finally he said, "I've never really thought of you as someone who would do something like that.

What are we talking here, Rory . . . bedroom, living room, swimming pool?"

Rory laughed in relief. Pretty sure he was about to get validation of his actions, he replied, "As funny as all of that would have been, I just dumped it on his garden gnome. Poor little guy is the centerpiece of a 2 foot-high, fifty gallon crap mound."

"Seriously, Rory?" Mark's voice had a true ring of concern, "That's a little over the top. I mean the shooting thing, you just snapped. That could happen to anyone. But saving fifty gallons of crap to put in your neighbor's yard . . . well that's something you thought about for a while."

"I didn't really plan to dump the crap on his yard. I just had it and he crossed a line."

"Why would you save it if you didn't plan to do something like that, Rory?"

Rory had to admit that while he hadn't really hatched the exact scheme until that night, he had entertained a number of nefarious scenarios in his head. Thunder's savings account had always existed for evil. Not knowing what face the evil would wear didn't excuse him from committing it. He asked, "What would you have done, Mark? I couldn't just let things keep escalating. It's really getting out of hand."

Mark shook his head. "I don't have an answer on how that could have been handled, Rory. But I do know that canine feces carry a lot of disease. Dumping a collection of them on someone's yard seems like a really bad idea. It doesn't seem like it's going to make things any easier with your neighbor. I certainly don't think it's going to end the escalation."

Rory sat for a while after Mark went back to the front counter. He was unhappy that Mark was making sense. Mostly he was unhappy because he'd wanted someone to approve of his handiwork. He wanted someone to snicker and pat him on the back and tell him, "Good show! That's too funny!" While Mark had said none of those things, what he had done was worse. He made Rory realize that not only was it unlikely that anyone would congratulate him, but that Rory couldn't even approve of it himself.

He sat in the office feeling sorry for himself for a while. After puttering about on the Internet, Rory halfheartedly read some email and did some paperwork. Eventually he rose to stretch thinking about a cup of coffee. He stepped into the doorway just in time to see Officer Doyle walking into the shop. She had an even angrier scowl on her face than she had after he'd mistaken her for a stripper.

He thought for an instant what lousy luck it was that they'd sent her to his shop. Immediately he rejected the notion of luck. *She probably asked them to call her anytime of day if my name came up.*

Rory turned back into the office hoping she hadn't seen him. He made a beeline for his ladder thinking to once again seek the comfort of his escape hatch. He pushed it upward only to let in an icy blast of cold air and snow. Rory looked down. His coat was on one of the wall hooks, which would be clearly visible to Officer Doyle. He was torn for a moment between escape and incarceration when he heard Doyle's voice below.

"Mr. Clark, I'd like to say that I'm displeased to see you in the midst of flight from a police officer, but I think we both know better than that."

Rory closed the hatch and started back down the ladder. He had little time to consider a strategy. He didn't know what she knew. He hoped she wasn't here to arrest him on some vague accusation of dumping crap in a neighbor's yard. So, he wondered, should he play it cool? *Officer Doyle, what brings you here?* Or should he tempt the jurisdiction rules, *You can't arrest me, this is Westminster, ha!*

He had no idea if a Broomfield cop could actually make an arrest a couple minutes into the next town. Playing it cool might give Officer Doyle the false impression that he was glad to see her.

Both sounded like bad ideas. So when Rory got to the bottom of the ladder he came up with a third option; he'd lie.

"Flight? That hatch popped open. There was snow blowing in."

"Really?" she asked, her hand on her hip somehow making it obvious she knew he was lying.

Rory was generally as wont to answer questions as he was to ignore non-questions. However in this case he decided it was likely best to remain silent. Officer Doyle was apparently accustomed to waiting for replies to her questions so the two of them stood looking at one another for a long while.

Rory was extremely proud of his personal stubborn streak. He once spent three days putting a cork back in an empty champagne bottle with no tools because Steph told him it wasn't possible. Still, seeing Officer Doyle unnerved him to the point that he spoke first.

"Officer Doyle, I'm still so sorry that we got off on the wrong foot last time we met."

"It's a bit late for that."

"You're right, there's no second chance for a first impression. But I'm a decent guy. I really am."

"Mr. Clark, decent people don't put piles of dog crap in their neighbor's yards."

Rory feigned confusion. He was pretty sure he was doing a bad job of it. Officer Doyle was the scariest police officer he'd ever met. Heck, she might have been the scariest person he'd ever met. Considering some of his fellow hockey players, that was quite an accomplishment. Still he tried. "I'd agree with that statement. Are you here because Davis Jennings decided to confess to his dog's acts in my yard?"

"Do you really want to play this game Mr. Clark? You know why I'm here."

"What game? Why are you here?"

"Have it your way. Last night an officer reported to your

house on a possible break-in. The call was cleared when you told him you were shooing a cat from your yard. This morning your neighbor, Davis Jennings, complained that he found a large pile of feces in his yard. Rory Clark, I'm placing you under arrest for criminal mischief, littering, unlawful disposal of animal wastes and trespassing."

"You've got to be kidding me."

"Am I laughing?"

Rory was pretty sure Officer Doyle had never laughed.

CHAPTER TEN

A BIT OF BARGAINING

The ride to the Broomfield Police Department was as short as it was unpleasant. This was Rory's first ride in a police cruiser. He would have preferred the front seat, but Doyle hadn't offered that option. The hard, fiberglass seat was as uncomfortable as the handcuffs. A fetid odor of old vomit and body odor didn't make the ride any more enjoyable. Of course the windows didn't roll down, but it seemed moot. While it might have helped with the smell, rolling down the windows in the blowing snow and cold would have given him pneumonia the way things were going lately.

Officer Doyle let Rory stew in his anguish without a word to him. He had no doubt that she would have been happy to cart him off to jail for jaywalking or even belching without a permit. On the first front he was correct. However on the second, which was not actually illegal, she would have simply told him he was rude and remained hopeful that he'd break an actual law. Regardless, calling her demeanor icy was akin to saying it was hard to find a good hockey game on the surface of the sun.

At the station, Doyle read Rory his Miranda rights and left him sitting in a rather warm room for a while. After the frosty ride this was a nice change. But ten minutes later it reminded Rory of the boiling rooms with broken thermostats back in high school. He tried not to think of Mrs. Harris, his terrifying four-foot-tall English teacher. Rory pondered whether his hatred of garden gnomes was the result of her following him mercilessly from middle school to high school. He was certain even to this day that her decision to change schools was solely based upon her desire to traumatize him for a few extra years.

Thus, despite having more serious problems, Rory couldn't shake the feeling that he was in high school detention. The glaringly bright fluorescent lights, stark white walls and institution-style, linoleum floor of an indeterminate color colluded to increase Rory's level of distress. At least they'd taken off the handcuffs and given him a glass of water. Something to read or a video game to wile away the time would have been nice. *Did they allow reading in detention?* Rory couldn't remember.

Rory felt nauseous. Never having been arrested before, he'd thought it a foregone conclusion that he never would be arrested —at least not for something he'd actually done. This change in status was somewhat depressing. Rory groused internally about how foolish he'd been. He was still certain that his act was righteous even if it wasn't right. His main concern was his lack of foresight. He never thought he'd be caught. Sure, he'd know he did it and so would Davis, but the police?

He thought to himself, *Why can't I let things go? I'm such an idiot. If only I hadn't been caught. Why did that cop have to see me going in the garage? If only Colette hadn't locked the door. Steph is going to make me sleep on the couch . . . I'm really hungry* and so on. As disturbed as Rory was by his mistakes, he was mostly disturbed by the fact that he didn't feel as disturbed as he thought he should.

Eventually, a man in a rumpled suit with an unwieldy stack of folders in his hands interrupted Rory's aimless grousing. He identified himself as Assistant District Attorney, Mike Evans. Evans set his pile of folders on the table where they yielded to the effect of gravity, cascading across the table in a tiny landslide of paper. The contents of the top folder fluttered to the floor. Evans cursed under his breath as he stooped to pick them up. He placed them back on the table haphazardly. After trying with no effect to smooth his wrinkled suit, Evans sat down across the table from Rory and shuffled through the mess of paperwork. Eventually he found what he thought he wanted.

"OK, Mr. Jackson . . ."

"I'm not Mr. Jackson," Rory interrupted. He fretted that Mr. Jackson was in for jaywalking, something Rory would have gladly pleaded guilty to in exchange for what he'd actually done. He instantly regretted not waiting to see what Mr. Jackson was charged with before correcting the Assistant District Attorney.

"You aren't?" Evans asked. Both the surprise in his voice and the uncertainty in his eyes implied that he wasn't sure if Rory knew his own last name. Rory might have found this amusing under better circumstances. In this one it was a little frustrating.

"Pretty sure that's not my name."

"Sorry, I guess I grabbed the wrong folder."

"That's my guess as well."

"Uh, what *is* your last name?"

"It's Clark, Rory Clark."

Evans shuffled folders and eventually replied, "Ah you're right, it is Clark." This did not come as a surprise to Rory.

Evans proceeded to scan the contents of the folder grunting slightly to himself or occasionally murmuring, "uh huh." It seemed to Rory that Evans had read Mr. Jackson's folder before sitting down, but that his own was fresh material. Finally, he set the folder down and looked up.

"So it looks like the arresting officer charged you with several misdemeanors, Mr. Clark. The exact charges are criminal mischief, littering, unlawful disposal of wastes and trespassing. These are all stemming from a pile of feces placed in the yard of . . .uh," he flipped open his folder, "David Jennings of 14230 Austin Court."

He waited as if a question were asked. Of course, one wasn't, so Rory did not respond. Nor did he feel compelled to correct Davis Jennings' first name for the man. They stared at each other for a moment. It was clear to Rory that Evans was less comfortable in his job than Doyle was in hers. Evans wasn't scary at all. The A.D.A. finally gave in and turned back to his folder.

"You were brought in specifically because of a couple of related incidents in the past few weeks which pointed to you as the culprit. The first of which involved you shooting a gun at your neighbor David's dog. Care to comment on that?"

"Not really."

"Mr. Clark, things will probably go better for you if you cooperate with me."

"What do you need to know?"

"Why you shot at your neighbor's dog might be a good start."

"First, I didn't shoot *at* anything. The gun only fires blanks."

Evans flipped through his folder again. "Yes, I see. And you were trying to scare off the dog because he was defecating on your front lawn?"

"Yes," Rory replied despite the non-standard question format Evans used.

"Did the dog continue to defecate on your lawn after that morning?"

"I never saw him doing his business after that day. I'd assume that a reasonable person wouldn't allow their dog to continue to crap on a neighbor's yard after being caught in the act. Wouldn't you?" Rory answered truthfully, though woefully inaccurately. While he'd never caught Thunder in the act, he had no doubt which dog was painting his lawn brown.

Evans half-nodded, then stopped and looked back in the folder. "So, you're telling me that your neighbor, was present when you shot at the . . . I'm sorry, fired your blank gun?"

"He arrived right after my warning shot, which might I add, I immediately regretted firing. We exchanged words and he said he was going to call the police. I guess it took him a while since it was a week before they showed up at my door."

Evans pored over the paperwork again, looking puzzled. He pulled out a pen and scribbled a couple notes on a legal pad. Rory wasn't confident that the man would be able to retrieve the notes if he needed them again. Evans put down his pen, picked up his pile of folders and headed to the door. He paused, turning back to Rory. "Give me a moment."

As if he had a choice, Rory nodded his head and went back to contemplating how lousy things were. He considered, *a lesser man would chalk all this up to bad luck.* The moment turned into several. He heard Officer Doyle swearing loudly in the hallway. Evans' voice was attempting to calm her down, but Rory detected an edge of anger in Evan's tone. This, he thought, might be a good thing for his situation. Another voice joined them sounding even angrier than Doyle had sounded. They trailed off down the hall after the third voice yelled loudly enough that Rory could make out the words, "These doors are thin."

A few moments later, Evans returned to the room. He didn't have his folders this time, just the legal pad. Without them he looked a little less rumpled. As he sat down, Rory surmised that Evans might be the one person in the world who had slept less than himself in the past month. The man had dark circles under his eyes, one of which was twitching slightly. His skin looked as saggy as his suit.

"So, Mr. Clark, here's the situation. The charges against you are all misdemeanors, but you're looking at serious legal repercussions. A criminal mischief conviction will result in revocation of your driver's license, three-months to a year in jail and up to a thousand in fines. Littering is going to cost you up to five hundred bucks. Class-three trespassing carries a fine of up to seven hundred and fifty dollars and a month in jail. Unlawful waste disposal *will* put you in jail for six months with no chance of parole and the fine is huge. It can be up to fifty thousand dollars. Essentially you're looking at the possibility of close to a year in prison and life changing fines levied against you."

Evans paused, seemingly for dramatic effect. Suddenly he seemed a little scarier to Rory. He continued, "However, your record was clean before this incident. Further, I can certainly understand what might lead you to do what you were arrested for. I'm not entirely sure I blame you. So I'm going to offer you a deal. Are you willing to plead guilty to lesser charges to reduce the fines and eliminate any jail time? We can take care of this right here and now. I don't think anyone here wants to see you go to prison for this."

That didn't carry any ring of truth to Rory. He was sure that Officer Doyle would like nothing better than to see him doing hard time. In fact, he was sure that Officer Doyle would like to see him spending lots of time in the Greybar Hotel with a very large man who answered to Nancy as his cellmate. Still, it lowered his stress level slightly. He sighed, "What are you offering?"

"I'll drop the unlawful disposal of waste and criminal mischief charges. You'll be on probation for six months, pay a thousand dollar fine and probably do a lot of hours of community service work, but you won't have to serve any jail time."

Rory pondered the situation. It smacked of a used car purchase to him. He certainly didn't want to go to jail. However, bargaining to have a couple misdemeanors on his record, was even less exciting than buying a used Saturn. He sat pondering for a while what might really be going on. *Does the City of Broomfield think that prosecuting me is a waste of money?* Rory wondered what it cost to prosecute and incarcerate someone. Unless they levied that full fifty thousand dollar fine for unlawful waste disposal, he was pretty sure they'd come up short. He was also pretty sure they wouldn't find that type of money in his finances—especially if he were in jail.

It all came down to their motivation. He pondered the question, *do they feel like they don't have enough to convict me or are they trying to save tax money?* The evidence against him, unless there was something he didn't know about, was all circumstantial. Yes, every bit of it pointed an accusatory finger at him. Further, yes, he'd done it. But there was no so-called smoking gun. It wasn't as if there was video footage or a neighbor had called to identify him . . . as far as he knew. But perhaps more importantly, Rory couldn't envision the government being frugal with taxpayer money. He did think that the charges were stupid and hoped that was a factor.

Poker faces, he decided, were the answer. Rory hoped he was a better poker player than Evans. The man seemed like an open book. Rory contemplated his adversary and decided that Evans was insecure about his job. He worked too much and slept too little in the hopes of hanging on to it. However, it was his lack of organizational skills and competence that had held him back, not his work ethic. He also noted that despite appearing to be in his late thirties to early forties, Evans wore no wedding ring. This, Rory surmised indicated that his work had either destroyed his marriage or prevented it from ever occurring.

So, used car dealer bargaining with a poker player it was. Rory asked, "Is that the best you can offer me?"

Evans was apparently taken aback. Clearly, he wasn't used to people bargaining over reduced sentences without jail time. His mouth worked a couple times, but nothing was coming out. Suddenly it dawned on Rory that some of the best poker players invented an inept persona in order to fool their opponents. Could Evans really be this bad at what he did? No one in Broomfield would ever go to jail if this were the case. Still, Rory noticed a twitch of Evan's right eyebrow.

"Mr. Clark, what I've offered you is more than fair given what you've been charged with. The city isn't going to debate with you over this issue. If you'd prefer to pass on my offer, we *will* take this to trial."

"Really? So that's it, your deal or trial?"

"Yes, Mr. Clark, that's it."

A little flicker of a half-smile unnerved Rory. Evans's eyebrow remained perfectly still this time. *Perhaps*, he thought, *I should just take the deal.* Still, Rory wasn't sure it was a fair price for justice. He wasn't the one who committed a grievous wrong here, Davis was. Another question might ferret out Evans's tell. Rory had to know if he was bluffing.

"What was all of the yelling in the hallway about?" Rory asked.

"I'm not sure what you're talking about," Evans replied. Rory had clearly caught the man lying in this case, unless there was so much yelling in the hall that Evans couldn't be sure which particular occasion Rory was referring to. Still, Rory noticed that Evans scratched his elbow while answering. He also took a deep breath before speaking, perhaps to buy a moment to answer dishonestly.

Thinking he had the A.D.A right where he wanted him, Rory asked, "How long do I have to think this over?"

"I need an answer now," Evans said, suddenly looking like the devil himself to Rory's eyes. No eyebrow twitch, no flicker of a smile, no deep breath, no itch to scratch just pure, unfiltered malevolence shown on the man's face. There was suddenly no doubt in Rory's mind that he should just take the deal. Evans was apparently telling the truth or he was a very good liar. He opened his mouth to reply when the door flew open.

"Don't say anything else, Rory."

Both Rory and Evans turned toward the door. The words came from behind a great, ugly beard perched atop a pair of wheels. Evans groaned, "Wheeler, what are you doing here? He didn't ask for representation."

"And yet here I am. A moment with my client please?"

Evans looked at Rory, who shrugged. He was pretty open to suggestions that didn't involve him being charged with a crime. He was also curious as to why Wheels had suddenly appeared. Was it to gloat? Was there some chance it was to help? Unlikely as that seemed, Rory was already in the lion's den. What could it hurt to fraternize with a second lion at such a moment?

Evans gave one last nasty look at Wheels, stood up and exited the room. Wheels rolled to the table. He was wearing a blue suit with a red tie. If not for the beard, he might have looked like a presidential candidate. Unlike Evans, Wheels' outfit was crisp and wrinkle free. However, Rory thought the beard looked even more ridiculous setting atop an expensive suit.

"So, you got yourself into a little trouble it looks like," Wheels stated. Rory wasn't going to answer the non-question, but Wheels didn't wait for an answer. Rory awarded him one point for realizing he hadn't asked a question. "He was offering you a deal, wasn't he?"

Rory nodded. "I was about to take it. I couldn't tell if he was bluffing about charging me."

Wheels smiled, at least Rory thought he did by the changing shape of his beard. "If he was offering you a deal on that mess of stupid charges against you they don't have anything, Rory. I'll have you out of here in fifteen minutes."

He spun the chair around but turned back when Rory asked, "Hey, how did you know I was here?"

"Your wife told Helen that you had been arrested. Helen called me."

"How did Steph know I was here?"

"That I don't know."

"Why did you come? I've been nothing but bad to you."

"I came because you needed me."

"Don't we need to talk dollars and cents? What are your services going to cost me? I don't even know if I can afford a lawyer."

"For fifteen minutes of work? It's only going to set you back a hundred and twenty five bucks. Now do you want out of here, or would you rather keep thinking of excuses for me to not help you out?" Wheels asked with a chuckle. He headed out the door leaving Rory to calculate the rate in his head. *Five hundred bucks an hour! I could live really well on ten hours a week.*

Wheels rolled back into the room a few minutes later. Evans was with him, looking a little dejected and somehow even more rumpled. Rory wondered if the suit was as depressed as Evans seemed and perhaps straightened up when its wearer was in a better mood. However, the suit remained silent on the subject. Evans did all the talking. "Mr. Clark, after speaking with your *attorney*," there was a twinge of malice in the word, "we've decided not to file any charges against you. You're free to go. I apologize for the inconvenience. Your attorney also convinced us that Officer Doyle owes you an apology. However, she's not currently in the office."

Rory looked at Wheels, who grinned. Even beneath the beard, Rory sensed that it was the kind of grin someone displayed right after saying, "I told you so." Though it was smug as ever, Rory found himself stifling a laugh. He still wasn't sure what Wheels was up to, but he found it harder to dislike him.

Evans handed Rory a tray with the personal belongings they'd taken when he'd arrived. When the A.D.A. left, Rory pocketed his phone, wallet and keys. Wheels chuckled as the door closed and told Rory, "At the risk of seeming insensitive, that man is inept. You need a ride?"

Arriving back at the rink, Rory thanked Wheels for the ride and offered to write him a check. To his surprise Wheels turned down the offer muttering the magical words everyone wishes their lawyer would say, "Pro Bono." As he pulled away Rory realized that perhaps Wheels wasn't muttering, but that his own attention span was very poor.

In truth the ride had been a little scary on several levels. First, he was riding with a man who had more electronics to control his car than Rory would have expected to see in the Starship Enterprise. Second, Rory wasn't entirely sure that Wheels hadn't saved him from jail in order to simply leave him murdered somewhere on the side of the road. Lastly, the snow was starting to accumulate and the roads were getting bad.

With so many things running through his head, the entire ride was a blur to Rory. Wheels had spoken quite a bit. What Rory did glean was that Evan's case came down to Jennings' word against Rory's word. The A.D.A. didn't think a man allowing his dog to crap in a neighbor's yard was going to come across as a creditable witness. Evans had been more disturbed when he found that Jennings had filed both complaints against Rory himself and attempted to do so anonymously. With only circumstantial evidence, the City and County of Broomfield wasn't interested in going to trial.

The rest of what Wheels spoke about was lost. Rory had given him the same sort of split attention that he would give to Steph if she were talking to him during an important sporting event. When Wheels had been speaking, all Rory was hearing was, "Blah blah blah blah blah." to which he'd replied, "Uh huh, uh huh, yeah."

Despite his previous record of doing so, Rory wasn't purposely trying to be rude to the man. In fact, he found himself somewhat intrigued by what Wheels was up to. The man had no reason to be kind to him, yet he was. However, Rory's interest in this phenomenon was trumped by the spinning of his brain. He did ponder his sanity.

Did I really save and dump fifty gallons of crap on my neighbor's lawn? Did I really get arrested? Am I really taking a free ride from my arch rival? Is he really my arch rival? I don't think so. Is my wife going to kill me? Is Wheels going to kill me? What are my employees thinking now that I was arrested in front of them? What on Earth is wrong with me?

And so went Rory's mind until he logically came to the conclusion that there actually *wasn't* anything wrong with him. No, it was his right to hold others accountable for being stupid, rude or ignorant. Perhaps it wasn't his duty to punish them if they didn't correct their personal issues. Still, he was pretty sure that the powers that be weren't going to take care of such matters. Neither the police or the HOA were competent enough to do the right thing. Was he a hero? No, but perhaps he was at least a champion of oppressed lawns.

In the end, Rory stood staring at the van pulling away in the rapidly intensifying snowstorm. He was pretty sure that he'd been rude to Wheels by omission. *What was he talking about during the ride here? I hope I didn't offend him again. I don't even remember if I thanked him. I'm a horrible person.*

The snow swirled angrily around him in the wind. Rory thought he saw a leering face as a cloud of white swept by him. The ethereal image leered angrily at him for a moment, accusingly even, before evaporating into a less menacing form. Shivering, more from the vision than the cold, Rory dashed into Lord Stanley's before it could return. The shop was quiet, which wasn't unexpected given the weather. Mark was at the front counter. He greeted Rory quipping, "That was interesting. I've never seen my boss arrested before."

"Yeah, let's hope you never get to see it again . . . at least for as long as you're working for me anyway." He started to head back to the office, then paused as a thought struck him. "Mark, did you call Steph?"

Mark nodded, looking a little unsure whether he did a good thing or not. Rory rounded the end of the counter. He slapped Mark on the back and pulled him into a one-armed embrace. It was as close to a hug as Rory was going to give him. "Thanks Mark. I appreciate it."

It was well past the end of Rory's shift so he collected his briefcase from the back room. As he finished up some quick tasks, he filled Mark in on how his day had transpired. Mark filled him in on the day he missed at the shop. Rory excused himself from the store after giving Mark the OK to close shop early due to the weather. He headed to the pro shop in the rink to pick up a new glove before heading home.

In the twenty-yards between his door and the rink entrance Rory found himself covered in snow. He knew he'd have to make a quick decision if he was going to drive the Porsche home instead of spending the night in it. Thus, he found himself dripping on the floor looking at the enormous selection. They had three goalie catch gloves in stock.

The first of the gloves was an abomination of day-glow yellow, lime-green, red and orange. Rory was pretty sure it was part of a Halloween costume. Perhaps someone dressed as a roll of Lifesavers five-flavors. With a groan Rory moved to glove number two. This one was navy blue and white. It wasn't the worst match with his navy, white and yellow set. He tried it on and found that while it appeared to be full-sized, it was apparently made for either Tom Thumb or a chimpanzee. He shelved it looking forlornly at the last blocker, which was black with metallic gold.

It should be mentioned that gold is a hockey color. However, in hockey the color gold refers to yellow. Had the glove been black and yellow it would have been less repulsive to Rory. As far as he was concerned metallic gold screamed, "Look at me, I'm flashy cool and never played a lick of hockey in my life. I'm also wearing a medallion the size of a clock under my jersey." He didn't even try it on opting instead to double check the fit of the navy-blue glove. When it still didn't fit, Rory picked up the black and gold one only to find that it was as substantial as a rolled up newspaper. If he used this one, he'd break his hand for certain. He eyed the five-flavors glove dubiously and wondered if he could spray paint it. He even flipped the price tag, just in case it was eighteen dollars or less. It was not.

The kid working in the shop looked over his magazine and asked, "You doing OK, man?"

Rory thought from his tone that the kid hoped he didn't need any help. Nonetheless he asked, "You really think someone's going to buy this atrocity for three hundred bucks?"

The kid shrugged. Despite the magazine in the kid's hand, Rory had momentarily forgotten he didn't really care.

"You have any other goalie trappers?"

"No man, just the full set in the window."

Rory knew exactly what the kid was talking about. The set had been there for at least fifty years. The leg pads, trapper and blocker were all signed by former NHL goaltender, Curtis Joseph. Rumor was, the pads had appeared mysteriously in that very spot before the building had even been erected. Rory was pretty sure they'd picked the ice rink location simply by the fortuitous appearance of Cujo's goalie gear. It bore a price tag of twenty-five hundred dollars. Apparently Joseph's signature was worth at least a thousand bucks, because fifteen hundred was on the high side of what the goalie set was worth when it was new—fifty years ago.

"Those have been there for a long time. Any chance of splitting them up?" Rory asked.

The kid shrugged. "I can call the manager to see. He might make you a deal."

Rory nodded toward the phone. "Do you mind?"

There was an audible sigh as the kid put down his magazine and went to the phone. He talked for a while, long enough that Rory figured he wasn't talking about the goalie pads. Maybe he was getting the score of the Avalanche game. All the while Rory was watching the snow pile up at astronomical rates. Pictures of people shoveling pathways between eight-foot high snow drifts flashed in his head. The kid laughed a couple times then finally hung up the phone.

"So here's the deal, man: he said if you want the whole set tonight you can have it for twelve hundred."

"He won't split it up?"

"Dude, that's a sweet set. Cujo signed them ya know."

"I know. That's the best he can do?"

"He said you might say that, man."

"And?"

"He said I can do a grand, but that's the bottom line."

"Bottom line, huh?"

"It is a sweet set, man."

"Yeah, Cujo signed them."

In the back of his head he knew that Steph was going to kill him. Another part of brain insisted he deserved a reward for staying out of jail today. And the thousand dollar price was the exact amount that his fine might have been. It seemed a fortuitous sign, if not a lucky one, *bah*. It wasn't every day he delivered vigilante justice *and* stayed out of jail. Rory cursed his goalie fashion sense as he reached for his wallet. "Will you throw in a roll of white stick tape if I buy them?"

The kid looked around as if assassins were tracking him. "Yeah, but the roll of tape stays between you and me, dude."

CHAPTER ELEVEN

THE LAWN FUDGE HITS THE FAN

"Rory, I thought we we're through with all of this!"

Steph was ignoring all of her rules again. Rory had no idea what stage this was. Yelling seemed to be a completely new one. He sat on the bed mute as she paced the bedroom like an agitated lioness. Even worse, he was the gazelle—about to be devoured.

For Rory, the drive home had been both tedious and exciting. It had fluctuated between the dullness of creeping along at six miles an hour in the near blinding snow and the thrill of having dark objects loom in front of him from time to time. He was pretty sure he'd almost hit a moose at one point, even though he was pretty sure no one had ever spotted a moose anywhere near Broomfield. The polar bear that had bounded across the road in front of him was equally confounding.

Steph arrived home a few hours after Rory. The fight ensued almost immediately and soon gravitated to the bedroom. For a change Rory was happy that Colette was drunk in front of the television since he had no doubts which side she'd take. Somehow she always picked blood over logic. The bedroom was the only place where they could fight in some semblance of privacy. He was grateful to Steph for giving him that at least, especially since he was apparently a gazelle.

It surprised Rory to hear himself answering her in a wavering voice. It came from him and sounded like him, but it was much angrier than he'd intended. "Steph, I'm tired of letting people walk all over me. How long did you propose that I let Jennings use our yard for a litter box? It isn't like you were the one cleaning up after his mutt every day. It isn't like the dog ate something that belonged to you. So don't tell me how I should have handled it."

"Who said you *needed* to handle it, Rory? It's embarrassing. Suddenly I'm married to the guy who dumps dog crap on neighbor's yards. How can I even go outside? I'm ashamed to show my face in my own neighborhood."

"Someone has to stand up to bullies, Steph. I'm sorry if you're embarrassed at me standing up for what's right." The vinegar in his tone belied his apology. In fact he was tired of not having anyone support him, especially his wife. He wondered, *What happened to for better or worse?*

"Rory, the police arrested you today. How is it that you don't realize what you did was wrong?" Steph's voice was rising to match Rory's ire now.

"That's all you can say, Steph? How about a little support. I was in a tough situation. Davis clearly wasn't going to change anything. You don't have to think I'm right, but you could at least offer me some kind of moral support here. I stood up for our rights and honestly I don't care if it embarrassed you. I'd do it again!"

Rory wished he could believe what he was saying. Even more he wished he could shut his mouth. The only thing that was clear in his mind was that he *didn't* know if he would do it again.

Things hadn't exactly worked out perfectly. For some reason he couldn't stop defending an act that he was pretty sure was actually a stupid one.

Steph sat down on the end of the bed. Though she was as far away as she could be from him, he saw her eyes were red. Rory realized she was crying. He moved to comfort her. It was a reflex action. It didn't matter how angry he was at her, it was still his role to comfort her. As he slid closer, she shoved him away. Her tears came harder and through now murderous eyes. "Leave me alone, Rory. I can't talk to you right now."

Thoroughly confused and profoundly angry, Rory retreated. He knew that opening his mouth further would only lead to words he'd regret delivered in a tone he abhorred. But leaving made him feel helpless. He despised the choice of leaving her upset or staying and making her more so, but chose the saner of the two. Before closing the door, he took one longing look back. Steph had collapsed on the bed, heaving silently with both hands over her face. For the first time in their marriage, he knew they'd be letting the sun set on their anger.

Steph was out of the house by eight in the morning. She'd left without a word to Rory who'd spent a sleepless night on the office futon. The only good news was that while Colette hadn't left, apparently she was also giving him the silent treatment. Rory was certainly not in the mood to listen to her prattle on about why vegetables from the supermarket caused cancer or how the people of United States needed to overthrow the CIA once and for all. He was unhappy enough without listening to her ridiculous agendas.

The doorbell surprised Rory about an hour after Steph left the house. He opened the door to a smiling man in holding an envelope. "Hey! Rory Clark, right?"

The question was asked with such enthusiasm that Rory was certain he must have known him from somewhere. Perhaps they'd had a class at the University of Colorado or worked together at Peaberry Coffee. He couldn't place the face though. "Yeah, how do I know you?"

The man handed him the envelope with a quickly fading smile. As Rory took it, he replied, "Never met you. I just have some legal papers for you. You've been served. Have a nice day."

As the man turned to walk away, an obscenely skinny woman bundled up against the cold was stomping up the walkway through the foot of snow that had fallen. As Rory was shutting the door she called, "Mr. Clark! Mr. Clark!"

Rory watched as the process server passed by her with a nod and she continued to the door. She too had an envelope. When she reached the porch she made a sour face. She held the envelope out to Rory who regarded it as if it were raw liver dipped in poison then set afire. He told her, "I don't think I want that."

She shrugged. "It doesn't matter if you take it or not. I'm with Sunshine Management Services. We operate the HOA in your neighborhood. The letter is a courtesy to inform you that we've placed a lien on your house in the amount of two thousand dollars."

"What?! How is that a courtesy?" Rory had no idea why or how they could do such a thing.

"Mr. Clark, you can play stupid with me all you'd like. I'm simply hand delivering this letter to you as a courtesy since you failed to respond to the many other letters we've mailed you in the past."

"I didn't get any letters from you in the past, I think I'd remember something about a two thousand dollar fine. All you people do is send vague threats about nothing specific. How can you turn that into a two thousand dollar fine?"

"It's all explained in the letter in my hand. Like I said, the lien is already on your property. The letter outlines that which you've previously ignored. Do you want it or not?"

Rory snatched it from her hand. With his proudest look of distaste he slammed the door, partly in disgust at her, partly in fear there were more bearers of bad news behind her. When he turned to go upstairs Colette appeared from around the corner with a drink in her hand. While it was still several hours short of lunchtime, Rory was pretty sure that it wasn't just orange juice in her glass.

She puckered her face and asked Rory, "What in the name of all things good is the commotion at your front door, Rory? I'm trying to watch Days of our Lives."

"Colette, you know what my favorite Ben Franklin quote is?"

"Oh do tell."

"House guests are like fish. After three days they start to stink."

"Huh, mine is 'A penny saved is a penny earned.'"

Rory shook his head and headed upstairs. In his home office he opened the subpoena. With trembling hands he read what turned out to be notice of a lawsuit filed by Davis Jennings. Interestingly, it didn't mention the monument to intestinal sculpture that Rory had erected in Jennings' front yard. In fact, the lawsuit had been filed two days before Rory had even confronted Jennings or contemplated his lawn decor revenge.

Jennings was filing a suit for the cost of intestinal surgery for his dog. As far as Rory could tell, with his limited vocabulary in legalese, Jennings had found the piece of the glove with Rory's first name on it in one of Thunder's defective Hershey's kisses. While Rory wasn't surprised to have proof that Thunder had eaten his glove, he was surprised that the dog had ever pooped in his own yard.

According to the subpoena, Thunder needed to have an operation to remove the rest of the glove. Jennings had the gall to sue him for the cost of the five thousand dollar operation as well as fifty thousand dollars in emotional damages. It would have been laughable to Rory if it was happening to someone else. Since it was happening to him, his hands were still shaking when he put down the subpoena.

How on earth does Jennings plan to convince anyone that I force-fed my custom glove to his dog? Did he have to find the world's dumbest lawyer to take his case? Won't the judge just throw it out? Did Colette really completely miss the point of me telling her that house guests stink after three days? Fifty thousand dollars!?

Rory picked up the envelope from the HOA. It informed him that they'd sent the same letter twenty times in the past two years regarding his fence, which was improperly constructed. The exact wording of this letter was:

```
        Mr. Clark,
    In   light   of   your   lack   of   action
regarding  the  item  below,  we  have  placed
a  lien  in  the  amount  of  $2,000  on  your
house.  Fines  and  further  action  will
continue   if   the   situation   is   not
corrected  at  once.  The following  text  was
sent  to  you  twenty  times  since  your  move
in  date  with  no  response:
        It  has  come  to  the  attention  of
Sunshine  Management  that  the  fence  you've
recently   constructed   on   your   property
does  not  meet  the  neighborhood  standards.
This  fence  must  be  torn  down  at  once.
Failure  to  comply  with  this  request  will
result  in  fines  and/or  liens  being  levied
against  your  property.
```

```
        Thank    you    for    your    cooperation
and  have  a  Sunshiny  day!
        Eileen  Phillips
        Neighborhood  Manager
```

While Rory had received half a dozen waste of time letters from the HOA, this was the first time he'd heard about the fence issue. He picked up the phone and dialed their number. A woman's voice answered and cheerfully told Rory, "This is Susie, it's a Sunshiny day at Sunshine Management."

"That's great, Susie. Because it's a crappy day here."

"I'm sorry to hear that, sir. How can I direct your call?"

"Send it wherever you send all the angry, oppressed homeowner calls."

"What neighborhood please?" she chirped happily.

"Shadow Ridge in the Broadlands."

"One moment, sir. I'm happy to connect you."

The phone clicked, rang once, clicked again, rang twice and finally was picked up. "This is Eileen. It's a Sunshiny day at Sunshine Management."

Rory instantly recognized the voice as the woman who had brought the letter to his door. "Really Eileen? You were just outside my door. Can't you see it's overcast?"

"Oh . . . Mr. Clark?"

"Yes Eileen, Mr. Clark. I just read the letter explaining the lien on my house. I'm still a little confused about the twenty letters you supposedly sent me since this is the first time I've heard anything about a fence being incorrect."

"I don't know what to tell you, Mr. Clark. We did send twenty letters to you."

"I never received one of them."

"I find that very unlikely."

"Maybe my mailman thinks it's funny to throw away mail from idiots?"

"Do you think that's what happened?" she asked, sounding

earnest to Rory. In fact, she sounded so earnest that he thought she was trying to gauge his mental health. He decided it was best to not to use sarcasm with her in the future. He also wondered if she was Canadian as he'd heard they didn't understand sarcasm.

"You know what, let's not worry about the letters for a moment. I haven't built any fences. My neighbor built one before we moved in. So I think you have the wrong guy."

"It doesn't matter who built the fence, Mr. Clark."

"How is that?"

"It's on your property line."

"So according to the letter I should tear down my neighbor's fence?"

"That would be one way to keep from incurring further fines."

Rory realized that he'd strayed into sarcasm again. He also realized that it was immensely difficult for him to *not* be sarcastic. *Why do people have to be so stupid?* he wondered.

"Listen Eileen, what is the purpose of the HOA?"

"To enforce the covenants of the neighborhood."

"To what end?"

"To keep property values high."

"Do you think making enemies of neighbors does that?"

"We'd never condone such a thing, Mr. Clark."

"You just suggested I tear down my neighbor's fence."

"Did you have another question? I'm quite busy."

"Sure, exactly what is wrong with my neighbor's fence?"

"Well I'm sure I don't know."

"Neither do I since you don't mention it in the letter."

"Well I'm certain the twenty previous letters explained that in detail."

"Where might I find those previous letters?"

"How would I know? We mailed them to *you.*"

Rory took several deep breaths. These were to keep him from tossing the phone through the window. He picked up his stress ball from the desk. It was a green alien with eyes and ears that bulged when it was squeezed. Normally this made him smile a little. This time, he crushed it with such force that one of its eyes popped and goo shot directly onto his shirt. Rory wiped the mess only to realize that the goo was the consistency and stickiness of molasses. The more he rubbed the worse it got.

"Crap," he said, this being one of his favorite shirts.

"I beg your pardon?"

"Sorry, that was not directed at you, Eileen. Listen could you fax me copies of the letters or something?"

"I'm in my car, Mr. Clark."

"Do you have a supervisor I can speak with?"

"Yes, but he doesn't know anything."

"Is there anyone in your office who does?"

"Only me."

"Fine, could you fax me those letters when you return to your office please?"

Rory hung up before she could reply. He'd felt his own I.Q. slipping merely from conversing with her. He set the phone on the floor. stood up and stomped on it approximately forty-seven times. As he did, he was *not* thinking of one his favorite Mark Twain quotes, "When angry count to four; when very angry swear." Nonetheless he was very angry and followed that advice passionately, swearing and stomping until the phone no longer resembled a phone.

Tuesday brought with it Rory's debut in the A-league. The first game of the season was supposed to be a joyous occasion. New goalie gear was also something to celebrate. However, for Rory it was a night full of nerves, anxiety, uncertainty and anger. Almost all of this was totally unrelated to what was about to happen on the ice. Rory was pretty sure that hockey was the best cure for a bad day. He also felt it was unfortunate that he couldn't play hockey all day, every day. For now an hour and a half would have to suffice. If only for a short time, competition would wipe the slate clean . . . at least he hoped it would. There was a lot of slate to wipe clean today.

Rory had shown up early, which was a good thing since Cujo's pads took a little bit of adjusting before they were comfortable—passably comfortable anyway. Rory remembered as he was getting dressed that he hated breaking in new pads. He hoped it wouldn't show in his game play and wished that he'd brought his old gear to use with the new glove.

Tim came into the locker room and looked at Rory's new rig. "Hey, aren't those Cujo's pads?"

Rory nodded, "Yeah, I needed a new glove and got a little carried away."

"I thought all the goalies were superstitious about those pads."

Josh agreed with him. "Yeah, I heard that too."

Rory didn't care about such things. Superstitions were the crutches of the weak. He needed superstition like he needed luck. He peeked into his bag to make sure that he had his jersey with number thirteen on the back. After he found it, he asked, "Why would anyone be superstitious about Curtis Joseph's pads?"

Josh answered, "I heard that was the last set of goalie gear that Joseph ordered in Saint Louis. He was traded to the minors right after ordering those pads."

Rory shook his head. "Two problems with that. First, from Saint Louis, Cujo went to Edmonton before he went to the minors. Second and more important, this set of gear is Toronto team colors, which means they were from *after* he was sent to play minor league in Vegas."

Tim interjected, "Yeah, Josh has that all wrong. The real reason is that Cujo has the most wins of any NHL goalie who never won the Stanley Cup. Guys think the pads are only going to get you to the final before you lose."

Rory was pulling his jersey over his chest protector. It took him a moment to get to get his head through the hole so he could inform his teammates of his opinion on the goalie pads. "You know what? I don't care what other goalies think of Cujo's pads. It isn't like any kind of luck, good or bad rubbed off in them. I'm the least superstitious goalie you'll ever meet."

Tim tossed him a jersey. It was an abomination of colors: black with yellow, red and purple stripes. Rory looked at the front where a logo in the same colors as the stripes read, "Fat Cats" above a little banner reading, "all out fun." He flipped it over. The number on it was zero. Zero didn't seem appropriate to Rory even if he didn't make a point of wearing number thirteen. Supposing this were this unimportant to Rory, the fact that it smelled like a combination of sweaty feet and the bottom of the dumpster behind a Greek restaurant certainly was.

He tossed the jersey back to Tim. "I have a jersey."

Tim returned it. "Now you have a *team* jersey."

Rory looked at it again and dropped it in his bag. He thought once he changed the number and laundered it he'd wear it. "It's a little ripe. I'll wash it and wear it next week."

"Next week, we're wearing white," Tim informed him. "I'll bring you the white one for that game."

Kelly heckled him, "Just suck it up, Rory. It's hockey. Your gear is supposed to smell bad."

He looked at Josh for help, but his old friend was simply nodding. Tim added, "It's our team sponsor. They paid for them so we have to wear them."

"Did you know they were this ugly when you agreed to that condition?" Rory asked.

"Just put it on," someone whose name Rory couldn't remember yelled from across the room.

Rory looked at it for a while dreading the moment he'd agreed to play A-league hockey. "Look, even if this thing didn't smell so bad it was going to make me blind, I always wear number thirteen. I've never played without that number on my back."

Josh laughed, his eyes rolling back in his head as he nearly toppled off the bench. No one else seemed to realize that anything funny had occurred until Josh reminded them, "That's the least superstitious goalie you'll ever meet, guys!"

It did dawn on Rory in warm-ups that the five flavors glove would have matched the horrendous jersey quite nicely. While this didn't make him sorry he hadn't bought it, the realization made him hate the jersey even more. Twenty minutes into the game his eyes stopped watering from the smell. The lightheaded feeling didn't fade until hours after the game was over.

Apparently any luck that Cujo possessed did not rub off on the set of pads that he'd left in Westminster. Rory of course, did not believe that luck could rub off on an inanimate object like goalie pads (even if there were such a thing as luck). Still, he was distraught by their lack of utility. At times, he found himself sliding uncontrollably when he dropped to his knees to make a save. Other times he couldn't kick his legs out fast enough or bring his knees all the way together. As a result, he felt as if his legs were going far too slow in a game that was far too fast.

If the leg pads were an abysmal disaster, the blocker glove by comparison was only a little tight. This created the unpleasant sensation of having his small finger twisted in a vise. Of course having your finger twisted in a vise is painful. Rory dropped his stick twice during the game as a result of this phenomenon.

The only piece of the new equipment that *was* working properly was Rory's catch glove, which seemed a little ironic. In the practice session a few days earlier, the borrowed catch glove was the only piece of gear that wasn't working for him. In all, Rory felt a little like a puppet fighting against the strings that were controlling him. Anyone watching might not see the strings, but if they did, it would be apparent whoever was pulling them was a fan of the other team.

Knowing that he was hopelessly outmatched until he broke-in Cujo's pads (which would take several weeks), Rory made some adjustments. He stepped up his play in areas that didn't involve using the goalie pads to stop other players. He spent a lot of time away from his net attacking loose pucks and challenging the other team. This was not a huge departure from Rory's normal play to be on the attack, but he took it to a new level to compensate.

Their opponents, *Flutterpucks*, wore white jerseys with Navy stripes. Despite the absurdity of their name, Rory couldn't help but notice that their jerseys were a perfect match for his new goalie outfit. Catching a whiff of his own malodorous jersey, he pondered whether Flutterpucks might consider a goalie trade.

The game went too quickly for Rory to gauge which was the better team. It was a pace unlike he'd ever seen before. Even the practice with the Fat Cats wasn't close to the speed of an actual game. He was, however, convinced that the only weak spot on either team was the goalie equipment he was wearing.

In the second period, Rory was firmly rooted in his attacking strategy. At one point he moved out of his net almost to the top of the zone anticipating a pass to an opponent who had eluded the defense. The technical term for such a player was cherry-picker. Rory had no idea why.

The would-be-cherry-picker caught the pass and turned to carry it across the blue line. Rory dropped to the ice, sliding on his side. Surprised, the opposing player attempted to jump over Rory but tripped. The puck bounced off Rory and he swatted it out of the zone with his stick. When the ref's arm went up, Rory was certain he was going to be called for a penalty. The puck went to a player on the other team who shot. Rory watched helplessly as the puck flew into the net. At the whistle he jumped up to protest.

"What's the penalty? That's not a goal."

"No penalty and no goal. It was a delayed offsides," the ref explained with a perplexed look as if he were tired of explaining why things were or were not penalties, "Nice play, though," he said with a small grin of appreciation.

Later in the game, Flutterpucks dumped a puck around the boards. Rory went behind his net to intercept it, only to realize that the largest player on the ice was barreling in on him. The skater was a behemoth of at least five-hundred pounds and perhaps eleven-feet tall by Rory's estimation. Realizing that this human freight train and the puck would converge upon his location at precisely the same time, Rory ignored the puck and chose personal safety.

He put his hands out in as a man might do if the moon were to suddenly fall from the sky directly at him. Eyes closed against the impending pain, Rory felt the impact. He was surprised at how slight it was. An instant later realized that he had taken the man completely off his feet and was lying on top of him. The puck still in play, Rory jumped off the player to make his way back to the front of his net. It cost him his stick as his large opponent pulled it out of his hand.

A shot put the puck directly in Rory's glove as he slid across the net mouth. The ref blew the whistle and handed out two penalties. Rory was awarded one for interference, which he protested, claiming truthfully that it was self-defense. The other penalty was awarded to the Titan who he fell on for holding Rory's stick.

Josh slapped Rory on the back. "Take it easy Ron Hextall."

Rory shook his head. "That's the first penalty I've ever taken. I was hoping to save that for a special occasion."

Mercifully, the game ended. Rory was not happy with his play. He tromped back to the locker room after shaking hands with the other team. The Fat Cats had lost eight to seven. Rory calculated that the leg pads had given up three goals and the blocker glove had yielded two. He only credited three against himself, but somehow that didn't make him feel better.

Tim tried to cheer him up on their return to the locker room. "Hey, don't worry about that one. It was just bad luck."

Rory sighed, "Yeah, that's it . . . bad luck."

It was close to midnight when Rory made it home. He figured Colette would be awake and drinking in front of the television. However, he didn't expect to see Steph. He wondered if he should sleep on the lumpy futon in the office another night or not. He figured whichever way he guessed would be the wrong one. If he went to bed, she'd kick him out again. If he went to the futon she'd be angry at him for not coming to bed.

It turned out that this was not a decision that he had to make. He walked into the house to find Colette and Steph sitting in the kitchen. The subpoena and HOA letter were on the table between them. Rory knew he was about to be ambushed. He thought, *If they had a couple more people this would be an intervention.* After running his hand through his hair, he headed to the table and sat down.

Colette was the first to speak. She seemed sober for a change. This was confusing and not at all comforting to Rory. She pointed to the letters and told him, "It looks like you've dug yourself quite a hole here. You planning on dragging my daughter into it with you?"

"I wouldn't worry too much about either one of those issues, Colette. The lawsuit is bogus and the lien is a mistake. They'll both be straightened out."

Colette continued, "I think that's where you get things twisted up, Rory. You worry about things that aren't important and ignore the ones that are.

"I took the liberty of having a little sit down with your neighbor, Davis. He's a reasonable person. He just doesn't like you, which by my reckoning doesn't conflict with him being a reasonable person one bit."

Steph interrupted gently putting a warning hand on her mother's arm. "Mom."

"I'm not gonna apologize. Rory, Davis will drop his lawsuit if you leave the neighborhood."

Rory had bitten his tongue reminding himself that Colette was important to Steph. But she'd clearly overstepped her bounds. She wasn't qualified to give advice to anyone on issues other than how to become a worthless alcoholic. She certainly had no right to talk to Davis. Rory was having a hard time holding back when he told her, "So you negotiated a settlement to the world's dumbest lawsuit that ends up with us having to move out of our house? That's quite a concession, Colette."

"You don't understand me, Rory. He just said that *you* need to leave the neighborhood. Steph can stay."

Rory looked at Steph attempting to reconcile his utter confusion at what Colette had just said. He asked her, "Is that what *you* want . . . for me to leave?"

She turned to Colette and put a hand on her arm again. "Thanks Mom, I think Rory and I need to talk alone."

Colette gave Steph a little squeeze on her shoulders and headed upstairs. Rory, taking this as confirmation of his deepest fear, felt his heart drop six-feet. His gaze followed it to the floor but he couldn't see it there. His entire world was spinning. He felt as if he'd been drugged, punched in the gut, stabbed in the chest and forced to drink a gallon of whiskey all at the same time.

Steph put her hand on top of his. He looked up through watery eyes to see that she was crying as well. He wasn't sure he remembered how to breathe properly, as it suddenly had become very difficult. She told him, "Rory, I don't know what else to do. You're breaking my heart every single day."

Rory nodded. She was right. What else could he do but agree? He told her, "Steph, I know I can make this go away. You just have to trust me."

She shook her head slowly. "Rory, I still love you. That's why you're breaking my heart. But with the way you've been acting and the decisions you're making, I don't think I have it in me to trust you right now. I think my mother is right. Even if you can make this go away, we need some time to figure this all out . . . time away from each other."

He wasn't going to take this dismissal without a fight. Even with his head spinning like an amusement park ride, he had to say something. "Please Steph, just tell me what I can do to make you change your mind. You know that I'd do anything for you. Tell me what I need to do."

"If you had to choose between the coffee shop and me, what would you pick, Rory?"

There was no question. Rory answered without pause, "You, Steph."

She nodded and asked, "And if you had to choose between me and hockey?" She slid the receipt for the goalie pads across the table to him. "You're obsessed, Rory. You bought these the same day you were arrested."

This wasn't all that simple. Rory knew that without hockey, he'd be impossible to be around. It was a choice between the love of his life and his only source of stress relief. Thus, it took him a moment to answer. "Steph, that's like asking me to choose between air or water. You know that I love you. But I'd be miserable to be around if I didn't have hockey as my stress relief. You'd hate me if I gave up hockey."

"I'm sorry, Rory. That's the problem; you're already miserable to be around. It's like you're going to explode at any moment. I don't know if there's anything that you *can* do. We just need some time apart. Both of us need to figure things out."

CHAPTER TWELVE

HOME SWEET HOME

It was Monday five a.m. Rory was swinging back and forth. He was disoriented when the alarm sounded on his cell phone. Momentarily uncertain where he was, Rory nearly toppled from his hammock. This might not have been serious had the hammock been swinging from a couple of palm trees on the beach. Sadly, this was not the case.

After spending his first uncomfortable night on the leather couch in Lord Stanley's, Rory rigged up the hammock in the back room the next day. He'd tossed and turned that first night on the couch barely sleeping due to the combined lack of comfort, the fact that his wife had evicted him and his propensity for insomnia. A month later, he had yet to realize the irony of an insomniac attempting to sleep in a coffee shop where the air was permeated with aerosol caffeine. As a result, he'd awoken both very tired, yet oddly energized each day.

Rory's embarrassment about the circumstances that led him to be living in a coffee shop had prevented him from telling anyone what had happened. He needed to wake up a few minutes before zero o'clock in order to stow away the hammock, shower and get out of the shop before it opened. Despite owning a coffee shop, Rory was not a fan of zero o'clock.

that he hadn't missed a beat serving warm, delicious drinks. Paying attention to anything else going on around him was something of another story.

For a week Rory had a nervous, nauseous twisting sensation in his gut and a vague lightness in his head. It was a feeling that he'd experienced most of the way through his freshman year of high school when he thought he couldn't live without Gina Trujillo. Much to his relief, by halfway through summer break he realized that he could live without her. This was a good thing since while he'd written her seventeen songs, twelve poems and a three-act screen play, he'd never been brave enough to actually speak to her. The only other time he'd had such a feeling was the result of intestinal poisoning from eating duck. He pondered for the briefest of moments how odd it was that food poisoning and love could feel pretty much the same.

While Rory was trapped in his reverie of unhappiness, Mark shook his shoulder causing him to spill a bit of steamed milk. Rory looked at him, slightly perturbed. Mark looked back quizzically and asked, "You alright, Rory? You've been in your own little world the last few days."

"What are you talking about?" Rory asked.

"I called your name four times."

"Sorry, I thought you were talking to someone else."

Mark pondered him for a moment as if he wasn't sure what to think. Rory thought from the look Mark was giving him there was possibly a large nest of spiders in his hair, so he smoothed it out. Eventually Mark told him, "There's a customer at the register waiting to talk to you. He isn't happy."

Rory handed off the milk pitcher. The register was only three steps away, and a short, balding black man was glaring in his direction. These things were generally easy. Unhappy customers just needed to be understood and to get what they needed. Despite the haze of self-pity he'd been enveloped in, Rory was confident as he stepped to the register.

"What can I help with?"

"I'm trying to order a coffee here."

"OK."

"And she's a moron."

Rory looked to Lisa who was clearly neither happy nor a moron. He paused for a moment considering punching the man in the face. After a deep breath Rory attempted to remember how to resolve an issue without anyone's feelings getting hurt or anyone's nose being broken.

"Sir, I'm sorry that things aren't going as well as you expect they should. I'll be happy to take care of you but if you insult one of my employees again I'm going to ask you to leave."

The man shot an angry look at Lisa and ordered, "I just want a regular cup of coffee please."

"No problem, what size would you like?"

"Regular!"

"So you'd like a medium, non-decaffeinated coffee, then?"

"I don't want decaf. If I wanted decaf I would have asked for it. You're *all* racists aren't you?"

"What?!"

"I know that the moron is. You don't look like one."

"I assure you I'm *not* one."

"The other guy looks like one."

"What?"

"A racist."

Lisa stepped in at this point. "Maybe you should meet my boyfriend."

"Now the moron racist is threatening me!"

"No, I thought you'd be interested that he's black," Lisa rebutted.

The man remained unimpressed replying, "That doesn't matter, you're just another kind of a racist."

Rory sighed and stepped in again even though he was pretty sure talking with this guy was about as smart as licking the fan belt in a running Mack truck.

"I'm going to have Mark get you a cup of coffee on the house. Then I'm going to ask you never to come back here unless you can speak to myself and all of my employees in a respectful tone, because none of us are racists or morons to the best of my knowledge."

And with that Rory headed back to the espresso machine to seek his refuge. Eventually Mark was able to calm the man down enough to slip him a cup of decaf (it was pretty evident that he didn't need any caffeine). He went on his way and agreed quickly to never come back again. Rory wondered if the free cup of coffee wasn't his plan all along. He momentarily worried that thinking that made him a racist before remembering that he didn't like the man because of how he acted, not because of the color of his skin.

Rory asked Lisa, "Is your boyfriend really black?"

She laughed and replied, "I don't even have a boyfriend right now. It was worth a try though."

Rory laughed before returning to his cocoon of obsession.

Ten minutes later a wild-eyed woman stepped up to the counter and poked her finger toward Rory. She was shaking either with rage or drug withdrawal. Her rather shapeless, colorless, hemp dress indicated to Rory that she probably came from Boulder. The scowl on her face indicated that she might be his second insane customer of the day.

"You! You're the owner, right?"

Rory wasn't sure he was up for another conversation after the last one went so well. Still, it wasn't as if he could blame Mark or Lisa for owning the shop. He sighed and answered sullenly, "Yes, that's me."

As soon as she spoke again, Rory knew who she was. She started, "I don't know what's wrong with you people but you've poisoned me for the for the fifth time!"

Rory stood there mute for a moment. With Steph still taking up 45,000 of his 50,000 thoughts for the day, Rory wasn't sure he had the spare brain power to devote to the clinically insane. If he had wanted to work with lunatics all day he would have been a therapist or a hockey coach. He clenched his teeth and tried to think happy thoughts. It didn't help.

"Let me guess: your coffee wasn't decaf?"

"Ha! That proves you make this mistake all the time!"

"No, that proves that I know who you are."

"So who am I?"

"You're the crazy woman who thinks she has to go to detox every time she drinks a coffee, but keeps coming back to the same place that supposedly poisoned her."

"Wha . . . how dare you . . .?"

"Are you supposed to be taking any medications?"

"Excuse me?"

"Can I call someone to pick you up?"

"I'm never coming back here again. You all suck!"

"Thank you very much. I for one will sleep better tonight knowing you won't be back."

With a little snort of contempt, she turned on her heel and walked out the door. Rory retreated to the espresso bar once again. For another thirty minutes or so he cranked out drinks until he realized that Mark was shaking his shoulder.

"Someone asking for you," Mark informed him.

Rory was gazing deep into the swirling milk in his steaming pitcher. He didn't want to talk to anyone else. *Why can't they just let me make drinks and contemplate how crappy my life is? This is getting ridiculous.*

"Rory?" Mark asked, apparently wondering if Rory was having some sort of minor seizure since he had stopped moving.

Rory was actually wondering the same thing. He was rolling around strategies in his brain to avoid talking to anyone else today. It was hard to figure out a way to not talk to lunatic number three. This rendered him temporarily immobile.

Eventually he replied, "Can you take care of this one, Mark?"

"I tried to, but apparently it isn't business related."

Rory sighed and handed the milk pitcher to Mark again. He looked up and instantly wished that the insane, caffeine-intolerant woman or reverse racist were back in the store. He took the dreaded three steps to the register and greeted his visitor.

"Officer Doyle, I'm a little surprised to see you."

Rory could practically hear the gears turning slowly in her head. He imagined that she was choosing from a long list of retorts. Perhaps sarcastic, *Really? You haven't broken the law for a full month?* or righteous, *You thought I'd continue to allow your evil ways?* There was always threatening, *I've got my eye on you, mister, you'll trip up eventually and I'll be there to put you away.*

Thus Rory was surprised when she forced a smile. Instead of implying she'd have him in handcuffs, Doyle apologized, "Mr. Clark, I'm here to offer my deepest apologies for arresting you. I know that it was an inconvenience to you. The arrest was baseless. On behalf of the department and myself I'm deeply sorry."

While it sounded rehearsed and wooden to Rory, it was nonetheless an odd sensation. He looked at her quizzically for a moment. Finally, he asked her, "Can I buy you a cup of coffee, Officer Doyle?"

She shook her head. "We're not allowed to accept any gifts on the job."

She left looking a little flustered. Rory stood at the counter for a moment feeling the same way. He had a nervous feeling that she would be back and that next time she'd be trying to make sure he was properly arrested.

Rory moved from one hiding spot to another. He was doing paperwork when Wheels rolled into the shop an hour after the morning rush ended. Apparently Mark had misunderstood Rory's request that he not be interrupted unless there was a major crisis. To Mark this must have implied, *Feel free to send anyone who comes in the shop right back into the office. I've enjoyed time-wasting idiots so much today that I'd like to see all of them!*

Wheels still had the same "I told you so" grin on his face when he sidled up to Rory's desk. "How are you, Rory?"

Rory was a little disturbed by the feeling that Wheels might suddenly consider them to be best pals. However, realizing the debt he owed the man, he put on his best air of civility.

"Good, how about you?"

"Doing alright, doing alright. I just wanted to make sure that Officer Doyle visited you today."

"Oh, that's what that was all about."

"So, she did come by and apologize?"

"Yeah, I thought it was a little odd."

"It was part of the deal I struck when they released you. I had to hound Evans to get them to follow up. They didn't really have enough to even haul you in like they did. I figured they should at least apologize. So I threatened them with a suit for false arrest."

"Really?"

Rob's head bobbed and his grin widened. Rory sat for a moment trying to gather it in.

"I do really appreciate your help, Rob."

"Not at all. Listen, how is everything else going?"

"I'm fine," Rory lied.

Wheels shook his head. "Rory, remember I have an inside track on what's going on through the nursing gossip hot-line."

Rory had indeed forgotten that Wheels knew far too much about him through Nancy. He pondered what Steph had been telling people she worked with. He sighed and looked through the one-way mirror. Both of his employees were busy. Still looking through the window he moaned, "I haven't told anyone that Steph kicked me out. It's miserable."

"You have a place to stay?"

"Yeah, got it covered."

Rory realized his eyes accidentally flicked to the hooks where he hung his hammock at night. He knew by now that Wheels was anything but stupid. He also noticed the man surveying the spot that Rory had involuntarily indicated with his glance. Wheels spun his chair to better face Rory and told him, "You let me know if you need a place to stay. I could always use the company."

When Rob departed, Rory found himself momentarily spending less time thinking about Steph. He was once again worried about what Rob *really* wanted from him. Rory couldn't fathom the man's motivations as hard as he tried. Even though Wheels seemed sincere it was hard for Rory to really imagine that he had any sort of nefarious intentions.

"This is Susie. It's a sunshiny day at Sunshine Management."

Rory wasn't entirely sure why, but wanted to choke someone every time that he had to call the management company. *No one who knows so little should be allowed to pretend to be so cheerful about it.* He imagined them all sitting in a giant boiling pot with some vegetables, smiling and answering the phone while their boss, who was approximately 40-feet tall, poured salt over their heads. This made him feel a little better.

"Susie, is it really that great at Sunshine Management?"

"Not really. How can I help you?"

"Would you believe that I'm an angry homeowner."

"Of course, what neighborhood?"

"Shadow Ridge in the Broadlands."

"One moment please."

The phone rang again and was answered, "This is Eileen. It's a sunshiny day at . . ."

"Yeah, I know Eileen. This is Rory Clark."

"How can I help you, Mr. Clark?"

"Well I finally have the twenty letters that you supposedly sent to me."

"If you have them obviously we sent them."

"Yes, you faxed them to me yesterday."

"And they were helpful?"

"Not at all."

"Why is that?"

"They don't tell me what is wrong with the fence for starters."

"OK and there's something else?"

"They were all addressed to 14279 Austin Court."

"So?"

"That's my neighbor's house."

"I see. Your neighbor didn't give you the letters?"

Rory imagined Eileen making a note to herself, "Place large lien on 14297 Austin Court for being a bad neighbor." He replied, "Obviously not, they had her name on them."

"I see. Well, that doesn't mean that you don't have to fix your fence."

"It does mean you shouldn't have put a lien on my house."

"Fix the fence and we will take care of that."

"That would be much easier if you'd tell me what's wrong with the fence."

"I'll make a note to check that, Mr. Clark. I'll call you once

his stick the entire game. Only his mind presented a significant problem. As much as he tried to reason with it, he couldn't persuade it to focus on the task at hand. It was as if his brain knew there were more important things than hockey at the moment. Rory cursed his brain for being so darn logical. It wasn't as if he could whine in the locker room about playing badly because his wife kicked him out of the house. Saying something like that in the locker room wouldn't garner any sympathy. A more likely reaction might be having all of his clothing stolen . . . again.

Moments later Rory wasn't sure how logical his brain was actually being. In the midst of warm-ups he was sure he spotted Steph in the stands. This distracted him for most of the first period as he strained to see if it was her or not. Oddly, she was watching the other team. Eventually he realized with no small amount of surprise that Dan was playing for the other team. Yes, Dan, piano-selling, pure-evil, Lucky Pucks team-captain who Rory had no warm feelings for. Rory wondered, *Does he really think he's good enough to play A-league? He was terrible in B-League.*

It was not Steph but Dan's girlfriend in the stands. That did answer the question of why Steph was watching the other team. It also answered the question about why she was wearing such a short skirt. Rory hoped the other team was as superstitious about her as the Lucky Pucks had been.

Despite realizing it was *not* Steph in the stands, Rory had no luck getting his brain to cooperate. Normally Rory's thought process during a game might proceed something like this: *OK, they have the puck now. They're coming out of the zone. Gotta watch that guy on my left. Defense should get him. Hmm, defense missed him. Is he going to pass or shoot? Still a guy open behind me. I think he'll pass. Shot! I got it. Uh oh, Deflection! Good, Tim has the puck. I should tell Tim the left wing is open. OK, he made the pass. I wonder what's on television right now?*

Anyone with a calculator could cipher that normally Rory normally spent about ninety-three percent of his thoughts on the game. However today's thoughts were more like this: *I wonder what Steph is doing right now? Does she really want me to choose between her and hockey? I wonder if she misses me? I know I miss her. Maybe if I just clean up Davis' yard and buy him a case of beer things will be all right. Is Thunder still leaving dead soldiers in my yard? I'd pick them up without complaining if I could go back home. I don't know how to live without Steph. This is all Colette's fault. She poisoned Steph's mind. Maybe I should learn to enjoy Greek food. Why am I so defective? Is that the puck in my net? I'm glad Steph isn't watching. I've never played so badly. Yep, that's the puck in my net. That little dimple on the puck reminds me of Steph's smile.*

This is how it was with everyday things for a week now. A woman with blond hair would enter the store. Rory would think of Steph. Someone would order a drink with chocolate or caramel in it. Rory would think of Steph. The sun would shine. A dog would bark. It was opening time. It was closing time. Pretty much every time something happened it caused him to think of Steph. The times when nothing happened, he was even more inclined to think of Steph.

Every time he thought of her it chipped away some vestigial piece of happiness or sanity inside of him. The sheer emptiness, which was much heavier than the happiness it replaced, spread from his chest to his ears and head. His head became as heavy as his heart. It was as if his sense of balance was fading. Sometimes it felt as if things were spinning out of control when he was sitting down. Constantly he thought he saw her from the corner of his eye. He'd turn to see some smiling face beneath a similar hairdo and for an instant he'd smile before realizing that it wasn't his wife. Once that instant passed he felt worse, for it only reminded him how much he missed her.

He'd hoped and believed that hockey would offer a respite from the thoughts gnawing away at him from inside. It always did. There was an hour every week when nothing else mattered. The pace of the game focused his thoughts in a singular direction. It did so not necessarily because the game was so important, but because each moment within the game contained so many focal points. But these were not enough to distract him tonight. He was so disturbed by this simple fact that he didn't even want to be on the ice after a while. Pucks regularly entered his net. He was slightly concerned by the fact that this did *not* concern him.

Glancing at the scoreboard, which reminded him the Fat Cats were losing eight to one, didn't bother him either. The only thing that did concern him on the ice was Dan, who had scored the first goal of the night despite being the worst player on the ice. Rory chose to simply blame Dan for his meltdown. His brain had informed him that if Dan could score tonight, *everyone* could score tonight.

Further evidencing that his brain really wasn't being very logical, Rory had also decided that Dan was to blame for all of his woes. It was of course, Dan who had replaced him with Wheels. It was Dan who didn't have the captain skills to lead the Lucky Pucks to a championship victory. He wasn't sure how, but he knew that Dan was also responsible for Thunder's Ho-Ho's in the yard, for Colette moving into the house, for Davis' lawsuit, for Steph kicking him out, for global warming and possibly for the assassination of John F Kennedy.

Rory decided that the next time Dan came anywhere near the net he was going to hit him. Never mind that Rory hadn't been in a fight since he was twelve years old. Never mind that Rory was sure some part of his brain was wrong in blaming Dan for everything. Never mind that he didn't even believe in global warming. He just wanted to escape the game early. Hitting someone seemed like the best way to do it. The only people he could even imagine punching in the face were Adolph Hitler or Dan. Fortunately, Dan happened to be on the ice.

He had however, forgotten a detail. Dan was good at making people hit *him*. Dan had been slashing and jawing at players all night. Further, Rory had failed to realize that most of the players on his team wanted off the ice as badly as he did. Blindly apathetic as he was, Rory hadn't realized that his entire team was playing as poorly as he was. Thus he was surprised and more than a little bit annoyed a few moments later when Tim was punching Dan in the face repeatedly. While Dan normally ended up in a ball on the ice protecting himself, Tim had a tight hold on his jersey preventing him from accomplishing this. Dan was thus forced to actually fight back, which he did quite poorly. Both players were thrown out of the game. Meanwhile, Rory shook his head at both the loss of the Fat Cat's best player and the intended target of his personal aggravation.

Rory finished off the game allowing a couple more goals just for good measure. These annoyed him quite a bit less than the fact that he had to finish the game. In the locker room afterward no one seemed as angry as they should have been. They handed out good-natured ribbings all around and made fun of the other team. But no one seemed terribly upset about the loss. Instead they were more worried about who would be last to the bar. Rory, more accustomed to feeling the scapegoat after a loss, felt a small amount of relief thanks to this attitude.

After showering and changing, he stowed his gear in the long-term locker he'd rented. Rory headed upstairs to join the team at Jackson's for beers. Before he made it across the lobby, Matt Morgan was approaching him. Rory was happy that he'd lost the desire to punch someone in the face. Matt's chin looked as solid as Mount Everest.

"Rory, I need a word," Matt said in a civil tone. Rory was pretty sure he was only being polite because he was in public. Even a jerk like Matt generally knew better than to be proud in public about being a jerk.

"Matt, you're here late tonight," Rory told him. It was pretty surprising to see Matt in the rink anytime after 4:59 p.m.

"You've been here late quite a bit yourself," Matt replied, "Can we talk in my office?"

Rory followed him across the lobby. He was feeling a little like he was just busted by the principal for hitting Jerry Sutton in the head with a paper wad. It was third grade, but Rory was still pretty sure that Jerry had it coming. The principal didn't see it that way and made him apologize in front of the class. That was a bad day. This one could be worse.

Still Rory was surprisingly numb as he thought, *Apparently Matt knows I've been sneaking in every morning. I hope I don't end up in jail. Does it really matter though? Could my life really get worse than it is now?*

Matt motioned to one of the chairs across from his expansive desk. Rory sat down. Matt did not. In fact, Matt seemed to pause in order to put on his angry face. He slowly shifted from a smile to a scowl. His eyes narrowed from friendly to glaring. Matt's eyebrows eventually furrowed into a uni-brow. His already enormous chin seemed to grow three inches. The effect might have been terrifying if Rory were still a third-grader. However, since by Rory's estimation it took Matt about sixteen minutes to arrange his features just so, it seemed a bit contrived.

Angry face in place, Matt finally chose to speak. "Alright Clark, you wanna tell me why you're sneaking around my rink in the middle of the night?"

"Me?" Rory protested lightly. He'd planned to follow that up with, "I don't know what you're talking about."

Matt didn't let him, interjecting, "It's impossible to tell that's you on the video, but your Porsche does kinda stick out like a sore thumb as the only car in the lot every night and whoever is in the video drives away in it every morning. Before you speak again, remember that you're on a short leash."

Rory nodded. Perhaps Matt would be sympathetic. It wasn't as if lying had done him a world of good lately. He launched into the explanation. "Look, I'm sorry, Matt. My wife kicked me out. I've been sleeping in the shop and showering in the rink."

Matt nodded slowly, his angry face slipped away to a more natural look of sympathy. Even though Rory was still convinced that Matt was a world class jerk, he found the sympathetic face more believable than the angry one. Matt sat down in the open chair on the same side of the desk as Rory. He whistled lightly and looked at the floor before speaking again.

"Rory, I was married four times. Every one of them broke my heart. I know exactly what you're going through."

Matt then talked to Rory for twenty minutes about his four ex-wives. He claimed to love all of them still. He also admitted to being caught cheating on each of them before being tossed out on his ear. The last two women he'd married were those his previous wives caught him having an affair with. Rory wondered how they could have expected him to be faithful given his track record.

Finally, Matt stood up and patted Rory on the back. He sent him off telling him, "Listen, we'll keep this between you and I. Just wait until the rink opens before you come inside to shower in the future. I don't want to call the cops on you."

Rory nodded. "That's a deal, Matt."

Matt smiled; it was an unnerving thing to see. It gave Rory the impression of a shark grinning at a mackerel. The shark told him, "Now get out of here."

Rory stood to go but Matt stopped him short adding, "And if you need any marriage advice, let me know. I've been there four times, Rory."

Rory wandered to the bar wondering two things: were any of his teammates still there, and did Matt really think that failing at something four times made him an expert?

The din in Jackson's was as oppressive as the food was bad. After sitting down amidst the raucous group, twelve of his teammates, Rory suspected that they were either drunk by the time he arrived or hadn't seen actually seen him play. Despite their insistence in the locker room that the last one to the bar was buying the first round, they refused to let Rory pay for it. Tim was the first one to come by and inform him of this. He set down a gargantuan beer (it was really more like three or four beers in one glass).

"Rory, I'm sorry about the game. We didn't do much to help you out tonight. It didn't help that I got tossed out for fighting. This one's on me."

Rory sipped the beer. Sunshine Wheat would not have been his first choice. However, after removing the orange slice from it, he found it fairly refreshing. Kelly spied the pale, cloudy beverage in his glass from across the table and yelled, "Who gave the goalie that girlie beer? What's wrong with you people?"

A moment later Rory had an equally large glass of New Castle Brown Ale in front of him courtesy of Kelly. This was a much tastier beer, at least in his opinion. It was also a more manly beer, at least in Kelly's opinion. He wasn't sure if he'd finish either of them and was relieved that he wasn't driving. He was only halfway through the New Castle when Josh set a second one in front of him. He slapped Rory on the back and told him, "Second round, try to keep up with us."

"Remember, I did get here last," Rory reminded him.

Eventually, Rory was working on the second New Castle. The Sunshine Wheat sat barely touched. He was surprised how good he still felt. The bartender came by with a Fat Tire Ale asking, "I poured this one by mistake. Who wants it?"

A couple of Rory's teammates pointed his direction. One of them yelled, "Give it to the Goalie."

At this point had Rory been sober, he might have wondered if this wasn't a conspiracy to make sure he got lost on the way home and never found his way back to the rink. He'd certainly made a pathetic showing in net. This wasn't something to be celebrated. But he did enjoy the feeling of belonging and the lack of finger pointing. Getting a good drunk on wasn't the worst way to stop his overactive mind from obsessing about Steph either.

After a few hours, Rory had finished all of the drinks in front of him. When he stood up and the bar began to spin, he realized just how much he'd had to drink. Rory was, however, too drunk to know that his alcohol-slowed brain was now only devoting seventy-percent of its reduced capabilities to thinking about Steph. What he did realize was that he was in no shape to walk. A few of his teammates were still there so he sat back down with a dopey grin on his face, feeling slightly warm inside.

Rory awoke on a boat, or maybe a ship. He was gently rocking back and forth. The sounds of the sea had roused him from his sleep. He lay there for a moment trying to remember how he could have ended up on a boat. Eventually he opened his eyes and wondered instead how he'd gotten back to his shop. Apparently he'd tuned the store music to the sound-scapes station, which was now playing seagulls and crashing waves. Even with a skull-splitting headache it was soothing. Slowly he realized that Mark and Lisa were staring at him.

He carefully sat up, holding his head as if he were concerned that the contents might spill out of it. He hoped Mark and Lisa thought he was simply attempting to conceal what he was sure was the most horrendous hairdo that either of them had ever witnessed. However, their perception was that they were witnessing someone with a tremendous hangover. This perception was quite accurate.

For a moment the three of them just looked at each other without speaking. Rory surmised that the situation was perhaps as awkward for them as it was for him. He looked down to make sure he was dressed and was reassured to find he was wearing sweatpants and a T-shirt. Pleased by this, he decided it was probably all right to break the ice.

"What time is it?" he groaned.

"Five-thirty," Mark replied, his mouth hanging open a little longer than it should have at the end of his answer. Rory was cognizant enough to realize they'd just walked in. The store would be open in thirty minutes.

"Let me just get out of your way here."

Lisa seemed quite confused about why her employer had been swaying in a hammock when she had arrived to work. Mark on the other hand didn't seem to display any real emotions on his face. He did however ask, "Rory? Why are you sleeping in the store?"

Not wanting to have this conversation before a shower, shave, trip to the bathroom and a lot of Tylenol, Rory slid carefully out of his hammock onto the cold concrete floor. He replied, "Steph has been snoring. It's like having a freight train in the room." Of course he really had no idea whether Steph had been snoring *or* what a freight train might sound like in a bedroom.

Mark wasn't buying the story by the look on his face. Lisa was still apparently struck mute by the situation. Rory was slightly embarrassed which made him want to leave in a hurry. He pulled down the hammock and started rolling it up. "Listen, just go ahead and clock in. I'm going to head home now."

This was indeed what Rory intended to do. It was his day off. Thus without any further explanations Rory stowed his hammock and headed to the restroom. A pause at the espresso bar had him walking out the front door with a four-shot Americano a moment later. His first stop was 24 Hour Fitness, where he procured a membership. This he immediately put to good use with the first of what he hoped were only a few daily shower and shaves in their locker room. He was a bit annoyed at himself for not thinking of this solution before having a run in with Matt. But then again he hadn't been thinking clearly in any respect for a while.

After cleaning up he stopped to replenish his cholesterol at Great Scott's. His Denver omelet wasn't quite as good as what he used to make at home. He doubted they could pull off the enormous pepperoni calzone either. However, the hash browns weren't bad at all.

As he sat in the comfortable booth, surrounded by too many Betty Boop pictures and Route 66 signs, Rory composed another letter. He wrote:

My Dearest Steph,

I'm thinking today of the first year we were married. It was hard at times. But there were so many good ones as well. Remember our joke: why are the people upstairs allowed to have a bowling alley and pet elephant while we get a call every time we listen to our television at a reasonable volume? I hope those people are now renting a house from a rock band that practices all night in their basement.

The first time we celebrated my birthday after we were married you took me to the Black Angus. I didn't think you'd have them sing Happy Birthday, but you'd slipped the waitress a note in the menu. Very sneaky of you! They brought that chocolate cake big enough for four people, remember that? It was worth the embarrassment of the silly birthday song just for that cake. Best chocolate cake ever, or maybe that was just because I was eating it with you.

We ate half the cake and took the rest home. Sadly, the box fell apart when I was getting out of the car and the cake landed on the parking lot. I was so mad that I kicked the cake twenty yards. You were mad because I tracked chocolate icing into the apartment. But you cleaned it up yourself since it was my birthday. Acts like that are just one of the many things that I love so much about you. The next morning when I went to the car a dog was eating my cake. It's funny now, but I was mad all over again.

I don't know why my thoughts of you so often include chocolate cake. Maybe it's something to do with the Sarah McLachlan song we used to listen to. How did that go? "Your love is better than chocolate", or was it "better than ice cream?" It doesn't matter, you've got both of them beat.

Even with what little we had back then, that apartment was too small for us. The time we both had the flu and had to share the single bathroom was a challenge. The kitchen was so small we only had room for fifteen minutes of food in the cupboards. We had to move the love seat to open the patio door. But I'd go back to living in that tiny, cramped place and having dogs steal my birthday cake if it meant that I could spend five minutes with you.

I miss your smile. I miss your laugh. I miss holding you at the end of a long day. I miss hearing you breathing next to me at night. I miss the beautiful way you smell. I miss everything

*about you· I'm empty· I'm broken inside· I'm so
profoundly sorry for failing you·*
I will love you always,
Rory

*P·S· I hope you know that I <u>will</u> give up
hockey if that's what you really want from me·*

Rory stuffed the letter into an envelope. He glanced at his watch. It was almost eight thirty. Steph would be on her way to work by now. As much as every fiber of his being longed to just have one glance at her, he knew that one glance would make him long for one kind word. One kind word would make him long for one touch . . . He knew that seeing her would somehow only make him feel worse for the reminder of all the desires he knew would go unfulfilled.

He paid his check and left Great Scott's with a little wave to a couple of the waitresses on his way out. After picking up a dozen red roses at the grocery store, Rory headed home. His one fear was that he'd run into Colette still freeloading in his house. Her expansive power of negativity was certain to undo any good that he might accomplish. Thus upon pulling up to the house and finding the parking areas to be free of green Honda Insights, he was quite pleased.

Rory pushed the button on his garage door remote. His pleasure quickly faded as the tiny green machine that Colette called a car sat parked in his side of the garage. Rory shut down the Porsche and sighed. Anyone who would have happened by in the next couple minutes might have thought that Rory had either died or was praying as he rested his head on the steering wheel for a full five minutes. Neither of these would have been accurate assessments. Meditating might have been closer to true. Rory was taking some time to collect himself for a confrontation with

Colette before heading inside. But mostly he was simply listening to Jeff Buckley's haunting rendition of Leonard Cohen's *Halleluja*. When it ended Rory turned off the radio and decided that it was the most depressing song he'd ever heard.

Eventually he felt composed. Roses in one hand, letters in the other, he went into the house. The family room, although it smelled of stale wine, was completely devoid of anyone resembling Colette. It was, in fact, completely devoid of anyone at all. Rory closed the garage door quietly and crept further inside. There were three distinct and new wine stains on the Berber carpet in the family room, a Merlot, Cabernet and a Pinot Noir if he had to guess.

While the television and all the lights were on, this didn't mean much. Colette was apparently immune to any thoughts that electricity cost money. He walked around the corner and looked into the kitchen. Dirty dishes were stacked to precarious heights, evidencing that Colette had been there. However while the evidence remained, she did not. Rory breathed a sigh of relief. Apparently Colette was sleeping.

He quietly found a vase. After filling it with water and roses, he placed it on the center of the kitchen table. He arranged the twenty-seven envelopes containing the letters he'd written to Steph just so in a fan around the flower vase. He wanted to leave without seeing Colette, but the kitchen was a disaster. Colette's belief that she should be waited on hand and foot wasn't fair to Steph. He tossed his coat over the back of a chair and rolled up his sleeves.

A few minutes later the dishwasher was loaded. Rory was making good progress on hand washing what the machine couldn't accommodate when he heard something behind him. He turned and ducked just in time to miss the wine bottle that Colette tossed at his head. Unfortunately, the window above the sink had much slower reflexes than Rory. When it failed to follow Rory's example of how not to be struck by flying objects, the bottle smashed through it. Rory watched the green vessel bounce off the deck and fall to the landscaping stones unbroken. He wondered why they couldn't make windows as tough as that bottle.

Colette was standing in her robe, an empty wine glass in her hand. "W-what in h-h-heaven's name?" she sputtered as she stood wobbling. Her robe wasn't quite closed in the front, revealing more of her copious belly than Rory had ever hoped to see. He looked toward the ceiling, but not before realizing that look on her face implied that she didn't recognize him. She was obviously quite drunk. Perhaps more drunk than Rory had been the previous night.

"What's wrong with you, Colette!?" Rory asked, making no effort to disguise the disdain in his voice. "You just broke my window! And fix your robe. No one wants to see that!"

She replied by throwing the empty glass at him. It was a weak toss. Even with averting his eyes as if she were Medusa, he managed to catch it. She stormed back upstairs yelling, although more slurring, "Get out of-f here. You don't live h-here anymore!"

Rory realized that aside from a broken window and a sight that he could never un-see, this was actually good news. Colette apparently had her nervous breakdown and would be going home soon. She certainly wasn't his ally in reuniting him with his wife and home. Nonetheless, if history repeated itself, now that Colette had lashed out at him, she'd make herself scarce. Each of her group nervous breakdowns in the past had ended this way.

Rory boarded up the window with a piece of plywood from the garage. He cleaned up the broken glass, happy that all of it seemed to have landed outside. A call to Toledo Glass elicited a promise for a more permanent repair the next day. He returned to finish the dishes and promptly cut his hand on the one piece of glass that apparently did not make it outside.

It wasn't a bad cut, but he yelled, "Thank you, Colette!" before finding a Band-Aid for it. She answered through the wall from upstairs with some unintelligible profanity that didn't make Rory feel any better. Finishing the dishes and seeing the kitchen clean for Steph however, did make him feel good. Good enough in fact that he tackled the wine-stained carpet with the portable shampooer.

While he had thought of putting some lasagna in the oven for Steph, it didn't seem as appealing after having a bottle thrown at him. He didn't want to make a meal that Colette would share. He pondered the possibility that if the bottle had struck him it might have been a good thing. Colette would have lost a lot of points and he would have gained some sympathy. On the other hand, he might have been knocked unconscious and Colette might have decided to dump his body in a river. Regardless, he decided that it was time to leave.

He took the kitchen trash out with him. The next day being trash day, he decided he'd move the big can to the curb as well. As he rolled it out of the garage, he stopped at what he saw. His anger at Colette was replaced when he realized that a month's worth of Thunder's butt biscuits had accumulated in the yard. It was a pile of frightening proportions. He sighed, went to the garage and retrieved the shovel and hoe. He was relocating tater tots and sewer trout from his yard when Davis Jennings strolled by with Thunder.

Thunder was straining against his leash, apparently trying to get to his favorite dookie dumping location. Rory jumped back a little seeing the massive dog straining toward him. Jennings shot Rory a look of distaste and told him, "See you in court, Clark."

Rory watched him walk away for a moment before yelling after him, "Hey, I don't live here anymore. I'm just helping out my wife, Davis. Isn't that what you wanted?"

Jennings held up a hand without looking back as if to indicate to Rory that he either didn't want to hear it or he didn't care.

CHAPTER FOURTEEN

OUT OF THE FRYING PAN

Rory had been sitting in the home theater room at Ultimate Electronics for two hours watching The Fellowship of the Ring. He sat there in a very comfortable leather chair. In fact, the chair was so comfortable the only thing that might have made the experience better was a cold beverage and some popcorn. Rory considered ordering a pizza. However, judging by the glances he was getting from the sales staff after two hours in the chair, he figured he better not push his luck.

Actually he was surprised they hadn't asked him to leave. One good thing about driving a Porsche was that people assumed you had money. When sales people see you pull up in one, they also assume you might spend it. They never assume you've spent most of your meager savings on a set of goalie pads, that you only paid the price of a new Ford when you bought your used Porsche, or that you live in a coffee shop.

When his cell phone rang, Rory fished in his pocket. It was wedged in such a way that it rang three times before he extracted it. He nearly slid off the chair onto the floor in the process. The display indicated that it was Steph. A thrill of excitement coursed through him.

He flipped the phone open. It flew out of his hands. He caught it then almost dropped it again. There was no disguising the joy he felt. He supposed she'd seen the roses. She'd likely read his letters so she knew that he was hopelessly in love with her now and forever. He had no doubt that the clean kitchen and carpet had earned him a few points as well.

It felt like a call back from a job interview that had gone well. However in this case, the interview wasn't going to result in working for someone who paid barely enough to keep him breathing. No, if all went well, Rory would be going home to the woman he loved. Despite expecting the call, now that it came he could barely contain himself.

Breathlessly, he put the phone his ear and answered, "Steph! I'm so glad you called!"

The homeless Hispanic man in the seat next to him shot an angry look and shushed him saying, "¡Callete Guey!"

Rory ignored him, anticipating Steph's warm reply. Just to hear her voice was something he'd longed for all week. This eagerly awaited revelation, perhaps that she couldn't live without him any more than he could live without her, had him on the edge of the leather seat. He was far closer than he needed to be to the hundred and ten inch screen. He felt like a child at Christmas ready to open his first gift. A smile on his face, his entire body trembled slightly.

However, when Steph spoke, her tone was much the same as that of the man next to him who had just told him to shut up in Spanish. "I can't believe you're still acting like such a child, Rory. What's wrong with you?"

Rory was stunned. He stood up and exited the theater room wondering if he'd heard her properly over the eight-speaker, twelve-hundred-watt Dolby surround-sound system. He moved toward the relative silence of the appliance section. Knowing there was no safe way to answer her question even if he did know what was wrong with him, he deflected asking her, "What are you talking about, Steph?"

"Don't play stupid with me, Rory. My mother? She doesn't even have anything to do with what's going on between us. Honestly, I don't know why it bothers you that she's in the house when you aren't even here right now." Steph sounded as agitated as he'd ever heard her.

Rory, on the other hand, felt like he'd had all the air sucked out of him. If he were that kid at Christmas he just opened an enormous box of underwear and socks and realized that there were no toys under the tree. Wandering into the appliance section, he gasped, "What are you . . ."

Steph wasn't done yet though. She kept talking right over him. "Look Rory, putting dog crap in a neighbor's yard might seem harmless to you. But, I don't think even in your stupidest moments you'd think that throwing a wine bottle at my mother could be harmless. I mean really, Rory! You broke the window with it. What would have happened if it hit her in the head? You could have seriously injured her, or worse."

Last Rory checked he was the one who could have been unconscious on the kitchen floor. He wondered, *How did this get turned around? Am I going insane?* The dishwashers around him were suddenly spinning. He was pretty sure that was just in his head. Flabbergasted, all that Rory could manage in reply was, "What?!"

"Look Rory, I don't even know what to think. I don't like what you're turning into. I don't understand it at all. I hate it, Rory!"

"Steph?!" Rory attempted to cut in. She wasn't having any of it though.

"How could you, Rory? How could you show up drunk at our house? How could you physically attack my mother and then leave her to clean up after you? I thought some time away would allow you to reflect on what you were doing. I thought that you'd figure out your priorities. But you're acting even crazier than before. You need to get help, Rory. I don't think I can talk to you while you're like this. Until you've seen a counselor or gotten some medication *don't* come around the house and *don't* call me. I'm not kidding."

With that she hung up the phone. Rory called the home number back in a panic. He couldn't believe that Colette was going to twist things around like this. Steph didn't answer. He waited for the answering machine to pick up and told her, "Steph, you've got this all wrong. Whatever your mother told you is nothing but lies. Why would I assault her on the day that I was dropping off letters and roses for you? How would that benefit anyone? Please Steph, think about which one of us is more reliable, your mother or me. Yes, I've been stupid lately, but I haven't lied to you about anything. I think you know that I don't lie to you. I *hope* you know that. I'm telling you right now that I wasn't the one who threw the bottle. It was your . . ."

The machine cut him off. Rory closed his phone and slumped back against a refrigerator. He sat there on the floor for five minutes sobbing lightly to himself. He would have sat there much longer but one of the store employees with a young couple in tow stopped in front of him. The salesperson bent down and quietly told Rory, "Hey, I'm trying to sell this refrigerator. You can get out of my way or I can have my boss call the cops to get you out of here. Your decision."

Rory balled his hand into a fist. The look in his eyes was enough though. The salesperson straightened back up regarding Rory with an intense and unmistakable look of fear on his face. He quickly turned and smiled at his potential buyers telling them, "You know I think he's going to take that one. There's another one in the next row that I think has everything you're looking for."

Rory took a moment to compose himself. After wiping his face on his sleeve, he stood up. He headed through the rows of dishwashers, ranges and fridges back toward the theater room. Upon returning to his seat his Hispanic movie companion looked him in the eye and asked, "¿Problemas con su espousa?"

Rory nodded. "Yeah, problems with my wife."

"You got to hit her, guey. I hit mi espousa once. I in jail for one semana. It was worth it. She never talk back to me more."

Rory filed that away in his head as possibly being the worst piece of advice he'd ever heard. He turned to the man and told him, "¡Callete Guey!"

For the first time in weeks Rory was preoccupied with something that kept him from dwelling almost exclusively on Steph. The anger that he felt at Colette overwhelmed him, but even that had always come back to Steph. He considered every conversation he could remember having with his wife since they'd been married. He analyzed every word he could remember ever speaking to her, wondering if any of them were misunderstood or left unforgiven. He did the same with every action and conversation he'd had with Colette. There were more questions than answers in his head when he was done. Frustration, anxiety, confusion and despair were the only things he found.

Unable to escape this line of thought he finally jumped in the Porsche and just drove. Eventually, as if the Porsche had decided for him, Rory found himself tearing along the Peak to Peak highway. The scenery buzzed by him at an alarming rate as the Porsche topped a hundred miles an hour every time a stretch of road even vaguely resembled straight. Rory braked, shifted and navigated the wild curves of the road alternating between a grimace and a grin. Aspen trees had a reason to quake as the car ripped by them, often with tires squealing in protest.

There was little doubt that much wildlife in the vicinity had to seek trauma counseling after Rory passed. He imagined squirrels and rabbits lying on a tiny couch unloading their problems to a sympathetic fox who promptly ate them at the end of their session. He knew how they felt.

Driving fast on the twisted pavement did something that the previous night of hockey and inebriation could not accomplish. It cleared Rory's mind. His knuckles were white on the steering wheel. The deep leather seats strained to contain him through the turns. His heart pounded as he accelerated to pass slower traffic at every opportunity. In one exhilarating, yet horrifying swoop, he passed eight cars at once. Afraid to look at their drivers he imagined them alternating between fist-waving rage, slight terror and a tad of jealousy. He slid back into the right lane just as the passing section ended approaching a blind hill crest. Safely tucked into the right lane, he started to breathe again.

The pace was terrifying and thrilling to him all at once. Every mile that ticked away was another mile without having to contemplate how miserable he was. Every second that he wasn't on intimate terms with the sheer drops beyond the guard-rail or any of the blue spruces lining the road was a pretty good one as well.

Rory wasn't suicidal, he just wanted to push the car close to its limits to keep his brain focused on something other than pain and unhappiness. But some small part of him did picture Steph and Colette peeking into his casket. If something did go wrong, he wondered if they'd mourn him or not. At least he'd no longer have to worry about anything if he *were* to miss a turn at a hundred and ten.

Some part of him hoped for an epiphany. He believed it might come while his brain was so occupied it was squeezing out almost every superfluous thought. Though he wasn't sure he believed there was a god out there sending him some sort of message, Rory wasn't closed to the idea. Certainly with all that was happening to him, he felt like something or someone other than himself was in control. No, if he were in control, things would certainly be better than this. For one thing he'd be driving a new Ferrari, not a used Porsche, and of course Steph would be in the passenger seat.

Perhaps some part of him thought that if he were silent, he might hear from this supreme being. He hoped whoever was pulling the strings in which he'd become so entangled would speak—would tell him if it was time to move on and in what direction he was meant to go. Though Rory listened for a clue— what to think, how to feel, how to carry on another day—he heard nothing. The click of the gear shifter, the roar of the engine, the hiss of air over the car, the scream of the tires and angry drivers yelling as he passed by all drowned out any possible answer.

Despite the hairpin turns and the low speed limits, in twenty minutes he had covered the seventeen-mile stretch from Blackhawk to Nederland. With the lack of any revelation, he thought of stopping at the Pioneer Inn for a bacon cheeseburger. The Porsche protested, instead pointing itself toward Boulder. None too reluctantly, he was flying down Boulder Canyon at a similar pace to that which had taken him up the mountains. Twenty-four minutes later, his stomach won an argument with his car. He parked in Arapahoe Village shopping center and let his feet guide him the rest of the way to Red Robin's, still thinking of a fat bacon cheeseburger.

It wasn't quite five yet, but the place was already filling up. He was certain that he'd be the only person eating alone. Most, if not all of the tables, were occupied with people who were smiling, laughing and enjoying the company of friends and loved ones. Rory felt all the more alone in a crowd of happy people. The inviting and whimsical decor seemed to shout, "No unhappy people allowed!" He spotted the mascot, a giant, fuzzy, red bird, and hoped it didn't come anywhere near him.

After being seated and ordering a lemonade, Rory made a quick trip to the restroom. As he was enthroned there, a father and son entered the next stall. The youngster was apparently quite inexperienced with using the facilities. His father praised him saying, "Good job getting up there all by yourself."

A moment later junior asked, "Dad, why is it green?"

"Your poop is green?"

"Yeah, how come?"

"I don't know."

"Look, it has white dots on it too."

The father sounded slightly concerned. "I see that."

"How come it has white dots?"

"I don't know."

"You know what, Dad?"

"What?"

"It looks like chocolate chip cookie dough."

"I don't think anyone would want to eat those cookies, buddy."

"Yeah."

Rory was never so relieved to exit a public restroom. He returned to his table, quaffed his lemonade and left five dollars on the table. The waitress was just coming by to take his order as he was putting on his jacket. "Is everything alright, sir?"

Rory nodded and told her, "Sorry, I'm just not hungry anymore."

As Rory stepped outside into the early evening his phone rang. Hoping it was Steph, he quickly retrieved it and opened it without looking at who was calling. "Hello."

"Mr. Clark, this is Eileen with Sunshine Management. I hope you're having a Sunshiny Day today!"

"I'm having a hailing softballs, raining hellfire kind of day actually," Rory told her.

"That's nice. I just wanted to follow up with you on the fence situation, Mr. Clark."

"Great," Rory replied even though he was pretty sure it was anything but great.

"The fence on the north side of your property doesn't have a top rail on it. That's why it doesn't conform with the architectural standards for your community."

Rory felt amazingly unconcerned given how much he'd come to despise the HOA. He asked, "So it's the fence on the north side?"

"Yes."

"And if I fix or remove that fence you will drop the lien?"

"That's correct."

"I don't *have* a fence on the north side of my property."

"Yes, it abuts your neighbor's property at 14325 Austin."

"Eileen, the property to the north of me is 14279 Austin Court, not 14325."

"I don't know if that's correct, Mr. Clark. I will have to check that address on a follow up visit. However, there were other issues that have come to my attention. First, you have a broken window that was repaired with a piece of wood. We'll be fining $50 for not keeping your property properly maintained."

"You've got to be kidding me," Rory protested. "That window broke this morning. The glass company will be there to fix it tomorrow."

"How would I know when it was broken? It isn't as if I live in your neighborhood. All I know is that windows must be made of a clear material. Wood is not clear. It's in the neighborhood covenants. If you don't like the rules Mr. Clark, perhaps you should petition the HOA to have the covenants changed in your neighborhood rather than complaining about them."

"I don't have an issue with the rules. I have an issue with the overly vigilant enforcement of them. What's the other problem?" Rory asked, reserving his final angry rant until he had the entire story.

"There was a large amount of dog waste in your yard and your trash can was out too early this morning. You will be receiving notifications of additional fifty dollar fines in the mail for each of these issues."

Rory thought about this for a moment. The timing indicated that she'd been essentially spying on him. "How many times did you visit my neighborhood today?"

"Oh, I wasn't in your neighborhood today, Mr. Clark. I found the information about the fence in your file. The other items were reported to me by the president of the HOA today."

Rory was afraid to hear the answer, but asked anyway, "Who is the president of the HOA?"

"That's your neighbor, Davis Jennings. Nice guy."

"Once again, you are wrong about pretty much *everything*, Eileen."

"Is there anything else we can help you with, Mr. Clark?"

Rory hung up on Eileen without another word. *Perhaps*, Rory thought, *I'm waiting for an answer that's been being given to me continuously. It seems like the entire universe is telling me to move out of the neighborhood.* Rory failed to consider the option that perhaps he should ask a question before searching for an answer.

An hour later Rory sat in the office at Lord Stanley's. He was choking down a Big Mac which he regretted ordering as it was one of the ten worst meals he'd ever had. The other nine, by some coincidence also involved Big Macs. He'd been staring at the computer screen for half an hour before he decided to turn the monitor on. It sat for another hour waiting for him to log in. During this time he sorted through the bills which he'd picked up from his visit to the house. He didn't really look at the bills per say. It was more like he was idly shuffling through a deck of cards.

Of course his mind wasn't idle while he sat there. He alternately raged at Colette, Davis Jennings, the HOA, the universe, slow drivers and how unfair life in general seemed to be. He also pondered why he kept ordered Big Mac when apparently he didn't like them. Mostly he wondered if his marriage was over and, if it wasn't, what he could do to save it. He was as close to having a nervous breakdown as he'd ever been in his life. He wondered if he shouldn't be looking through brochures for mental hospitals before Steph made the decision for him. He'd hate to end up in a mental hospital that didn't have a pool.

After a while Rory realized that the envelope he thought contained his water bill was actually from the City of Broomfield Court. He tossed it aside, unsure if he wanted to know what the court might want from him. He'd been conditioned lately to believe that the only news was bad news.

Instead he thought about his drive. There hadn't been any answer. The only thing to do was continue to fight for Steph. With no new plan in mind, he pulled a piece of paper from the printer tray and started writing:

My Love Steph,

To say this has been a tough day wouldn't begin to cover it. I don't want to write about that though, because lies don't seem important in the face of the simple truth that I love you. I'd do anything for you.

I took a long drive today, trying to find an answer, the way to win you back. But as I sit here and write, I'm not sure what the question really is. If you still love me, it should be simple. We can work through this. We can work through anything with love. But if you aren't willing to talk to me how can we resolve this?

Some months ago, I pulled up next to a couple guys in a 968 Cabriolet. I yelled over to them, "Hey, what year is yours?" They looked at me and laughed before driving to the next light. I remembered at that point that I was not driving my car, but taking your PT Cruiser in for an oil change and brake job. When I pulled up beside them at the next light and yelled, "I have a '93 coupe at home. This is my wife's car," the passenger replied, "Is your wife's name Richard?" Then they ran the red light and drove away laughing.

It was a little embarrassing. Actually it was very embarrassing. The PT isn't a manly car by anyone's estimation. But it didn't matter. It made me feel good to take care of you, Steph. Whether it was making you breakfast, making sure your car didn't break down, installing the security system in the house, or just paying the bills, it felt right. There's still nothing that I wouldn't do for you. Let me take care of you.

Don't shut me out, Steph. The truth is in the fact that I love you now and forever.
Always yours,
Rory

Rory put the letter in an envelope and sealed it. After dropping it into his briefcase, he contemplated another letter—the one from the Broomfield Court. Rory glared at it for a few moments. If it were a small child or animal it would have no doubt run away from the sheer force of his glowering gaze. However, since it was a letter it felt nothing, instead simply resting on the desk unafraid.

Eventually, Rory decided that no matter how intensely he stared at an inanimate object it probably wasn't going to go away. He reached over and picked up the envelope. Perhaps it was good news. Davis had told Colette that he'd drop the lawsuit. It could be official notice that he'd done just that. As badly as Rory would have liked to believe this to be the case, any optimistic part of his being had been beaten down so repeatedly in the last weeks that it had gone into hiding.

Carefully he opened it, much like an old lady might proceed with a gift after claiming, "My what lovely wrapping paper. I'm going to save this!" Thus fifteen minutes later, he was reading a document with the City and County of Broomfield Seal at the top. Rory scanned it finding the gist of the letter was to inform him that the lawsuit Davis Jennings had filed was postponed by a week. Interestingly, Jennings' lawyer had postponed the case at his client's request. The request had been placed two days ago, a full five days after Rory moved out.

Rory wasn't entirely surprised that Jennings hadn't dropped the case. He more or less indicated such when Rory had the dire misfortune of seeing him earlier in the day. However, Rory did wonder how deep Colette's treachery ran in this circumstance. He wondered, *Did she even talk to Davis, or was the whole thing fabricated to get me out of the house?*

Mark stuck his head in the office. "Hey, we're about to close up. You want me to do the end of day paperwork?"

It was a nice way of asking Rory to get out of the chair so Mark could do his job. Rory didn't mind. He needed to get out of the shop anyway. He stood up with a weak, forced smile. "I'll get out of your way, Mark."

Mark put a hand on Rory's shoulder as he passed by and asked, "Rory, you have a place to stay tonight?"

"Yep," Rory answered. He wondered if Mark knew how poorly he'd worded his question. He thought to himself, *I've had a place to stay every night. A wonderfully uncomfortable hammock in the back room of a coffee shop.*

CHAPTER FIFTEEN

INTO THE FIRE

Rory wandered into the Ice Centre. He settled into the stands among the eight other spectators in the blue rink. It looked like a B-league team warming up on the ice, but he wasn't paying much attention. He flipped his phone open. Finding his parents in the directory, he sat for a while trying to decide if he really wanted to call them. He tried to excuse himself from dialing because it was too late, but they'd moved to San Diego after his father retired. It was just past seven in the evening there.

He remembered the last time he'd called someone while sitting in the general area he now occupied. It was a couple months earlier when the Red Wings were in town to play the Avalanche. Like most teams, they'd stayed in the Westin next door and practiced on the center rink. He'd dialed his best friend, Wayne, now living in Cleveland, to gloat about watching a pro level hockey practice from right behind the glass. That was the last time he'd talked to Wayne. He considered calling him, but realized that a nine p.m. call might be a bit annoying to a guy with three kids under five years old.

Rory sighed loudly enough that a woman watching the game looked to see if he was all right. Rory smiled weakly at her and dialed his parents. His mother picked up on the second ring. "Hello?"

Rory was glad to hear her voice. It seemed like the first friendly voice he'd heard in a month. "Hi, Mom."

"Who is this?"

"Your only son, Mom. It's Rory."

"Hello?"

"Can you hear me, Mom?"

"Can you hear me?"

"Yes, can you hear me?"

"If you can hear me call back. I can't hear you."

Rory hung up the phone and dialed again.

"Hello?"

"Mom, it's Rory. Can you hear me?"

"Can you hear me?"

"Yes."

"Good. I couldn't hear you last time, Rory."

"How are you, Mom?"

"I'm not doing too well Rory . . . "

Rory had forgotten his rule to never ask his mother how she was doing. It was hard because it was pretty much how he greeted everyone. "How are you?" It was like, "Hello" to him. In his mother's case it was a bad idea though. She'd been a borderline hypochondriac for twenty years. The last ten she'd graduated to full-blown imaginary invalid. With the slightest amount of encouragement, she'd let you know about forty or fifty new infirmities she was now afflicted with.

". . . I think I'm going to the doctor tomorrow, Rory. I'm pretty sure I have a detached retina. I keep seeing things in my left eye that I don't in my right. Your father says I shouldn't worry about it. I'm thinking better safe than sorry though . . . "

While Rory considered whether it was normal to see things with one eye and not with the other, she ranted on for another fifteen minutes covering topics from a broken thumb to brain cancer and Parkinson's disease. Despite being on the phone, Rory nodded much more than he spoke. Finally, she seemed to have covered the vast array of ailments she suffered and medications she should and shouldn't have been prescribed.

"But that's enough about me. How are you, Rory?"

"Maybe you should put Dad on the phone. I have pretty big news."

"Oh, are we going to be grandparents?"

"It's not the good kind of news."

"Oh," she replied, sounding unhappy for the first time in the entire conversation. As long as she had a personal malady to talk about she was pleased. Someone else with bad news tended to rain on her parade. He heard her yelling in the background, "Keith, pick up the phone. It's Rory."

Rory's father picked up the phone. "Hey son! How are things going?"

Rory's father was much the opposite of his mother. At least in the fact that nothing ever seemed to bother him. His health had generally been pretty good. Even when it wasn't he didn't complain about it. However, the opposite side of this was the fact that Rory's father didn't seem to care about anything either. They hadn't had a meaningful conversation since Rory was about seven years old. And really, how meaningful could a conversation with a seven-year-old be?

"Hey Pop. I'm hanging in there."

"So what's this news then, Rory," his mother cut in, worry tinting her voice.

Rory paused. Saying it aloud to his parents made it feel so real that he wanted to hold it in for a while. He stood up and headed toward a quieter corner of the rink before answering.

"Steph and I split up."

"Split up? You're getting divorced?" his mother was clearly confused and displeased.

Rory felt his eyes watering and blinked to keep the tears from spilling out. "I don't know. I hope not, Mom. I'm having a hard time believing it, but we've been apart for a month now."

"What did you do to mess that up, Rory?" she asked.

Rory noticed that his father hadn't turned down the television. He wondered if he'd speak again during the conversation. He wondered if he was even listening.

"It's a long story, Mom," Rory replied, thinking that she'd want to hear it all nonetheless. He planned on telling them all the details. How he'd shot at the neighbor's dog, yelled at a man in a wheelchair, piled dog crap in a neighbor's yard, was oppressed by the HOA, been sued, gotten arrested and was finally outsmarted by Steph's alcoholic mother. He wanted someone to listen. He needed someone to tell him honestly that he'd made mistakes but the punishment was far worse than his crimes.

His father vaguely mumbled, "Uh huh," into the phone.

"You turn off that television and pay attention. This is important!" his mother yelled, her mouth too close to the phone.

"I'm watching CSI. It's almost over, Jean."

"I don't care what you're watching. Your son needs you to listen."

"Hold on, let me turn on the VCR."

"For crying out loud, Keith!"

Rory visualized his father turning down the volume while he pretended to listen to the phone conversation. It *was* CSI after all. Further, Rory knew as well as his father did that the likelihood of him getting the ending properly recorded on the VCR was pretty low. His father's skills with electronics were frighteningly slim.

To Rory's surprise, his mother didn't let him tell what had happened. She simply launched into a long bout of advice. Her advice wasn't entirely unlike her health complaints. Much of it seemed obvious, like buying Steph flowers, and helping out around the house more. All of it was theoretical. Rory would have noted that these had been tried and fallen short had she given him a moment to speak. The only thing she said that made sense to him was, "You have fight for your wife, Rory."

When she finished, he was again surprised as his father spoke, "Jean, let me talk to Rory alone please."

"Rory, you call me if you need to talk," his mother said, "and don't you let that girl get away."

"Thanks Mom. I'll talk to you later."

"I love you, Rory. Goodbye."

After she hung up, his father asked him, "Rory, did you cheat on Steph?"

"Of course not, Dad."

"Good, I'd drive out there and give you a swift boot to your backside if you had. Not that there's any shame in it. Better men than you or I struggled with remaining faithful to their wives."

Rory wasn't sure why his father thought there was no shame in something as long as better men had struggled with it. He was also starting to wonder if he wouldn't have been better off unloading his woes on some anonymous stranger. It had worked pretty well for Forrest Gump.

"Rory, I came very close to losing your mother due to infidelity."

"What?!"

"Hear me out. Your mother already knows about this, that's the point. I was in another woman's hotel room on a business trip . . ."

Rory most certainly had no interest in making sex the topic of the first real conversation with his father in twenty some years. His Dad skipped "the talk" during his adolescent years deferring the uncomfortable subject to his mother. Rory was pretty sure he didn't want to hear whatever his father had to say now and asked him, "Is this relevant, Dad?"

"Shut up and listen, Rory!"

"OK."

"Nothing happened, but I came really close to ruining twenty years of marriage for a few minutes, Rory. My point is, if you did mess up, you need to come clean. There can't be any secrets in a healthy marriage. You understand? Steph cannot forgive you if you don't apologize."

"I'm not sure it's relevant, Dad. I don't *have* any secrets from Steph."

"Huh, well I don't know what to tell you then."

Rory hung up the phone a few minutes later, sorry he'd called. While both of his parents were well intentioned, they hadn't paused to wonder *why* he and Steph were separated. It made Rory wonder if they hadn't expected his marriage to fail all along. He didn't move for a while as he pondered what it all meant. *Why do my parents think this is all my fault? Is there something wrong with me that I don't know about?*

After a while Rory realized that he was sitting on the downstairs floor next to the elevator. Four feet away from him were a set of wheels and some feet. He looked up at Rob who was gazing down on him with what appeared to be concern. Rory tried to smile.

"Comfortable spot there?" Rob asked.

"Comfortable enough I guess," Rory replied. "I suppose you've still got the inside scoop on my life?"

"Not so much," Rob replied. "But if you want to talk about it, I'm always willing to listen."

Rory looked at the fluff-faced man for a moment. He still didn't entirely want to trust Rob. Rory knew that if he were in Rob's shoes he'd have it out for Rory (which confused him since there were two Rory's and no Rob in this theoretical situation). Nonetheless, there was something in his gut that believed that Rob was responsible for keeping Matt informed about any and all transgressions he committed. It dawned on him that Wheels probably figured out he was sleeping in the shop. He certainly had the opportunity to mention this to Matt. On the other hand, he might still be in jail if not for Rob's intervention. Everything about Rob confused him.

Realizing that he still hadn't been able to tell anyone about his woes, Rory opened up. "Let's see, the latest is that I'm being sued, I live in a coffee shop and my alcoholic mother-in-law is using subterfuge to destroy my marriage."

Rob nodded and his whiskers twisted into something resembling a smile. "Being sued sounds like fun. That's something I can help with. Backstabbing mother in law, well that sounds interesting too. I'll tell you what, let's grab a couple beers and you can tell me all about it."

Rory stood up and pushed the elevator button. As the doors slid open, he told Rob, "Deal, but I'm buying the beer."

Upon arriving in Jackson's the bartender waved at Rory and shouted, "Hey goalie! Glad to see you're doing alright."

Rob parked at a nearby table while Rory walked up to the bar. He greeted the bartender, "Hey Steve," as this was what his name-tag read, "how are you?"

"I'm doing alright. What can I get you?"

Rory ordered a couple of small Fat Tires. Steve delivered the beers to the counter swiftly. These it turned out were the same size as the large beers but cost a dollar more. Slightly confused, Rory started to head to the table, but paused turning back. "Steve, did you see me leave last night?"

The bartender nodded. "Yeah a couple of your teammates practically carried you out. You were messed up! You're not planning on doing that again tonight are you?"

"Not for a very long time," Rory told him and headed back to the table. He set one of the beers in front of Rob telling him, "I hope Fat Tire is OK."

"Geez, I woulda liked a Sunshine Wheat."

"Really?"

"No, that's a chick beer."

They chatted for a while. Rory found himself telling Rob more than he expected. He wasn't just giving him details about the lawsuit and Colette. He was dumping all of his woes upon a man who was practically a total stranger. Wheels listened to all of it sympathetically. Occasionally he'd ask Rory to clarify or expand on something, but mostly he just listened.

Eventually Rory's tap of anxiety ran dry. He was out of words, but he felt as if a carcinoma had been cut out of his soul. He wasn't cured, but he was somewhat refreshed. Wheels took a sip of his beer and nodded, offering some advice for the first time in the conversation. "Let me take care of the lawsuit. But you need to take care of getting your wife back and reconciling things with your mother-in-law. It will likely go easier if you can convince Steph to take you back first. Of course that's going to be hard unless you can convince Colette to confess her lies.

"As far as sleeping in the coffee shop goes, I have a comfortable couch and can always use the company. It's yours if you want it."

Rory considered the offer of the couch for a moment. It would be nice to not have to drive ten minutes to get to the shower. But he didn't feel comfortable accepting it. Further, he still had the lingering question of why Rob was anything but cruel to him. This night it would go unanswered because it remained unasked. He thanked Rob for the help with the lawsuit and the advice, gracefully declined the offer of the couch and headed back to his hammock for the night.

Rory woke up on time. He gently rolled out of his hammock and slipped to the cold, sealed concrete floor in his bare feet. Unlike the previous trip to Jackson's he'd limited himself to a few sips of beer. For the first time in two weeks he'd slept fairly well and felt refreshed.

He pulled a coat over his sweats and headed out the door. He allotted twenty-five minutes to hit the gym where he planned only to shower and shave. This gave him thirty-five minutes to grab breakfast and get back to the store. He decided that Einstein's bagels might be a more timely choice than Great Scott's. It was also less likely to give him an eventual heart attack. He made it back to the shop just as Lisa was getting out of her car.

"You didn't sleep here last night?" she asked.

"Maybe," he replied cryptically."

"Maybe you didn't or maybe you did?"

"Yes."

Lisa gave up on an answer at that point.

Rory's workday passed slowly, as most of them had since he'd been living in the shop. But it did pass and at 2 p.m. he left the store in Mark's capable hands. He headed off to start the fight to get his wife back. Ten minutes away she was working at the hospital.

Saint Anthony North was something of a mess when Rory arrived. It wasn't a mess like a hospital in Manhattan might have been after Godzilla tripped over the bus terminal at rush hour. It was not full of people on gurneys who wanted desperately to be reassembled. It was full of men in hard hats with nonchalant attitudes about how long it might take to have a hospital reassembled. Rory had forgotten Steph's complaints about the remodeling project until he walked into the hospital. It dawned on him that he'd only half-paid attention most of the time when she was complaining. Given the chance now, he'd sit at rapt attention.

Rory crossed the drastically reduced lobby, which was bisected by a sheet of plastic, and waited at the front desk. After a long enough time that he'd probably be unconscious if he had a real emergency, a nurse finally greeted him. He recognized her but didn't remember her name. She made a bit of a face when she recognized him. After looking over her shoulder, she told Rory, "Steph is pretty busy."

Rory didn't appreciate her attitude. Obviously she was going to play gatekeeper. He reminded himself that he was here to fight for his wife. After putting on what he thought was a nice smile, but was unfortunately more of a sneer, he told her nicely, "Let her know I'm here please. I'll wait as long as I have to."

She gave him what he could only describe as a death glare. The only thing that might have made the look on her face scarier would have been seeing it on a Doberman Pinscher. Rory glared right back and sat down in one of the ugly, green chairs that were welded together in a row along the wall. He picked up a fifteen-year old copy of *Highlights for Children* and began paging through it still glaring in her direction. By the time he got to the hidden picture puzzle Rory gave the magazine his full attention.

After finding all of the items in the hidden picture except for one comb, and reading all of the jokes (he only found a couple of them funny), Rory started looking for another magazine. The offerings were limited to *Fly Fisherman* or *Glamour,* neither of which appealed to him as much as *Highlights* had. He was reaching for *Glamour* on the table when a pair of nursing scrubs walked up to him.

He looked up to find Steph filling them quite angrily. She had a hand on her hip. Her face matched the rather unfriendly demeanor of her stance. It wasn't quite a death glare, but perhaps as close as Rory had ever received from her. Her jaw jutted out. Her eyes burned. Rory never thought she looked better.

"Steph . . ."

She cut him off. "Why are you ambushing me at work? Which part of, 'I don't want to see you' didn't you understand, Rory?"

He stood up reminding himself that he came to fight for her. "All of it, Steph. I didn't come here to argue with you. I suppose your mother threw away the letters and flowers?"

"What are you talking about?"

"It wasn't your mother who cleaned the house, Steph. It was me. I left you a dozen roses thirty letters I wrote you, one each day. You mother was drunk and threw that bottle at me, Steph."

"Rory, I don't know what you expect to gain by coming in here twisting my mother's words . . ."

"I don't know what *I* expect, Steph. I do know that I love you and I'm not giving you up without a fight. I do know that I've never lied to you and I'm not going to start now. I would hope that you'd think about all the facts and consider the big picture before you condemn me."

"So now my mother is a liar? I'm done with this conversation, Rory. Get some help!"

She turned to leave but he grabbed her arm. She tried to pull away and he quietly told her, "Steph, just take this and promise me that you'll talk to your mother before you decide what the truth is."

She took the letter he offered her. With one quick look at him she walked away. Rory had not expected Steph to fall sobbing into his arms to ask his forgiveness. Nonetheless, he had expected things to go a little better then they had. Sick to his stomach, Rory walked out of the waiting room with the fifteenth heartbreak he'd had in a month.

Rory was considering another aimless mountain drive, maybe he'd try to shave a minute off his Blackhawk to Nederland time. While his mind was meandering about how to escape the oppressive world closing in on him, the oppressive world called his cell phone. Rory pulled into the parking lot at Hyland Hills golf course as he picked up the phone. Seeing it was Mark he flipped it open.

"What's up, Mark?"

"Matt Morgan is here looking for you."

"Tell him I'm in Casper, Wyoming."

"You better get here fast, Rory. It's pretty serious."

"What's going on?"

"He's talking about closing the shop."

Rory gritted his teeth. He knew Matt's act was too good to be true. Matt was a world class jerk and world class jerks don't have hearts. Rory silently berated himself for believing that Matt was suddenly a kindred spirit. *How could I have momentarily trusted a man who betrayed and lost four wives?*

"I'll be right there," Rory told Mark. He flipped the phone shut and tossed it on the passenger seat. Anger and adrenaline pumping through him, Rory stomped the gas and slipped the clutch, launching the Porsche in a half moon power slide back toward Sheridan Boulevard. Leaving a cloud of white smoke, he ran the stop sign leaving the parking lot.

Rory stomped the brake pedal when he realized he was doing sixty in a thirty-five mile per hour zone notorious for sneaky police speed traps. He smiled a little as he saw the front of a police cruiser poking out slightly from 98th Avenue. The smile was short lived when he realized that there were flashing lights in his rear view mirror.

He eased the Porsche over, turning off on 98th. The officer pulled in behind him just as his comrade in the sneaky, speed-trap cruiser pulled out with his lights flashing. Rory shook his head, incensed by the injustice of it. This was nothing but pure commerce in the guise of public safety. He made a mental note to move to Germany as soon as possible where they didn't care so much how fast you drove.

It was about three months later when the officer finally delivered Rory a summons and a stern warning to drive more slowly. Rory thanked him (although he had no idea why) and pulled as carefully onto Sheridan as he had onto any road in his life. A few minutes later he was pulling into the parking lot at the

Ice Centre. While he'd only been five minutes away when Mark called, it had taken him almost an hour because he was driving too fast. The irony of this was lost on Rory at that particular moment.

After parking, Rory ran to the shop. Matt was there with a man wearing a work shirt. The patch on the man's shirt read, "Hank," which Rory didn't deem important. However, the other side a patch read, "Jiffy Locksmith." This Rory thought might be significant as Hank was working on the front door to Lord Stanley's.

"What's going on, Matt?" Rory demanded.

"Nice of you to bother to come by," Matt replied snidely. "I'm evicting you right now."

"For what? I though we had this worked out."

"That was before I realized that the roof was leaking."

"What's that have to do with me?"

"It's leaking along your little, secret path to my rink. Apparently this type of roof isn't created for heavy foot traffic."

"And you couldn't have just billed me for repairs?"

"Oh, I already have."

"You know you're a complete waste of air, Matt?"

Matt smiled proudly and looked at his watch. "You have fifteen minutes left to grab what you need. We're going to hang onto all of your equipment as collateral until your insurance company pays for the damages and you settle up on the remainder of your rent."

Rory ran inside and yelled to Mark, "Run end of day and bag all the cash for the deposit including both cash drawers and petty cash."

Mark jumped into action pulling the cash drawer from the register and running to the office.

"Lisa, you want some coffee?"

She looked at him quizzically so he told her, "Box up all the coffee beans and fresh food and put them in our cars. I'd rather you and Mark take them home than throw them away."

He tossed her his keys and she went to work.

Rory went back out front. "You have paperwork on this I assume, Matt?"

Matt produced a rather thick sheaf of legal papers outlining several hundred reasons for the eviction. The most significant of these were code violations for sleeping in the store, distribution of liquor without a license, running an illegal gambling operation and unauthorized use of adjunct facilities. Among the odder items Rory found were unauthorized overnight parking and cruelty to animals.

"Come on Matt, you just made half of this up."

"I don't think so."

"Cruelty to animals?"

"Your table scared a poor bulldog nearly to death just a few weeks ago. I know *everything* that goes on here, Rory."

Rory threw his arms up in despair. "There's nothing I can do to persuade you to change your mind?"

"I doubt it," Matt replied.

"Are you looking for a bribe?"

"Are you offering one? I'll be glad to add bribing a city official to the reasons we're evicting you."

Thus, twenty minutes later Rory had a small car filled with coffee, pastries and three computers. Matt was no doubt sitting in his office rubbing his hands together and laughing maniacally. Lisa was crying and Mark was angry. Rory promised them that he'd sort things out one way or another. He gave Lisa a hug and shook Mark's hand patting him on the back.

After they drove away, Rory looked forlornly at the Porsche. Driving fast in a Porsche was fun. Utilizing one for your bedroom held significantly less promise. Rory pondered, *I have to find a place at 24 hour fitness where I can hang a hammock.*

CHAPTER SIXTEEN

A NEW DOGHOUSE

Rory had been trying for thirty minutes to re-arrange the hatch area of his overladen Porsche. While the 968 was as practical as any sports car, it still wasn't meant to hold two desktop computers, twenty-five pounds of coffee, eight bagels, two muffins, four danishes, three cinnamon rolls, two dozen cookies and a coffee cake. For a moment Rory was thinking he needed to check the bagel order for next week to make sure they weren't normally ending up with eight of them this close to closing time. Then he realized he needed to cancel all of the standing orders. As far as the car went, there was no way he could determine to recline the seat into a reasonable position for sleeping.

Rory picked up his cell phone and laptop computer. With one last disapproving look at the Porsche, he headed into the ice rink. His first stop was the public bathroom where he sat in the back stall and wept for fifteen minutes. Being evicted was just another pebble on top of the landslide. The hardest part was not having Steph's shoulder to cry on. It was a very difficult cry and not nearly as cathartic as he'd expected because he had to stop wailing every time that he thought he heard someone walking in. The last thing he wanted was pity from a fellow hockey player.

After crying, Rory headed to Jackson's. For the next hour he called every vendor to cancel standing orders. He made a note in the computer about which accounts he had contacted. He also verified the amount payable to each one of them. He checked the balance in his business bank accounts. There was enough to pay his vendors, his employees' paychecks, the home mortgage, settle the year and half of remaining rent with the rink and buy a couple Big Macs. It made him sick.

Rory pondered how long he could stay alive on stale bagels and pastries. He supposed if he froze to death it might be better than starving to death. Of course, either way, he'd be dead which seemed unpleasant. While he was currently less opposed to the idea of being dead than he was the day before, it still didn't seem like a good idea.

He contemplated how a man with no home went about finding a job, which he apparently now needed since he had no home and only enough money to eat for about three days at best. At least he was paid up for a year of showers at 24 hour fitness. Despite his hopes that he'd only be using their facilities for a few weeks, the sign up offer was so good he took the full year. He figured he could always work out there if he didn't need a place to shower.

He pulled up a couple job search websites on the laptop thinking how foolish he had been to not inquire with his vendors if any of them needed help. So, for several hours, he updated his resume, made notes about who was hiring and applied for jobs. He hated the idea of going back to work for someone else almost as much as he hated the idea of starvation . . . but not quite.

Concentrating on the task of finding a job was difficult at best. Most of him alternated between wanting to be in a quiet corner weeping or throwing a public rage by smashing something and screaming. The waitress came by and refilled his lemonade a few times. He barely noticed her until the third time when he got her attention and asked, "Hey, are they hiring for any positions here?"

She shrugged. "I think we're pretty much always hiring waitstaff." Then after a glance over her shoulder she told him, "But that's because it's pretty much the worst job on the planet."

As she walked away Rory thought to himself, *Welcome to the world of having a job.* He'd loved being a business owner. People came into his shop greeting him by name. As friendless as he often felt, many of his customers treated him like a friend. He'd miss that as much as any part of owning the shop.

After an indeterminate time of perusing an assortment of rather repulsive opportunities, Rory noticed that Wheels was rolling up to the table. "I thought I might find you here. Things at your usual sleeping establishment don't look so good."

"What do you mean?" Rory asked, immediately suspicious of Rob. He wondered how Rob knew he had been evicted so quickly after the fact.

"Sorry, I thought you knew already. There's a big sign on your door that says the shop is closed and the contents have been seized by the City of Westminster," Rob replied looking a bit uncomfortable about having to break the news to Rory.

Rory hadn't noticed the sign. When he walked by to return to the rink he had been pretty much in a daze. He had no interest in looking at the shell of his shop, the place where all his hard work had been reduced to ashes. His suspicion simmered somewhat. "Yeah, I knew about it. I'm in here trying to find a job and wondering what people without a home generally do when looking for one."

Rob nodded slowly. He then backtracked slightly and asked, "What happened, Rory? Why did they evict you?"

"Matt Morgan happened. He's the biggest tool I've ever met. Yesterday he was acting like my best friend and today he's blaming me for a leaking roof."

"For the roof?"

"I did walk on it quite a bit."

"Uh, why?"

"To get to the shower in the morning . . . before the rink was open."

"Rory, I'm not taking no for an answer. You're sleeping on my couch tonight."

"I don't know, Rob. . . "

"Where are you planning on staying?"

"My car."

"How long has it been since you looked out there?"

Rory turned around and looked out the window. There was a full-blown blizzard outside. In the time he'd been in Jackson's it looked like almost a foot of snow had fallen. He groaned inwardly. *It's only October and we're having a second big snowfall, really?* Rory sighed, "Apparently I've been in here quite a while."

Rob waited a moment before speaking. Had Rory been paying attention he might have realized that Rob was waiting for the reality of the situation to sink in. It was cold outside. There was a lot of snow on the ground. No one in their right mind thought that sleeping in a car was a good idea. Of course had Rob been pondering whether all these things were sinking in, he might have also wondered if Rory was in his right mind. Really, who'd blame him if he wasn't?

Eventually, Rob spoke again. "Come on, Rory. They're closing up in thirty minutes here. You can follow me home."

"I don't know, Rob."

"Rory, you still don't trust me, do you?"

"I'm sorry, Rob, I want to trust you. You seem like a decent guy, but you don't owe me anything except maybe a black eye."

"Sometimes you don't get what you deserve," Rob replied. Rory wasn't sure in this case if getting something other than a black eye was a good or bad thing. He was pretty sure that a place to sleep wasn't what he deserved, but neither was having both knees broken with a tire iron. He wondered which of those two items Rob was actually thinking about.

"So Rory, a couple days ago you trusted Matt?"

"Yeah, I guess."

"How'd that work out for you?"

"Not so well obviously."

Rob nodded gravely and replied, "I can't force you to trust me, Rory. But ask yourself a couple questions. Did Matt have a record that indicated you should trust him? And have I ever given you a reason to not trust me or is that based upon how you think you'd feel in my shoes?"

Rory slowly nodded to himself. Yeah, he didn't really have much to lose at this point. But that being the case, sleeping in the car was almost easier. The simple fact was that Rob had a point. He'd never shown Rory a hint of malice. Although he did seem to have a bit of stalker in him. Rory wanted an explanation for that before he agreed.

"Alright Rob. Just explain one thing to me."

"Fire away."

"Why are you always here?"

"At the rink?"

"No, how is it that you are you always here to rescue me?"

Rob's beard bobbed slightly as he chucked. "Rory, I'm just here to play hockey. I was going to ask why you always need to be rescued when I'm here."

Rory smiled genuinely for the first time in a while. He stuffed his laptop in its case and stood up. "Alright Rob. I accept your offer."

Rob patted the arms of his wheelchair. "Good, I wasn't sure how I was going to make it to my van in this snow. You know this thing doesn't have four wheel drive."

As it turned out, the Porsche wasn't going anywhere in the snow either. Rory grabbed the pastries and a five-pound bag of Sumatra. He jumped into the van and rode with Rob. It seemed that Rob was taking him to his own house until they pulled off Sheridan a couple blocks too early.

Their destination turned out to be a rather plain-looking, brick ranch. Rob pulled into the garage which, though big enough for three cars, held only the van they arrived in and an old, partially-dismantled Corvette. The garage was fully loaded with black and white floor tiles, a flat screen television, large, stainless fridge and more tool chests than Rory's mechanic likely owned.

"Quite the man cave," Rory remarked.

"Yeah, I don't spend as much time in here as I used to." To Rory, Rob looked a little saddened with this admission. Neither of them commented further. After the ramp lowered Rob out of the van, he rolled into the house. A golden retriever greeted him happily when Rob opened the door. He petted the dog with a smile.

"Rory, this is Cody."

Rory, not being a huge fan of dogs recently, grinned weakly and followed Rob inside, his arms laden with pastries and coffee beans. While the house seemed rather plain on the outside, it was stunning on the inside. Rory was pretty sure the dining room with its towering vaulted ceiling, was big enough for a game of football, although the hickory hardwood-floor would have strongly dissuaded a tackle game. The house was tastefully decorated. While the style was minimalist, it was definitely not the masculine vein that the garage had exuded. Everything was immaculately clean.

Looking out a wall of glass at the back of the house, Rory realized that it sat on the same golf course that snaked through his own neighborhood. Where Rory's house was across the street from the golf course, Rob's backed up to a lake that cradled the green of the second hole. The view was pretty much stunning even in the dark, through the falling snow.

Gazing out the back window Rory sarcastically noted, "No mountain views, huh?"

Rob was still scratching Cody who had followed him into the kitchen. With a chuckle, he replied, "Yeah, we almost passed on this lot because of that. But the mountain view from the roof is outstanding."

Rory regarded Rob quizzically. He was unsure which subject was more important. Rory wondered, *Who does he mean by we?* Instead he asked, "So you spend much time on the roof then?"

Rob chuckled, "I used to, but the chair kept rolling off with me in it. Hey, you wanna set that stuff down or is carrying it around part of your workout plan?"

Rory realized that he still had breakfast in his hands. "Oh yeah, where do you want it?"

Rob nodded to the kitchen counter. As Rory placed the bags there, Rob started rolling away. "Let me give you the grand tour."

The house, it turned out, had two spare bedrooms upstairs. Rob told Rory that the basement was finished. There were three more bedrooms each with their own bathroom, a great room with a wet bar and an office there. That he was apparently sleeping on the couch in a house with five spare bedrooms was slightly annoying. The fact that Cody, who had apparently gotten his fix of ear scratches, now alternated between sniffing Rory's butt and crotch was somewhat more annoying.

Rory tried forcefully to remove the dog's nose from one area only to have it migrate to the other. Rob scolded the dog a couple times. He apologized to Rory. "He won't do that once he gets to know you. Sorry."

Rory didn't want to talk about Cody. He just wanted Cody to go sleep in the garage or something. There was little doubt in his mind that Cody would be sharing the couch with him that night. He knew that the most evil thing about dogs was that they sensed who didn't like them and responded by jumping on, licking and sniffing them. That Rob had a dog, was just the way his luck was going. Regardless, he still wondered about the feminine touch to the decor and told Rob, "You have a really nice home. Did you decorate it yourself?"

Rob shot him the same look that any hockey player accused of home decorating might. However, Rory caught a slightly sardonic look in Rob's eyes. It passed in a flicker. He softened and told Rory, "No, my wife decorated the house."

There was a detectable sadness in Rob's voice. Rory wasn't sure what it meant, but he did consider that the question of how Rob had a girlfriend *and* a wife might not be that big of a mystery. He suspected his wife was an ex-wife.

"Sorry, I didn't mean to pry, Rob."

"You didn't know. No one from hockey really does."

"I'm still not sure that *I* know."

"Grab a seat."

Rory settled into one of the leather couches in the living room. Rob rolled up across from him. Cody circled a couple times and settled in at his feet. Rob opened his mouth as if to speak, then seemed to change tact. "Sorry, I should have asked, do you want a drink? I think I have a few beers in the fridge."

Rory nodded. "That sounds good. Want me to grab them?"

Rob shook his head as he rolled away. "I got it. I keep the beer on the bottom shelf. Otherwise Cody would have to get it for me."

Cody turned his head and watched his master, but didn't get up. Rory pondered for a moment if or how a dog could fetch beer from the top shelf of a fridge. While it didn't really matter, he considered all of the most comical possibilities in the short time Rob was retrieving the beer: stilts, trampoline, roller skates and a ramp, forcing a cat to do it at gunpoint. Sadly, none of these really amused him.

Rob rolled back with two bottles of Left Hand Milk Stout in his lap. He rolled up to Rory, flipped the top off of one with a blue, aluminum bottle opener in the shape of a shark. After handing it to Rory, he backed up to the coffee table and opened his own beer. Rob tilted the bottle back, wiped a little foam from his facial hair and asked, "How long have you been married, Rory?"

"Six years," Rory replied interrupting his first sip of the beer.

"I hear that's about the time when things get tough."

Rory nodded. Although he hadn't heard that before, he certainly wasn't in a position to disagree with Rob. Both of them sipped a little bit of the frothy, smooth beer. Rory noted with his coffee tasting palette that the drink had a smooth, creamy texture, hardly a trace of bitter hops. It was laced with a pronounced chocolate layer, a hint of caramel and a clean milky finish. He noted with his beer drinking palette that it was really good.

Rob launched in on his story. "Rory, my wife, Christina, was killed in the car accident that put me in this chair. We'd been married for five years at the time. I guess you could say that the honeymoon phase wasn't over yet since we hadn't faced any of the issues that so many people seem to have at the six-year point. It's easy for me to romanticize things and believe that we never would have struggled. It's also easy to forget the times we did now that she's gone. I loved her more than anything.

"The guy who hit our car was drunk. He tested at a point four alcohol level an hour after the accident. In case you don't have them memorized, that's enough to be lethal even to someone who isn't driving. He was driving a pickup so big that it pretty much drove right over our car. Christie died before they could get her out. I was in and out of consciousness, but I knew she died beside me. There was nothing I could do. I never felt so helpless in my entire life as I did sitting beside my wife watching her die.

"Our two-year-old son, Nathan, died in surgery the next day. They had to put me into a medical coma to keep me from causing myself further spinal injury. When I woke up a week later, the doctors told me that I'd likely never regain the use of my legs and that my family was dead."

There were tears in Rob's eyes. Cody looked up and whined slightly. Rob patted the dog then fiddled with one of the bottle caps in his hand idly. He stopped making eye contact with Rory. Rory was surprised that Rob was sharing this, trusting him with it. Despite how unbearably bitter it was, it also made him feel important.

Rob continued, "You ever see the Mel Gibson movie, *Payback*, where he essentially kills everyone who tried to leave him for dead?"

Rory nodded. "I love that movie."

"Yeah, that's pretty much how I felt after a few weeks of wishing I had died along with my wife and son. My purpose in life before that accident was to protect and provide for them. Everything seemed so futile in light of how it turned out. As much as a we might want something, nothing is really in our control. Lying in that bed and being forced through physical therapy, I had no purpose. I didn't want to get up, get out of that bed. I didn't care if I'd ever walk again.

"Then I found out the guy who hit us didn't have a scratch on him. I raged at the universe for being so unfair. I screamed at God, not even knowing if there was a God. Finally I came to the conclusion that I could make that driver pay even if the universe or God wouldn't. I knew I wasn't going to drive to his house, walk through the front door and shoot him. But I could do something even scarier; I could take everything he held dear. I am a lawyer after all.

"I worked like a dog after that, trying to recover. In three months I was out of the rehabilitation center and getting to work on my case. I argued a civil case and won a judgment of fourteen million dollars against him. He lost everything he owned. He had to sell his house. He lost his job. His wife left him and took his kids. A few months after all of that he was sentenced to five years in jail for two counts of vehicular manslaughter. He's still in jail now."

Rob stopped talking and took a long sip from his bottle. Rory had been completely absorbed by the story. He didn't know what to say or even if he should say anything. Eventually Rob continued.

"In the movies that always seems to be enough, doesn't it, Rory? Giving someone what they have coming is supposed to make you feel better."

Rory nodded in agreement.

"It didn't work for me. I didn't think it was possible, but it made me even more bitter. His insurance paid me four million dollars. He sold everything he owned and raised another million. After that he pretty much owed me everything he'd make in the rest of his life and then some. I had utterly and completely destroyed that man. His life was as devastated as mine, worse perhaps since at least I had money and freedom and the people who he loved had rejected him. I was rich by most people's standards, had reduced the man who ruined my life to ashes and I still felt completely empty.

"I was lost again. Not knowing where to find happiness, I spent money like there was no tomorrow. I dated a different woman every month. I took long trips. I drank too much. I did insane things like skydiving, white water kayaking and learning to fly (none of that's not easy without working legs by the way). But nothing completed me. Nothing could fill the emptiness that losing Christie and Nathan exposed in me."

Rory started to feel a little nervous. Was this the part where Rob revealed he had also retrieved his favorite pistol from the kitchen? To Rory this confession of not finding happiness in revenge sounded like the ranting of a madman. *Why wouldn't destroying your enemies make you happy? Maybe the wheelchair is a complete ruse. What if he can actually walk?* Rory pondered, *He probably has the bodies of fifty hockey players buried in the basement.*

"So you know what I did to him next?" Rob asked.

Rory was pretty sure he didn't want to know at this point. *Why, oh why did I trust you?* he wondered. *If you're going to kill me, make it quick. At least my life was already ruined. There's not much left to miss and there aren't too many people who'll miss me.*

Rory nodded, unaware of the wide-eyed look of terror on his face. Then realizing that he had no idea what Rob had done, Rory stopped nodding. He opened his mouth to reply. His voice crackled, a raspy, "No." He tried to smile to cover his fear. It looked more like he had gas. He tried to cover his discomfort with another sip from the bottle. His hand trembled slightly.

Rob apparently didn't notice Rory's distress and continued. "I visited him in prison and I forgave him. I told him I was canceling his debt to me. I invested, saved and eventually was able to put five million dollars into a high yield account and haven't touched it since."

Rory almost fell out of his chair in relief and surprise. He gasped deeply and realized that he hadn't been breathing for five or six minutes. Once the blood returned to his brain, Rory set down his beer. It dawned on him that he was quite confused. *Why would Rob do that?*

"You forgave him?"

"Yes I did."

"And you're going to give him back his five million dollars?"

"Only a million was actually his."

"But you're giving it back?"

"I'm going to try to help him get his life together when he gets out of prison. I'm not going to hand it over to him, but it's there for him if and when I decide he's ready for it."

"Is this some kind of joke?"

Rob laughed before replying. "Nope Rory. It's the best thing I ever did. I haven't stopped forgiving people since."

The light bulb suddenly went on. Rory realized why Rob had taken him in. He took a long drink from his beer, slightly saddened to reach the bottom. However, he was more reflective of what this all meant.

"Rob," he asked quietly, "you took this interest in me because I was so cruel to you, didn't you?"

Rob smiled and nodded. "I wouldn't have put it that harshly, Rory. I took an interest in you because you were so human. And Rory, I forgave you the day you apologized in the Rock Bottom, so don't worry about anything you might have done to me. I'm not sure I remember it anyway."

Rory felt himself tearing up a little with this revelation. Rob was right. Sometimes people didn't get what they deserved. Rory still didn't understand why, but he knew that he was fortunate to know this man. He sat there feeling slightly better about life for the first time in weeks. In light of all that had happened to his new friend, Rory's life suddenly didn't seem all that bad. He didn't even mind the fact that Cody was in his lap licking his face.

CHAPTER SEVENTEEN

MENDING FENCES

Rory awoke to the annoying chirping of his cell phone. Unlike previous days where it had served as his alarm clock, on this occasion, it was serving as his phone when it interrupted his slumber. He looked at the clock in the downstairs bedroom where he was sleeping. (As it turned out, Rob didn't really intend to make him sleep on the couch at all). The red numerals on the digital clock dutifully informed Rory that it wasn't quite eight in the morning. He picked up the phone. Despite not recognizing the number he answered groggily, "Yeah."

"Mr. Clark, this is Eileen with Sunshine Management. I hope you're having a Sunshiny Day."

"Is the sun even up yet?"

"It's eight in the morning, Mr. Clark. Of course it is."

"That's great, Eileen. Why are you calling?"

"I wanted to let you know that I visited your neighborhood yesterday . . ."

"I hope everyone who visits my neighborhood doesn't start calling me first thing in the morning."

"Excuse me?"

"Never mind, you were saying?"

"You were right. There is no fence on the north side of your property, Mr. Clark."

"It's a relief to know I was right about that."

"Also, the managers met today to discuss your lien."

"Why would you have to do that, Eileen?"

"To decide if we could remove it."

"That sounds like a great use of time."

"Meetings are very important, Mr. Clark."

"Get on with it."

"Unfortunately . . ."

"There better not be an unfortunately."

". . .we cannot refund your lien since you haven't paid it yet."

"You don't need to refund it, you need to cancel it."

"We thought you should pay it and we'd send you a refund."

"If I pay it you still have to cancel it."

"True."

"Why not just cancel it?"

"I'm afraid we didn't discuss that."

Rory wasn't surprised. The HOA never did anything that made sense. Why would the company they hired to manage the neighborhood do *anything* rational? He wondered if the employees of Sunshine Management had the good sense to fear for their lives. It was only a matter of time until they pushed some poor homeowner over the edge and he stormed into their offices shooting. It was hard for him to not point this out to Eileen. However, he realized in an uncharacteristic moment of clarity it would sound like a threat, making himself a prime suspect when it eventually did happen. He decided that it sufficed for him to understand what might make some lunatic eventually snap and end up in the national news.

"Eileen, why don't you call me back after you've discussed doing that." Rory snapped the phone shut. He was tired of hanging up on Eileen. It wasn't normally in him to be so impolite. It was just something about Eileen and Sunshine Management.

Rory rolled out of bed. For the first time in a while the walk to the shower was an enjoyable fifteen feet. He felt like he was staying at an expensive hotel. Rob had told him to take the biggest bedroom on the lower level. He had a bedroom that was probably five hundred square feet and his own private bathroom. Outside his door was Rob's great room with a pool table, pinball machine and big-screen television. While the upstairs decor clearly belonged to Rob's wife, the lower level was all Rob. It was ironic since it was so hard for him to get to the lower level in the wheelchair.

After a shower and shave Rory wandered into the great room. Another wall of glass led out to the backyard from the lower level. He looked outside, per his normal morning custom, to estimate what sort of day it might be. The snow had apparently tapered off after they'd arrived at Rob's house. By Rory's estimate there had only been another inch or two beyond the earlier foot. The October sun was already doing its work, illuminating the white fluff, which shone like crystals. The drooping trees danced slightly shaking the uncharacteristically-heavy snow from their shoulders.

Rory stood gazing out the window, looking over the pond to the deserted golf course. He vaguely noted the thermometer on Rob's patio read forty-four degrees already. The snow wouldn't be around long. His mind was already spinning at 8000 RPMs, contemplating not only the weather but his personal woes when Rob called him from upstairs. "Rory, you awake?"

"Yeah, here I come."

Rory trudged up the stairs to where Rob and Cody waited. He felt remarkably refreshed. While he still had more burdens than he thought any man deserved to carry, they were somehow lighter today. He even paused to scratch Cody behind the ears at the top of the steps.

"Sleep well?" Rob asked.

"I did. It's the first time that's happened in a while."

"Good, now we need to get some ground rules straight for while you're here," Rob told him. "First, there is absolutely no cleaning up after yourself. I have a daily maid service and I'd hate to not get my money's worth.

"Second, aside from the stuff you brought when you came, I don't want you to buy any food. I have a service that drops off pre-made meals that I heat and eat. They don't make meals for one, so I end up throwing half of it away most of the time anyway. You're doing me a favor if you eat it.

"Third, you can stay as long as you need to in order to get your life back together. However, I do expect you to be *putting* your life back together. I am a Republican. If you want a lifetime handout, you're going to have to find a friend who is a Democrat."

Rory chuckled. "Wow, your hospitality sucks. I think I'm just going back to my car."

"Oh, speaking of your car, we're going to the lunch pickup game. I assume you don't have anything pressing. I'm going to teach you a little something about goaltending."

Rory raised one eyebrow and sneered at Rob. "Oh really? You wake up a little cocky, don't you?"

Rob rolled into the kitchen with Rory behind him. "You know what they say, 'It isn't cocky if you back it up.' You better have yourself a big breakfast my friend. You're going to have to bring your A-game to beat me today."

The snow was apparently just enough to keep the other goalies away. Rory and Rob were the only pair on the ice for the afternoon pickup session. The player benches, on the other hand, were pushing close to capacity. The result was a pretty excellent session of lunchtime hockey.

Rory knew most of the players on the ice, but only a few of them by name. For the most part, he'd assigned them colorful nicknames to keep them straight in his mind. For instance, one guy with a spectacularly-large, light-blue, perfectly-round Jofa helmet was "Bucket Head." Another guy who fell down every time he stopped leaning on his stick for balance was "Tripod."

Some other players were Pinocchio, Goggles, Captain America and Anti-Gretzky, all of whom were so self-explanatory that Rory overheard other people calling them the same thing. Perhaps the one exception was Captain America, who someone else had dubbed Mike Eruzione, captain of the 1980 Olympic team whose jersey Captain America wore. These were both nicknames of the ironic variety, since the guy had as much hockey talent as a Mike Eruzione's *empty* jersey might.

Even with Captain America, Tripod and Anti-Gretzky on the ice, the session had good flow. Rory and Wheels faced a large number of shots against. While Rob didn't move as fast as Rory, his chair presented a huge obstruction in front of the net. Much to Rory's surprise the goal tally against each of them seemed pretty even.

Halfway through the session Rory and Rob switched ends. At center ice, they bumped gloves as they passed. Rob told Rory, "Good luck down there. They aren't playing much in the way of defense."

"It looked like you did OK," Rory replied.

"Yeah but I'm a better goalie than you are," Rob told him with a chuckle. Rory shot him a look as he rolled away.

Fifteen minutes after they switched ends, Bucket Head and Captain America collided with one another in the corner to Rory's left. They jostled for the puck until Bucket Head managed to get it away. Captain America, in a very non-superhero move, whacked Bucket head in the back of the leg with his stick. Rory wasn't sure it was meant to be as dirty a play as it appeared to be.

Bucket Head collapsed like he'd been shot. Rory noted that apparently there was no padding on the back of the guy's legs. It made sense since there wasn't any padding on the back of his goalie pads either. He was surprised when Bucket Head jumped back up, his anger seemingly overriding his pain. He gave Captain America a shove yelling, "What's your problem?"

At this point Captain America probably could have put a cease to the hostilities. He might have said, "So sorry, there was a spider on your leg." Or perhaps asked Bucket Head, "You alright? I was trying to hit someone else with my stick." However, he did neither of these instead opting to yell back, "I barely touched you. If you can't take a little contact you should go play bridge!"

This put asunder any thoughts that Bucket Head might have had about how much his leg hurt. As Rory watched, Bucket Head's eyes actually turned red an instant before he was swinging his gloved fists at Captain America. In a moment both players were pummeling one another with unabashed fury. Rory rolled his eyes and retrieved the water bottle from atop his net, taking a sip as he watched the fight with minimal concern.

Several of the braver players (or perhaps those more interested in hockey than their personal health) interceded, taking their fair share of punches for their intervention. With great effort the two combatants were finally separated. They skated to their benches, but before arriving there, more words were exchanged resulting in a second flurry of punches. Other players once again moved in and divided them. Eventually, hockey continued.

Some minutes later, Rory was racing to a loose puck. A large player who was unanimously nicknamed, "The Orient Express," was bearing down on him. This moniker was the result of his Sumo Wrestler appearance and inability to turn or stop quickly. Knowing that his opponent wasn't too nimble, Rory's plan was to poke the puck to the boards and let him skate past it. It was a simple strategy that almost always worked.

Unfortunately, as Rory was poking the puck and coming to a hard stop, he lost his edge. His skates came out from under him and he slid into the Asian giant's feet. The man landed on him with a thud that would have knocked the air out of a tractor tire. Rory, not having quite as much air in him as a tractor tire, forgot his name for a moment. He thought he heard the sound of raspy weeping and eventually realized it was coming from his own throat.

The puck skidded to the corner of the ice. Players stopped to see if everyone was all right, save the one guy who made a point to shoot the puck into the empty net. Tripod looked down at Rory and muttered, "That's not pretty!"

Once the giant rolled off of him, Rory immediately apologized, well as soon as he'd caught his breath anyway. "Sorry. I lost an edge. You alright?"

The Orient Express smiled at him and helped him to his feet. "No problem, goalie. Nice play."

The game ended without any further drama. However, Captain America and Bucket Head were still yelling at each other when Rory left the locker room thirty minutes later. A string of profanity chased him out the door. Rory met Wheels in Jackson's, where his new friend proclaimed himself the victor of the day. Rory was about to protest when Rob introduced the idea that the winner was buying lunch. Remembering the contents of his bank account, or more accurately the lack thereof, Rory quickly nodded and said, "Yeah, you killed me. You're the man in net. In fact you should start your own goalie school."

Rob nodded as if either he didn't care or didn't realize that Rory had pulled a fast one on him by not arguing. As Rory dropped into a chair across from him, Rob asked, "What did you think about the session?"

"It wasn't half bad. There were a few guys that should have been sent down to the minors, but all in all not bad. The fight was a little stupid."

"I thought so too," Rob noted. "How hard is it to just apologize instead of punching someone?"

The waitress came by to take their orders. Rory was thinking how good the New York Strip sounded, but was loath to overstep Rob's hospitality. He ordered a cheeseburger. Rob handed his menu to the waitress and told her, "New York Strip, medium rare and a side salad with ranch."

As she walked away, Rob returned to the subject. "I thought you might have your own little tussle there. How's your head after having Chen land on it?"

"Chen?"

"Yeah, Chen, The Orient Express."

"Oh, my head is fine, Rob. He landed on my gut."

"He's a terrible skater, but it's a good thing he didn't take offense to you taking him down."

"Oh, I just apologized right away."

Dimly, Rory was aware that maybe Rob was making a point.

The snow along Colorado's front range is notorious for melting. Not so much just melting, but for doing it rather quickly. At times when the conditions are right, the snow is polite enough to simply evaporate, minimizing the messy necessity of puddles. This particular day being one of those occasions came as a relief to Rory.

By the time he and Rob left Jackson's the parking lot was pretty well clear of snow and the temperature was over sixty. Even the copious amounts of white stuff, which Rory was pretty sure Matt had ordered the plow driver to deposit on top of his car, were entirely gone. While the snowfall was about a foot, his car *had* been covered with about seven feet when they arrived for hockey. Rory dropped into the seat of the Porsche, the leather warm from the sun.

He turned the key and sat for a moment preparing himself for what he had to do. He'd decided at lunch, with Rob's counsel, that he needed to start forgiving people in order to move on. Rory wasn't convinced that it would work, but he was desperate enough to try anything. Officer Doyle's apology the other day had certainly helped point him in the proper direction. After talking with Rob, he'd decided that starting with the most difficult one to forgive wouldn't be a bad idea. At least everything after that would be easier.

Fifteen minutes later, he arrived in the neighborhood attached to his mortgage payments. Rory eased into the driveway to his house and sat in the car for a moment rehearsing what he'd say one last time. He stepped out of his car and walked around the corner of his house. Rory gazed across the street at Jennings' house where his now soiled garden gnome grinned evilly. Rory muttered, "What are you looking at?"

Jennings was on the list, but he wasn't Rory's task today. Rory breathed in the cool winter air deeply. He proceeded up the stairs to his house and rang the doorbell. After a moment he unlocked the door and walked in. He called out, "Colette?"

Colette was sitting at the kitchen table, a cigarette dangling from her lips and a halo of smoke lingering about her head. Rory didn't know that she even smoked. Although infuriated by the fact that she was doing it in his house, he bit his tongue. He came here to mend fences, not throw wood on the fire. He was thankful that at least she was fully dressed this time.

"So the buffoon returns," Colette said looking up at him. "What do you want this time?"

"I just want to talk, Colette."

"Suit yourself."

She nodded nonchalantly to the chair across from her. The kitchen was somehow in worse shape than it had been the last time he had arrived. The stacks of dishes were even higher. Moreover, there were pieces of mail, magazines and papers on almost every horizontal surface in the kitchen. The mess had spread to the Family room which hosted a couple TV trays with dirty dishes on them. Rory moved a stack of newspapers from the chair so he could sit down.

Colette was scrutinizing him as if he had an agenda that she didn't approve of. While outwardly she was brazen, exuding an unaffected air, Rory sensed a defensiveness from her. She was nervous. It dawned on him that perhaps she was jealous of him. Perhaps she wanted more time with Steph and viewed him as an obstacle to that. He wondered, *Could it be? Does Colette hate me, or is she just so in need of a friend that she's manipulating her own daughter?*

Rory took a moment to collect himself, then promptly forgot everything that he had planned to tell Colette. The only thing that remained in his head was forgiveness. If Colette was so pitiful that she'd stoop to ruining her daughter's marriage out of loneliness, she needed compassion from someone. As rueful as he was for that to be him, he started talking.

"Colette, are you doing alright?"

She cocked her head as if he'd just asked if she'd ever been visited by extraterrestrials. Obviously she hadn't anticipated this line of conversation, nor was she certain how to reply. She hardened her features and snorted, "What do you care?"

He nodded understanding this reaction more fully that he expected he would. "I haven't been good to you, Colette. I know that. You've reached out to us for help and all I've seen was someone leeching our happiness. I owe you an apology for that. I should have done more than half tolerate your presence here for the sake of my wife.

"Colette, I was always fond of you. When Steph and I were dating, you were always a great hostess. You used to invite us over for those amazing, home-cooked meals; just thinking of your meatloaf makes my mouth water. You were always there for us to help ensure that things were going well. It's not fair that I deserted you when things took a turn for the worse. I'm sorry for that, I really am.

"I know that things right now might seem irredeemable between us. What you did between Steph and I was the most horrible thing that I can imagine. I'm not sure why you did it either . . ."

Colette opened her mouth to protest, "I don't know what you're talking . . ."

Rory didn't let her continue, speaking right over her interruption. "Colette, I didn't come here to argue with you. We both know what you did. We both know it was a horrible thing. The hurt that you did to my relationship with Steph might never recover from what you did. But I'm not even here to blame you."

Colette looked at him baffled. Rory could see more than a flicker of doubt in her eyes. She was still playing chess, trying to figure out what his gambit was. She looked him in the eyes, analyzing his play carefully as he spoke. Finally she asked, "Then why are you here, Rory?"

Rory tried to smile, but there was a tear in his eye as he told her, "I'm here to forgive you, Colette."

CHAPTER EIGHTEEN

AWKWARD MOMENTS

How do I feel about this situation? I'm lying here in a spare bedroom inside the house of someone who I barely knew a week ago. I'm mooching off a man in a wheelchair. My life is in shambles, but I have been rescued from homelessness. Still I lie here for hours asking myself the same question over and over again, "What am I going to do now?"

I should be embarrassed by this situation. A man is supporting me for no apparent reason other than that he's a decent person. I should be ashamed that I can't help myself, but I'm just relieved that someone else has helped me. I should feel guilty for freeloading, but he won't allow it. I should feel completely alone since I've lost everyone and everything that was important to me. Yet I feel like I have a new friend.

What am I going to do now?

It had been eight days since Rory moved into the basement. He had been searching for a job, but Rob discouraged that line of action, telling him, "We need to find you a new location for your shop."

"There's an issue with that, Rob."

"What issue?"

"All of my equipment is locked up in the old location."

"Why?"

"Matt seized it."

Rob nodded and a slight grin formed on his face. "Then we need to fix that issue first I guess." He started to wheel away from the table, then stopped, turned back and told Rory, "Oh yeah, by we, I mean me."

For a man confined to a wheelchair, Rob had an extraordinary abundance of energy. At times Rory thought Rob either had ADD or was actually the world's largest hummingbird. Either way, even though he was always sitting, Rob was never sitting still.

As far as the shop went, Rory didn't bother Rob with the fact that if he paid off his old lease to get back his equipment, he wouldn't have enough money in his business account to sign a new lease on a even tool-shed. It was just further evidence that his existence on the planet was as important as that of . . . well a pile of rump raisins from a large black dog. Besides, he wasn't a hundred percent sure about the value of Rob's advice.

Rory had forgiven Colette a week ago and nothing had changed. She was still occupying the house that he should be living in. Steph hadn't called him to invite him back into it and his contrition didn't seem to have had any impact on that fact. If he thought about it though, there was a certain amount of peace that he'd gained from forgiving Colette. It was the one annoying thing in his life that he was done with. He'd forgiven her and stopped ruminating on why she'd done what she'd done. There was nothing more that he could do. That felt good in itself. Deeper still, and perhaps he didn't realize this part yet, the weight of his grudge was lifted. He felt better for that alone even if he didn't know it.

Rory sat at the table a little while longer, eating a quiche with his right hand and typing absently on the computer with his left. He'd become an ambidextrous eater from years of multi-tasking in the food industry. Now he was looking at a job posting for a truck stop and wash manager, which didn't exactly sound promising, when he heard a crash from the direction of Rob's room.

Rory bolted out of his chair. He ran to the source of the crash and was disturbed to find Rob on the toilet, his wheelchair somehow resting in the bathtub. Rob looked at him sharply. It was the first time that Rory thought he saw a flash of anger in Rob's eyes. This was confirmed when Rob barked, "Get out!"

Rory was embarrassed and quickly told him, "Sorry." It was the first time that he felt like an intruder in Rob's house. He backed quickly out of the room.

Rob called after him in an apologetic tone, "Hey, do you think you could grab my chair out of the tub before you go?"

Rory put the wheelchair back in reach and headed to the kitchen table. After a short while Rob wheeled back out. He looked a little grim as he rolled to the table. "Sorry Rory. It's kinda hard to get on the toilet sometimes, especially if I'm in a hurry. I guess that quiche didn't suit me too well today. I didn't mean to yell at you. It's just that I've tried so hard to be independent so it's embarrassing when I can't."

Rory nodded. Although he felt there was more to it, a need for independence was certainly something that he could understand. "Rob, sometimes it's hard to make it without help. I'd be living in my car if it wasn't for you. Anything you need from me, you can ask it. I'm not going to judge you."

"Even if I need help getting on and off the toilet?"

"I didn't say I'd *do* everything you asked, just that I wouldn't judge you," Rory replied with a grin.

Rob smiled. "Fair enough, Rory." He paused a moment before continuing, "How is your forgiveness list going?"

Rory had told him about Colette already. There wasn't anything to add at this point. He told Rob, "Nothing new on that front."

Rob nodded. "It's hard to do, Rory. But it's easier if you keep up your momentum. The longer you wait between people on your list the harder it becomes to do. At least that was the case for me. I'd suggest that you keep working on it regularly. Eventually it will become second nature."

Rory wasn't convinced. He hadn't seen stellar results with Colette and wondered if he should even continue. "I don't know if it's working for me, Rob. I don't really feel like anything has changed since I spoke to Colette."

It took a moment for Rob to answer. Rory thought he was reflecting on the proper words. Eventually he spoke. "First off, I think something *has* changed. It might not be obvious to you, because it isn't what you're expecting, but I've seen it. I think you've changed. Maybe not a lot . . .. and maybe I'm wrong because honestly, I haven't known you very long But I don't think you should expect world-shaking changes from your first step down the path.

"You should also know that not everyone on your list is going to react to you in the same way. Some people will be grateful, some will be indignant and self-righteous believing they haven't done anything to offend you. On the inside those people probably know better and some of them will come around in time. Some people won't care one way or the other.

"The other thing that you should know is there's a second part to what turned my life around, Rory."

"And you were waiting until I was worthy to teach me in this second part, Sensei?" Rory mocked lightly.

Rob chuckled, "I started attending a church partway through my forgiveness list."

The paranoia meter in Rory's head started registering a little fear once again. Hockey players weren't religious people. Rory had visions of himself being carted off to some mountain town where they put him in a yellow robe, shaved his head and told him that the last fool who tried to escape was eaten by bears.

"I didn't know you were religious, Rob."

"Well, religious is an ugly word. I'd never say that."

"So it's an *atheist* church?"

Rob laughed aloud. "No it's a Christian Church. You're welcome to come Sunday. I'm pretty sure it's not what you'd expect a church to be. For starters, it meets in a shopping center in Lafayette, in what used to be a farm supply store or something. The band is outstanding and the pastor has a great sense of humor. It's kinda like going to a rock concert and comedy act with a spiritual message. No obligation, Rory, but I think you might get a lot out of it."

Rory wasn't sure what to think about church. He hadn't been to church since he was sixteen and back then it was just for Christmas or Easter. The impact on him was such that he couldn't really remember which it was. Oddly, at least oddly to Rory, he was actually considering going to Rob's church. His first thought had been that Rob had waylaid him into living with him simply to proselytize him. He quickly dismissed this as a crazy notion thinking, *If Rob were some sort of insane zealot, he would have tried to shove a giant Bible down my throat days ago.*

There were, in fact, two things compelling Rory to give Rob's invitation a chance. First there was the simple fact that he didn't want to offend Rob by simply dismissing the invitation. Rob had been nothing but hospitable, checking out a church was the least Rory could do to thank him. Second, there was a certain emptiness in Rory that had been there even before he'd lost everything. The lack of purpose and love in his life revealed to him the glaring depth of it. He had questioned the existence of God more often lately, but come to no real decision on what the answer might be.

Thus he replied earnestly, "I'll think about it."

"Fair enough. I do have one favor to ask you."

"Fire away."

"I want you to sub for me tonight."

"For The Lucky Pucks?"

"Yep."

"Why can't you play?"

"I know my digestive system pretty well. I'll be sick tonight."

Rory nodded grimly. He didn't want to let down Rob the first time he asked for help. On the other hand he didn't want to play on Dan's team. He'd clearly decided that Dan was the enemy. He was conflicted.

"That's tonight for The Lucky Pucks?" he asked as if there were something to clarify.

Rob nodded. "I need a good goalie to take my spot."

Rory remembered that Dan was on his list. He wasn't sure he was ready to forgive him yet, but Rob was clearly giving him a chance. He found himself nodding, even though his brain was shaking its head.

Rob grinned widely enough that a couple teeth showed through his massive beard. He told Rory, "I need a good goalie, but I'll settle for you."

Dressing in the Lucky Pucks locker room was something that Rory never thought he'd do again. Regardless, he was the first one in the locker room. He found himself sitting half-dressed when Dan became the second person to enter the room. Rory nodded to him. "Hey Dan."

The expression on Dan's face registered considerable confusion. Obviously, Rob hadn't informed the team of the last moment switch. Dan sat down across from Rory and looked at him. Rory wondered if having Dan show up first was good or bad luck. He shook his head remembering there was no such thing as either.

"How are you, Rory?"

"I've been better. But things are looking up."

"So you're filling in for Wheels tonight?"

"Yeah, Rob's feeling sick and asked me to play."

"I've gotta say I'm surprised you agreed."

"Me too, Dan."

Dan started retrieving some of the gear from his bag and Rory almost let the moment pass. He cleared his throat though. When Dan looked up Rory started slowly.

"Dan, last time I saw you things didn't go well."

"You mean the A-league game?"

"No, I meant the team meeting."

"Oh, yeah. Sorry about the mix up, Rory."

"I appreciate that, Dan. I was really mad about it."

"Yeah, I felt bad about it." Dan's words clearly didn't match his actions. His gaze had turned back to the bottom of his bag. He rummaged through it as if looking for something. Rory could tell he was simply avoiding eye contact.

"Well, I just wanted to say, I forgive you and I'm sorry about the way I acted. It was appalling and I apologize for it."

Dan looked up. His face looked even more confused than when it had first spotted Rory. The rest of Dan looked pretty much the same as normal. Perhaps his face was confused why his body lacked a neck, but Rory suspected that it had given up wondering about that years ago. It seemed more likely that Dan had never been forgiven of anything in many years. He was, after all, a piano salesman.

The mouth on Dan's face opened and some words came out. They were, "You really have no idea, do you?"

"I guess not," Rory replied, wondering what he was apparently in the dark about.

"You shouldn't forgive when you don't know what you're forgiving, Rory. I knew that Rob was coming back. I just wanted to make sure we didn't have to play against you. I figured we had a chance to win the championship, but not if you were on a team we had to play. I waited to the last second so that all the teams would have goalies lined up. I wouldn't have even considered taking on Wheels if he didn't pay the league fees for the entire team. You were the best goalie in the league . . . "

Rory had never heard Dan talk so much and certainly not in an apologetic, human-like voice. He usually was trying to come across as wise and assertive, but it just came out as smug. This was somewhat confusing.

Dan continued. "The issue was that several of the guys on the team weren't sure they could afford to come back to play and since Wheels always sponsors the team, I decided to let him take your spot. I should have been straight with you, Rory. I'm sorry."

Rory smiled at the realization that Wheels was right. It *was* good to forgive people. Maybe Colette didn't take it as well as Dan had, but this was going well. In fact, Dan had confessed something that Rory didn't expect. He could almost see a screen of smoke between them dissolve. Rory felt as if the pile of stones that rested on his chest had just become slightly smaller.

He stood up and crossed the room to Dan. Dan seemed to think he was about to get pummeled until Rory stuck out his hand at Dan and told him, "Thanks for telling me all of that, Dan. It's alright. I already forgave you. Now shake my hand. Let's forget about water under the bridge and go play some hockey tonight."

The game proceeded at what seemed a slow pace. After weeks in the A-league, it took Rory a few minutes of play to adjust to the slower B-league. He was able to recover from a couple of mental gaffes caused by the extraordinarily patient tempo. At least this was the case until about five minutes into the contest. However, the mental gaffe was not his own.

A shot from the opposing team had resulted in the puck resting partially under Rory's right leg pad. Despite the puck not actually being covered up, the referee blew his whistle stopping play. As Rory stood up, the player who had initially shot the puck swiped at it and knocked it into the net. Oddly, the ref blew the whistle again and pointed indicating a goal.

Dan immediately was on the ref protesting, "How can they score after the whistle? The play was dead."

All of the Lucky Pucks, including Rory, joined in angrily protesting the call. The other team had a look of indifference that indicated they didn't believe it was a goal either. However, one thing that Rory had learned over the years was that referees might apologize, but as a rule referees don't change calls. The two officials conferred and after a moment decided that the first whistle was never blown. The goal would count.

Neither team was able to score again in the first period. As they switched ends in preparation for the second, Rory stopped by the penalty box where the refs were nursing their water bottles. Rory knew they didn't want to see players (or goalies for that matter) between periods, but he wasn't there to berate them. So even though Johnson tried to close the door when he approached, Rory was not deterred. Fortunately, Johnson's immense mustache kept him from moving very quickly anyway.

"Hey guys," Rory started. Johnson started to grunt something. His partner that day was a young, red-haired kid with a pasty complexion. Rory wondered if the kid were old enough to even play in the adult league, let alone ref it. He'd been the one who made the error.

"Except for that one mistake it was a good first period. I just wanted to let you know I'm not worried about it. You shouldn't be either. I know you try to not make errors and fully trust you to have a great couple periods to finish the game."

They both looked confused. The kid mumbled, "Thanks." Rory felt like the kid should have probably mumbled, "Thanks, sir." He wasn't compelled to mention it though and skated off toward his net.

Halfway through the second period, the score still one to nothing, there was a scramble in front of Rory's net. After fending off three shots, Rory made a tremendous stab with his glove and caught the puck. However, his entire glove was inside the net. Clearly it was a goal. As he fell on his backside he pushed the glove out of the net.

The kid in the striped shirt was two feet from the action. Rory saw him there even as his glove was still in the net. They made eye contact. The corner of the kid's mouth turned up slightly, a moment before he blew his whistle. Rory fully expected him to point to the net, indicating a goal. Instead, he waved his hands, signaling that the puck *hadn't* gone in. The score was corrected from the previous error. Rory and *Ginger the Ref* both knew it.

The game increased in intensity in the third period with the Lucky Pucks still trailing by a goal. Rory ratcheted his own play up a level. He made three glove saves that brought his team to their feet yelling and pounding on the dasher boards with their sticks. After making a deposit in Rory's goalie glove, one unfortunate shooter told him, "Come on goalie, that was too good a shot to not go in."

Rory eventually caught the other team changing lines on a weak dump in pass. He handled the puck making a sharp pass to Mike, the team's only real talent. Mike streaked down the open side away from the bench and stuffed the puck past the other goalie. Things were even, at least for the moment, and Rory had an assist. He prided himself in being an offensive talent at goalie even if it was a bit of a stretch. He did, however, manage a couple assists in a typical season.

The Lucky Pucks were barely done celebrating Rory's assist and Mike's goal when the other team raced down ice on a two on one break. Rory wasn't happy to see that Dan was the one defender against two of the other team's better players.

Nonetheless, Dan put in a solid effort, taking away the opportunity for the other team to pass.

The player with the puck shot hard and low. Rory figured he was hoping for a rebound that his partner could finish. He dropped to make the save. When he felt it strike his stick he was pretty sure he'd made the perfect play. The puck would have split the difference, going right by both his opponents . . . it *would* have done that, had it not bounced off of Dan and right back to the second man.

The second man was familiar. Rory didn't place him at once, but suddenly realized that he had changed his appearance; his pants were no longer purple. The puck had landed at his feet. Fancy Pants, skating full speed, kicked it up to his stick in a perfect shooting position.

Rory pushed toward the open side of the net to stop the attempt. He knew he had a chance, but it would be a near miracle save. Glove and goal stick outstretched, he made a final dive in that direction just as the shot came. It was a hard rising shot, destined for the top corner of the net if Fancy Pants had his way.

Things didn't slow down for Rory as they had the last time he faced his once purple-panted nemesis. In a fraction of the time it might take to blink, Rory poked his goal stick into the air where he thought the puck might go. There was no time to react to the shot, he simply had to preemptively guess and hope he was right.

Even as he felt the satisfying smack of the rubber puck hitting his stick, he realized that there might be bigger issues. Dan had hooked Fancy Pants across the chest pulling him off his feet. The man was flying at him skate blades first. As the puck skittered into the corner of the rink, they collided. Adrenaline coursing, Rory didn't notice that it hurt. As he scrambled back into position, he vaguely thought that it probably *should* have hurt.

Rory popped back up ready to make the next save. Before anyone even touched the puck the ref blew the whistle. Ginger dashed off the ice with the urgency of a man who finished three

Big Gulps and was headed to the restroom. Johnson came to Rory's net. "You've gotta go."

"Me? I didn't do anything wrong! Don't you make another bad call," Rory found himself yelling. He wasn't so sure why he suddenly felt so defensive.

"I'm not calling a penalty. You can't play while you're bleeding!"

"I am?" Rory exclaimed almost more than he asked.

Looking down Rory realized that the crease was now blue with small, red polka dots. He felt fine. *Why do they make players leave when they're playing well? I don't want to go. I need to finish this game. I need to win.*

"I'm fine. I can finish."

Johnson shook his head. Rory realized that Ginger had dashed off to get help. One of his teammates was pressing a towel against Rory's neck. Everyone had the look on their face that Rory might have expected if he were looking at them from inside his own coffin.

He looked down again and realized that there were a lot of polka dots on the crease. He pondered, *How much blood is that? How much is in the human body? Why do I feel lightheaded? This really is bad luck, no no no, there's no such thing! How much blood can I spare?* He didn't feel like he was doing a good job with the math to calculate blood loss estimations. Determining whether he could finish the game before passing out was too hard, so he sat down.

"The ambulance is on the way, Rory," the scorekeeper told him. A couple guys with gloves were behind him with a First Aid kit. Rory was thinking to himself, *I really should have gotten a Kevlar neck guard. They aren't <u>that</u> uncomfortable. I'll pick one up before the next game.*

CHAPTER NINETEEN

BACK ON THE BOAT?

Rory woke up on a boat . . . again. The boat was a 1958 Chris-craft Continental; this he knew as his uncle owned a 1958 Chris-craft Continental. The Continental was a fine, old, wooden speedboat. This one was every bit as meticulously restored as his uncle's. However, while the boat was pristine, the situation seemed pretty dire.

Dark clouds hurled rain down while the wind and waves batted the boat none too playfully. Rory looked down at his feet where several inches of water sloshed over his goalie skates. He wondered, *why am I wearing my skates? Why does that seem odder than the fact that I'm on a boat? Are we water skiing in a thunderstorm?*

Rory checked out the other occupants of the vessel. In the front of the boat, Davis Jennings sat behind the wheel. The engine wasn't running, but Jennings didn't seem at all concerned about this fact. He turned the wheel slightly as if they were clipping along at twenty-five knots. A wave dumped a copious volume of water on Davis, but he was unfazed.

Next to Jennings was Matt Morgan. Matt had a young woman in his lap. She was holding her hand out to look at the rather large diamond ring on her finger. Both Matt and the woman were laughing hysterically, drinks in their hands.

The second row of seats contained Officer Doyle. She was glaring at Rory. She pulled out a citation book from her pocket after a moment. Rory had no idea why, but he was pretty sure that she was writing him a summons.

Sitting next to Doyle was Thunder. The great dog was slobbering all over the place. An enormous, gooey, orange life jacket was haphazardly fastened about the black dog's neck. Thunder dropped from the seat. He splashed over to Rory and peed on his leg. After a single angry bark the pooch returned to his seat.

Next to Rory in the rear, triple row of seats was Colette. She sneered at him, blew cigarette smoke in his face then turned away and laughed. In her hand was a large glass of wine. Despite a significant amount of sea water splashing into it, she chased her cigarette smoke by emptying the contents into her gullet and returned to laughing.

Sitting beside Colette was Steph. She alone looked concerned at the rapidly rising water in the boat. Rory's heart soared to see her there. He caught her eye. She smiled the special smile that he knew to be his alone. Even if the boat were to sink everything would be all right. That smile said more to him than a million words could convey. *Steph still loves me! Nothing else matters as long as I have that.*

Suddenly, Rory realized that everything *did* matter. If Steph did love him, he didn't want the boat to sink. Dying without her love wasn't a big deal. Living without her was hard. But if she loved him, it was a reason to carry on. They had to start the engine before the water was too deep. The engine pump would keep the Chris-craft afloat long enough for them to make safe harbor.

Steph was still looking at him as he realized this. He started to bail the boat with the wooden scoop that had materialized in his hand. Steph stood up. She sloshed to where he was scooping water and told him, "I cannot be that, Rory."

Rory stopped scooping and stood. He watched dumbfounded as she stepped over the side of the boat and into the waves. Steph swam away from him, pausing once to flash that special smile at him. It didn't make him feel good this time.

What does she mean? Where is she going? How do I carry on from here? If she loves me, how can she just leave? Rory watched her swim away until the speck she'd become on the horizon evaporated between two waves.

He looked back to the now swamped vessel. Everyone carried on as if nothing was out of the ordinary. The water inside the boat was level with the gunwales now. Gentle waves lapped over the top of the boat. The rain had slowed and a rainbow stretched across the now-quiet sky. Thunder dog paddled alongside.

Rory yelled at them, "What's wrong with all of you?"

They looked at him and laughed.

Rory awoke from the dream. He was on a boat thinking, *again?* He tried to remember how he got on a boat this time. Eventually he remembered that he was actually dreaming last time. He was on a hammock in the coffee shop and *not* on a boat the time before that. That couldn't be the case this time, could it? This could be the first time that he woke up on a boat without knowing how he got there. He felt the mattress, he certainly wasn't on a hammock.

Eventually he remembered that he'd left the rink in an ambulance. They'd poked him with an I.V. and driven with the siren on. The I.V. wasn't so great, but the siren was pretty good . . . although he didn't really remember anything after that. Still he correctly came to the conclusion that he was in the hospital. He vaguely wondered what the sound of the ocean was doing there with him.

He also wondered what they'd done with his hockey gear. It would be a shame if they cut up Cujo's goalie pads. Idiots at the hospital were prone to doing things like that. He'd lost a favorite shirt to a pair of medical shears when he broke his arm at age twelve. He still was wary of hospitals because of this. To his thought it was some sort of scheme they worked out with the clothing makers who perhaps gave them kickbacks for destroying favorite shirts.

Rory opened his eyes. The television was playing one of the videos his dentist played for patients in the chair. It was nothing but ocean waves lapping on various beaches. He momentarily wondered why anyone other than a dentist might buy something like that. He looked across at his roommate in the other bed curious what sort of person it might be. It was his dentist.

The dentist hadn't noticed him since he was intently watching the relaxing scene on the television. Rory suspected he might cheer if the next set of waves were to come rolling in with a little more vigor. Not wanting to interrupt his dentist's show, Rory turned his head the other direction. He was even more surprised to find that Steph was asleep in the chair next to his bed.

Looking beyond her through the window, Rory gauged that it was early in the morning. She was still dressed in her scrubs indicating she'd probably spent the night at his bedside. It moved Rory to see her there. He realized something that he had wondered about in light of the recent events—she did still care about him.

The dream flooded back. He wondered what it all meant. Rory vaguely remembered calling Steph's cell phone a couple times to tell her that he was doing all right. Anesthesia, it was way more potent than liquor for drunk dialing people. He wasn't sure what he'd told her, but apparently it wasn't too bad if she was here. He suddenly felt a hope that had been missing. Perhaps this was the nudge they needed to reconcile things. He was certain the dream was the result of his phone conversations with her.

Without realizing it, Rory groaned. It wasn't a groan of discontent or pain. Instead this was an involuntary expression of joy manifested in the only voice his dry throat would produce. Steph rolled over slightly and looked at him. He tried to greet her.

"Hi," it came out as a hoarse whisper.

Her look was one of pure shame. Rory didn't know what to make of it. *Is she ashamed for kicking me out? Is she embarrassed at being caught by my side—embarrassed that I know she still cares?* The look was gone in a flicker, replaced by a smile that could infect a funeral with joy. It wasn't quite the one from Rory's dream, but it was close enough. She stood up and came closer.

"How are you feeling?" she asked, instinctively pouring him a glass of water as she did.

Rory took a drink and was relieved to find that his voice returned, somewhat. "I guess I'm OK. I think this hospital stay might be the least of my worries, although I'd have a better idea about that if I knew why I was here."

A look of concern crept across Steph's face. If there was any doubt before that she cared, this erased it completely for Rory. "You had a pretty serious injury at hockey."

"I remember bleeding a lot, but I felt fine."

"A skate nicked your carotid artery, Rory."

"It wasn't that bad. I wanted to finish the game."

"You almost *died!*"

"There were only 15 minutes or so left in the game."

"Rory, be serious. If the EMT's weren't already at the rink because someone broke their leg, I'd be at your funeral instead of your hospital bed."

"I thought *you* were the one joking."

Her tone was stern. "Rory, you passed out from blood loss right after they got you on the ambulance. If they'd taken another thirty seconds to get to you or if that skate blade cut you any deeper, you would have died on the rink. You don't know how lucky you are."

Rory thought of reminding Steph that he didn't believe in luck. Further, he considered telling her that if he *were* lucky he would still have a wife, a home, a business and a yard without crap in it. He'd also have finished the game and not left the rink in an ambulance. It seemed like if there were any sort of luck his was all bad. He also thought of telling her it would have been bad for his team if he'd died. Of course he didn't know if they won or lost anyway. While deflecting with humor was what he tended to do in the face of hard truths, it somehow seemed a little trite in this situation.

As a result he was at a loss for what the appropriate words were. He looked at Steph, lost inside her eyes for a moment. There were more important things to be talking about than whether his team won or lost or what might have happened but didn't or how he was feeling. His neck didn't really hurt, it didn't hurt when it happened and it didn't really hurt now. His heart hurt though.

He looked at her, a little moisture welling up in his eyes. He hated crying. It made him feel less a man, but it was the way he'd been wired apparently. He cried at the end of almost every sports movie he'd ever seen. Even *The Rookie* got him a little bleary eyed and it was a baseball movie. To Rory, that made it *barely* a sports movie.

"Steph," he started, "none of this matters. What matters is that we reconcile our marriage. I love you. Not having you in my life is the most painful thing I've ever gone through. I don't know if I can keep doing it."

He reached out his hand toward her. She pulled her own hand away nodding toward the dentist in the other bed. Rory turned his head to look. The dentist apparently found their conversation more interesting than his ocean video.

"Hi Doctor Mike," Rory said.

The dentist turned back to his program with a nod. Rory turned back to Steph. He didn't really care if the dentist listened in on their conversation. It was the hygienists who he figured might be gossips. He reached out for her hand again. She did not offer hers.

Instead Steph told him, "I'm not interested in talking about that right now, Rory."

Rory stiffened and pulled his hand back. "Steph, we've been married for six years. How can you just walk away? You're the single most important person in my life."

The ashamed look was back in her eyes. While Rory was only very good at reading people as long as he wasn't married to them, there was no mistaking it. She sighed. "I'm sorry, Rory. I'm just not ready for that."

He nodded. At least she had the sense to be ashamed. That seemed a good sign in some small way. He asked her, "When do you think you might be ready?"

She shook her head and bent over to pick up her purse. "I don't know, Rory. I just don't know."

She left in a hurry. Rory wondered if she was crying. It didn't matter. She'd stayed at his bedside while he was injured. That counted for something. It would have been nice if she'd said she was happy that he was still breathing though.

Doctor Mike turned back to Rory after she'd left and asked Rory, "How are your teeth?"

Rory feigned interest in the video in the hope that the dentist might think he hadn't heard him.

A few hours later, Doctor Mike thought he had good reason to be excited. Most of the Fat Cats came walking into the room. They had a broken hockey stick they'd all signed for Rory. As Josh handed it to Rory, the dentist exclaimed, "You're all hockey players!?"

A couple of them replied in the affirmative. Doctor Mike turned off tidal TV for a moment and eyed them carefully. After a few moments of conversation, he sighed, "You all have all of your teeth still?"

Tim simply drew the curtain between the two beds in answer. Kelly set a bottle of whiskey on Rory's chest. "Here's a little something to wile away the time in here. "

Tim added, "We wanted to bring you some beer, but figured you didn't have a fridge."

When checking out of the hospital a couple days later, it seemed a little odd to Rory that not one of The Lucky Pucks showed up to visit him in the hospital. The team that he'd bled for, and apparently almost died for, didn't deem it important to visit him. He realized that the Lucky Pucks got together once a season for beers after the game. The Fat Cats got together after every win or loss, early or late game. He wasn't sure what it meant, but he appreciated his new team all the more.

It seemed ironic to Rory that someone in a wheelchair was picking him up from the hospital. Still, he was glad for the ride from Rob, even if it had felt a little strange wheeling down the hall next to him. He was trying to decide if he could make a joke about lawyers making patients leave hospitals in wheelchairs without offending Rob on both fronts.

Before he could decide, it was Rob who said, "If not for stinking lawyers, at least one of us could have walked out of here today."

Rory grinned at him. "You?"

Rob simply shot him a angry glare which quickly dissolved into a chuckle. "So how long until you can play again?"

"Later this afternoon," Rory replied with a grin.

"Seriously?"

"No, not seriously. At least a week."

"You going to wait a week?"

"Maybe. How did the Lucky Pucks do by the way?"

"Won it in a shootout."

"Who took over at goalie?"

"Fred Wray."

"Seriously?"

Rob nodded.

"He's odd. Even for a goalie," Rory commented.

"Yeah?"

"I accidentally showed up an hour early for a pickup game once. I decided to toss my gear in the locker room and kick back in the shop for an hour. When I got to the locker room, Fred was dressed in his goalie gear from the waist down, just staring at the wall."

"That is a little odd."

"Have you ever seen him getting on the ice, Rob?"

"No, what's he do?"

"He hops over all the lines, Patrick Roy style. Then he talks to the goal for a little bit. Maybe I'm wrong because I think superstition is dumb, but superstitious goalies should at least have their *own* superstitions. I wouldn't be surprised I found out he has a shrine in his house with Patrick Roy pictures and some candles."

Rob laughed and told Rory, "I used to hop over all the lines too. It's much harder now."

Rob dropped Rory off at the rink. He was somewhat relieved to find that his car hadn't been towed. After all, it had been sitting in the lot for a couple nights. He wouldn't have put it past Matt to have it towed away just out of spite.

Rory sat down in the leather driver's seat of the Porsche. With his hands on the wheel, the reality of his injury finally started to set in. Life was a fragile thing and for the first time in his history, Rory began to realize it. He'd lived a charmed existence, cheating death three times now.

His first brush had been at twelve years old when he and some friends were playing tag on a house being constructed near his neighborhood. He had climbed to the top floor and when his buddy, Mark, who was "it" came to tag him, Rory dropped through the joists of the garage planning to swing down between the studs to the safety of the first floor. It was an excellent plan aside from the fact that the joist came loose from his weight. He ended up falling head first two stories. The only thing that saved him was a perfect landing on the sloping grade to the foundation, which had not yet been back filled.

He remembered his friends looking down at him as he lay in the trench awkwardly, his head against the concrete, feet straight up on the dirt. It was a position he wasn't sure was natural, but nothing hurt. His friend Chris was yelling, "Oh crap! Clark is dead!" Much to their surprise and slightly to his own, he'd risen, dusted himself off and was ready to play another round. They'd all concluded that maybe it was a stupid game by that point however and decided that they'd go shoot each other with their B-B guns instead.

His second brush had come at seventeen. He was driving his father's cantankerous old pickup truck to work. His morning shift started at 5:30 and there had been a blowing snowstorm the night before. The roads were mostly clear, but as he turned onto the highway entrance on the Boulder Turnpike, he'd hit a patch of black ice just as he'd cautiously shifted into second gear.

The truck spun and hurtled backward down the steep embankment before he knew what happened. Cleverly the vehicle stalled straddling both lanes of the highway. At any other hour the mistake would have likely been a fatal one. As it was, the one car that was coming toward him honked angrily and swerved, narrowly missing him. Rory had pulled to the shoulder and sat there for ten minutes to try to get his heart to slow down before heading to work.

Somehow at the time, neither of those events had given him any sense of his own mortality. But today the full weight of that reality descended upon him as if it were a load of bricks unceremoniously dumped from the back of a truck. He didn't know why, but there was suddenly a sense of urgency to completing his task of offering the forgiveness he'd been holding back.

With a sigh, Rory realized that Matt was on his list. He'd rehearsed his words for both Colette and Dan dozens of times before his encounters with them. This time he simply exited the car, hopeful that he'd know what to say when the time came. The walk to the rink seemed longer than normal. Rory didn't want to see Matt Morgan at all, let alone forgive him. It felt like Matt had made Rory's destruction his personal mission.

As Rory passed by the space formerly occupied by his shop, he noticed a sign in the window that read:

Coming Soon
Starbucks Coffee

He shook his head as he walked by. Maybe Matt had some sort of deal brewing all along. Rory wondered if the roof ever even had a leak. He was determined not to dwell on these things since the task at hand was difficult enough without this new information.

A moment later he was knocking on the door to Matt's office. Matt looked up at Rory unsurprised. "What can I do for you, Rory?" He asked it like they were old friends.

"You mind if I sit down?" Rory asked, moving toward the chair.

He expected some sort of dismissal, Matt claiming to have a meeting or something. Apparently, Matt was either extremely confident or totally disinterested. He nodded to the chair and Rory slipped into it.

Matt eyed him with vague interest. Rory wondered if maybe Matt enjoyed confrontations. Perhaps they were a way for him to assert his power, to feel better about himself. Rory assumed a relaxed posture even though he was anything but relaxed.

"Listen Matt, the last time you and I were in here I felt like we had a real connection. I shared things with you that I was embarrassed to tell anyone. I felt like you opened up to me as well. Up till that moment our relationship had always been, well . . . adversarial."

Matt nodded to indicate he was paying attention. He was leaning forward in his chair slightly. *Interesting*, Rory thought, *he's actually listening. I wonder if Matt has any friends?*

"I really appreciated that you cut me some slack. It even occurred to me that you and I weren't all that different when we were talking that night. As odd as it seemed to me, I thought that perhaps we could even become friends if we weren't always at odds with our business relationship."

Matt was fully engaged now. "What are you getting at, Rory?"

"Apparently I almost died a couple days ago. I'm just trying to clear some things up with the perspective change that I've had . . ."

"You can't sue the rink, Rory. You signed a waiver."

"Even though you and I both know waivers aren't worth much, I hadn't even thought of it, Matt. I'm talking about setting things right between you and I."

Suddenly Matt was confused rather than confident. He still tried to paste on the swagger though, abruptly asking, "So, what's your point?"

"I felt like you were trying to ruin me when you closed my shop. It felt very personal to me, Matt. One day you were acting like a friend. Next thing I know, you're tossing me out on the street."

Matt almost looked sad when he told Rory, "Sorry, it was just business."

"Friends can do business more honestly than that, Matt. But I didn't come here to accuse you or argue. Like I said, I just want to set things right. Regardless of your motivations I think you could have handled things better. But I'm over it and wanted to tell you that I forgive you."

For the first time in Rory's experience knowing Matt, he didn't have any sort of angry or glib comeback. Matt sat looking at him for a few moments, perhaps to gauge if Rory was serious, perhaps to assess the possibility of any legal liability from being forgiven. Eventually he nodded and smiled slightly. "Thanks for that, Rory."

The successes with both Matt and Dan bolstered Rory's confidence in Rob's advice. Though it surprised him somewhat, he found himself agreeing to try Rob's church. A major part of the decision was based on the fact that he'd almost died recently. Things like this apparently made one consider the existence of God, at least for Rory this was the case. Rory figured it might be a good thing to greet Him in His house on Earth before meeting Him in the afterlife.

That night Rob spoke more about his personal forgiveness project after asking Rory if he'd like to go to church with him in the morning. There was no pressure and had there been, Rory probably would have passed on the invite. Instead, he'd asked Rob what made him start attending church.

"Remember I told you how empty I felt after Christie and Nathan died?"

Rory nodded.

"After all the things I tried to fill that space I finally found God. I thought church was a place filled with perfect people who had perfect lives. Someone invited me to join them and I found a place full of broken people leading broken lives. They were just like me."

"That doesn't sound like a fun place," Rory interjected.

Rob smiled. "But that's just the thing. I was tired of stumbling around the lies that people put up to make themselves think they're happy. We try to push all the bad things about ourselves under the rug, to hide them from each other. We don't want people to know that we aren't perfect. It doesn't make sense since we're all the same. No one is fooled either. They walk into our house and know the rug is bulging with all dirty little secrets. We don't wonder if anyone has them.

"That's the difference with my church. We acknowledge that we all have our flaws, that we all make mistakes. More importantly, we don't judge people by their flaws because the bottom line is that God sent his Son, Jesus to atone for our mistakes. We've all fallen short and we're all forgiven if we simply follow and believe that Jesus is Lord.

"Rory, we all long for God, whether we know it or not. He created us and we are incomplete without Him. He's the *only* thing that can fill the emptiness we all have."

Rory wasn't sure it was all that simple. This wasn't how he remembered church. But for the sake of his new friend and benefactor, he was willing to give it a try. He certainly understood the emptiness that Rob was talking about.

In the morning, not having a shirt and tie handy, Rory dressed in a polo shirt and pair of Khakis. Rob was sitting at the kitchen table when he got upstairs. Rory felt a little self conscious about the possibility of being under-dressed.

"Hey Rob, do you have a blazer I could borrow? I don't have one for church." Rory was oblivious to the fact that Rob was wearing a pair of jeans and tee shirt that read, "I think the goalie might be hurt!"

Rob looked up from a bowl of oatmeal, his face twisting into a smirk while he chewed. He swallowed and replied, "Rory, if you put on a blazer you'll be the best dressed person in the place."

Rory remembered church as a place where everyone dressed in their best. His mother made him wear a jacket and tie last time he'd been to church. It wasn't the only reason he didn't go back, but it was a reason. A polo shirt and pair of jeans was certainly more in his comfort zone than a shirt and tie.

Thirty minutes later they were pulling up to a shopping center off South Boulder Road. If Rory were to have judged simply by the number of parking attendants festooned in orange vests, they were pulling up to an amusement park rather than a church. The building, as Rob mentioned, was clearly a large commercial store at one point. From the outside, only a sign reading, "Flatirons Community Church," indicated that its purpose was no longer for shopping.

Inside, the building certainly didn't resemble a church either. Televisions hung from the ceiling displaying information to guests. A busy bar was serving bagels and coffee. There was a glaring lack of pretty, red carpets, pipe organs and stained glass. In fact, in the auditorium (Rory wasn't sure calling it a sanctuary was proper) the atmosphere was more dance club than cathedral, save for the thousand plus chairs in the way.

He noted curiously that there were earplugs available in the lobby. That might have been a nice thing in the church of his teen years. Back then it would have kept the service from interrupting his nap. Rob explained that in this case it was because the music was a little loud for some people.

In the auditorium, a huge screen was displaying videos to go with the music, neither of which were anything like what he remembered from church in the past. Eventually the screen took on the appearance of something from the Matrix movie. A five-minute countdown started on the screen and the live band filtered out onto the stage.

At the end of the countdown the band immediately fired up their instruments opening the service with . . . it took Rory a moment to place the song, not because he didn't recognize the song, but because it was so out of context. It was akin to running into a childhood friend who was suddenly assigned the next cubicle at work or seeing the nanny at a cigar bar. Nonetheless, after a few strains he realized that they were playing "Sweet Child of Mine." Oddly, they weren't just playing it, they were nailing it, hitting every nuance. Eyes closed, it was easily as good as any live show from Guns and Roses themselves might have been. It was also every decibel as loud.

Someone who Rory assumed was the preacher, jumped on the stage after the song ended. He whooped, "I bet there aren't too many churches that opened with Guns and Roses this morning. Some of you who are here for the first time might be wondering if you're in the right place. What are these people doing? This is nothing like grandma's church."

He proceeded to make a few announcements and asked everyone to wish those around them a good morning. The band moved on playing three songs which, though Rory classified them as religious music, were for the most part as electric as the Guns and Roses number had been.

The service proceeded as the preacher, a thin, curly-haired man apparently in his mid forties who apparently never heard of decaffeinated coffee, retook the stage. Rory noted that Rob hadn't been exaggerating about the dress code. The preacher was wearing a pair of jeans and a Broncos T-shirt. A tattoo appeared to be peeking out from under his shirt sleeve. The message was well delivered with both humor and passion. It was also pretty simple.

He illustrated the message drawing on a whiteboard. This was blown up on the huge video screen behind him so the fifteen hundred people in attendance could actually see it. On the left side, he drew a stick figure and said, "That's me, see—curly hair."

People laughed and he snarled tongue in cheek, "What, you can draw better?"

On the right side he drew a smiling head with a crown perched on a robe. "That's God." Adding a beard told the audience, "Everyone knows God has a white beard."

Then he started writing words to describe God, "just, loving, merciful, perfect." Beside the picture of himself he wrote, "unjust, unloving, not merciful, imperfect."

He continued. "If God is all of these things and we are all of the things I wrote beside the picture of me, how can we get to God? We can't possibly enter His presence as the imperfect people we are. Imagine a judge presented with giving a verdict to someone they love. If he decides to let that person go free, he isn't just. If he decides to prosecute them, then he is unloving.

"The question is, how can God be both, yet merciful *and* perfect, right? Let's say a cop pulls you over for speeding. You were going a hundred in a school zone—shame on you! He writes you a ticket for five hundred dollars, then says, 'hey, let me take care of that for you,' and hands you five hundred bucks. That's how God is! He looks at you and says, 'The verdict for what you've done is death, but I'll send someone else to pay the penalty for you. Here's my Son, Jesus.'

"That is what makes Christianity different than any other religion. Christianity is the only faith that recognizes that we as people cannot make it to God on our own, because we'd have to be perfect. Show of hands, how many of you are perfect? No, put your hand down! You cut me off in the parking lot this morning. No one else?

"Bunch of sinners!" He smirked before continuing. "I'm not here to disrespect other religions. Correct me if I'm wrong though, every religion aside from Christianity claims that a man must become righteous in order to get to heaven." He paused pointing to the whiteboard then vehemently added, "We can't do that!

None of us can. There was only one perfect man in the entire history of the world—Jesus!"

He drew a canyon on the whiteboard between himself and God and wrote, "Sin," inside it. Then continued, "Sin is the gulf that divides us from God. Since none of us is perfect, none of us can come before God who *is* perfect. Romans 6:23 says, 'For the wages of sin is death . . .' Fortunately, it says something more."

He placed a cross from himself to God, like a bridge. "The only way to get to God is through Jesus. Remember that cop who was going to pay your fine? Did you have to take that five hundred dollars? Nope. Now call me crazy, but you'd be a little crazy not to take it! Right? It's the same thing with Jesus. God offers to pay your fine. Romans 6:23 continues, '. . . but the gift of God is eternal life through Jesus Christ our Lord.' If you take His offer you get eternal life. That's the whole point! It's God's righteousness, not ours that makes Christianity different."

The man behind the podium punctuated this saying, "I imagine one day I'm going to get to heaven and meet some other people there. They might say, 'Hey, how did you get in?' I'll answer them, 'I screwed up and God forgave me,' and they'll say, 'Awesome, me too!'"

Rory found some comfort in this message. He'd spent too many hours in churches that excelled in identifying what other people did wrong. It seemed oddly refreshing to have an imperfect man delivering the message . . . or at least one who so willingly admitted he was imperfect.

Underneath, the message was the same one that he'd heard on the few occasions he'd been in a church. They clung to that whole crazy story where baby Jesus was born on Christmas then got crucified some years later around Easter and eventually rose from the dead. That part, the existence of God and Jesus being His son, still seemed a bit dubious to Rory, but at least he was somewhere that people weren't all over-stuffed, superior individuals.

CHAPTER TWENTY

FORGIVENESS

Walking out of the strangely disarming church, Rory bumped into Lisa, his former employee. She smiled and gave Rory a hug. This was a surprise to Rory as he hadn't been hugged by a former employee since the last time that Lisa gave him a hug . . . which was the first time that he'd been hugged by a former employee.

"I didn't know you came to church here, Rory," she said, letting go of him. There was no doubt that the smile on her face was genuine. He was happy to see her as well.

"First time," Rory admitted. "Are you doing alright?"

She nodded. "I have a part time job. I don't like it as much as I did working for you and I really need something full time. Any chance you'll be reopening the shop?"

Rory started to shake his head, but Rob cleared his throat, so he made introductions instead. "Lisa, this my good friend Rob."

Lisa smiled. "I've seen you around the rink before. Nice to meet you."

"Likewise," Rob replied. "Lisa, I'm also Rory's lawyer. I think we're pretty close to finding him a solution for getting the shop opened again."

Rory looked at Rob dubiously. This was the first he'd heard of any progress. Did Rob even know that Starbucks had laid their claim to the location? But he had figured out that Rob kept close as much as he shared. He was still an enigma.

"That's awesome! Let me know how it goes. I'd love to come back to work for you. I've gotta run though. Mike is taking me to brunch." Lisa nodded over her shoulder to a skinny young man who smiled and gave a little wave when they looked in his direction.

"You'll be one of the first I call when I know something," Rory told her. "It's good to see you."

She was still smiling, but there was a trace of sadness in it now. "I'll count on hearing from you. I've been praying for you and Steph. I won't stop until you let me know my prayers have been answered."

She paused for a moment, as if pondering whether it was her place to say what came next. She lowered her voice as she told him, "Rory, sometimes a woman pushes a man away to see how hard he'll fight for her. Giving her space might not really be what she wants. Just a thought." Her smile returned to its full radiance as she told him, "It's good to see you too, Rory."

With a little wave she turned and took Mike by the arm. As they walked away, Rory felt an odd warmth inside. *Someone is praying for me.* It felt oddly reassuring. A few weeks ago he would have thought differently, along the lines of, *that's a nice thought, but why waste your time sending your hopes into the ether of the universe where there is nothing?*

Something was different now though. Perhaps he'd reached the epitome of hopelessness. Was it desperation that made him grasp for anything? Or was it the realization that everything seemed so hopeless without some higher power? He wasn't sure, but it felt good that someone cared.

They made their way to Rob's van, which was quite a task. Rory, apparently in a biblical state of mind thought of Charlton

Heston parting the Red Sea and how helpful that type of action would be in crossing the sea of people in their way. Once in the van, the exit was still reminiscent of leaving the Disney World parking lot at the end of the day.

Rory was astounded that there were so many people at one place looking for, or having found, something Godly. *Are all these people here because they're lost too? Or are all these people here because they found something? Where did all these people come from!?*

He mentioned this to Rob who laughed and further surprised him with his response. "There are actually five more services. They had two last night, three this morning and another tonight."

Rory wasn't sure what to say about that other than, "Wow!"

"So what did you think?"

"It was different than what I expected."

"Different good?"

Rory nodded as he replied, "The band was amazing. But I think, more importantly, I felt like the minister was speaking right to me sometimes."

Rob nodded knowingly and thumped his fist lightly over his chest. "Some days it gets me right here."

"It surprised me. It also surprised me that Lisa was praying for me."

"Rory, there are other people praying for you. Personally, I've been praying for you and Steph since our run in at the Rock Bottom. I'd guess that she and I aren't the only ones praying either."

The Rock Bottom—that seemed like half a lifetime ago. Rory once again felt bad about the way he'd treated Rob. He looked over at the bristle-faced man driving the van. No one had ever shown him such kindness in his life, especially not anyone who he'd been so angry at.

"Rob," Rory started, his words sputtering a little, "I'm so sorry for the way that I treated you the first times we met. I hope this doesn't sound too sappy, but you've done so much for me that I didn't deserve. You're truly the best friend that I've ever had. I don't know if I would have survived all of this without your help."

Rob grinned slightly. "Rory, if you ever apologize to me again I'll give you a black eye. It's water under the bridge."

Rory knew that this was hockey talk. It wasn't unlike a couple of guys, who when discussing "Desperate Housewives" at the water cooler, quickly changed the discussion to the Chicago Bears if someone happened past. It was also code that perhaps he *was* being a little too sappy.

Rob continued, "Rory, I didn't want to throw too much at you in one bite. I think you're ready for the reason that I do what I do now. The forgiveness thing, that's just part of my faith. I try to live like Jesus would. I don't always manage to get it all right . . . honestly, I don't even get close most of the time. But I felt like God wanted me to reach out to you. I felt the calling to do more than just forgive you. Not everyone who I forgive ends up moving into my house."

Rory thought Rob was blinking away some tears as he finished up, " . . . and truth be told, you're probably the best friend that I've ever had too."

Rory patted Rob on the shoulder and told him in a self depreciating manner, "Now that is sad."

Rob gave him a sharp look. "Don't even think about trying to hug me."

Rory laughed and replied, "Wouldn't dream of it."

Rory spent much of the day contemplating the fact that forgiveness had always been a challenge for him. He came to realize that most, if not all, of his issues lately pretty much stemmed from that inability. While he was still dubious about the whole Jesus thing, Rory did realize that every time he forgave someone a great weight was lifted from his chest. There were still quite a few people on his list.

There was one thing he feared with forgiving people. While things had gone well it seemed only a matter of time until he bumped into someone who didn't think they needed to be forgiven. He wondered how that might turn out. *Hey, I'm here to forgive you for being rude to me. . . You're calling* me *rude? Go home and look in the mirror, buddy.* He didn't want to be the one coming across as self-righteous. He just wanted to relieve the weight on his shoulders.

It was late. Rob and Cody had turned in several hours earlier. Rory stood in front of Rob's refrigerator. He'd been considering a late night snack, but ended up ruminating about Steph. He pondered the dream he'd had in the hospital. *Am I supposed to figure something out from that dream? What did it mean?*

He considered that all the people in the dream were meaningless. They didn't care if his boat was sinking. The one exception to this would have been Steph. She'd always been there for him. They were supposed to be bailing out the sinking boat together. She was the only one who could save him. Instead, she'd deserted him with the cryptic last words, "I cannot be that."

What can't you be? Rory wondered as he stared blankly at the fridge. Eventually, Rory realized that the refrigerator was covered with dozens of plastic labels—old labels from one of those ancient hand held devices which required the user to spin the dial for a letter and then press with all their might to emboss it on the label. Every one of the labels displayed a quote about forgiveness. There had to be a hundred of them. Wondering why he'd never noticed them, Rory read a few:

Know all and you will pardon all.—Thomas A'Kempis

To forgive is to set a prisoner free and discover the prisoner was you.—Unknown

A Christian will find it cheaper to pardon than to resent. Forgiveness saves the expense of anger, the cost of hatred, and the waste of spirit. —Hannah More

Sincere forgiveness isn't colored with expectations that the other person apologize or change. Don't worry whether or not they finally understand you. Love them and release them. —Sara Paddison

"I can forgive, but I cannot forget," is only another way of saying, I will not forgive. Forgiveness ought to be like a canceled note—torn in two, and burned up, so that it never can be shown against one. —Henry Ward Beecher

Forgiveness is the fragrance that the violet sheds on the heel that has crushed it. —Mark Twain

He found himself slightly disturbed by a Mark Twain quote that was poetic rather than humorous. Nonetheless, Rory was moved somewhat by what he read on the refrigerator. He grabbed himself a beer and headed back down to his room in the basement.

Rory fell asleep reading the Bible that Rob had picked up for him at church. He figured that if Jesus had this forgiveness thing so right, maybe there were a few more things he could learn from the Bible. He didn't know if he was willing to buy into the Son of God part, but he didn't really have any issues with Jesus. He fell asleep with the Bible on his chest that night thinking about forgiveness. He dozed off with a vague determination that he'd finish his list the next day.

Despite staying up until well into the morning hours, Rory awoke at six, feeling refreshed and invigorated. He showered, shaved and headed to the kitchen to start brewing some coffee.

Cody pattered out to greet him. Rory sat down at the kitchen table, absently scratching the top of the dog's head as his laptop booted up.

He pondered the thoughts that had come to him in the night. In that odd half-dreamed, nocturnal clarity that he so often experienced, he'd composed the perfect words of forgiveness for everyone on his list. As was so often the case, now that he was fully awake it became a half-fog of obscurity. He felt a little sad that sublime cognizance had departed him. Rory did remember one important thought.

Though he had been very good at applying the concept of forgiveness to his business, without thinking of it as such, he'd failed to apply it to the rest of his life. It was just common sense that if you wanted to keep a customer, you smiled and nodded when they complained. You did this even when they were obviously wrong. Yet with the people in his personal life, he'd constantly failed to recognize this same principal as a sound one. The one epiphany that *did* stick with him from the previous night was this one.

He wondered, *Why was it so easy for me to let things roll off my back in business, yet so hard to do the same thing in life?* As a business owner, he'd realized that he was giving up a little to gain a lot. If someone ordered the wrong drink, it was more profitable to fix their mistake knowing they'd be more likely to return. Even if he had to take the blame for the mistake they made, Rory did this. It was simple enough most of the time. The one obvious exception to this was insane customers who claimed they needed to go to detox for caffeine. There were times when he had to simply cut his losses. Still this seemed analogous for forgiveness. In life wasn't it just as wise to forgive small things to have a bigger relationship with someone?

He poured himself a cup of coffee and returned to the table. There was a lot to do today. Despite forgetting all of the profound things he thought he might say, Rory intended to finish off his list in one day. This put Davis Jennings, Eileen from Sunshine Management and Officer Doyle square on his list. It also dawned on him that he needed to forgive his wife for tossing him out of the house. He'd been so upset at losing her that he didn't really realize how upset he was *at her* until he started this entire process.

Rory found the Broomfield Police department phone number on the Internet. He dialed it on his cell phone. It was answered by a rather gruff sounding male voice, "Broomfield Police."

Rory tried to be cheerful, but between the task at hand and the thinly concealed anger in the voice on the other end of the line it was tough. He was pretty sure the guy who answered was thinking, *Who would dare call the police station before seven in the morning?*

"Good morning, I'm hoping to speak to Officer Doyle please."

"Regarding what?" the gruff voice asked.

"I'd just like to set up a meeting to talk to her, on a . . . personal matter."

There was a pause on the other end. "Hold on."

Rory waited for five minutes before the gruff voice came back on. "I'll get you her voice mail."

The phone transferred to an extension where he was greeted by a generic message. He hadn't really thought through what he was going to say. He stammered a bit leaving the message, "Officer Doyle, this is Rory Clark and I . . . you probably remember me as the guy who mistook you for a stripper. . . geez, sorry . . . I just feel like there is some bad blood between us and was hoping that we could get together . . . er, that I could talk to you in person. Nothing weird, just take about ten or fifteen minutes of your time. If you could give me a call back I'd appreciate the opportunity to sort this out."

He left his number and hung up wondering if he sounded nearly as stupid as he felt. *Apparently, I should have let the coffee hit my bloodstream before I used the phone.*

After a quick breakfast, Rory was on the road before Rob was even awake. He knew that Thunder would be out doing his business shortly and thought it might be a good time to catch Davis Jennings. Well, catch wasn't really the appropriate term. He'd caught him already. This time he wanted to forgive him for the things he'd caught him doing in the past.

Rory parked the Porsche just up the street from Jennings' house where Steph wouldn't think he was stalking her if she looked out the window. In fact, he wanted nothing more than to knock on the door. He longed to see how she was doing but he tried to give her all the space she wanted. She made the rules and it seemed that every time he violated them it just pushed her away. He had no idea what else to do.

He still wrote her a letter every day, but he'd been tossing them in the mail. He still came by to put out the trash and pick up the bills too, but made sure to do it when she wasn't home. It was the hardest thing in the world for him to not make these visits an excuse to see her. But for her sake he did it. He did make it clear in every letter that he wanted nothing more than to see her, but was respecting her wishes for some time apart. He hoped she understood how hard it was. Regardless, he'd see her later in the day to forgive her if all went as planned.

Jennings poked his bald head out of the house about twenty minutes after Rory arrived. He had to admit to himself that Davis Jennings made him more nervous than anyone else on his list. Jennings was the one person most likely to react with indignant pride and insist that he'd done nothing that required forgiveness. Although on the other hand, Rory was pretty sure that deep down the man knew that he was wrong.

As he climbed out of the car, Rory realized there was another possible reaction from Jennings—fight or flight. It wasn't impossible that Jennings would react in fear. Nonetheless, Rory called out to him, with as friendly a tone as he could muster, "Morning Davis, do you mind if I talk with you for a moment?"

Thunder was out the door behind Jennings, amazingly, on a leash. Jennings swiveled his bald pate, a look of surprise on his face. Rory thought he spotted a twinge of fear as well. Regardless, Jennings' face quickly shifted to one of contempt. "What do you want?"

"I just want to talk to you for a moment, Davis."

Jennings sneered as he replied, "You can walk with us, but I doubt you have anything to say that I want to hear."

"Fair enough..." Rory replied.

Rory nodded and bent down to scratch Thunder behind the ears. The dog looked at him with thoughtful brown eyes. For a moment Rory felt like Thunder knew something he didn't. Perhaps dogs never doubted the existence of God. It would certainly explain their propensity for instant forgiveness.

Jennings gave the leash a little tug and started walking. Rory jogged a couple steps to catch up with him. "Davis, I don't expect you to drop the lawsuit as the result of anything that I say to you today. That's not what this is about. I just wanted to tell you I forgive you . . ."

Jennings stopped abruptly. The glare in his eyes would have been convincing had Rory not noticed the flicker of confusion followed by a scant smile right before he put on the mask he wore now. He also knew that Davis tended to turn as red as a fire truck when he was truly angry.

Still, Davis put on a pretty good front of righteous rage. He wheeled on Rory. "You're forgiving me?! I'm the victim here, remember. You have a lot of nerve coming here and trying to make me out as the bad guy."

"Davis, you're right, absolutely right. I've done things to you that you didn't deserve. If you're honest with yourself, we've both done things that weren't exactly neighborly. But, I'm trying to take the step that I should have from the start. I should have forgiven you rather than reacting in a retaliatory manner. I'm truly sorry that it took me this long to come to my senses. I should have forgiven you from the start. I know that I made things worse for both of us."

Rory watched Davis' face for a reaction. There was a trace of sadness in his eyes, perhaps remorse even. Playing poker only afforded so much practice, people didn't generally show much remorse at the table, but that was Rory's best guess. Jennings increased his pace. Without turning back he gruffly replied, "You can take your forgiveness and shove it, Clark."

It certainly didn't feel as good as the other talks he'd had, but Rory knew that Davis would be a tough case. He stood watching the man walk away. "That's fine, Davis. You're still forgiven." Rory wondered if the man wouldn't soften up once things set in. It didn't matter, forgiveness was all he could offer him.

The question on Rory's mind was, *How do I forgive a corporation?* Really he wondered if he was mad at the corporation or just Eileen. Eileen was essentially the face of the corporation as far as he was concerned. She wielded her power covertly. She placed the blame on the rules or her superiors, but Rory was reasonably certain that she had more power than she alluded to possessing. He picked up the phone and dialed.

"It's a sunshiny day at Sunshine Management, this is Susie. How can I direct your call?"

"Hi Susie, it's Rory Clark. How are you today?"

"The usual, Mr. Clark, sunshiny as can be." There was no attempt by Susie to mask her sarcasm, "How are you?"

"I'm sorry to hear that. I'm doing well. Could I speak to Eileen please?"

"One moment please, and have a nice day, Mr. Clark."

The phone rang only twice before Eileen picked up and answered, "It's a sunshiny day at Sunshine Management."

"Hi Eileen, this is Rory Clark."

The sunshine faded in Eileen's voice, assuming that there had been any sunshine in her droll delivery. It was more a case of her moving from cold to frigid. "Mr. Clark, what can I do for you?"

Rory immediately regretted not just writing her a letter. He'd somehow forgotten the thick-skulled nature of his discussions with her in the past. It always seemed to him that the dialect of English that she understood was far different than the one he spoke.

"Eileen, I just wanted to forgive you."

"Oh well, thank you."

Could it really be this simple? Rory was taken aback. Then Eileen said, "I'm sorry, you're giving me what?"

"I'm forgiving you."

"Did I do something?"

"Um, you put liens on my house."

"That wasn't wrong, it's the rules, Mr. Clark."

"I hate to disagree, but there's never been any *real* reason for you to put liens on my house . . . look, I'm sorry. I didn't call to argue or justify my position. Suffice to say I feel like you could have done a better job. I release you from the fact that I feel like you didn't treat me very well. You're forgiven."

Eileen as well did not attempt to hide her sarcasm. "That's a great weight off my shoulders, Mr. Clark. Did you need anything else?"

Rory backtracked a little. "Listen Eileen. I know that you have a difficult job. You're stuck between the homeowners and your superiors at work. I wasn't helpful with my attitude by any means. I just wanted to let you know that I'm sorry for the way I acted and that I don't hold any animosity toward you."

There was a silence on the other end of the line. After a moment Eileen replied, "You're not messing with me?"

It was the first time that she'd made anything resembling a human response or statement that Rory remembered. "No, I'm not messing with you."

"In that case, thank you, Mr. Clark."

They spoke for a few moments longer. It was actually almost a pleasant conversation. Rory hung up the phone feeling much better than he had after talking to Jennings. He almost dropped the phone when it immediately rang. He answered and found himself speaking to Officer Doyle. She was, as he expected, all business.

"Mr. Clark, I had a message from you. I'm not sure exactly what you want."

"Officer Doyle, I was hoping we could sit down and talk."

"Why?"

"I just feel like things between us are unresolved."

"You need closure?"

"Sure, kind of."

"We weren't dating, Mr. Clark."

He wasn't sure if he should laugh. "No, nothing like that."

There was a long and hesitant sigh on the other side of the phone. "Are you sure you want to do this, Mr. Clark? I don't have any issues with you that *I* feel like discussing."

"I do feel like this is important." Rory left off at that.

After a long pause where Rory was pretty sure he'd been disconnected, she replied, "I will be at Gizzi's Coffee, 144th and Lowell at 10 a.m. tomorrow. Does that work?"

"I'll be there," Rory replied. *He wondered why she sounded so ominous when she suggested the place and time.*

CHAPTER TWENTY ONE

A GOOD DAY?

Gizzi's coffee, only a few blocks from Rory's former (and hopefully future) home, was surprisingly crowded at ten in the morning. Rory felt a little self-conscious when he walked in. It was as if everyone knew that he *used* to own a coffee shop. They all stopped what they were doing and looked at him for a moment. He pushed through the doorway convincing himself that no one knew or cared about his history. *I just imagined everyone looking at me. Why* would *they be looking at me?*

Officer Doyle was sitting at table with her back to a set of shelves displaying merchandise. Rory appraised the small collection of Bodum products, travel mugs and a couple Capresso coffee makers finding it a rather unimpressive collection. He acknowledged Officer Doyle, who didn't look at all happy to see him. She did look a great deal less like a walking refrigerator in her civilian clothes than she had in uniform. Apparently blue polyester was not as flattering as Rory might have once believed. At the very least, blue was not her color.

Noting she didn't have a coffee, Rory nodded toward the counter. "Do you want anything to drink?"

"I'm fine," she replied, somewhat tersely.

He was going to order a drink but sensing her uneasiness, he decided to sit down instead. Perhaps she had somewhere else to be. Regardless, he didn't want to make this any more difficult than need be. He had thought that things would be easier with Doyle than they had been with Davis, but after the limited success of yesterday's meeting, he found himself quite a bit more nervous than expected. He slid into the chair and put his hands in his lap so she wouldn't see they were shaking.

"Thanks for meeting me."

"So what is this about, Mr. Clark?"

"I've made a mess of my life and I'm trying to fix it."

The face Officer Doyle made was the same one he'd expect to see on someone who'd bet the farm on three of a kind, only to see the flush draw come up on the river. He'd describe it as slightly-fearful uncertainty. He wasn't sure what it meant in this context and it made him feel a bit of fearful uncertainty himself.

"So I'm meeting with the people I have some sort of grudge with," he continued.

"Me?! Why?" she asked. "You know I was just doing my job."

It sounded like an excuse bordering on an apology. He kept moving forward. "I know you were doing your job. It just felt a little more personal than it should have. I know that the way I acted when you came to my front door was offensive, but I felt like you were out to get me for something I didn't do. I know I was imagining it, but I felt like you were going to jump out from behind every corner to try to catch me doing something wrong."

"And?" he noticed *her* hands were shaking now.

"I just wanted to forgive you in person. I know you were doing your job. I know you believed, and maybe still do, that you were right. I didn't come here to protest my innocence. I just wanted you to know that I appreciated your apology and I forgive you."

"Seriously?" she asked.

"Yeah, that's all."

"But why?"

"Like I said, things haven't gone well for me lately. My wife kicked me out of the house, I lost my business and recently I almost died in a hockey accident," he said as he pointed to the bandage covering three hundred stitches on his neck. "It kinda puts things in perspective. I made a list and started forgiving everyone who I felt wronged me."

Doyle looked him in the eye for a moment. Rory was pretty sure she was trying to judge the veracity of his statements. She almost smiled at the end of her scrutiny. She stood up and said loudly, "It's alright guys, false alarm."

Everyone else in the coffee shop, save one man reading the paper stood up. They made their way out the door chatting loudly and laughing. Rory realized they were all Broomfield cops, the man hiding behind the paper was her doughnut toting partner. Rory groaned, "Oh. You thought I was up to something bad, didn't you?"

Now Doyle really did smile. "You can never be too careful when some nut calls and wants to sit down with the officer who arrested him. It's pretty much procedure. I'm still wearing a wire, so be careful what you say."

"Wait, you're calling me a nut?"

"Let's see, we had everyone but the SWAT team out here, I told you I'm wearing a wire and that's all you're concerned about? Do I *really* need to answer that?"

"Point taken."

She chuckled. This was somewhat surprising to Rory as it seemed totally out of character.

"They going to send me a bill for all the man-hours?"

"Naw, you're a taxpayer. And we're all relieved that you didn't come in here planning to shoot. Although I think I'm more relieved than anyone else."

She nodded to her partner before telling Rory, "It's a tough job, being a cop. Lots of people hate us for trying to do what's right. That's no fun. Sometimes, we screw up. Nothing feels worse than when you realize that you might have arrested the wrong person. No one likes to be hated, right?"

Rory grinned. "So you're saying I'm innocent now?"

"You're as innocent as I am skinny, Clark. But you're alright in my book." She started humming and gave him a little wave as she and her partner left the coffee shop.

Feeling oddly euphoric after being the focus of a major police action (major at least for the city of Broomfield), Rory was anxious to talk to someone. It felt like things were looking up. He longed to share that feeling with someone. While Steph was his emotional choice, the emotions associated with that choice weren't all good. They brought one thought to the forefront; he needed to forgive his wife. It was time for him to complete the final step on his road to redemption.

While he didn't think that talking to Steph was going to present near the challenge that the other people on his list had, he was more nervous about speaking with her than anyone else. Obviously the stakes were higher. She was the only person on the list who could really return his happiness to him. At least this was what he thought.

Rory pulled out his cell phone and checked the time as he walked to the Porsche. It was quarter after ten. Try as he might, Rory couldn't remember if it was Steph's normal day off after a late shift or if she was working the day shift. She'd always insisted that her schedule was simple.

He tried to remember it. *It's four ten-hour night shifts followed by four ten-hour day shifts the next week, or is that the next month? I don't remember.* Never mind that the days she had off in these shifts sometimes changed, it was hard enough for Rory to remember if she was working days or nights on any particular week even when they lived in the same house. Keeping track now was pretty much impossible.

He dialed the number to the house, but quickly hung up before it started to ring. If she *had* worked a graveyard, she'd be asleep for at least a few more hours. If she worked a day shift she'd already be at work. He decided that he'd swing by the house around six. He'd catch her regardless of whether she was waking up or coming home at that hour.

So, feeling excited about how well things were going, he decided to head back to his lodging. The best way to kill part of the wait was to tell Rob about how great he was feeling. They hadn't really talked for a couple days. Rory had seen him the night before, but Rob complained about being tired and went to bed early. Rory suspected that his friend was sick. Tough bird that he was, Rob wasn't one to ask for help or admit to being under the weather. He'd looked a bit pale though and his energy level wasn't quite at its usual hyperactive peak the last few days.

Rory slipped into the leather seat, turned the key and headed back toward his temporary abode. It was warm out. Rory drove with the sunroof open, windows down and stereo blaring. He found himself singing along to Boston's *More Than a Feeling.* He didn't know how loudly or off key he was singing until he realized that a jeep load of laughing college girls pulled up beside him. Rory wondered momentarily why they were dressed as vampires before remembering it was almost Halloween. One of them mimed singing passionately into a microphone before blowing Rory a kiss.

Any other day he might have slumped down to the floor mat in embarrassment. But today wasn't any other day. Instead he sang a little louder, laughed and waved. The girl yelled, "I think I love you, Superstar." While clearly she was mocking him, Rory took it in good grace. He winked at her and left fifty feet of rubber at the intersection when the light changed. Impressed or not, the jeep's horn honked and they flashed their lights as the Porsche sped away.

A motorcycle cop going the other direction was certainly *not* impressed. He gave Rory the universal slow down sign, like he was patting an invisible small child on the head. Rory panicked for a moment before realizing that the officer wasn't turning around. Apparently there was nothing that was going to go wrong on this day. Even leaving a traffic light in a cloud of smoke wasn't getting him a ticket.

He pulled up to Rob's house a few minutes later. The mail truck was pulling away as Rory rolled into the driveway. After retrieving the mail, Rory headed into the house. He was surprised to find a couple of large envelopes with his name on them intermingled with the junk mail. Folding Rob's mail under his arm, he slid open the first of them as he walked to the front door. The envelope contained legal documents based upon what Rob had been doing for him. A cursory glance indicated that his equipment was being released from the Ice Centre. He leafed through it a little further and found a check refunding him the full amount of his deposit as well as the final month's rent. It also appeared that they were going to pay his relocation expenses. Suddenly, Rory wasn't flat broke.

Almost too stunned to open the other envelope, Rory walked through the front door. He called out, "Hey Rob, you here?"

Rob didn't answer. It wasn't surprising. Rob was always up to something. Nonetheless, Rory was a little disappointed that he wasn't home. He sidled up to the kitchen table and opened the second letter. This one contained documents regarding the lawsuit that Davis Jennings had filed. Again, it wasn't exactly written in plain English. The gist of it, as far as Rory could tell, was that Jennings had dropped the case.

Rory set down the second letter for a moment. He returned to the first one and read it again. He looked at the check. After a moment he looked at the second letter again. He thought, *Can this be right? After all the days of pure hell I've been through, could this many good things possibly happen to me at the same time? I don't deserve this, do I? Rob said sometimes you don't get what you deserve though.*

He gyrated from ecstatic to looking at the ceiling with pure expectation that it was about to collapse on him. It felt oddly like he'd won the lottery. There was enough money for him to relocate the shop and sign a lease on a new one. If he were honest with himself, Starbucks was *welcome* to the old location. He'd picked it on sentiment rather than solid business practices. It simply never supported his business model the way he'd hoped. He was pretty sure that Matt Morgan put a good coat of whitewash on the location to get them interested.

This was a good day. But he felt he didn't have any right to these things. He'd deserved most of what happened to him. That was one thing that he'd determined. Besides, he'd read somewhere that a huge percentage of lottery winners ended up broke a few years later. There had to be a giant shoe coming down to squish him any moment. He pushed the papers away to seek some consolation that this wasn't going to be the case.

Rory picked up the phone and dialed Rob's cell. He could hear Rob's cell phone playing Journey's "Keep on Running." He'd be amused by Rob's ironic choice, if he weren't so annoyed at the fact that the phone was not with him. Steph constantly did the same thing to him. He was pretty sure she'd planned it out though. She only forgot her phone when he locked himself out of the house or befell some equally annoying disaster.

The worst of these examples came to his mind in a flash. He couldn't find his car keys. He'd turned the house upside down but failed to find them in any of the normal places. When he finally called to ask her if she knew where his keys were, he found the phone. He was jumping up and down, swearing loudly when she came in the house and asked him what the problem was.

Rory was embarrassed to tell her that his tantrum was about her not having her phone when he needed her to find the keys he'd lost. She was embarrassed to tell him that she took his keys instead of the phone. She realized both issues when she reached into her purse to call him. Rory had asked, "Why were you going to call me?"

She smiled coyly and told him, "I just wanted to tell you I loved you."

Even though she'd returned before even getting to girl's night out and he hadn't yet left for poker night, they both decided they'd rather stay home with each other instead.

Rory smiled at the memory and hung up the phone realizing that Rob wasn't going to answer a phone that he didn't have with him. As a consolation he headed to the refrigerator to contemplate a snack. He spotted a bumper sticker under several lists stuck on the door. He read, "Forgiveness is free, failing to forgive costs everything." Rory considered this for a moment. He decided he agreed with it before opening the door.

Peering into the depths of the fridge Rory began to wonder if he was just being picky or wasn't actually hungry. Nothing looked interesting. He was feeling antsy. He needed to tell someone what a great day he was having. But beyond Rob, he couldn't think of anyone who might want to celebrate with him. As he closed the fridge, he realized that Cody had crept up beside him.

He reached down to scratch the dog behind the ears. Rory wasn't sure how a dog could look dejected, but Cody was clearly not happy. This was a state Rory had never witnessed in him before. He contemplated the normally cheerful pooch for a moment. Cody whined and pattered back toward Rob's bedroom. The dog paused and looked back as if asking him to follow. Fear suddenly washed over Rory.

He ran back to Rob's bedroom. The door was open but the curtains were still closed. The sun tried to creep through the gaps in the fabric, but the best it did was to cast an eerie half-light upon the scene. It took Rory's eyes a few moments to adjust. He could make out the shapes of the furniture in the room. There was an odd, slightly-musty, sickly-sweet scent in the air.

He could make out the bed, in the dim light. But he couldn't tell if he was looking at his sleeping friend or just rumpled sheets. Rory flipped on the light switch. Rob was lying in bed. His flesh was pale, his eyes were open and dull. The missing spark in Rob's eyes was all that Rory needed to see. He knew that his one true friend on Earth was gone. He didn't have to check for a pulse. Rob was dead. Rory felt the air go out of him as he surveyed the scene. Aside from the realization that Rob was gone, he wasn't able to process what he saw for a few moments.

Cody sat on the floor looking at the empty shell that once was his master's body. He whimpered again. He looked back at Rory as if perhaps he could fix the situation. Rory knew exactly how Cody felt.

While Rory's mind told him Rob was gone, his heart didn't want to believe it. He stood there for a moment trying to deny the obvious. Eventually logic overrode denial. Rory found himself crumbling to the floor. Obviously, he couldn't provide Cody the resurrection of his master. The real question to Rory was whether he possessed enough strength to leave the room.

Even being in a wheelchair, Rob was as virile as anyone he'd ever known. Rory tried to put aside the gnawing feeling that had he not left the house early, Rob might have still been alive. *How could this have happened? What if he was in his room struggling for life and I walked right out on him? Have I killed my only friend by not being here?*

For a long time, man and dog sat on the floor together mourning the loss of their mutual best friend. Rory hugged Cody, who attempted to lick away the tears that rolled down. Cody's worries may have revolved primarily around who was going to feed him and pet him. Canine love was simple and absolute. Rory realized that he felt somewhat the same way.

Who is going to stand up for me? Where can I turn for help now? The one person that I can trust when everything is going wrong is the biggest thing that's going wrong right now. Am I poison? Did Rob die simply from knowing me? What is wrong with me, even when I try to do the right thing disaster follows me every step of the way . . . Oh God, I'm not strong enough for any of this! Help me!

He felt like someone had scooped out his insides, like he was a pumpkin being turned into a jack-o-lantern. What was inside him was unimportant. Whoever was picking him clean apparently decided that his innards were in their way. His soul was being strip mined. Everything good within him was hauled off. Whoever was taking it didn't care if they destroyed him completely in the process. Rory knew that there was every possibility he *would* indeed be destroyed by it. He found himself uncharacteristically poetic, thinking, *How many blows can one man take? How much loneliness can one man feel before he simply shrivels up and blows away like the remnants of an autumn leaf crushed under a boot?*

Strangely, Rory didn't feel sad for Rob. Rob had lived his life to the fullest. Rory had never met anyone who he was so sure would be in heaven five seconds after leaving his body. Rob didn't really leave anyone behind either . . .well, anyone but Rory. Though he tried not to take this personally, Rory was appalled by how short the most important friendship of his life had been.

He couldn't help but wonder why it had happened. It seemed like the most unfair thing that could have ever befallen anyone and even more unfairly, here it was happening to him. He wept because there were no answers. Who did you ask about such things? God knew the answer, Rory supposed. But God didn't really seem to go around talking to people these days. As far as

Rory knew it had been several thousand years since anyone had had a conversation with a burning bush.

He knew that he should call 911 to report Rob's death. But emotion had taken a toll on him. Rory sat on the floor for an hour weeping until there were no more tears to come out. He wondered how many low points his life could reach before he finally hit the bottom and could start ascending again. He'd been sure that he had already hit the bottom, so this new lower level was extremely surprising to him.

Cody had settled in with his head on Rory's lap. They'd commiserated long enough apparently. At the same time that Rory decided he'd been on the floor long enough, Cody stood up. Rory went to the bed, not sure what to do. It wasn't as if he'd ever seen a dead body outside of a funeral. He'd certainly never discovered his closest friend dead before.

He stood looking at Rob's body for a while. Thinking how he'd promised never to hug the man brought a near smile to Rory's face. He started to pull the covers over Rob's head, but paused, looking at the beard. There was a chunk of unidentifiable food in it. Rory went to the bathroom, found an electric trimmer and cleaned up his friend's beard. Done with that he dressed Rob in a nice pair of pants and a clean shirt.

With a deep sigh, Rory told him, "I always meant to tell you that your beard was ridiculous. Now I can send you off with a little dignity. I hope you don't mind. You're the best friend I've ever had and the best man that I've ever known, Rob. Thanks for everything."

After pulling the sheet over his face, Rory noticed an envelope on Rob's nightstand. His name was written upon it. He hesitated for a second wondering why Rob had written it. He wondered when Rob had written it as well. A pang of panic washed over him. *What if Rob killed himself?*

Rory couldn't imagine Rob doing that. Why would he end himself after all the other tough things he'd prevailed over.

Hesitantly, Rory picked up the envelope and peeled it open. A glance indicated it wasn't going to be a quick read, so Rory moved to an overstuffed chair, turned on the light and sat down.

```
Rory,
    I'm sorry if you're the one who found
me. I've been fighting colon cancer for a
while now. As I write this letter it has
been      several     months     since     it
metastasized. My treatment options have
been exhausted. It's now a matter of
weeks, maybe even days before I will
leave this body behind.
    Please don't mourn for me. I go with
the knowledge that my place in heaven is
reserved. Life is hard but my reward
awaits by God's grace. There are few
things that I will be sad to leave
behind. Your friendship is among them.
I've felt truly blessed to have gotten to
know you these last weeks. I know that
you've      been    through    the    toughest
challenge of your life recently. I expect
my passing will not help improve things
for you. I'm sorry for that.
    I want to make sure that you know
you've never been a burden. It was so
helpful just to have you here that I
don't think I can put it into words.
You've been like the brother I never had.
It was good to have someone to talk to
during my last days. Honestly, my
loneliness was almost unbearable until
you moved in.
    While I told you I'd never ask you to
try to pay me back for my hospitality, I
do need to impose upon you slightly. If I
```

weren't indisposed by the inconvenience of being dead, I wouldn't ask. However, I cannot take care of two things in my current state. Please take care of Cody and call my lawyer who will make arrangements and execute my last will and testament. His card is enclosed in the envelope.

I've been working hard to get your life back to you, as much as I can from a legal perspective. I hope my efforts will alleviate some of your burdens. It will be up to you to heal the relationships. However, I've been praying daily that I will last long enough to keep you out of trouble on the legal front. Also, you don't need to be in any rush to leave the house. My attorney can speak to you on the specifics of that subject, but rest assured, you're not going to have to go back to living in your car.

I will offer you one piece of advice if you don't mind. Actually, you don't have much choice unless you're going to stop reading this now. Here it is, LIFE IS SHORT. Don't wait until tomorrow to decide what to do with it. I think you're on the way already. But don't think that you'll be done when you've crossed off the people on your list. You'll have to figure out what comes next. Once you do, I encourage you to run toward it with all your might.

You're at a crossroads in your life, Rory. Forgiveness is the first step in the right direction. Don't make my death an excuse to take a wrong turn. Remember that hate and anger are never going to heal you. Look toward the truest source

```
of  love  and  forgiveness  every  time  you
need to make a turn.
    Thanks   for   your   friendship,   Rory.   I
hope you'll find peace soon. I've pointed
the  way,  but  the  last  step  is  up  to  you
to make.
            Your friend,
            Rob
```

Rory read the last part of the letter twice. *What is next? How do I find it? The only person I could have asked for advice on the matter left me more of a question than an answer. Could you have been more cryptic, Rob?*

Perplexed somewhat, he walked back to the nightstand and fished the business card out of the envelope. *Alf Lawson*, his first name was a little odd, but his last name seemed pretty apt for an attorney. Rory dialed the phone. He explained the situation to the attorney who apparently knew Rob very well. Alf told him, "Give me 20 minutes. I have to clear my schedule and I'll be right there."

CHAPTER TWENTY TWO

REDEMPTION

Rory opened the door to a thin man with a long nose. His drooping ears seemed to be attached a little too loosely. The man had a face that could have landed him the role of Ichabod Crane just about anywhere regardless of any lack of thespian aptitude. His suit looked expensive despite draping from him as if he were a wire hanger. Somehow Rory had expected Rob, as a lawyer, to have hired a more imposing lawyer for himself. Alf, if there was ever a more fitting physical description for a guy with that particular name, Rory would have been surprised.

It was impossible for Rory not to wonder if Alf had been someone on Rob's list. He wondered what one lawyer might forgive another of doing. Perhaps it didn't even matter. Maybe they had met by chance rather than knowing each other professionally. On the other hand, for all Rory knew, the relationship was purely professional. Speculating was futile.

Alf shook Rory's hand after stepping over the threshold. "I'm sorry for your loss. I know Rob valued your friendship greatly."

Rory was surprised that Rob had spoken about him, let alone so highly. He was a little embarrassed even. *What did I ever do to be valued? Mooch off a guy in a wheelchair?*

The lawyer ushered Rory into the living room, gesturing with his hand. It was much like one might guide a woman or child, but not typically another man. Under normal circumstances it would have felt demeaning. In his dejected state, Rory didn't care at all.

The lawyer opened his briefcase and retrieved a folder from it. He started, "Apparently you found Rob's letter. Did you have any questions for me before we start?"

The first question that popped into Rory's head was, *What are we about to start?* However, the thing that had bothered him most was that Rob hadn't told him that he had cancer. That certainly had the potential to plague his thoughts. So he asked, "Why didn't he tell me he was dying?"

Alf shrugged slightly. "Rob was a good friend. Even though I knew him for years, I never felt like I completely understood him. While Rob shared things with me that many people might not, sometimes I think he held back at least as much. Do you know what I mean?"

Rory nodded. He'd felt that way sometimes. It wasn't as if Rob was hiding anything. It was more of a case of him not having enough time to put the seemingly boundless operations of his mind into words. Rob was someone who seemed too busy doing things to talk about them.

Alf continued, "I don't really know for certain why he didn't tell you. From what I gathered you were going through a tough time though. Rob probably didn't want to add to the burdens that you were already facing. Whatever the reason, I think we both know Rob well enough to know it was selfless. He certainly wouldn't have wanted to dump more stress on you."

Rory nodded. A part of him felt like Rob didn't trust him with it. But Alf was right. If Rob thought it would have been better for him to know he was dying, he would have mentioned it. It still stung a little that Rob hadn't shared it.

"So what are we about to start?" Rory asked.

"I thought I could read you his will as you are the only individual named in it . . . unless that seems indelicate so soon. We can certainly wait until later," Alf told him.

Rory's head spun. *I'm the only person named in Rob's will?*

It immediately disgusted him that for an instant he once again felt like he'd won the lottery. He'd give it all away if he could turn back time, cure Rob's cancer . . . it didn't matter that he had no idea what Rob actually left him. For all he knew Rob left him nothing more than Cody and gave the rest to charity. On the other hand he knew Rob had millions. Rory would have been content to pass on that for one wish.

He thought about the letter his friend left. Two things came to mind. "Don't mourn for me" and "LIFE IS SHORT. Don't wait until tomorrow to decide what to do with it."

He nodded to Alf and told him, "I'm still processing all of this, Alf. I don't know if I'm ready to hear it yet. But Rob wasn't one for waiting around. I think he'd want you to read it now."

Alf nodded in agreement. He pulled a pile of papers from the folder and flipped through them for a moment. "Here we go." He looked at Rory and continued, "You do know that Rob was rather . . . well, wealthy?"

Rory nodded.

"OK, here's your first section, I leave male golden retriever, 'Cody' to Rory Clark."

Alf looked up at Rory who didn't have a reaction, already knowing this part of the bequeathal. He flipped the page and continued, "Let's see, disposition of property . . . I leave Rory Clark my house at 4635 Castle Circle and all belongings within, my 1963 Corvette, the shopping center at 28th and Arapahoe Road in Boulder, Colorado. I also leave him the balance of my Wells Fargo Bank account ending in 4368 to cover any expenses associated with inheritance taxes, title changes, building maintenance, etc."

Alf looked up again. This time Rory knew he had reacted. He had no idea how much money was in the bank account.

However, he was suddenly a landlord who owned a second house *and* a shopping center. He was speechless and once again a little ashamed for feeling that way.

Alf continued through Rory's speechlessness. "I won't have all the details, such as the balance of Rob's bank account for a week or so. He did indicate to me that there was about a two hundred and fifty thousand to three hundred thousand dollars in that account normally. It will also take forty-five days for his will to become binding. However, Rob did stipulate that you should continue to live in the house. As the executor of his estate, I will make sure all the bills are paid. He also asked that I assist you with any other incidental costs you might incur up to the time that the inheritance is finalized.

"The other beneficiaries were all non-profit organizations. However, he did leave several million in trust for the man who killed his wife and son . . . I believe Rob had mentioned that to you in the past?"

Rory nodded.

"Rob asked that you execute that portion of the estate. You are free to decline as such a request is not legally binding by any means. If you'd rather not do it, I am named as the secondary executor and will be glad to carry out that portion as well."

Rory nodded again. He was still trying to regain his power of speech. The two of them sat for a few moments before he could reply. "It's a lot to swallow in one day."

Alf nodded sadly.

"Listen, would it be alright if I left for a little while? I need to talk to someone. I'll get back to you on that last part."

Alf stood up. "Of course, Rory. I will take care of things here. You have my number if you need anything. Call me anytime."

Rory and Cody drove back past Gizzi's Coffee to the house in which he once lived. He'd been so happy driving the other direction earlier that day. Now he felt like he couldn't have the conversation he'd wanted to with Steph. Everything that had been going right had been obliterated by Rob's death.

Still, he could think of little else than how much he needed her as he got closer to the house. It was an unseasonably warm day, much like the one when he met her. Aside from the brown tint of the front lawns, shedding foliage of the deciduous trees, and Halloween decorations it could have been May.

Rory pulled up in the driveway, it was the closest place he could park with a low likelihood of being spotted from the house. It wasn't that he wanted to be sneaky, he just needed a moment to collect himself, to calm the flock of butterflies and grief cavorting in his gut. He stepped out of the Porsche and was greeted by a steady, warm breeze. He inhaled deeply, wondering why he was sweating. It was sixty-eight degrees, not ninety-eight. Cody, by his side, was looking at him as if he wondered what the delay was.

He started to run through the script in his head for the hundredth time in the last few months. The words seemed hollow in light of the day's events. *Steph, I need you. I cannot live without you. Oh yeah, and my only other friend just died.* Rory gagged on the thought.

Sometimes these last months felt like a day, most times they felt like a hundred years. Time had lost importance to him. Almost everything seemed inconsequential. The depth of his heartache had rendered so many things meaningless. He'd spent so much time worrying about that, he'd lost his focus on pretty much everything else. With his brain turning over thoughts of Steph at a hundred miles an hour, everything else often seemed to be standing still.

The words from Rob's letter played in his head, "LIFE IS SHORT." He'd wasted too much life already. He reminded himself that lightning strikes, cars crash and sometimes people even choke to death on a delicious piece of steak. There was no promise that tomorrow would come. With this realization, time was one of the most important things he had. Money could be re-made. Things could be replaced. But time was truly finite. Once time was gone, he couldn't get it back.

He suddenly felt a fool for waiting for the right time to talk to his wife. He suddenly didn't care about waiting until the right time for anything. If the thing was right, the time was irrelevant. He needed to fix his marriage before more time passed. He'd do whatever it took. More importantly, he knew he needed to fix his life and he'd do whatever was required of him to accomplish that.

Rory realized that he had become obsessed with his misery. Despite the vow he'd made to himself, he'd failed dreadfully to fight for Steph. He'd ruminated over the issues. He analyzed the failure of the relationship from every possible angle. He questioned things with no answers. He made plans but never enacted them.

His thinking was eclipsed by a feeling of negative helplessness. It tossed him into a spiral of inaction and depression. Steph was the most important thing on earth to him and he'd more or less given up on her.

As he considered this, the dream surfaced in his head once again. He remembered Steph stepping out of the boat telling him, "I cannot be that, Rory." *What was I thinking right before she said that?* It came back to him in a flash. It was like lightning, searing his soul. I was thinking, *Steph still loves me! Nothing else matters as long as I have that.*

That isn't quite right, is it? Can one person possibly be everything to another? Steph knows me better than anyone else ever might. But can one person <u>really</u> know another? Even though I try to give her every part of me, it isn't possible. No matter how much I love her, I will always have small secrets. If only by simple omission, secrets will exist. It's impossible to share all the minutia of life with another person. Our feelings are ours alone, and often *inexplicable even to ourselves. Is it possible to even know ourselves? Our memories are far from perfect.*

It isn't fair to her for me to expect her to be everything to me when I know that I cannot be everything to her. It's impossible because we are mere people, flawed and incomplete. Steph cannot define my life anymore than I can define hers. How could I have failed her? I would have done anything for her. Without knowing, did I want more from her than she could give me?

Somewhat to his surprise, Rory suddenly realized that there *was* something more important than Steph. He immediately knew that she could never completely fill his life. *No one could possibly do that. No matter how transparent I try to be, there is no one who could know my every thought. There is no one who can ferret out every truth and lie. There is no one with a perfect memory and understanding of me. God knows me better than I know myself. More importantly, God, who knows all of my dark secrets, loves me. God, who is perfect in every way, accepts me in spite of my imperfections. In fact, He'd sent his own Son to atone for them.*

Rory had always pictured God as a judge weighing the rights and wrongs that everyone committed before flipping the up or down switch on the elevator to the great beyond. But at Rob's church, the preacher had explained that it didn't work that way. The only people who got into heaven on merit were those who had been perfect. There had only ever been one who qualified—Jesus.

Perhaps Rob had put it into the simplest of terms, "If you rob a bank, you go to jail. It isn't as if the judge looks at all the things you've done and makes naughty and nice columns. He doesn't compare the good things to the bad. We don't excuse crimes because someone gives a lot of money to charity, or has a family, or spends a great deal of time volunteering. God is the same way, except that He sent us a *get out of jail free* card.

"Since He knows we're all imperfect, He knows we can't do it without His help. So He gave us the gift of his Son. Jesus lived a perfect life and died to bridge the gap of our own mistakes, which separate us from God. All we have to do is accept the gift that is given. It's kind of like when you told me you didn't deserve my forgiveness, Rory. But it's much, much bigger than that. With Jesus we don't get what we deserve. We all deserve condemnation but we're offered salvation instead."

For the first time in his life Rory found himself praying to God, who he was until recently, uncertain even existed. He was pondering all of this before he whispered the prayer. It was a volume that he was sure God could hear, but no one else would. "God . . . Jesus, I know that I've messed things up. I've messed up almost everything in my life. I know that you're the only one who can fix me. You're the only one who can pull me out of this mess. Jesus, please take the wheel . . ."

He felt momentarily stupid quoting Carrie Underwood in his first conversation with God, but continued, "Dear God, thank you for the gift of your Son. Please guide me today. Help me to do the right thing in the future. Thank you, God . . . um, Amen."

It was a simple prayer, none too elegant by Rory's estimation. Yet it moved him in a way that he hadn't expected. He'd heard the supplications of preachers a number of times. They always seemed to know the right words, but it never impressed him. Half the time he felt like it was just an act put on for those in the pews rather than a real prayer. However, his own simple words moved him inexplicably to tears.

While he'd whispered his prayer quietly as to not appear too odd in front of any neighbors who might stroll past, he now crumbled uncontrollably to the hood of his car. In a moment he was reduced to a puddle, eventually sliding to a sitting position on the driveway. He sat heaving, sobbing loudly, unable to stem to flow of his own emotions. Cody whimpered beside him for the second time today.

He'd cried at least a few dozen times since Steph had tossed him out of the house, but these tears were different. For starters, he didn't know exactly *why* he was crying now. A depth of emotion he couldn't explain or understand had swept him up like a small child hurt child being pulled into his father's arms. A purifying warmth flowed through him. Despite his inability to arrest the flood of tears, his emotions were no longer those of hopelessness.

He felt as if the tears were stripping away layers of grime that covered him. It was cathartic. The wave of indescribable emotion was cleansing him. He'd always be imperfect, but what was done was behind him. It was forgiven. The Creator of the universe loved him and had a plan for him. It was in His hands now. This was infinitely better than Rory having to be fully responsible for the plan of his life. Recent events had clearly indicated he himself wasn't up to that task.

He was crying aloud, tears streaming down his face. The dry Colorado wind was licking them away when he became aware of someone talking to him. A pair of shoes appeared in his blurry vision. He suddenly felt foolish sitting on the driveway weeping and began to wipe his face.

He looked up and saw Steph's legs rising from the shoes. She was gazing down upon him with a quizzical mixture of confusion and sadness upon her face. He felt a second wave of warmth as she stood looking down at him, sharing in his breakthrough if only as an observer. He didn't know how long she'd been there or how many times she'd called his name. Finally she bent down to his level. Looking into his wet eyes, she put her hand on his shoulder. "Rory? Are you alright?"

He looked up and smiled at her despite, or perhaps because of the tears. "Yes, yes I am. I just figured out the next step and took it."

Rory carried in the groceries that Steph had just brought home. She regarded him as if he'd grown an extra head, a really odd looking extra head, in fact. There was no telling why he'd been slumped in the driveway weeping with an odd grin on his face. She'd never seen him cry like that before. Sure, he'd teared up at pretty much every sports movie they'd ever watched, but this time he'd been shaking and wailing. That was new. As far as she knew he always had an odd grin on his face while he wept that hard.

Still she couldn't overcome the feeling that there was something changed about him . . . something other than the fact that he'd begun crying aloud. She'd have guessed he was a broken man, that something inside of him had given up if she'd only heard that he was sitting on the driveway weeping. But having seen it herself, she knew the tears he shed were not those of a broken man. The man carting in the groceries seemed to her to somehow be a deeply thoughtful, strong-hearted man. There was no one thing that she could put her finger on, to point to an obvious change. But she was certain that this was a very different person than the wholly-thoughtless, strong-*willed* man she'd thrown out of the house. Somehow she could tell; something had changed.

The many letters he'd written signaled a start of the change. She'd been able to see it in the words he chose. His tone had evolved over time to one that she recognized from a younger Rory Clark, the one she'd fallen in love with. Whatever had been started in him was obviously completed moments before she had returned home.

The dog sitting quietly at her feet? Well that was a mystery as big as anything about this stranger in her kitchen. But was he really a stranger? She'd loved him for years now. She couldn't have been that mistaken, that blind for all that time. Rory Clark, the man she knew better than anyone, had thrown off a layer of cynical tarnish and emerged anew. She caught herself smiling a little.

What Rory couldn't know was that something had changed in her as well. She'd been reluctant, even embarrassed to tell him. However, seeing the man that she loved in this new light, she knew that she must, regardless of the outcome. She had made mistakes as well. Would he be able to forgive her?

She sat at the kitchen table ruefully considering the weight of her mistakes. She pondered what she'd done and shuddered inwardly as Rory put away the groceries. He'd insisted on doing it alone. "Not because I don't want to do it with you, but because you deserve to be waited upon," he'd told her. She wondered what he might think she deserved once she confessed her mistake.

Rory finished putting the groceries away. There was a lump in his throat when he started the process, but by the time he finished, he felt almost like they'd both just come home from a day at work. He grabbed a Wienhard's root beer from the shelf in the fridge. At least the kitchen was clean. He wondered what that meant. *Has Colette left the house finally? More likely Steph got up early to clean the mess. What a way to spend a day off!*

As he walked toward the table, he couldn't help but smile at her. In spite of what might have been the worst day of his life, it cheered his heart to be near her. She returned his smile, perhaps even warmly. It was both pleasing to him and a little off putting. What did a smile mean from Steph these days? He shrugged logic aside. She'd clearly been upset to find him crying in the driveway —upset in the good way that seemed concerned about why he was hurting rather than the bad way which wondered what he was doing in her driveway.

"Remember how long it took us to find this table?" he asked. It had indeed been a long time before they found the round, slightly-distressed, walnut table that sat on the hardwood floor in the kitchen. After more than a year of searching, they'd spotted it at American Furniture. They knew at once that it was the table they'd been looking for.

She smiled. "We had a nice dance floor here for a year and a half and never once danced on it."

Rory set down the root beer and walked to the family room. He turned on the stereo, walked back to Steph and held out his hand. "May I?"

Steph stood up and he took her into his arms. They danced awkwardly for a few minutes. It was partially awkward because neither of them were quite comfortable with the baggage between them. But mostly it was awkward because the only way that Rory was capable of dancing was awkwardly. He was neither gifted with grace or rhythm. Cody wandered around their feet at first. Steph hadn't asked the obvious question of why Rory had a dog with him. He was thankful for that. Cody was on the lower end of his priorities.

Eventually the distance melted into familiarity. They settled into a close embrace with Cody curled up safely under the table. This was when Rory felt the weight of the day hit him once again. He would have been angry about crying for the third time in one day if he wasn't so sad already. He tried valiantly to blink away the tears, but it was in vain. When they began falling on Steph's shoulder, she stopped dancing and put her hands on his face. It was much the way that someone might look into the face of a young, crying child to tell them they were all right. Rory found this comforting.

Steph asked him, "Rory, what is going on?"

It warmed him and terrified him all at once. It was time for him to pour out his heart. All of the practiced and well thought out words left him in an instant. He took a deep breath and prayed silently, *Lord, give me strength and wisdom.*

"Steph, it's been the most . . . interesting day of my life." He wasn't entirely pleased with the word *interesting*, but nothing else seemed to fit. So he continued, "Today I lost my best friend, the only person who I could really call a friend in the last couple months. But I found something new in the process. Until today, I didn't know how to keep existing without you."

"Didn't? *Didn't* know how to live without me? Why not *don't*?" she asked sounding agitated.

He felt the tears welling up again. "Steph, I still don't *want* to live without you. But when you found me in the driveway, I had just figured out that me *being* unable to live without you was a problem. I wanted you to fill a void inside of me that you're simply not capable of filling . . .

"Don't take that the wrong way, please. I have no doubt that you came closer than any one person who ever existed could. The problem is that it's not a part of me that *any* person could make complete. And because I was incomplete, I could never be the man you deserved."

"I don't know what you're telling me Rory," Steph said as she moved to the table and sat down. She fiddled idly with his root beer bottle, seemingly afraid to look him in the eye.

Rory turned his head from her for a moment and wiped his eyes. He sat beside her, took the root beer and covered her hand with his own before he continued. "I came here to tell you that I forgive you for sending me away. I don't understand why you did it, what happened or what you expected from it. I didn't like it, not at all. I felt like my heart and soul were crushed. It seemed like my entire world crumbled.

"I was nervous coming here, Steph, because I had so much at stake. I didn't want you to tell me that you decided you never wanted to see me again. I got out of the car and couldn't walk to the front door on my own. I did something that I've never done before. I started praying. I've been almost completely worthless as a person lately. It isn't what I wanted to be anymore, but that's over. I realized that I wasn't strong enough to walk in here and be your husband without help.

"When you found me there, crying . . . well, I guess I had just become a Christian."

"You guess?" Steph queried.

Rory smiled. "No, I'm sure. I just was surprised a little when it happened. I guess I've been kicked enough lately that I realized something had to change. I cannot do life on my own. Ten minutes or so ago I finally figured out what it was that needed to change."

Seemingly unsure what to make of this, Steph slightly changed tact. "Rory, if anything, I'm the one who should be begging your forgiveness. You weren't perfect, but I was the one who took bad advice from my mother. I should have been listening to you. I should have trusted you. I wasn't sure that what she was telling me was right. I doubted her advice, but I took it because I was mad at you. It wasn't my greatest moment.

"Yesterday she told me that she lied about talking to Davis Jennings. She never even spoke to him, let alone made any sort of agreement with him. My mother told me to throw you out based upon a conversation that never took place. You told me she was lying and I didn't believe you. I should have listened and I'm so sorry.

"She also confessed to breaking the window herself. I'm so sorry I doubted you. My mother has . . . serious issues. I guess we already knew that. She told me it wasn't even that she didn't like you. She did it all because she resented you having all of my time. She was lonely and jealous."

Rory nodded gravely. He had to admit he was somewhat pleased by this vindication. A part of him wanted to say, "Ha, I told you so!" However he knew that Steph was probably almost as confused by this revelation as he had been when she asked him to leave. She'd just found out her mother was a malicious, manipulating liar. That had to hurt. "Is she still staying here?"

Steph shook her head. "She checked into Centennial Peaks Hospital for the next three weeks for mental health counseling and alcohol rehab. She told me that when you forgave her for the horrible things she did, she knew it was time for her to make some changes. Just so you know, she does feel really bad about what she did."

"How are *you* feeling about it?" Rory asked her.

She smiled a bittersweet smile. "The rehab? She needs it and I'm glad that she realizes it. But she's my mother so I'm heartbroken that she needs it. As far as her lying and manipulating me, I'm furious. There are just so many things I'm feeling right now, that I don't know if I can put my finger on all of them. I don't know how you forgave her, Rory. I'm not sure that I can do that myself. It's going to take some time."

"Steph, I came here to forgive you. Even if you hadn't told me all of that I would have, in fact I forgave you before I got up off that driveway. I appreciate you letting me know what happened."

She paused, her expression becoming more wistful. "What changed in you, Rory? If there was one thing about you that drove me really crazy it was your inability to let things go. Now you've forgiven my mother and you've forgiven me for being the worst wife in the world. What is behind all it?"

"First you aren't the worst wife in the world. Second, it's more of a who than a what."

"OK, who then?"

"You remember Rob Wheeler?"

"Of course."

"I've been living in his house since I got kicked out of the shop. He's the friend that I lost today."

"Wait, you were living in the shop?"

"Yeah."

"And then you moved in with Rob?"

"Yep."

"Rob who you insulted more than once in public?"

"Who better to teach me about forgiveness?"

"But he's mad at you now and kicked you out so you came here?"

Rory shook his head sadly. "Steph, Rob didn't kick me out. He died this morning. He had terminal cancer."

Steph sat silently for a while. Eventually she sighed, "That makes sense. That would be how he met Helen. She must have looked at his records and found out he was terminal. She dumped him a few weeks ago, but she's spent half of her time at work crying lately.

"I'm so sorry Rory. Are you alright?"

An hour earlier, he'd have been lying if he said yes. But he found himself answering, "I think I *am* alright. I'm sad of course, but I'm happy at the same time. It's hard to explain. I just know that Rob is in a better place. I know people say that, but in regards to Rob I really do know it.

"So Steph, the only question left is where are we?"

She took it in for a moment. "Neither of us is blameless here, Rory. I'm sorry for the way I treated you."

He smiled and put his hand back on her hand. "Steph, I told you it was done before I walked in the door and I meant it. I'm sorry too. Can you forgive me?"

She nodded and told him her last secret, "I was going to call you today to tell you it was time for you to come home. I don't know how to live without *you*, Rory." It was her turn to cry, but Rory joined her an instant later.

It was half an hour before she remembered to ask about the dog. Cody felt left out for those thirty minutes but was quick to forgive them both.

EPILOGUE

It would be nice to think that there were nothing but cute puppies and sunshine for the remainder of Rory and Steph's days. That the air was filled constantly with the pleasant aroma of warm chocolate chip cookies, the house was pristine as ever and guests came by for parties often would be pleasant to believe. It would make us smile to consider they never had another fight for the rest of their happily married lives, which were spent in good health even when they'd both surpassed a century of existence. In truth, things were better, much better even; but they were not perfect. People are flawed. Perfect lives are impossible for imperfect people. Life was still challenging. That's just how life is.

Steph gave the forgiveness challenge a try on Rory's advice. She eventually found herself sitting in a strangely disarming church with Rory. Not too long afterward she decided that Jesus was indeed the only way to God. They are both finding that marriage is still sometimes challenging even with God at the center, but it's a lot easier than it was without Him.

You may recall that Rory's inheritance from Rob included a shopping center. This shopping center turned out to be the very place where the coffee shop in which he once worked resided—the very shop where he'd met Steph. He bought the coffee shop from the company running it and hired Mark to manage it. With the equipment and furniture from Lord Stanley's, he opened a second shop across town a few months later. Lisa now manages that shop.

Cujo's pads survived the hospital visit with minimal damage. Rory, eager to stifle talk of them being cursed, went ahead (against all odds) to win the championship with the Lucky Pucks. The Fat Cats managed to sneak into the championship but lost one to nothing in a defensive battle. Oddly, or perhaps *not* so oddly, Rory found the second place result for the Fat Cats more rewarding than the first place victory on a team that offered no real camaraderie. He also played much better when he realized there were more important things in life than stopping pucks. He is now determined to keep the importance of hockey in perspective (especially as it pertains to keeping his wife happy).

Cody has settled in nicely. Although he wanted to help Rory get dressed at first, he quickly discarded this habit realizing that it did not please his new master. Part of the problem was Cody's tendency to bring Rory Steph's clothes. There was one regrettable incident in which he ate an entire *Enormous Pepperoni Calzone*, but he's been forgiven. Further, the incident seems unlikely to repeat itself as the amount of cheese in an Enormous Pepperoni Calzone tends to cause an amount of canine intestinal distress that no one in the family is likely to forget.

Rob did leave five million dollars in a trust for the man who had killed his wife and son. Alf told Rory in the firmest possible terms that he was under no legal obligation to manage the trust or meet the man even though Rob's will asked him to do so. Rory took up the torch without a second thought. It was the only thing Rob had asked of him and in some small way a chance to return the kindness that Rob paid him.

Colette hasn't had a drink for seven months. Steph is teaching her about forgiveness. Her other two daughters are learning about it from Steph as well. All three show a great deal of promise. Most importantly, Colette hasn't felt the need to instigate a nervous breakdown, (group or otherwise) since her time in rehab.

Davis Jennings was removed from his position as President of the HOA after an emergency meeting. Apparently there were a number of complaints about him allowing Thunder to defecate freely in various yards and common areas of the neighborhood. The homeowners felt that a man spreading canine feces over the neighborhood was *not* a good choice to represent the their interests. They also replaced Sunshine Management with a slightly less incompetent HOA. While they would have preferred a competent HOA, apparently such a thing does not exist.

Jennings is also displeased that Rory and Steph moved into Rob's house. It was not that he missed Rory. He was displeased that they rented out their home to a family who he found even more irritable than the Clarks had been. Thunder misses both Rory and Cody but still leaves gifts for them in the lawn every time he gets the chance.

Officer Doyle was promoted to Detective. With the low crime rate in Broomfield, she occasionally stakes out Davis Jennings' house. While she has no doubt that Rory Clark dumped a huge can of turds in his yard, there's a feeling in her gut that something isn't kosher about that man. Besides, she lost interest in arresting Rory Clark (who seemed a decent enough guy) after she began finding random derrière donuts in her own yard.

Eileen, who quit working for Sunshine Management in favor of a smaller, friendlier company, ended up winning the account when the Broadlands hired a new management company. After making sure the Clark's liens were all corrected, she levied approximately $40,000 in fines against Davis Jennings. However, she's planning on forgiving them as soon as he stops letting Thunder soil neighbor's yards. She's currently engaged to a nice man she met who, although divorced several times, swears he's never been as deeply in love as he is with her. His name is Matt Morgan.

While sometimes you don't get what you deserve, sometimes you do.

ALSO FROM SCOTT NOBLE

Hockey for Weekend Warriors: a guide to everything from skates to slap shots to separated shoulders

Goalie for Weekend Warriors: a guide to everything from gear selection to glove saves to groins pulls (coming soon)

Scott Noble is published by Walk on Water Books

Walk on Water books is a Christian Publishing house with the vision of spreading the gospel of Jesus Christ. If you'd like someone to pray for you, or you'd like a free Bible to see what John 3:16 is all about, please email us at walkonwaterbooks@gmail.com